Exile

Evil Toad Press

This novel is a work of fiction. All of the characters, organizations, and events portrayed herein are either products of the author's imagination or are used fictitiously. Any resemblance to actual people, places or things, in this solar system or another, is purely coincidental.

EXILE: THE BOOK OF EVER

Copyright © 2014 by Evil Toad Press

All rights reserved.

Cover design by Evil Toad Press

Published by Evil Toad Press

ISBN 978-0-9905963-2-5

First Edition: August 2014

Acknowledgments

This book has been a long time coming, and as much as I would like to say that there is a long list of people to thank, there is really only one—the person to whom this book is dedicated. Without her, not only would this book not exist, but I would not be here to write it. If I were here at all, it would be as a denizen of a dark, unfriendly land, devoid of hope and true happiness, seeing only confusion. It is true that even at the best of times we look through a glass darkly, but sometimes the universe sends us a light. She is mine.

J.C.

To my wife, who believed.

Exile:

The Book of Ever
Part 1

A Novel by
James Cormier

Ever Oaks' Diary
First Entry, 19 Month of Gold

It's two weeks since they breached the walls, and my hands still shake when I think about it. I think deep down I'm glad to be leaving. Bountiful doesn't feel safe anymore—if it ever did. The High Council says the Marmacks will return, and in force.

I never thought of Sainthood as burdensome. Who am I to judge the gift that God has given me? I've always tried to do my duty, to be like the Savior, to help and love and heal my brothers and sisters as I know He would want. But with the journey to the North looming over us, I find myself scared, truly scared for the first time since my parents were killed. Even more so, maybe, because then I was too young to really know what was happening. Now it's all I can do to keep focused on the present. Every minute of the day it's a struggle to not obsess over all the possible outcomes, all the dangers that lie ahead of us.

We're traveling into the Desolation, and I am afraid.

Elder Hales says the journey will be difficult, and that the snows will likely come before we reach the heart of the Maine. The Women's Society have helped prepare our expedition in such a short time; it was hard work they insisted on doing themselves, leaving those of us who would be going to take care of other things. Most of our supplies have been inventoried and packed. There's a small mountain of dry goods, clothing, medical supplies, and camping gear stacked neatly in Storehouse Three, waiting to be loaded onto the packhorses.

Horses are dear in Bountiful; it was a great sacrifice for the community to spare any at all. There was no question of making the trip on horseback. Not only does Bountiful need the animals more than we do, the roads are ancient and hazardous and filled with the rusting hulks of the motorized carriages the Old People used. We will likely be forced to walk at some point in any case, so it's no great loss. The packhorses will at least lighten our load.

Erlan seems nervous about me leaving, now that we've come down to it, though he won't admit it. I wish I could say that he was nervous about losing me, but I'm not sure it's me he's worried about so much as the future he expects for himself. I wish I could say that I'll miss him, even so, but the truth is I don't know. How am I supposed to feel, I wonder? We leave in three days, and I'm no closer to understanding what he expects of me, let alone who he is inside. We might have known each other since childhood, but for all intents and purposes we're getting to know each other for the first time.

The advice my Sisters have for me is well-meant, I suppose, but it isn't helpful. Bishop Royce began the ordinance of marriage but told us there wouldn't be time to seal our union in the temple until I return in the Spring. The marriage won't be complete until then. So I'm half a wife, and my husband is half a stranger.

Erlan accepted the Bishop's decision obediently, as always, and seems to think it was just unfortunate timing. The sealing ritual takes time to prepare, and so on—better not to rush such an important event. I think Bishop Royce knew exactly what he was doing, but I can't tell Erlan that. Since we were joined he's gotten more and more touchy, as if it's strange to him that I'm still the same person.

It makes sense, from a tactical perspective, as Elder Betenson would say: if we're not sealed, we're not really married yet, and there's no chance of me getting pregnant. It was difficult enough to convince the Elders' Council that I'm capable of making this journey as I am. If I were with child the matter would have been decided for me. But the fact that Erlan and I have been joined in the ordinance, and our union begun—our "betrothal confirmed," as Bishop Royce put it—means that I can travel in the company of unmarried men without a chaperone.

Some of the girls I know presume I was disappointed—disappointed by an incomplete marriage and by having to leave my husband so soon. They don't seem to remember that I chose this. They've all conveniently forgotten that I was the one who went into the Bishop's chambers and told him I had to go. Their mothers see me as some kind of paragon of feminine courage, but the daughters think only of the fact that I won't be able to make a home for my husband.

I didn't correct them. I let the ones who wanted to believe that I was a victim believe it. There was no point in trying to convince them otherwise. Some of them—Cambree Betenson, for one—told me to pray to Heavenly Father for patience and help.

The truth is I'm relieved to be going. For all of his selfish anxiety, I think some part of Erlan is too. We share a bedroom now, if not a bed, but there is a space between us wider than Marvel Sound.

I always wake first, in the morning, and I look at Erlan and wonder what my future holds, and if it is truly meant to be tied to his.

Second Entry, 21 Month of Gold

Tonight our Society held a Thanksgiving dinner for us, since we will miss it, and we all stuffed ourselves on turkey and sweet potatoes and herbed stuffing. Bishop Royce blessed us, Elder Bingham, Elder Higbee, Elder Belnap, and myself, and tasked the Elders to keep a watchful eye over their "faithful sister." Then he shook their hands, and when he came to me he took my hands in his and said quietly that despite the danger I must realize that it was the Divine Will that had chosen me for this journey, and that my light and love must hold our little group together. He said it just like that, my light and love. For a moment all of my trepidation was gone and I squeezed his hands and felt like there was hope, and that we would all come back safely.

After dinner I walked home with Erlan. Our cabin is on the Northeastern edge of Bountiful, near where the forest sweeps down to the ocean and you can see over the wall. On clear winter nights you can see the water through the trees from our little garden, sparkling between the bare branches like it's winking at you. I know because the Bishop assigned us to the cabin I grew up in. It had been empty since they died, because it was smaller than some of the other open cabins and it needed some work, and when I asked the Bishop gave it to us. Erlan let me choose.

When we got inside Erlan poked the fire back to life and sat in his chair and began his nightly prayers. I waited for a few minutes to see if he would talk to me, but when he didn't I went out back and looked through the trees for the water. The sky was cloudy, though, and all I could see was darkness. I sat on the pine log bench my father built so many years ago, wrapped in the woolen shawl Cambree knitted for me as a wedding present, and wondered why I couldn't cry. No tears would come, even when I tried to force them. After a while I heard the back door creak and Erlan came out. He didn't sit down, but put a hand on my shoulder gently. I looked up at him.

"I'll wait for you, Ever," he said. "If God wills that we be sealed, then we'll be sealed." The way he said my name it sounded like he was saying *I'll wait for you ever*, like *I'll wait for you forever*, but I knew that's not what he meant.

1

At the edge of the forest, where the march of pines halted suddenly at the gentle slope of Brokeneck Beach, Ever Oaks stopped to remove the light coat she had put on to fight the morning's chill. The sun had grown hot, and the woolen bodice of her dress was already damp with sweat. The Northeast Kingdom was beautiful in the Month of Gold and Ever loved the crisp weather that usually accompanied it, but this year the summer heat of Bounty Month and Harvest Month lingered. The weather could not seem to decide what it wanted to do, which was a problem when the majority of your clothing was made of wool.

Ever stuffed the coat into her already heavy satchel and slung it back over her shoulder. Brushing a stray pine needle off of her apron, she stepped down onto the rocky scree at the top of the beach and carefully began making her way down. It was low tide and several minutes' walk to the water line, where green waves lapped gently at Brokeneck's dark gravel surface.

The rocks at the head of the beach, a tumble of small granite boulders whose configuration changed with the tides, were not easy to navigate in a skirt, but Ever made a fine job of it until the screaming started. Her breath catching, she teetered precariously between two rocks, one foot in mid-step, and just managed to drop down onto a flat stone a few feet away without falling over. Ever froze, crouching behind the larger of the two rocks, and listened until the sound came again. When it did it was louder, a screeching noise halfway between a yelp and a gobble.

The sharp tension that had formed in her shoulders and her chest relaxed when she realized it wasn't a person but an animal, and not far off from where she stood. Silently rebuking herself for being so girlish, she traversed the remaining rocks and hopped down onto the rough sand a few minutes later.

Why was she so jumpy? The fact that she had left the village without an escort was hardly a big enough infraction that she should startle like a toddling child at every noise. A healer had to have a strong constitution, Sister Hales had once told her, and Ever agreed. She had sown arrow wounds and helped bring babies into the world through cuts in their mother's bellies. It wouldn't do to let loud noises faze her, or worry so much about a walk in the woods.

The screech-gobbling continued, and Ever turned left, looking North up the beach. She had come out of the woods on the south side of a small point, where the beach stuck out slightly into the sparkling green chop of Marvel Sound.

She paused for a moment to catch her breath and enjoy the cool air blowing in off the ocean water. Nerves or no nerves, she was glad to be away from Bountiful this morning. The entire community was buzzing like honey bees in a hive over the upcoming return of the Haglund Mission, and every pair of idle hands was being put to work doing whatever was necessary. Ever was hardly a stranger to hard work, but the Women's Society would expect her to spend every moment she had free from the infirmary baking cakes, decorating halls, and sewing party clothes for the welcome feast.

It wasn't that she resented having to do women's work, or so she told herself, but she did try to give her primary duties priority, and it *had* been over a month since she had last visited Elder Barrus.

She looked to the right, where the old wooden dock was just visible down the beach near the remains of the ancient causeway, then to the left, where the sound seemed to be coming from. It was only a few minutes out of her way to round the point and find whatever creature was making the awful noise. Whatever it was, it was obviously in pain. She hesitated only a moment before walking left, up the beach, around the rocky point of land.

The view northward was excellent: the broad water of Marvel Sound stretched between the peninsula where Bountiful sat and the long island known as Golden Neck. It was mid-autumn, and the old trees on the Neck were at their most beautiful: the island was a riot of crimson and orange and gold. An old memory suddenly came to her, and Ever found herself recalling a trip to that very beach with her father many years before. She couldn't have been more than—what, eight years old? It must have been around this time of year. They were searching for smooth rocks of similar size and loading them into a wheelbarrow; her father was going to use them to rebuild their cabin's crumbling chimney.

Is it called Golden Neck because of the leaves, Papa? That sounds like a good reason to me, dearest, her father said. *But is that why the Old People called it that, Papa?* she asked. Her father bent over to heave a rock into the wheelbarrow, then stood, massaging his lower back with his thumbs, and looked at the island. *I don't rightly know what the Old People called it, dearest. But I remember my greatfather telling me that in his greatfather's time, before the Fall, lords and ladies of the Old People lived there. You can still find some of the foundations of their palaces out there in the woods.*

And were the palaces made of gold, Papa? Her father had smiled. *Maybe so, dearest. But they certainly had a lot they didn't rightly need, and when the first Blessed arrived here after the Fall they named the place Golden, after the god those people worshipped. And so we see what happens to those who disobey the First Commandment.*

What, Papa? Ever had asked. Her father narrowed his eyes and drew close to her ear. *The trees devour them!* he whispered, and tickled her belly suddenly. Ever had rolled in the sand and laughed until she could hardly breathe.

Ever stopped, her sturdy shoes sinking into the wet sand. She had wandered toward the water line in her reverie. Her father had never finished the chimney, she remembered now. Less than two weeks later he and her mother were both dead, murdered in their cabin by Marmacks. Ever licked her lips and started walking again. With an effort, she put aside the memory and returned to the task at hand. It had taken her years to learn to control the images, the sudden, vivid recollections that were all but waking dreams. She would not let them take back control now.

She found the bird lying in the shade of one of the huge immobile boulders that dotted the middle of Brokeneck Beach, flapping its glossy wings in a futile attempt to take off. It screeched again as she approached it, one glassy eye focused on her, thick, scaly legs clawing desperately at the sand.

Ever cooed quietly at it, met its eye, and slowly folded her apron under her knees to kneel down as close as it would allow. She hummed a little and brushed the nearest, long primary feather with her fingers, gently. The bird tensed, fluttered nervously for a moment, and then seemed to relax, folding its wings onto its body and waiting.

She thought it was a young male from the color of its feathers, but it was hard to tell. It looked injured and generally unhealthy, and as she stroked it the bird rolled slightly to reveal a dark stain on its breast. As it lifted the wound off the sand Ever wrinkled her nose at the unmistakable smell of rot.

She rolled the animal over gently and saw that its other leg ended in an awkward club. It had two eyes on one side of its head, both milky white and useless. Only the eye pointed at Ever looked functional. Its beak was strangely twisted. One of the Damned, then—a poor, twisted victim of the Fall.

Many in Bountiful thought all of the Damned were inherently evil, but Ever couldn't help but pity them. There were even human Damned—crazed, rotting creatures that subsisted on whatever raw flesh they could find, truly dangerous only to those stupid enough to be caught alone and unarmed in a group of them. For every one that was fast and strong there were three who were stunted, slow, or crippled. But even they had some scrap of awareness buried in their twisted minds. Even they deserved pity.

And animals that suffered from it? Even more so, in Ever's mind; the Adversary had infected them almost as an afterthought, it seemed to her, innocent creatures with no knowledge of right and wrong.

As she thought this she continued to stroke the poult's rippling feathers, easing its wings against its body when it startled and making soft shushing noises to comfort it. She thought of how much the creature had suffered, how long it must have lain on this beach in pain. She saw the ragged edges of the wound and knew it had been attacked by something small and vicious, some cowardly scavenger only brave enough to attack it because it was lame.

Ever felt her palms grow warm, the soft-edged, comforting heat that soothed; she felt the crackling sensation grow, the same pent-up energy that children goosed each other with after rubbing their woolen socks on woolen blankets, the popping, cracking power....

The turkey was entranced, now, lulled by Ever's hands, and as she pressed her palms onto its breast she heard a hurried shout from behind her. She straightened up, as startled as the bird, and got to her feet awkwardly, nearly tripping on her apron as she twisted to look behind her. Even as she moved she heard a sharp whistling followed by a soft thud and the poult's frightened squawking cut off abruptly.

She had felt the wind of the arrow; it had missed her by less than two feet. It was lodged now firmly in the turkey's breast. The long, wrinkled neck was slumped on the ground, and the young tom's milky, mutated eyes stared up at her, dead.

She turned at the scrape of a boot heel on stone, where the archer was making his way down to her from the woods.

Jared Meacham was seventeen, one year her junior, and a close friend of Erlan Ballard. He treated her respectfully but there was something about him that made Ever want to avoid him. Which was difficult, since Erlan and his father kept sending Jared after her when she went outside the walls.

"Sister Oaks," said Jared, stepping down onto the sand and gravel and slinging his bow over his shoulder. The bow was one of Elder Blackham's new recurves, a single, sinuous piece of polished maple that shone beautifully in the midday sun. *Next they'll be giving him a rifle*, Ever thought. There was something about the way he held himself—the cant of his neck, the look in his eyes—that made her dislike him. "You left the community without an escort again. Erlan asked me to look after you."

"I'll thank you to not shoot arrows in my direction, Brother Meacham. I doubt very much that Erlan would like you endangering the life of his betrothed." Now that Ever had had a few moments to think about it, the near miss with the arrow had scared her. Jared's sudden presence there scared her.

"You were never in any danger," Jared said flatly. "I've taken the winner's garland in Archery in the Harvest games two years running."

Imperious, Ever thought. *That's why I don't like him. He's imperious. He acts like everyone should naturally want to obey him.*

As if in direct contradiction to her thoughts, Jared grinned.

"It was a good shot, you have to admit," he said. He looked like a little boy who'd caught his first fish. Ever felt herself frowning.

The meaning of something he said suddenly occurred to her.

"Have you been following me, Jared?" Ever asked.

"I caught up with you shortly after you left Bountiful," Jared replied, as if this should have been obvious.

"You *stalked* me through the woods?" Ever was more than a little shocked, both at Erlan's presumption and her own failure to detect him. She was considered to have good woodcraft, for a woman.

"Calm yourself, Sister Oaks," said Jared. "I was only following Erlan's instructions. Erlan knows you don't like being escorted, but the Council has declared that all unmarried females now require an escort to travel outside the walls. He only wanted to"—here Jared seemed to search for the right words—"preserve your illusion of privacy."

The various ways Ever would have liked to respond to this statement roiled in her brain like the sea in storm. *Preserve my* illusion *of privacy? Who do they think they are? And why only "unmarried females"? Do they think I'm out here having some apostate tryst?* With an effort that was almost certainly visible to Jared, Ever took control of her emotions and responded with as much decorum as she could muster.

"My person and my…virtue…are quite safe less than a mile from home, Elder Meacham," said Ever. Jared tried to interrupt, but she spoke right over him. "However, if the Elders require it, then I will obey." Obedience was a virtue among the Blessed; sometimes Ever thought that the Elders thought obedience was the only virtue that really mattered for women.

"That still doesn't excuse you nearly skewering me," Ever finished.

"Impetuousness doesn't become you, Sister," said Jared, squatting down to look at the dead turkey. Ever resisted the temptation to push his face into the rough, wet sand. She did *not* sound impetuous.

"What were you doing with this animal?" he asked.

"I was about to try to heal it," she said, "until your arrow made that impossible."

Jared looked up at her from his crouch, and for the first time since his face expressed something other than arrogance. He looked confused.

"But it's Damned," said Jared, gesturing at the bird's twisted beak. The poult's milky mutant eyes stared up at them. Ever shivered.

"So?" she said. "I might have been able to—"

"To what?" Jared interrupted. His imperious expression was back. "Heal it? Fix it?" He stood up abruptly, brushing sand and gravel off of the padded knees of his hunting breeches. "Even Saints can't heal the Damned, Sister Oaks. If it was God's will that this animal not be Damned, it wouldn't be Damned. But as we can clearly see, it is."

He folded his arms across his chest and looked at her, his dark eyes serious.

"You should be more careful," Jared said. "This thing could have attacked you. And you were *touching* it. I got here just in time."

"It's a *turkey*, Jared," Ever said. "And it was in pain. It wasn't going to hurt anyone."

"Then I spared it suffering," he said. "But it doesn't matter what looks like. It's a creature of the Devil." Jared squinted for a moment as if he were in pain, then looked at her again, pleadingly this time.

"I'm a hunter, Ever," Jared said. "Even the meekest Damned can be vicious. Even dead they can be dangerous. This arrow's useless." He made no move to retrieve it. Ever waited until he looked away and rolled her eyes.

"What are you doing out here, anyway?" he asked. Ever collected her satchel, which had tumbled to the ground when Jared surprised her, said a silent prayer for the dead bird, and started walking back the way she had come.

"I was on my way to see Elder Barrus," she said. "The Society sent me to check in on him. His heart gets weaker every year." Elder Barrus was a surly old loner who refused the safety of Bountiful's walls, preferring instead to live by himself in the thick woods of Golden Neck. He turned out for church meetings and the occasional funeral, but otherwise they rarely saw him. He subsisted on what fish and fowl he could catch on the Neck. He had already been very old when Ever was a girl; now he was downright ancient. He never asked for anything, but the women of the Society cared for the well-being of all the Blessed of Bountiful, even the ones who made it difficult.

"Something tells me they didn't intend for you to go all by yourself," Jared said, jogging a little to keep up with Ever. She realized she was walking very fast and made an effort to slow down. It wasn't Jared's fault that her overzealous husband-to-be had dispatched him to follow her. There was no reason to punish him for it. No good reason, anyway.

"They trust me to know my own business," Ever said. If she was short, well, she was still getting over the fright Jared had given her, wasn't she?

"I'm sure they do," Jared said. Ever cut her eyes at him sharply, searching for signs that he was mocking her, but Jared kept his eyes straight ahead.

They reached the old jetty a few minutes later. It was early enough in the season that the small rowboat was still tied to the dock. It bobbed at the end of it, wood clunking hollowly against wood. Ever found the sound comforting. She tossed her satchel into the bow and hopped gamely in after it. She bent over to untie the aft lashing and stopped. Jared was still standing on the dock.

"Are you coming?" she asked him. He looked down at her uncertainly.

"We should go back," he said. "It's getting late."

Ever looked at him incredulously.

"It's barely past noon," she said.

"There's a storm coming," Jared said.

Ever made an exasperated noise. "So?"

"Look there," he said, pointing south. Past the ruins of the causeway, where Marvel Sound met the ocean, she could see a dark smudge of storm clouds near the horizon. They hung like a bruise in the distance. "It's moving this way. We don't want to get caught out in it."

"A little rain never hurt anyone," Ever said. Given the sweat-sodden state of her clothing, a little rain would not go amiss. "Look, you can wait for me here if you want. I'll be fine. It's an island, after all. And Elder Barrus isn't *that* unpleasant." She continued working at the knot, got it loose, and then moved to the forward lashing. Jared jumped in just as the little boat's stern began swinging out into the water. Ever gripped the gunwales to keep herself upright and glared at him.

"If you're coming," she said, adjusting her apron as she sat on the forward bench, "then you can row."

2

Twenty minutes later Ever jumped out of the boat into the shallows and splashed up onto Golden Neck. The cold water soaked into her shoes and stockings, but it felt good: the sun was still hot. She put her satchel over her shoulder and watched as Jared stowed the oars and beached the boat. He checked his bowstring, frowning at one point as he ran his fingers down its length.

A trailhead opened onto the short beach, marked by a boulder rolled into place for that purpose. When Jared was finished obsessing over his bowstring, they made their way up the beach and into the woods.

The path was flat and smooth, and there was gravel spread in the low-lying areas. They crossed two small streams, both of which were bridged with sturdy bound pine logs sawn flat across the top. Elder Barrus took good care of his home on Golden Neck, and as he was the only one who lived there it was a good thing he did. The rest of the Blessed of Bountiful thought the place was bad luck.

Ever shook her head as they climbed a short set of stone steps that looked like they had been repaired recently.

"Elder Barrus pushes himself too hard," she said. "Living alone out here would be hard work for a young man, and he's not young. His heart isn't strong enough for this kind of labor. He's going to kill himself."

"It would kill him to *stop* working," Jared said from in front of her. He had insisted on going first. "He's an ornery old man, but his testimony is true. My father says he lives out here because he thinks living in the community makes you soft. 'The slothful man's desire kills him, for his hands refuse to labor.' " He turned his head slightly and Ever could see that he was smiling.

"He learned his scriptures from Elder Barrus," Jared explained. "My father, I mean. The Elders say his recollection of the Word is closest to the lost books of all the Blessed in Bountiful."

"I'm surprised to hear you speak so well of him," Ever said.

"Why?" asked Jared. They reached another set of drystone steps; the trail mounted a small hill in several well-planned stages, making an otherwise difficult hike into an easy walk. The trees of Golden Neck were mostly hardwoods, and the midday sun shining through their bright fall foliage turned the trail into a colorful tunnel through the forest. "Because people think he's strange?"

"It is a bit strange, wanting to live out here by yourself, isn't it?" Ever asked.

"Perhaps he feels that God is company enough." Ever took advantage of her place in the rear and made a frustrated gesture heavenward.

"He never took a wife, you know," Ever said. "And we know what the scriptures have to say about that."

"Who told you that?" Jared asked over his shoulder.

"Sister Higbee."

"Sister Higbee's *your* age—"

"Not that Sister Higbee, her mother."

"She's still half Elder Barrus's age," Jared said. "She doesn't know what she's talking about."

"And you do?" Ever asked sweetly.

"My father says he did have a wife, a long time ago. She died when they were both still young—just a little older than you, I think. He never remarried."

"I've never heard that before," Ever said, honestly surprised. "Why don't more people know that?"

"Probably because they listen to too much Women's Society gossip," Jared said, managing to sound both annoyed and like he'd won a point somehow.

"Well, I think it's romantic," Ever said. It *was* romantic. To think, irritable old Elder Barrus had spent his whole life alone, waiting to be reunited with his one true love.

Now it was Jared's turn to roll his eyes, which he did, coming to a full stop and looking at her incredulously before shaking his head and continuing on.

"Sometimes I think I'll never understand womenfolk," he muttered. Ever smiled. *And that's exactly the way the "womenfolk" like it.* She had a sudden image of Jared as a small bantam rooster, strutting around self-importantly, and stifled a laugh. He growled something she couldn't hear. Ever didn't ask for clarification.

They reached the top of the hill a few minutes later, coming out of the trees into a wide, grassy clearing. Elder Barrus's cabin was small but well-built, of seasoned logs and pitch; there was a vegetable garden on the kitchen side and a shed built up against the trees on the other. Beyond the cabin a corridor of trees had been topped or cut down, giving the little house a view of the ocean down the eastern slope of the hill.

Jared stopped as soon as he entered the clearing and held out a cautioning hand to Ever. At first she was confused, and was about to ask what the problem was, but then she looked at the cabin again and saw that the front door was ajar. She had overlooked it in admiring the tidiness of the clearing.

Jared held a finger to his lips and quietly slipped his bow off his shoulder, knocking a black-fletched arrow from the quiver strapped to his back. He put tension on the string without drawing it fully, and started forward, motioning Ever to follow him with a jerk of his head. She knew enough to keep her mouth shut. Jared was probably being paranoid and overcautious, but it wouldn't do to take unnecessary risks. For a man like Elder Barrus, leaving his front door open was like anyone else tracking mud into the Women's Society meetinghouse.

The packed earth of the path led right up to the door. They made very little noise approaching the house. The clearing seemed very quiet; the sound of a cicada starting to buzz off in the distance was almost startling.

Jared held out a hand again when they got to the door and tried to peer into the cabin. After a moment he backed up, drew his bowstring to his cheek, paused, then abruptly kicked the door in hard. It swung open almost all the way with barely a creak, stopping when it banged into some obstruction they couldn't see. A moment later Jared was through the door, sweeping the point of his arrow around the tiny house in all directions. He seemed to know what he was doing, but Ever couldn't help but be scared for both of them. He disappeared behind the door and Ever waited, holding her breath.

Jared looked pale when he reappeared, stumbling slightly as he crossed the wooden threshold.

"What?" asked Ever anxiously. Jared only shook his head.

"I don't think you should…" he began, swallowing, but Ever was already pushing her way past him into the cabin.

The cabin was a single large room, with a fireplace on the left side, a table in the middle, and a separate cooking hearth on the right, hung with iron pots and pans. A number of canisters had tumbled off of a shelf onto the floor, and a large sack of flour was torn open, coating the far wall and floor in a layer of off-white powder. Embers still smoldered in the fireplace. Elder

Barrus's single small table was just behind the open door; one of the chairs had been overturned.

Elder Barrus, or what was left of him, was on the other side of the table, stretched out in front of the cold hearth. Ever clapped a hand to her mouth instinctively.

His face was a swollen red mess; one eye was completely shut. His simple buff shirt was stained in several places from what looked like stab wounds, and a dark pool of congealed blood trailed out onto the clay tile that made up the bottom of the surround. Ever swallowed her shock and rushed over to kneel next to him. He wasn't breathing. She turned his face gently and saw that the far side of his skull was horribly misshapen.

"Someone caved his skull in," Jared said, sounding dazed. Ever jumped. She hadn't realized he had followed her back in.

"There were no birds singing," Jared said, as if that explained everything. "The whole glade was...just quiet. The woods are never quiet."

"There's nothing I can do," said Ever. She had known he was dead as soon as she laid eyes on him. The blood on the floor, which had begun to seep slowly into the hem of her apron, was thick and cold. She took his hand gently; it too was cold, his wrist stiff and unyielding.

"He's been dead for hours," Ever said, feeling as useless as she'd ever felt. She stumbled to her feet awkwardly, her shoes slipping in the blood. Her apron was a sodden mess. Near Elder Barrus's feet some of the blood had mingled with the spilled flour, creating thick pink sludge that looked uncomfortably similar to bread dough.

Healing was Ever's calling, but this made her gorge rise. She had treated wounds before, even injuries Bountiful men had gotten in fights with apostates and Damned, but nothing like this. The sheer brutality of it.... She swallowed hard and turned away.

"We have to..." but the words wouldn't come.

"We have to get out of here," Jared said, seeming to come out of a trance. "Now."

"But the body..."

"We have to tell the Council. They'll send men. Right now we have to *leave*," Jared said. "We messed up the tracks in the flour coming in, but this was more than one man. Whoever...whatever...did this could still be in the area."

Ever didn't object when Jared took her arm and hurried her down the path toward the trees, then stopped suddenly.

"What is it?" she asked.

"They didn't take anything," he said.

"What?" Ever said. Jared's grip on her arm was comforting, but now that the horrible spell the scene inside the cabin had cast over her was broken, she wanted nothing more than to follow his advice and get off of Golden Neck as quickly as possible.

"Whoever did this," Jared said. His eyes were unfocused, as if he were doing figures in his head. "Elder Barrus had three months of supplies in there, at least. There were dry goods on the shelves. The trap door to the root cellar was closed. He even had a bottle of firewater on the table. They didn't take any of it."

"Elder Barrus drank firewa—" Ever cut off mid-sentence and shook her head. It didn't matter. Elder Barrus was dead. Who cared if he had broken a commandment? "So what, Jared? You're right. We need to get out of here." She tugged on his arm, but Jared ignored her.

He frowned for a moment, then nodded his head as if he'd decided something.

"Look," he said, "I want to check around back of the cabin and do one circuit of the clearing."

"Jared, no," Ever said urgently. "You were right the first time. Let's go!"

He took her by the shoulders and looked her in the eyes.

"We'll stay together," he said. "Keep close behind me. This could mean something very important. We've got to check it out. I didn't see any tracks on the trail hiking in. There might be something…we might be able to find something to explain this. See where they came from, at least."

Ever's fear was mounting, and despite how sure he sounded Jared looked just as shaken as she was. Seeing that she wasn't going to change his mind, she nodded. Jared spun around, knocked his arrow again, and kept his bow at the ready.

There wasn't much behind the cabin other than a woodpile and a rain barrel. The hillside was steep on this end; there were fresh stumps along the edge of the hill where Elder Barrus had taken down more pines to make his view. Off to the left, toward the northern side of the clearing, was another trailhead leading north. This path was traveled less frequently than the trail to the beach, being useful only for Elder Barrus's own wanderings around the Neck, and even the very beginning of it was muddy and partially overgrown. Several feet in Jared found boot prints in the mud and broken underbrush where someone had cleared the path.

He crouched above the prints and examined them closely.

"They don't look more than half a day old," Jared said. "They're partly trampled, but you can see where they walked in and walked back out. At least three of them. Probably more." Staying in a crouch, he looked down the length of the trail, which disappeared in a dogleg to the right after a few dozen feet.

"We need to follow them," Jared said, looking up at Ever.

Ever squeezed her eyes shut and prayed for guidance.

"Jared," she said, as firmly as she could, "I don't even have the words to describe how stupid this is. What are you thinking?"

He sighed and rose from his crouch, transferring his bow and arrow to one hand and fingering the hilt of the hunting knife sheathed at his belt absently.

"You're probably right," he said finally. "It probably is stupid. In fact, I *know* it's stupid." The wave of relief that Ever felt was short-lived, however. "But if that storm passes this way, and it will, we might never find out where these tracks lead. The rain will wash all the evidence away."

"It's a *trail*, Jared," said Ever. "On an *island*. Whoever the Council sends can follow it whether there are footprints or not." Jared was already shaking his head.

"We don't know for sure that they kept to the trail," he explained. "For all we know they only came across it when they neared the clearing. They could have come from any direction on this side of the island. The Neck isn't huge, but it's big enough that even a large party could waste a day searching it for tracks. And they could be gone already, and we'd never know."

Ever could see that he was convincing himself even as he spoke the words. She needed to reason with him.

"And if whoever did this is still out there?" she pleaded. "You said yourself there are at least three of them. Three grown men, by the looks of it, who could do the same thing to you that they did to poor Elder Barrus." Jared's face grew cold.

"I can handle myself," he said.

"Don't be foolish!" Ever said, raising her voice.

"Besides, they'll never see me, even if they are still here somewhere. I know how to move in the woods."

"But what's the point, Jared? Why risk your life? For what? Some misguided sense of justice?"

"No, Ever—that's not what this is about. Look, I think there's more to this than it seems. You know how the Elders' Council held a special meeting last week? About the Marmack Apostates?"

"So?" she said.

"Scouts have been reporting movement. There are new settlements within two day's walk of Bountiful. The Elders are worried."

"Get to the point, Jared!" Ever shouted.

"Keep your voice down!" he hissed in response.

"Look...this could be related, somehow. They could be scouting us. Trying to find a...a muster point. Somewhere to attack from. Somewhere we'd never expect." He gestured widely, with both arms.

"Just wait here. Keep in sight of the clearing and the trail, but stay in the trees. I won't be long."

Before Ever could argue further, Jared turned and began striding down the trail. After a few dozen feet he disappeared into the surrounding woods and she couldn't see or hear him any longer.

Suddenly feeling cold and not quite believing that he had left her, Ever wrapped her arms around herself and moved off the trail into the underbrush, trying to make as little noise as she could. She found a tumble of mossy rocks near a large pine and sat down, facing the direction Jared had gone.

Sitting there, listening to the occasional chirping sparrow—the woods *had* seemed quiet, now that she thought about it—Ever wondered how her foster parents would react when she finally got home. Would her foster father be angry? Elder Orton—whom Ever called Father, out of respect—was a kind man, if an unimaginative one, but he brooked little nonsense. His wife was caring and sweet, but she had the ferocity of a field mouse and the depth of a trout stream. It wasn't a secret that Ever liked to leave Bountiful without an escort, but as it had never been an issue in the past—and because even years later most of the community still pitied her for the loss of her family—she had been allowed to get away with it. The Council changed the rules periodically anyway, depending upon how much of a threat the apostates were, though the most recent ruling did have a ring of finality to it.

Ever sighed, feeling overwhelmed at all that had happened today and not a little depressed at the fact that sneaking in a solitary morning hike might have cost her her freedom.

When the hand clamped over her mouth, she had no warning other than a sudden rank smell, which she realized in hindsight she had first noted a minute or so before. The man was suddenly on top of her, his grimy, crack-nailed paw gripping her face like a vise. She tried to scream, but he only squeezed her in a powerful bear hug until she felt lightheaded, and then she felt something sharp prick her side.

"Look down," a husky voice growled. Ever's eyes rolled frantically, hoping against hope that Jared was about to return, that God would strike the man dead, but all she saw was empty woods. They were alone.

"Look down," he repeated. He wasn't even lowering his voice. How had he snuck up on her so easily? Fighting down an overwhelming feeling of shame, shame at being caught so easily, shame at putting herself in this situation to begin with, Ever finally looked down.

Past the scarred, sunken knuckles of the hand over her mouth, Ever could just see the man's right hand holding the point of a rusty knife against her side.

As she watched, he pressed it slowly but firmly into her flesh just below her ribs, and she saw a rosette of blood soak the light wool of her dress. She didn't even feel pain.

"Yeh scream 'gain, yeh move w'out my say-so, I shows yeh what yeh insides look like," the man snarled. He pushed his face forward over her shoulder and she could feel harsh whiskers scratching her cheeks. His breath was rotten, not unlike the odor that she had smelled from the turkey's wound a couple of hours earlier. "Yeh un'stan', baby?"

Ever had never considered herself fainthearted, but for the first time in her life she felt like she might pass out from fright. Through a supreme effort of will that she did not know she possessed, she gave two sharp nods to say she understood. Her attacker cackled in response.

"Goo' girl, baby, goo' pretty holygirl, nice pure swee' girl," he murmured in her ear, almost cooing. Ever swallowed and focused on breathing through her nose and tried her best to ignore the man's roving right hand.

"Now," he said, spinning her to face him—he handled her as easily as he might have a child—while keeping his greasy hand over her mouth, "I take this hand off yeh pretty lips, yeh gon' keep 'em press *shut*, ain't yeh baby?" Ever nodded frantically, snorting indelicately through her nose, unable to control the tremors rippling through her body. His hand was still clamped around the bottom half of her face, but she could see him now: his hair was long and greasy—it looked like it had never been washed—and the mangy black beard that obscured his face framed a mouth full of twisted brown teeth. He grinned when he saw her looking at them, running his tongue over them lewdly.

"So we straight then, baby?"

Ever nodded again and mumbled a muffled assent into his dirty palm. She found his apostate patois difficult to understand, but his meaning was clear. Slowly, his blade still pressing through the thin material of her apron and dress, he lightened his grip on her face and then slowly pulled his hand away, taking advantage of its freedom to scratch at his hairy neck. His hair was patchy and thin, and Ever could see where the scalp beneath it was red and irritated. He almost certainly had lice.

Now that she had a brief opportunity to look at her captor—for that was what he was, Ever realized suddenly; she'd been taken captive as certainly as a baby stolen in the night—she had to resist the instinct to recoil in disgust.

He was a short man, she saw, likely due to a lifetime of poor nutrition, but despite his general repulsiveness he was not one of the Damned. He wore a long, patched hide vest over a shirt of rough, dirty homespun and his boots were crude moccasins wrapped in rawhide thongs. Around his waist, however, he wore a finely made leather belt fastened with a bright brass buckle. It was the buckle that caught her eye, though the fine black tanning of the leather was also as good as a signature: it was stamped with the sun, moon, and stars sigil that Ever had seen every day of her life, in one form or another.

"Fine make, baby—you like?" the man grunted, fingering the buckle. "Yeh holy ones do da fines' makes." The Blessed limited their contact with the apostates as much as possible, but those who were called to duties outside of their communities had been known to do acts of charity for apostates who didn't threaten them. Ever found it hard to believe that the man's belt had been a gift, however. Likely he had robbed someone. It was a man's belt. *Which means he killed whoever owned it*, Ever thought. Her eyes dropped to his knife involuntarily. She could see now that it was as crude as the rest of him: a jagged shard of metal sharpened on both sides with a cord-wrapped grip.

A strange trilling sound pierced the air suddenly; it sounded like birdsong, but not from a bird she recognized. The apostate looked up suddenly, scanning the woods around them, then grabbed Ever by the arm and began tramping through the trees toward the cabin. He could obviously move silently when he wished, but he made no attempt to do so now. Ever told herself it was because of her presence, because she couldn't move the same way, if only to avoid thinking about the alternative: that there were enough other apostates on Golden Neck today that it didn't matter whether anyone had heard him, now that he had caught her.

They broke out onto the trail, where the man dug in his belt and removed a small, carved wooden cylinder. He put it to his lips and blew, producing the same trilling sound they had just heard, except in short, staggered bursts of sound. The distant call came again and the man responded.

They reached the clearing, which was still deserted, and waited just outside the trailhead. Another whistle came, closer this time, and another, even closer but from a different direction. This one cut off abruptly, sounding unfinished even to Ever. The man stiffened, and then they heard the scream. Ever's captor cursed foully and jerked her close to him, bringing the blade of his knife up against her bodice again. They backed toward the cabin until there was at least fifty feet of space on all sides. There was another scream, then shouting that couldn't have been more than a few hundred yards away, and then there was silence.

The clearing was again empty of wildlife; they waited in tense silence for whatever was coming to reach them. Ever felt a dim surge of hope: could it be men from Bountiful? Had Jared gone for help? Were they coming to rescue her?

Her captor was growing increasingly anxious. After a moment he wrapped his left arm around her waist and brought his knife up to her neck. She gasped, feeling the sharp, rough edge against the delicate skin of her throat. Her gorge began to rise as she felt warm blood run onto her chest and all thoughts of rescue fled her mind. She could only hope the man wouldn't slit her throat by accident. She tried to pray, asking Heavenly Father desperately for help, but her thoughts seemed to shatter as soon as they formed. All that seemed real in that moment was the knife, the stink of the man behind it, and the clearing around them, silent as a grave.

Just as the moment seemed ready to stretch into forever there was a dull snap from behind them, and for the second time that day Ever heard the controlled shriek of an arrow's flight. There was a spray of something warm, a quiet gurgle, and then the apostate was falling sideways. Ever brought her hands up to protect her throat but the blade only nicked her knuckles as it fell away. She looked down and saw the man on the ground, an arrow neatly bisecting his Adam's apple, the black fletching still quivering above his lifeless face. He'd been shot from the left side.

She turned and then Jared was there, only Jared, and he took her hand quickly and told her they had to run.

3

Sister Hales' round face hovered over Ever's own, her soft, motherly features pinched in concern. Ever let her dab her forehead with a cool, wet cloth and drank the broth that she foisted on her, more to appease Sister Hales than out of any real desire to drink it.

She could barely remember their flight back to Bountiful, though the trip must have taken over an hour. She had never been so scared in her life. There were only flashes: trees whirring by, their feet churning the sand on the beach, Jared heaving against the oars with all his might. Then more woods, the walls of Bountiful suddenly looming, and Sister Hales, Bountiful's Mother Healer, wrapping Ever in a warm, doughy embrace and showing her onto a cot in the infirmary.

She had slept, she thought; the sun was low in the sky through the small, square window near her bed.

"There's someone here to see you, dear, if you're up to it," Sister Hales said. The way she said "if you're up to it" clearly implied her willingness to scare off any visitors Ever didn't want to see. But the shock of her experience was already fading, replaced by worry that she'd been left out of whatever decisions the Elders were now making in response to the day's events.

"I'm fine," she said, hoping it was Jared, or someone with news. Sister Hales finished fussing at her forehead and took the broth away, disappearing through the doorway that led to the storeroom and kitchen. A few minutes later Erlan came in and approached her with a look of dramatic concern on his face.

"You're awake," he said, taking her hand.

"Yes," she said, not knowing what else to say. "Has Jared reported to the Council?"

"It's lucky I sent him after you," said Erlan, as if she hadn't asked the question. "Do you understand now why everyone is so concerned about your little solitary journeys? If Jared hadn't been there you'd be dead."

Ever withdrew her hand and tried her best to project the placid acceptance she knew Erlan wanted to see. It was hard. She wasn't sure she succeeded, either, given the look on Erlan's face. Beneath the surface, anger warred with a whipped feeling. After what she'd been through, this was how he greeted her—his future wife? She wondered suddenly if he'd even bothered to ask Jared the details of what happened, or if he had started blaming her for it as soon as he heard there had been trouble. Ever had never thought of herself as having a particularly fiery personality, but at that moment all she really wanted to do was hit Erlan over the head with a bedpan and walk out.

"I'm glad to see you were so worried about me," she said.

Erlan squinted, his mouth a crooked line. She had trouble reading him at the best of times—was this rebuke? Confusion? He had plain features, an oval face, brown hair and brown eyes; he had never been accounted particularly handsome, but when Elder Orton had first proposed him as a suitable husband for her Ever had thought of his plainness as purity, and had transformed his stern countenance into nobility.

In the six months since their engagement, however—on the rare occasions that Erlan relaxed enough to actually talk to her—Ever had realized that what she had first seen as purity of character was in fact a distinct lack of curiosity about the world, and what she had thought of as noble seriousness was a narrow rigidity that now made her recoil. In short, she was having serious doubts about their compatibility as husband and wife, and spent most nights praying for guidance.

"Of course I was concerned about you, Ever," he said reproachfully. "We're...we're *promised*." Ever remained silent, looking at the fringe of the blanket covering her legs.

"Perhaps you need more rest," Erlan said, after an uncomfortable pause. He fidgeted at his waistcoat, obviously ready to leave. Ever didn't bother trying to explain how she felt; the time and effort it would have taken to make him understand would take energy she simply didn't have at the moment.

"Maybe I do," she said finally. "Can you tell me one thing, though?"

"What?"

"What is the Council going to do?"

He shook his head. "I don't know. Brother Meacham—Jared—told Bishop Royce and his advisors what happened as soon as the two of you returned. He's giving his report to the full Elders' Council right now. You know as much as I do."

Would they call her to address the council? Somehow she didn't think so. The feeling of being left out of something came back, stronger than ever.

After saying a polite, passionless goodbye, Erlan left. Ever counted to one hundred, then got out of bed.

The Elder's Council building was one of the largest structures in Bountiful, second in size only to the chapel and the largest of the storehouses. The Council chamber itself was housed in a large hexagonal wing containing tiered seating around a circular chamber floor. It was large enough to house every worthy adult male in Bountiful, and then some. The Women's Society building was much more modest, a fact which Ever found both troubling—why weren't they the same size?—and appropriate—men thought power was all about size.

Ever trotted through the unoccupied anteroom—a simple entrance chamber with a couple of wide tables for Council secretaries—and down the main hall to the Council chamber.

The wide oak doors were closed, and guarded by a pair of Deacons. One of them was her foster brother, Dallin Orton. His eyes widened when he saw her. He took a step forward, then thought better of it and straightened up.

"Sister Oaks," Dallin said, with a seriousness only a twelve year old boy could muster.

"Deacon Orton," Ever intoned, in her best church voice. Then, knowing that Dallin was struggling between wanting to give her a hug and minding his duties as a door warden, Ever grabbed him in a bear hug and kissed him on the cheek. He blushed fiercely, though his fellow Deacon, a dark-haired boy whose name escaped her at the moment, didn't seem surprised. Elder and Sister Orton often felt more like a dear aunt and uncle than parents, but she had loved Dallin since before he could walk. He was a bright boy, and dear to her, and had never seen her as anything but his big sister.

"I'm glad you're okay," Dallin said, looking worriedly at the bandage on her throat. It was a shallow cut, but it had bled freely.

"I am too," said Ever. "Dallin, I need to go inside." Dallin hesitated.

"I can't, Ever. It's a closed meeting. I'm not supposed to let anyone except Council members in."

"Look Dallin, they may not know it, but they need to hear from me," said Ever. "I was there too, and Jared and I were separated for a little while. There might be something I could add, to help."

Dallin chewed his bottom lip, looking conflicted.

"Do it for me, little brother," she said, "I've had a heck of a day."

"You'd never get past the inner wardens," Dallin said after a moment. "But the balcony's empty. I could get you up there. You could at least listen." Dallin looked at the boy on the other side of the door, who shrugged apathetically.

"Good enough," Ever said. Dallin took her hand, led her down a narrow hallway to a set of stairs.

"There's a door at the top. It leads onto the viewing balcony. If you're quiet they'll never know you're up there."

"Thank you, Dallin," said Ever, giving him a quick hug.

"If I get in trouble I'm telling them you beat me up," said Dallin.

Ever smiled at him and winked.

"And they'll believe it, too," she said.

Dallin went back to his post as Ever crept up the staircase. The door at the top was ajar. She bit her lip as she eased it open, but the hinges didn't creak. The viewing balcony ran along the section of the council chamber's hexagon that was connected to the rest of the building; she was sitting right above the doors where Deacon and his friend stood guard.

It was lucky that Dallin had been on the door. In her hurry to get to the council building, she hadn't considered the possibility that the meeting might be closed.

The balcony was the perfect spot to eavesdrop: it was unlit, deep enough to hide from view but open enough that she could see most of what was going on below.

Bishop Royce sat on a small dais with his advisors on the far side of the circle. The room was almost full; almost every Elder in Bountiful was here. The chamber had wide, low windows along the top of each wall, but the sun had sunken below them only moments before. A young Priest—the holy office immediately above Deacon in the priesthood—was lighting the oil lamps that lined the walls in sconces. After a few minutes the chamber took on a warm, if slightly eerie amber glow.

Jared was standing in the middle of the council floor describing the scene they'd found in Elder Barrus' cabin, addressing his account to the Bishopric dais. As she settled quietly into one of the wooden chairs arranged in rows up to the railing, a collective gasp swept through the assembled Elders.

"His skull was caved in. It looked like they'd beaten him badly before he died. Sister Oaks..." here he paused before continuing, "Sister Oaks estimated he had been dead for some hours before we found him."

As disturbing as it was to hear Elder Barrus' body described, Ever was glad she'd arrived when she did. She still had no idea what had happened to Jared when he left her to follow the apostates' tracks.

A few of the older men made disapproving noises when Jared described his decision to leave Ever in the clearing to follow the killers' tracks, but were quickly silenced by a raised hand from Bishop Royce. Jared explained his reasoning, which seemed to mollify the dissenting brethren.

Jared's father, Elder Tanner Meacham, sat on the Bishop's right hand on the dais. He had been appointed to the Bishopric several years earlier as First Counselor, and so far had been very popular. Now, sitting above his son as if in judgment, his handsome face was unreadable.

"As you know, the back trail leading out of Elder Barrus' clearing runs north along the island and comes out on the old ocean road," Jared said. "The tracks led me from there down to Granite Head, the point next to the ruins of the old castle."

"How did you manage to track them across the ocean road?" asked Elder Cardon, Bishop Royce's other adviser, who sat to his left. "Is that road not still paved with the remains of the Old People's tar cement?"

Elder Cardon's face resembled that of a hungry rat. As unpopular as Tanner Meacham was well-liked, the rumor—among the Women's Society, anyway—was that he only remained in the Bishopric because Bishop Royce hadn't come up with a reason to release him yet. Even the oldest citizens of Bountiful found Elder Cardon's views a bit "traditional" for their taste.

"It is, Elder," said Jared, "but even the hardest surface can leave traces. The apostates' boots were muddy from the trail, and left clear markings across the blacktop. Even if they hadn't, it would have been a simple matter to search the far side of the roadway until I picked up their trail again. No mortal footsteps are beyond the sight of the skilled tracker."

Jared sounded like he was quoting someone with the last bit, which, Ever decided, might best have been left off. *Petulance has no place in Elders' Council, especially when you're talking to Elder Cardon.*

"A skilled tracker?" repeated Elder Cardon. His voice was skeptical, almost snide. "Such as yourself, Brother Meacham?"

"Yes, Elder Cardon," said Jared. "My father trained me well." A ripple of laughter passed through the crowd. Elder Meacham seemed to be holding back a smile. Elder Cardon frowned, but waved at Jared to continue.

"The path leading to Granite Head was covered in tracks," Jared said. "I'd say a dozen men at least, but some of the tracks were older. I kept to the trees from that point on, and when I came out at the point I saw them."

"What did you see?" asked Bishop Royce. "Take care that you describe it in as great detail as possible."

"Four men, all apostate, one of them Damned, and a beached longboat. They'd been there at least half a day."

"How do you know that?" Jared's father asked.

"There were no drag marks in the sand behind the boat from when they beached it. The tide was low, and hadn't reached the high water mark yet. They'd also built a cookfire in a pit, small and tented to hide the smoke.

"I couldn't see what if any provisions they had in the boat, though there were several parcels, and I wasn't close enough to hear their conversation. I could tell from looking at them that they were grim, serious types, though," said Jared.

"Fighting men?" asked Jared's father. Jared nodded.

"I'd say so," he said. "They weren't well-armed, but each had a crude bow and at least one large blade. Their cloth was poor. They were bearded and unkempt. I saw no obvious tribal markings, but they had the look—they must be Marmacks."

"Your place is to report your observations, not draw conclusions," intoned Elder Cardon. Elder Meacham frowned and glanced at his fellow counselor sidelong, but said nothing.

"Respectfully, Elder Cardon, who else could they be?" asked Jared. "Of all the warlike tribes, the Marmacks are the closest and the most hostile. We know they want our land. And why weren't they wearing clan emblems or sashes?"

"Perhaps because they are mere drifters. Perhaps because they wish to conceal their clan affiliation—"

"Exactly," said Jared. "Why would vagrants from some distant tribe conceal their markings? They take pride in their tribes, their clans. Only Marmacks, who we keep special watch for, would take that precaution."

Elder Cardon began to respond, but Bishop Royce raised a hand for silence.

"Enough," he said. "I'm inclined to agree with the boy. We'll move on for now. What happened next, Jared?"

Elder Cardon, far from mollified, sat back in his chair and glared at Jared. Ever couldn't see Jared's face from where she was hiding, but she hoped he kept it civil. Elder Cardon wasn't one to take even a reproachful glance lightly. Jared cleared his throat.

"Well, Bishop, seeing as I was alone, and had Sister Oaks to think about, and there were four of them," he said dryly, "I figured that was as good a time as any to get out of there." There were chuckles from the audience. The Bishop's smile was small, but it was there.

Ever fidgeted with her skirt nervously. By this time in Jared's narrative, she would have already been taken prisoner by the unnamed apostate who now lay dead in Elder Barrus' clearing. She tried not to think about the harsh smell of him, his gravelly voice, and the way his hands moved on her body, but images kept intruding into her thoughts. She closed her eyes and tried to focus on Jared. She still wanted very much to know what had happened to cause the shouts and screams she'd heard in the woods.

"I didn't take the same route back," Jared continued, his voice echoing hollowly up to where Ever sat. "I was on the lookout for scouts on the way down to the beach, but I didn't find any. I found some on the way back." The room grew quieter, the muffled conversations of the listening Elders dying down as Jared continued.

"They weren't scouting the way we do, they were too close together. Like they were just wandering through the woods at random. They stayed in sight of each other. There were huge swaths of forest where they wouldn't have seen me, but I just happened to go right between them. I tried to sneak past them, but the cover was sparse...."

"Go on, son," said Elder Meacham.

"I...I shot them. They started whistling, some kind of scout language. After a few exchanges I realized they'd spotted me. I still don't know whether they were better than I gave them credit for or just lucky. I stood up from cover and shot the first one I saw, the one on my left. I got him through the heart. He died quiet. The other one saw me and screamed, and then I shot him too." Jared was silent for a long moment. Ever looked around the room from her perch: all eyes were fixed on him.

"I knew Ever could be in danger too, so I got back to the clearing as soon as I could, while still keeping to cover. She was—another one of them had her. He had a knife to her throat. I circled around to the side and shot him through the neck."

Ever realized she had her hand over her mouth, her eyes wide and hot. Whether it was because of Jared's blunt retelling of the killing he'd done, or because it brought her back to the moment the apostate had his dirty knife against her throat—or both—she didn't know, but she had to clench her teeth and breathe slowly and deliberately for several minutes before the panic in her chest started to loosen and fade.

She must have been on the verge of swooning, because by the time she got herself under control Jared had already finished his tale and was waiting for a response from the Elders. Feeling not a little embarrassed, she tried to take hold of herself. *Here I am acting like a little girl, and Jared is down there calmly describing killing people.* The thought of Jared killing someone was outrageous to her. Jared Meacham, a boy she had known since...as long as she could remember, friend of her fiancé, the boy who won archery contests shooting at straw targets on feast days, had *killed* someone? And not just someone, but three someones—three *Marmack Apostates*.

She tried to think of what he must be feeling and didn't even know where to start.

Down on the dais, the three members of the Bishopric were deliberating amongst themselves. Elder Meacham seemed to be arguing, quietly but fiercely, with Elder Cardon, but when the Bishop spoke they stopped. After a moment Bishop Royce addressed Jared.

"We will have to deliberate on this matter further, Jared, but for now I have just one question: were you followed on your return from Golden Neck?"

"No, sir," answered Jared. "There were no other men that I was aware of in our immediate area when...when it happened, and it would have taken the men at the beach at Granite Head several minutes to reach the others. Ever and I were off the Neck within minutes—we ran back to the boat—and I used every method I knew to make certain there was no one pursuing us on the paths leading back to Bountiful." Jared lowered his head for a moment.

"But there's no reason to think that they don't—"

"That will be all, Elder Meacham," said Bishop Royce. The Bishopric thanks you for your honest testimony. Please make yourself available to members of the Bishopric at their request."

"Sir," said Jared uncertainly, "if I've given offense, or…or sinned, I—"

"Your actions were as God willed them," said Bishop Royce, not unkindly. "Your choices were sound, given the circumstances. If you have questions or doubts, I urge you to address them to our Father in Heaven through prayer."

Recognizing this as the dismissal it was, Jared nodded his head, turned around, and walked out of Ever's view toward the entrance doors below.

Bishop Royce rose, and addressed the entire room.

"Brethren," he said, "As you know, Brother Meacham only returned a few hours ago; the Bishopric has had barely more notice of these events that you have. With that in mind, if there is nothing else before us, we will recess at this time to discuss Elder Meacham's account more fully. Please return to your homes and duties, and pray that Heavenly Father may guide us in our deliberations. This council will reconvene tomorrow at nine o'clock. In the meantime, I'm sure you all have as much to do as I do before Elder Haglund and our younger brethren arrive."

With that, the Bishop seated himself. Elders Meacham and Cardon leaned in to speak with him quietly again. The rest of the Elders populating the council tiers began to rise—slowly—and make their way toward the exit.

As the men in the room prepared to leave the volume level rose; a dozen conversations began at once and suddenly the peace of the chamber was shattered. Ever found herself standing at the railing of the balcony, looking down on the chamber as it stirred and mingled in adjournment.

Her voice was small and faint at first. She had to repeat herself, almost shouting, before any of the men looked up. The buzz in the room grew and then began to subside as Bishop Royce looked up.

"Wait!" she yelled, surprising herself with the volume of this final cry.

"Sister Oaks," said the Bishop, when the clamor had died down. He alone seemed unsurprised to see her. "It would please me very much to speak with you. If you would see me in my office—"

"There is something else, Bishop," Ever said, unable to keep her voice from quavering. "Something Brother Meacham didn't share, because he didn't know."

"Are we to understand that you have been eavesdropping on this entire council meeting, Sister Oaks?" asked Elder Cardon, which produced a rumble of disapproval among the gathered men.

"Yes, Elder Cardon, but—"

"You are old enough to know better, Sister Oaks. The deliberations of this council are not for the ears of women. You—"

"Elder Cardon," Bishop Royce said quietly. Cardon broke off and looked questioningly at his superior. "Under the circumstances, I think we can forgive Sister Oaks this small infraction."

"What would you say to us, Sister?" said the bishop, looking at Ever and nodding. Ever was too nervous to feel grateful to Bishop Royce for his patience and forbearance. Instead she focused on getting out what she had to say before she lost the opportunity.

"The man...the apostate who...took me," Ever said, searching for the right words. "He wore a belt. A belt of Blessed make. It bore the symbol of the Three Kingdoms, the sun, the moon, and the stars."

"An Elder's belt," said Elder Meacham, looking at Bishop Royce.

"Is that all, Ever?" Bishop Royce said.

"He was a dangerous man, Bishop," Ever said. "Not the sort who'd accept charity, even if offered, if he could take what he wanted by force. He stole the belt."

"Did he admit that to you?" asked Elder Cardon.

"No, Elder Cardon," said Ever, looking down at him. "But if you'd been there, if you'd seen him, felt his knife at your throat, you'd know it too."

"With all due respect to *women's intuition*, Sister Oaks—" began Elder Cardon, but Bishop Royce again stopped him midsentence. This seemed to be a frequent occurrence; none of the assembled Elders seemed surprised.

"Thank you, Sister Oaks," said the Bishop. "If you will return to the infirmary, I will visit you there shortly."

Her cheeks warm with embarrassment now that she'd said her piece, Ever quickly excused herself, hurrying down the stairs and out of the building before any of the Elders could corner her.

4

The back of the Orton family cabin looked out on a small cove on the western side of Bountiful, its yard a mossy, level patch at the top of a tumbled slope of sea grass and granite that ran down steeply to the water. The wooden walls were a bit lower here, arranged on a ledge of cliff below where Ever stood that still allowed a decent view.

Ever stood at the top of the slope, watching the dark waves crash against the rocks as the sun sank into a molten puddle in the western sky.

After leaving the Council chamber, Ever had returned to the infirmary and submitted herself to the remainder of Sister Hales' treatment, which mostly seemed to consist of pushing broth, bread, and vegetable pasties on her until she was so full she could barely breathe.

Bishop Royce had been as good as his word: less than an hour later he had walked in the door, pulled a chair up to her bedside, and listened to her tell her entire story. When she was finished he apologized that he hadn't been able to see her sooner, and said that he had been concerned about her condition. Ever felt relieved and satisfied for a moment, until it occurred to her that, good intentions aside, the Bishop was merely humoring her. He evaded her questions about how Bountiful would respond to this new threat, and had encouraged her to put her trust in the priesthood. Thinking back on it now, Ever only felt more determined than ever to make sure that her voice was heard. If the Elders weren't taking this seriously, someone had to make them see sense.

She sighed and wrapped her arms tightly about herself. The air was growing chillier. She considered going back inside, but quickly rejected that notion. Her family was just sitting down to dinner; she had begged off, explaining to her mother and father that she was stuffed from Sister Hales' ministrations, and needed time alone to clear her head and pray. Elder Orton had agreed on the condition that she not leave the cabin grounds. There was a very serious lecture coming on the dangers of traveling unaccompanied, Ever knew. Up until know she had avoided it, and would avoid it for a day or two longer, most likely, if only because her parents and everyone else in the village were worried for her sanity after her encounter with the Marmack. But it was coming, as surely as were the first snows of the new season. The days grew shorter and colder as winter loomed, and perched over the ocean as they were, Bountiful could be a cold place to live.

The community, a holdfast village home to over three hundred souls, was situated on a point, a thick, drumstick of rocky, wooded land jutting out into Marvel Sound from the larger peninsula that stretched out north and east from the mainland. The walls that surrounded the village were stout and thick. On the three sides that were open to the water the land fell away in treacherous, craggy rock tumbles and sheer cliffs.

The community of Blessed that had become Bountiful had not always been located in this spot, a fact every child of Bountiful learned in Primary. It was the relentless harassment of the Marmack Apostates that had driven them to this, the eastern edge of the Northeast Kingdom. The Marmacks were an inland tribe, strangely cautious around the sea; when her people had first settled this spot and built Bountiful, many had believed they had put themselves forever outside the reach of the Marmacks and all others who would harm them or their way of life.

That had proven sadly wrong, as the more pragmatic brethren of Bountiful had always known it would be, but for many years there had been relative peace. It was only in Ever's own lifetime that the Marmacks had finally found them again, making their way from their river communities inland and conducting periodic raids. Testing their defenses, Elder Betenson, Bountiful's Master at Arms, said. Aside from the raid that had killed Ever's parents, the Marmacks had never breached Bountiful's walls. But even the most devout among them, those who believed that Heavenly Father would literally defend their lives with choirs of angels if need be, had begun to realize that they were no longer as safe as they once were. We're living on borrowed time, according to Elder Betenson, she remembered Father—her foster father, Elder Orton—saying once at dinner. *If Bountiful is to survive, we can't stay here forever.*

"I wonder where we'll go? I wonder when it will happen?" Dallin had said, around a mouthful of bread, his eyes wide with excitement. His most prized possession, a crude wooden model of one of the Old People's flying machines, sat next to his plate. Their younger sister, Airie, barely three years old at the time, made a comically frightened face. Ever had put her arm around her and whispered comforts in her ear.

"Don't scare your sister," Father had said, and changed the subject.

Ever no longer had to wonder when it would happen. She knew. That apostate and his knife had shown it to her, as clear as day. She had an unshakable feeling that everything she knew—everything she had ever known—was about to change.

She heard a twig snap behind her and turned to find Jared standing there.

"Getting a little sloppy, aren't we?" Ever said, with more humor than she felt.

"I didn't want to scare you," said Jared. "Where's Erlan? I thought he'd be with you."

"He's come and gone," said Ever. "I told him I wanted to be alone." Which wasn't precisely true. Erlan had indeed visited again after she returned to her family's cabin, but upon discovering that Ever still evinced the same lack of remorse for her actions that he had encountered earlier, he had begun lecturing her. Ever ended up telling him that if he couldn't offer her comfort, she would rather that he left. After a few moments, he left.

Erlan was strangely literal; Ever tried not to take it too personally. She chose to believe that he was being respectful by honoring her wishes, even though part of her knew all too well that what she really wanted was to be held and to have someone tell her everything was going to be all right.

Jared looked troubled.

"He's my friend and all," Jared said, scratching his head awkwardly, "and older than me, and about to be an Elder, but sometimes...."

Ever gave him a resigned smile. Jared seemed to understand. He was good that way, Ever realized suddenly; it didn't take much on her part to get her feelings across to Jared. Sometimes, speaking to Erlan felt like trying to communicate with a crab, or a spider—something totally alien, something with whom she shared little common experience beyond gravity, or the need to eat food. With Jared, she could always just...*talk*.

"Look, Ever," Jared said. He moved next to her and looked down at the water. "I wanted to say that I'm—"

"Don't," she said suddenly. Ever would have been lying if she had said that she hadn't felt annoyed, even angry at Jared at first for leaving her on the Neck, but in hindsight the issue seemed much clearer to her.

"Don't apologize. You saved my life. I should be thanking you."

"I shouldn't have left you," Jared said stubbornly. "I should have gotten you off that island, and then you would never have…he would never have…." He trailed off, as if the wind had gone out of his sails. "I'm sorry, Ever."

"I said don't say that," Ever said. "You were right." She turned and looked at him. "You were right, Jared. If you hadn't followed those tracks when you did… we'd know nothing about those men. And you saved me. That's all that matters."

"That's not entirely true," Jared said. "Scouts reported in an hour ago. They found tracks less than a mile west. Half a dozen men, at least. About two days old. They explored the whole base of the peninsula. Looks like they came by boat, too. Made shore at Red Rocks."

"The same men? Or others?" Ever asked.

Jared shook his head. "No way to know."

"The Elders told you this?"

"No," Jared said. "You know Brother Snow? Elder Snow's son? He was the one scouting that area with his father. He told me."

"What are they going to do?" asked Ever.

"Bishop Royce sent out to scouting parties: one back to the Neck, the other to the south to investigate Red Rocks and patrol the area. Both were heavily armed. Other than that, I don't know," said Jared. "There's something else, though."

Jared took her gently by the elbow, looked over his shoulder to see if anyone was nearby, then leaned in close.

"My father let something slip earlier. About the Haglund Mission. The Bishopric is worried."

"Worried about what?" asked Ever. "They're not due back until at least this Sunday. And they're coming from an entirely different direction—they made it to Serai in one piece, why wouldn't they make it back?"

"I don't know, but I get the sense there's a lot more to it than we know," said Jared. He was quiet for a moment.

"They wouldn't let me join either scouting party," Jared said.

Ever glanced at him worriedly: she approved, but didn't say so—Jared was still young, after all—but she knew it must be a huge blow to his ego.

"I'm sorry. I know you must be disappointed," she said.

"Yeah, I suppose," he said. "Mostly I'm just worried. Something's about to happen, Ever, and I don't think it's going to be something good." His words were so close to her own feelings just before he arrived that she looked at him sharply and felt a surge of fear return.

Jared checked the horizon, saw that the sun had all but set, and gave her shoulder a friendly squeeze. She looked at him, trying to read his face.

"I'd better go," he said, turning to leave. He got a few steps then stopped.

"If you ever need to talk…about Erlan, or…anything," he said, "You know where to find me."

"Thank you," said Ever. Looking at him now, limned by the last rays of the setting sun, Ever wondered how she could have thought him imperious. In the fading light he only seemed kind.

"And Jared?" she said suddenly.

"Yes?"

"Let me know, will you. What happens. With the Scouts, and…with whatever else." He nodded once, then walked around the cottage toward the lane that led into the village proper.

After he was gone, Ever felt strangely restless. It wasn't just anxiety over the frightful events of the day—that was certainly there, but buried away, forced down by her need to regain some semblance of safety. It wasn't ripe for feeling yet, was one way to put it; Ever could only hope that when it was it wouldn't be too burdensome.

No, if she was honest with herself, the main thing she was feeling was frustration. She couldn't get past the feeling that her part in all of this—whatever *this* was—was over. She was just a young woman, not privy to the councils of the Elders; her opinion was no longer relevant, if it ever had been. It was a powerless feeling, like being in a boat with no oar. It shouldn't matter; she was being selfish.

But it does matter.

The clink of plates through the small, shuttered windows reminded her that her family was enjoying dinner without her. She didn't really want to go back in, but she didn't want to stand outside alone, either.

Looking at the warm glow that shone through the slats of the shutters, her family suddenly seemed symbolic, as if they represented her entire people, not only Bountiful but the Blessed as a whole: the thousand men and women scattered among the last three holdfasts of God's chosen. She wondered suddenly if there was another girl in Serai, or Camora, or even among the apostates, who also felt like she was outside looking in.

And if there is, what does it matter? I'll never meet her. I'm here, now, and my options are what they are. Why is it so hard to choose?

Up until that moment, Ever couldn't honestly have said she was trying to *choose* anything, but now that the thought had occurred to her, she couldn't shake it. Inside she was trying to make a decision. Both the question and its answer eluded her, but the feeling was there nonetheless. Why?

Maybe because you're not trying to choose anything. You're just bellyaching.

Ever couldn't help but smile. There was always a little voice that told her the truth, deep inside. When the Bishopric talked of the Spirit, and letting it guide you, that voice was what Ever always thought of. Everyone had it, in some form, though the trick was learning to hear it. And then learning to listen.

For Ever, the voice was almost always her own, and it usually came in the form of a nagging whisper in the back of her mind, mild but persistent, trying forever to lead her in the right direction.

The gift of being Blessed is that you always have a guide, Ever reminded herself. Trying her hardest to keep the dry humor she suddenly felt out of her voice, she whispered aloud to the darkness behind her house.

"Thy way is in the sea, and thy path in the great waters," Ever recited, "and thy footsteps are not known." *Unless you* look *for them.*

Lost in her thoughts, she walked slowly back into the house, sat down at the table amidst her loud siblings, and helped herself to a piece of bread.

By the time she finished helping their mother with the washing up, both Dallin and Airie, who now at five years old still snuck into Ever's bed some nights, were asleep on the narrow cots in the room the three of them shared. Ever often lay awake for an hour or more, but tonight she fell asleep only moments after she lay down.

The dream, when it came, was quick and powerful, more a sequence of images than a running narrative. They came in rapid flashes, as if with each blink of her eyes she was whisked to some new place.

She saw a little girl with ice blue eyes. She smiled, blinked, and became something *else*: the same girl, but translucent like white crystal, her hair like needles of captured moonlight, her eyes featureless fields of deep cobalt that glistened like tide pools. The girl that was not a girl blinked again and she was holding a bough, though from no tree Ever knew. Its bark was smooth and silver, with trefoil leaves the color of spring. Its parent tree was nowhere to be found, but the bough was alive anyway. As the girl held it, several of the perfect green leaves fell from the branches and disappeared.

She saw a great field of ice in front of a forest; a mountain loomed purple and white in the background. Ever knew somehow that the mountain was the destination, if not the goal. Beneath it was a sea of stars, first midnight blue and gold then black and silver. Ever felt herself drawn into it. There was a rushing sensation, then silence.

She saw a figure—male, though how she could tell she didn't know—born of hate clothed in love. She could perceive these things with her senses, in the manner of dreams, though she would be unable to describe them in detail later.

She heard a child's voice calling from a deep well, and the well was surrounded by wolves, and the wolves were lean and hungry.

She saw a strange vessel, a ship of some kind, and a great blossom of flame. She saw three saplings torn from the earth by a strong wind and cast into darkness. She saw a spider's web torn apart and rewoven.

She saw the great ruins of the cities of the Old People, carpeted in rust and green and crawling with Damned.

She saw Jared in pain, and the children of Bountiful, Dallin and Airie among them, naked and wild-eyed, living like animals in the forest.

She saw the walls of Bountiful, riven and burnt, a horde of Marmacks rushing through the breach to terrorize the faithful within.

Then she woke up, to screaming and the smell of smoke.

5

Jared put an arrow through the eye of the first Marmack to reach the gates. He made the shot despite an odd angle: he was positioned a few dozen feet down the wall east of the gates, aiming almost horizontally. The main archers' group was deployed to the western side, where Elder Betenson thought the largest force would come from. The walls were weakest there, where the terrain was uneven, and from that side they had the clearest approach to the gates.

The Marmacks had appeared with the sun, and Bountiful's fighting men had responded with impressive speed. Elder Betenson's drills were showing their value today.

Depending on how you looked at it, the Elders had ordered him to the eastern wall either because they wanted to keep him out of the worst of the action or because they trusted him to pick his own shots. Jared was one of the most talented of the archers of Bountiful, but he was also one of the youngest. It didn't really matter; he preferred to choose his own targets anyway. Firing volley after volley with two dozen or so other men from below the walls was frustrating in comparison.

Elder Betenson called out for the first volley a moment later, and the archers released a rain of projectiles with a harmonious *thrum*. They were angled high, and well, and a few seconds later they fell amongst the onrushing Marmack attack party to a chorus of screams that made Jared want to sing a hymn.

He didn't rebuke himself for taking pleasure from the battle; there was time enough for that when it was over. He had never killed a man before he and Ever got caught on Golden Neck. The shame and fear he had felt hours later—only last night, which was difficult to imagine now—were still sharp in his memory, but now, just as then, he felt only the need to draw his bow.

Firing a few more shots over the edge of the wall into the first rush, Jared scuttled farther away from the battle and scanned the woods to the east.

Bountiful's rampart was a stout wooden affair, built from hardwood logs planted vertically into the ground and joined together with tar and heavy iron spikes. The walkway that ran along the top of it was just wide enough for the men that manned it to be able to fight without fear of falling off the back. The parapet was chest-high and crenellated. It was from these convenient notches between the tarred logs that Jared aimed his bow. The wall was over twenty feet high, with a hundred yards of cleared ground on the landward sides. To the Marmacks, whose own settlements were usually unfortified or at best surrounded by heaps of rubble, it was a formidable barrier.

Or so Jared told himself, if only to keep his mind on what he was doing. The Marmack tribe were unsophisticated warriors. Most of them were brawlers and berserkers rather than real fighting men. They charged into the fray wielding whatever rusty piece of sharpened metal they could scavenge, screaming war cries that chilled the blood until you realized that half of them were drunk on the white liquor they distilled from wood and roots and corn and the other half were too stupid to do more than slash at the first man who presented himself. They were frightening, and loud, and fearsome, but they were unorganized and valued brute strength over precision.

Nonetheless, they had the numbers. *The numbers and enough fear of whoever leads them to storm our walls when they could be hunting easier prey.* The fact that they had attacked Bountiful at all was worrisome. The community had withstood worse raids than this one, but not for many years. If the Marmacks were getting this desperate, they had bigger problems than one raid on the walls.

Movement at the edge of the forest caught Jared's eye and he scanned the treeline again. Nothing moved. The Marmacks' main force numbered around fifty men, aside from a few loners who hurling rocks and shooting small arrows from weak bows at isolated parts of the wall, hoping, no doubt, to distract the defenders away from the gates. A larger force than they'd seen in a long time, but nowhere near as large as the one that had attacked the community and breached the walls when he was only a boy. Ever's parents had been killed during that raid, Jared remembered. He wondered where she was, and if she was all right.

He tried to put everything out of his mind but the battle, tried to find the center that he relied on to make the shots he made. Aim, draw, release. See, pull to cheek, let go. Nothing else mattered.

The first two volleys from the archers had weakened the Marmacks considerably, and now the Elders manning the section of the wall over the gates themselves, where the majority of the Marmacks were massed, heaved heavy baskets of stones over the parapet and onto the heads of the grisly men below.

They appeared to have no real plan of how to enter the village. Jared made out two shoddy ladders being brought up to the wall, both of which were thrown down easily as soon as they slapped against the parapet. *Where's the battering ram? Are they even going to try getting through the gates?* Even as he watched, a small group of apostates hauled something up behind their main force. He shook his head in disgust.

They had indeed brought a ram, but it was a single tree of no great width, its bark still on, its tip inexpertly torn and hacked away. They held it by the stubs of broken branches. It was almost comical. The gates were indeed the weakest part of any wall, but Bountiful's gates were six inches of solid oak, barred with a heavy oaken beam strapped in iron. If there were even enough of their men left to provide cover when they got it up to the gates, it would take them hours to break through with that. It seemed almost...

...*too good to be true.* A line of men was emerging from the eastern woods, where he'd been looking only a few moments earlier. There were at least as many of them as were in the group already attacking the gates, and unlike their ravening companions, these men stepped out from under cover as one unit, as silent as they were unexpected, all of them carrying longbows. The man at the head of the line knelt, did something with his hands, and with startling speed a line of fire leapt up in front of the archers.

The forest's edge was farther from the walls where they emerged, perhaps a hundred and fifty yards from where Jared perched, but he could still see that they were dressed similarly in dark, dun colors. Camouflaged.

He watched, frozen, as they nocked arrows to their bows. The arrowheads seemed oddly large to Jared, and it was with a dawning horror that he realized their plan. Even as they knelt, as one, and dipped their arrowheads in the line of flame, Jared began screaming.

He turned and stood, giving up his own cover to wave his arms and yell for Elder Betenson. They needed to get men to this side of the wall; they needed to...*do* something. What? He saw Betenson acknowledge him, saw him wave a detachment of Elders toward Jared's position, but even as a dozen men set off in a run Jared knew it was too late.

He turned back just in time to see the bowmen loose. Their arrows had become flaming missiles that streaked the morning sky in bright orange, arcing up in slow grace over the cleared ground between the woods and the wall. They weren't aimed at the men on the wall, Jared saw; the archers' target was farther away than that. A substantial portion of Bountiful's homes and buildings were well within the range of those bows.

He turned, dropped, and slammed his back against the parapet out of instinct, facing the village of Bountiful from atop its walls. He sat and watched as the arrows alit in the roofs of the Blessed, setting old thatch and cedar shingle afire with ease.

The bright flames that had begun spreading over the village were oddly beautiful. Jared felt as out of breath as if he'd just sprinted a mile, though he had barely moved since seeing the line of bowmen. He felt nailed to his spot. For the first time since the attack began, which could only have been a matter of minutes earlier, though it felt like hours, Jared had no idea what to do next. The battlefield analysis that had been running through his mind moments earlier was gone, replaced by numb immobility.

The dozen men that Betenson had sent his way were pounding down the wall toward him now. Women and children too young to fight were already mobilizing to fight the flames in the village below. Elder Betenson was nowhere to be seen. The men that had manned the sections of wall near to him were either busily engaged with the enemy or gone.

Taking a deep breath, Jared wrapped his fingers around the grip of his bow. With a strength he didn't feel, he made himself get up and face the Marmack archers, who had leapt over the quickly fading fire trench and were now advancing on the wall. With a strength he did not feel and a focus he was surprised to find he still had, Jared bent his bow and began firing into the line of men who were coming to kill him.

Ever's foster father had sheathed a large knife at his belt and was checking the bore of his rifle when she emerged from her bedroom. Dallin was holding his leather shooting vest and staring at him wide-eyed while Airie cried in their mother's arms.

"Father," Ever said. Elder Orton looked at her and smiled ruefully.

"I'm sorry to have to wake you, Ever," he said. "God knows you need the rest." To hear her him use Heavenly Father's name so casually surprised Ever. Elder Orton was among the most devout of the Blessed in Bountiful, and he kept the commandments strictly.

"What's happening?" she asked.

"The Marmacks are here," said Dallin, who looked more excited than scared. Airie hid her face in her mother's neck.

"A large group of them are attacking the gates from the west," her father explained as he loaded precious cartridges into his rifle. Ammunition was almost as invaluable as firearms in Bountiful. Most of the guns they did have were well-tended antiques, relics of the Old People kept in perfect condition over the centuries since the Fall. The carbines Elder Betenson and the village blacksmith had been able to reproduce were inferior and unpredictable; metal was scarce enough that they had a hard enough time replacing the bullets they lost. Which was why they only used guns when absolutely necessary.

"I have to report to Elder Betenson," her father continued. He had taken his vest from Dallin and buttoned it up, rolling the sleeves of his homespun shirt up past his elbows. Securing a pouch of ammunition to his wide leather belt and slinging his rifle, he ruffled Dallin's sandy hair and put his arm around their mother.

"Aethan," said her mother, her face betraying her concern.

"It will be well, Dalee," he said. "Pray for us. Keep the children in the house. Make sure they all have a weapon. Dallin, you have your bow?"

Dallin hefted his half-scale flatbow hopefully.

"Keep it at hand in case you need to flee," said Father. "Don't try to draw it inside, or in haste." Looking back at his wife, he said: "You remember the escape plan?"

Ever's mother nodded. All of them knew it, and knew it well; they practiced evacuating the cabin and village regularly. Not all of the Elders were so conscientious with their families, but there was a reason Elder Orton was on the High Council.

He came to Ever and hugged her briefly.

"Be safe, daughter," he said. Pressing her cheek to the old leather of his vest, she realized she had to go with him.

"Sister Hales will need me at the infirmary," she said.

"I'll check in with her soon," said Father. "For now I want you to stay and help your mother."

Ever only hesitated for a moment.

"No, Father," she said. Elder Orton, who had turned to leave, looked back at her in mild surprise. "I have no business hiding in the cabin while I could help with…I'm either a Saint, or I'm not," she finished. "It's my duty." Hardly as eloquent as she would have liked, but it got her point across.

Elder Orton looked at her appraisingly, then nodded.

"Very well, Sister Oaks," he said, and laid his hand on her head. "I bless you in the name of Heavenly Father. May he keep you safe." With that, he walked through the door of the cabin briskly and closed it behind him. Sister Orton stared after him for a moment as if he had just walked off of a cliff.

It only took her a few moments to gather the things she would need in her satchel. Putting on a fresh apron, she slung it over her shoulder, hugged her mother, kissed Airie, and gave Dallin a kiss on the cheek. Less than five minutes after her foster father left, Ever was out the door herself, striding with purpose toward Sister Hales and the infirmary.

Making her way down the lane toward the village common, she heard the thrum of bowstrings and the muffled shouts of men beyond the walls, followed by a series of thumps and hoarse cries.

None of it seemed real yet. Except for the occasional cry of pain—whether from inside the walls or outside,

Ever couldn't tell—the sound of the battle was rather like the commotion of the Harvest Fair. The steady roar of the crowd, the snap of bowstrings.... *A comforting illusion.*

It was cut off as something bright and orange flashed through the sky over her head. Fire arrows. She saw the flaming bolts soaring in a neat flock high over the wall, dropping from the sunny sky toward the houses and cabins of Bountiful clustered below.

As the first roofs caught fire, and the screams of Bountiful's children began, all thought of fairs left Ever's mind and she started running.

When he felt the bowstring slap hard against the bracer on his left wrist, Jared reached for another arrow and realized his quiver was empty. He'd lost track of the men he'd injured or killed, a fact that still hadn't quite sunk in, but all of his shots had found flesh. He hadn't wasted any arrows. The line of Marmack archers had advanced to a position closer to the walls, fired another volley, then disappeared back the way they had come. He wasn't surprised, given that they had neither cover nor any kind of siege equipment, but the damage was done. At least a third of the village was on fire. The Women's Society had formed a bucket brigade starting at the village well, but they were fighting a losing battle. At this point, unless someone else had any bright ideas, they'd have to rely on the firebreaks built into the village to keep the flames from spreading.

The group of Elders that had rushed to relieve Jared at the appearance of the Marmack archers had spaced themselves out along the eastern wall. The volleys over the gate had decimated the main assault force, the remains of whom had retreated to a safe distance. They appeared to be trying to construct some kind of protective shelter over their battering ram using cut pine boughs.

Jared took advantage of the lull in the action to squat down behind the wooden parapet and take a long drink from his water skin. The sun had risen higher in the sky and the air was growing warmer. It promised to be another unseasonably hot day. Jared had already sweated through his shirt and waistcoat. Wiping his damp brow, he looked toward the village green. He could see his father's tall form assembling a group of riflemen beneath the big maple near the well. He hoped it wouldn't come to wasting ammunition, but so far nothing had gone as expected.

Elder Betenson hadn't been completely unprepared for a split assault, but the Marmacks had never shown any such sophistication in the past, so the men posted at sections other than the gates where minimal. Like Jared's, their purpose was more to warn and inform than fight, so that the appropriate forces could be maneuvered.

At least they didn't have to worry about the seaward sides of the community. The wall surrounded the whole village, but the cliffs of Bountiful's peninsula were a formidable obstacle all on their own.

Jared let the man nearest to him know that he had to leave the wall to restock his quiver, then climbed down the closest ladder and jogged to the green. Elder Blackham, who served as both bowyer and fletcher to Bountiful's bowmen, had set up a resupply station near the center of the green. The lanky old greybeard, who was several inches taller than Jared's father even with the hunch that age had given him, was in the process of sorting a large basket of arrows into bundles when Jared came up.

"I'm out," Jared said, without preamble.

"Already?" said Elder Blackham pleasantly, looking up. "I don't why I'm surprised." He gestured at the bundles as if Jared had asked him for an apple and bent back to work. Jared passed over the shorter, softer arrows issued to the rank and file brothers who had yet to distinguish themselves with the bow and filled his quiver with a dozen of Elder Blackham's finest black-fletched poplar shafts—a privilege the old man reserved only for those archers he deemed worthy.

Bishop Royce was deep in conversation with Elder Betenson near the assembled riflemen, and after he finished preparing his men Jared's father joined them. Elder Cardon was approaching with Elder Ballard—Erlan's father—and Erlan himself. Seeing Erlan standing awkwardly outside of the circle of Elders as his father and Cardon joined the others, Jared walked up to him.

"Erlan," he said, waving. "Are you all right? How's your family?"

"Our house wasn't hit with the fire," Erlan said.

"Good," Jared said. "I don't know if your father's got you doing something for him, but we could certainly use another bow on the walls if you're—"

"I'm observing," Erlan said. "And taking notes." He brandished a small, leather bound notepad. "For the minutes."

"The minutes?" Erlan was a year Jared's senior, but he had only recently received his first calling as an adult member of the community. Unlike Jared, who had shown interest and aptitude for scouting and shooting early on, Erlan had always been more…bookish. His father had recently secured him a position as secretary to the High Council. Had Erlan been instructed to "observe" the Bishopric's administration of the battle, or was he just avoiding having to pick up a weapon?

Jared felt some guilt at the thought—Erlan was his friend—but he set his teeth and didn't dismiss it. It made no sense to ignore your friends' flaws, even if you were willing to overlook them. Jared bit his tongue and stood awkwardly for a moment, during which time Erlan returned to eavesdropping on his betters.

Jared was about to return to the wall—the Marmacks might have been temporarily stymied by the village's defenses, but they weren't broken yet—when he noticed Ever hauling buckets of water from the well toward the infirmary.

"Did you know Ever's out here?" asked Jared.

"What?" said Erlan. "Oh. Yes. I think she's helping Sister Hales in the infirmary." It made perfect sense: Ever's abilities were…miraculous, to say the least. But she was a Saint; miracles were to be expected around the Saints. There was a Scout who lived near the southern wall who could make his skin like tree bark, and he wasn't half as well known as Ever.

"Have you...talked to her?" Jared asked.

Erlan looked at him as if he had sprouted wings. "What?"

"I mean, have you...you know...asked her if she's okay?"

"Jared," said Erlan, "I'm sure you're needed back at your post."

He wasn't wrong—Jared himself didn't entirely understand why he was wasting time questioning his friend about whether he'd comforted his own betrothed in the middle of an apostate attack—but he couldn't help himself.

"Very true," said Jared, and left. Erlan didn't appear to notice. Jared ran across the green to the infirmary, where he caught Ever just as she was about to enter.

"Are you all right?" he asked, taking the heavy buckets from her and carrying them inside. She was flushed and sweating, like everyone else, but otherwise she appeared to be alert and focused.

"Yes. Thanks," she said. Jared put the buckets down near the big hearth, which already had a big fire roaring within.

"Your family?" he asked.

"Fine. My father's with the riflemen."

"Good," said Jared. "Then be safe. And make sure you're the one who tends to me if I get wounded." He squeezed her shoulder, smiled at the expression on her face, and walked away.

He had just begun climbing the ladder back to the top of the wall—no one was moving up top, so the Marmacks must not have reappeared for a second go, yet—when he heard a woman scream.

The water had already begun to bubble in its cauldron before Ever was able to clear thoughts of Jared from her head. Why had he suddenly appeared like that? Just to see if she was all right? In the midst of all this? Was it bad that she now felt like judging Erlan, whom she had seen near his father across the green, for not even looking in her direction? Her supposed betrothed?

Sister Hales appeared from the main wardroom as if by magic. Her doughy face was red with exertion and several damp tendrils of her brown hair had escaped her tight bun to plaster against her forehead.

"Is the water boiling yet?" she asked.

"Almost, Sister," said Ever. The water was in fact just reaching a rolling boil. Ever collected a variety of jars from the shelves nearby and put them on the large work table. Willow bark for pain, calendula flowers for dressing wounds to prevent infection, honey for burns. They hadn't received many wounded yet. Only two men lay in the beds in the infirmary ward: one for a superficial arrow wound through the shoulder and another, an old Elder whose name Ever was blanking on at the moment, who had begun having chest pains at the onset of the attack. One sister had come in for a dressing for some mild burns but had left quickly to rejoin the bucket brigade. Ever knew there would be more serious injuries yet, however.

The scream split the air like lighting, even from inside the infirmary building. It seemed to come from the back of the village, near the cliffs. But that didn't make any sense, there was barely anyone left in that area. Everyone was either on the green, or fighting the fires, or on the walls, fending off the apostates.

"Heavenly Father!" exclaimed Sister Hales. "That'll mean more for us, no doubt." Collecting a bundle of the clean dressings Ever had cut and laid out, she disappeared back into the wardroom. A few minutes later two young brothers burst through the door carrying Sister Flowers, a beautiful young woman slightly older than Ever who was four months pregnant with her first child and who appeared to be unconscious.

"She was clubbed over the head," said one of the young men. Ever didn't look closely enough at them to even determine who they were.

"Bring her in here," said Ever, leading them into the ward. "Lay her on this bed, carefully. How long ago?"

"Only moments."

"Was the she the one who screamed?"

"Yes," said the first boy, who she now recognized as Brother Smoot, an older boy Dallin liked to follow around, when he wasn't busy idolizing Jared Meacham.

Ever felt Sister Flowers' pulse, which was weak, peeled back one of her eyelids, and called for Sister

Hales. The plump woman hurried over, leaving the man with the arrow wound, who was convinced he was dying despite their most fervent assurances to the contrary, to moan in despair.

Sister Hales bent over Sister Flowers' prone form from the other side of the bed, feeling tenderly at her head through her golden hair. It was matted with dark blood on one side of her head.

"What's happening?" asked Ever while Sister Hales assessed the situation.

Brother Smoot swallowed.

"They're coming over the northern walls. Near the cliffs," he said. His companion stood in dumb silence, staring at the pregnant woman on the bed before him in horror.

Ever had no time to respond.

"Her skull is broken," said Sister Hales, her voice flat and grim. "Badly. I'm afraid her brain…I could try to relieve the pressure, but the child…." Ever had rarely seen the unflappable Sister Hales unsure of what to do, but that, she realized with shock, was exactly what was happening.

"Let me try," said Ever quietly. Sister Hales looked at her worriedly.

"Can you…but it doesn't always come when you want it to," she said.

"Does she have a chance otherwise? Or the baby?"

Sister Hales thought for a moment, then shook her head.

"Even if I try to drill into her skull," she said, upon hearing which the younger, silent brother promptly hurried into the other room with his cheeks bulging and a hand over his mouth, "there's no guarantee the damage to her brain isn't already beyond helping. And the child is too young to be born."

"Then that makes it an easy decision," said Ever. Sister Hales nodded.

"What do you need?"

"Just space," said Ever. Sister Hales took Brother Smoot by the arm and led him away, leaving Ever alone with Sister Flowers.

"Heavenly Father give me strength," she whispered, then grasped the pretty face before her in both of her hands, her fingers reaching into the hot, wet blood that defiled her hair, and closed her eyes.

Ever breathed in deeply through her nose, then exhaled through her mouth, and focused on the woman's breathing. She could feel the thready pulse, the damaged tissue of her scalp, the seeping, slowly-congealing blood, the horrible broken landscape of her skull. She focused harder, and she could hear her heartbeat itself, beating slowly, as if with difficulty; and beyond it, a faint echo, a second heartbeat, a tiny flutter of the life that grew in her womb.

The power never came in exactly the same way. She couldn't always predict how well it would work or whether it would come when summoned at all, but when it did, it was almost always in response to a strong emotion on Ever's part. Looking at Sister Flowers, the girl that had been Harvest Maid two years running when Ever was still in pigtails, the young woman who had married the handsome Brother Flowers to all the village girls' envy, the radiant mother who had announced her pregnancy to the Women's Society only weeks before—looking at the mess some Marmack savage had made of her perfect head, Ever felt only anger.

It swelled in her chest like fire and swept upward; she could feel it in her cheeks and behind her eyes. She clenched her teeth together until they felt like they would break against each other. And then it came, the warmth, the Spirit, and it flowed from the place deep inside of her where it lived and ran down her arms and through her dry palms and into the woman beneath her. Ever was aware of a sharp intake of breath, and a deep moan, and a quiet cry. Vaguely, as if at a great distance, she heard the sound of gunshots and more screaming, but filtered through the golden light of the power as words through a waterfall.

Then there was only darkness.

6

"They killed Brother Rowley silently," said Elder Betenson, his voice cracking. "A...knife wound to the throat. They came over the walls at the northern tip of the point, where the cliffs are the steepest, exactly where we...where *I*...least expected them."

Jared forced down a surge of nausea with difficulty. He had seen the body, had run to defend the village when they realized what was happening. A Marmack had slashed the boy's throat savagely coming over the wall. They weren't alerted to the sneak attack until they heard screams from the women who were working nearby.

He had known Brother Rowley—not well, they were a year apart in age, Brother Rowley the younger. But he had known him, the way everybody knew everybody in Bountiful. Now that the battle was over it was becoming more and more difficult to stomach all of the violence that had occurred—not only that committed by the Marmacks, but the lives he had taken as well.

Elder Betenson was speaking to what was supposed to be a meeting of the Elders' High Council, but which had turned into a general gathering of nearly every man and most of the women in Bountiful. Those who couldn't fit into the Council chambers were lining the halls; every able-bodied person who wasn't manning the walls, tending the sick, or assisting with the last of the firefighting efforts appeared to be in or just outside of this room. The Bishop had made no move to throw anyone out.

Ever, from what he understood, which wasn't much, was resting in the infirmary. The women were abuzz over something she had done during the attack, apparently after Jared had left her with her buckets of water, but he hadn't had a chance to ferret out what it was yet.

He wondered if it had something to do with Sister Flowers, who was being escorted into the chamber now. He thought he had seen two boys carrying her away to the infirmary, but he hadn't been looking closely. She seemed fine now. Several other women were flanking her, one holding her arm, though it didn't look like she needed it. Her attendants seemed somewhat upset. One of them was whispering something in her ear. Sister Flowers, however, moved with purpose. An Elder gave up his seat on the bottom row of the stadium seating, and Sister Flowers sat down defiantly, one hand protecting the gentle swell of her belly.

Elder Betenson noticed her come in and faltered briefly upon seeing her. He cleared his throat and continued, looking like nothing so much as a guilty child admitting that he had struck a sibling.

"Elder Meacham was able to rally the rifle corps to the back of the village, and thankfully the apostates were defeated without further losses to our people. Every raider who set foot inside the walls of Bountiful lost his life for it," said Elder Betenson. "I can say that much, at least. Many of those outside the walls did as well."

Bishop Royce cleared his throat and interjected.

"For the, ah, benefit of those who have joined us, Elder Betenson, could you please report briefly on the state of our defenses now," said the Bishop.

"The watch has been tripled," he answered, "with every section of wall given equal priority. Additional braces have been installed behind the main gates. Every third man on the wall has a rifle, and the others have bows. Elder Blackham has recruited a second apprentice to assist with arrow production. The lanterns are burning brightly, and will be kept lit all night until further notice. They'll need a lot more than what they brought today to get past us again."

"And just why were they able to get past 'us' today, Elder Betenson," asked Elder Cardon, peering down from the dais at him over the heavy lenses that served him as eyeglasses. He said it snidely, as he said most everything, but for once the Bishop did not censure him.

"Because I failed you," said Elder Betenson. The crowd murmured quietly, and Jared heard a woman sobbing. The Elder turned slowly, addressing the entire community. "I failed you," he repeated.

"I won't insult you by making excuses. I didn't anticipate the extent of the Marmacks' attack, nor the sophistication of it. I assumed they would attack as they have in the past, and I left the least likely points of attack all but undefended. I was wrong."

"If it is the wish of this Council," he continued, turning to the Bishopric, "I will humbly tender my resignation as Master at Arms." But for the woman sobbing, the people were silent.

After a long, tense moment, the Bishop spoke.

"No, Elder Betenson," said Bishop Royce, "that is not the wish of this Council. We were all fooled by the apostates' belligerence and guile. You cannot take the blame completely on yourself. Please, speak no more of giving up this most important calling."

"Elder Betenson," said Elder Meacham, leaning forward in his chair on the dais, "do you have any new information on the Marmacks' movements?"

"No, Elder," said Betenson. "But there are scouting parties out as we speak, attempting to acquire just that. They left the village an hour ago, through the secret gates." There was only one main gate through the walls of Bountiful for the use of the general population of the community, but it was an open secret that Elder Betenson and the High Council had constructed clandestine methods of ingress and egress for emergencies and the Scouts.

"In your opinion," asked Elder Meacham, "what can we expect from the remnants of the Marmack force that attacked us?"

"I am...disinclined to speculate, Elder Meacham, particularly in this forum," said Elder Betenson.

"Come now, Elder," said Elder Meacham. "The people of Bountiful deserve to know. Your opinion is still respected and vital to the defense of this community. There will be no panic." Elder Meacham scanned the crowd upon speaking the last line, as if underscoring his words. Bishop Royce nodded curtly in approval.

"In that case..." said Elder Betenson, "I believe it's unwise to presume that we have caused any lasting damages to the Marmacks. I think this was a test, the last and most relevant of the feints they have been waging over the last few years. Their newfound tactics speak of a change in leadership, someone who is intent on securing Bountiful's resources for his own use. We've known for years that they crave the contents of our storehouses. Up until now, the distance between us and their main settlements has been too great to merit committing a large enough force, but as we all know, the Marmacks have expanded. They've begun settling land only miles from Bountiful, in small groups. It seems they may've finally decided they will have our home for their own, whatever it takes."

This was the first open, public confirmation of facts everyone in Bountiful had known for several years. There was uneasy murmuring in the audience, but as Jared's father had predicted, there was no panic.

"Excuse me, Elder Betenson," said Elder Cardon, "but am I correct in understanding that when you say that this horrible assault our community endured this morning was a *feint*, you mean that our enemies attacked us with less than their full strength?"

"There are more than enough Marmacks in the Northeast Kingdom to take this community if they want it badly enough, Elder Cardon," said Elder Betenson. "Up until fairly recently, we've been too remote to occasion their interest. It seems that has changed. There's no way to know for certain, but I think that this morning's attack was primarily intended to test our ability to respond to a more coordinated assault. Certainly there was the possibility that it may have succeeded, but the mess at the gates struck me as a distraction more than any real attempt at breaching our walls."

"In short, Elders," finished the Master at Arms, "they will be back. And it will only get worse. It is time that we start seriously considering our options."

Without waiting to see if there were any additional questions from the dais, Elder Betenson bowed slightly and excused himself, walking out of the hall without another word.

Jared was left, along with every other soul in the room, to ponder what Elder Betenson meant by "options."

• • •

For the second time in two days, Ever Oaks woke up in Bountiful's infirmary. Sitting up slightly, she pressed at her temples. Despite obviously having slept for some time, she felt exhausted, and she had a dull headache that felt like the remainder of something far worse. She saw that she was the only patient still in the room and began edging off of the cot gingerly.

"Oh no you don't," said Sister Hales, thumping through the archway noisily with a covered tray in her arms. "Not until you eat something, at least."

"How long was I out?" asked Ever, resigning herself to another enormous, bland meal. Sister Hales believed that simple food was best for the sick, which was undoubtedly true, but sipping broth and eating bread and boiled chicken was hardly Ever's idea of a feast.

"Most of the day," said Sister Hales, setting the tray, which had little legs on either side, on Ever's lap and then plumping the pillows behind her. "It's almost dinner time." Once she was satisfied that Ever's pillows were sufficiently fluffy, she whisked a cloth off of the tray and took the lid off of an earthenware crock.

To Ever's pleasant surprise, the food before her was anything but plain. The crock turned out to contain a hearty portion of Sister Orton's turkey stew, a mouth-watering concoction of tender meat, root vegetables, and herbs. There was also fresh bread, a smaller crock of whipped butter, a wedge of the sharp, yellow cheese that Elder Collins made, and a wide slice of Sister Higbee's honeyberry pie.

"Your mother and your brother and sister spent most of the afternoon with you," said Sister Hales, pulling a nearby chair up to Ever's bedside. "They only left half an hour ago to begin the cooking."

Ever began sampling the fare before her only to find, to her surprise, that she was ravenous. While she ate, Sister Hales caught her up on what had happened since she passed out. The community's casualties had been blessedly few; the biggest problem was finding shelter for those families whose homes had been damaged or destroyed by fire. Twenty-odd houses had burnt to the ground, Sister Hales told her sadly, despite the bucket brigades and the fire breaks designed into the village layout.

"But no one died of fire," she said. "No one died at all, except for that poor Rowley boy. They lost their house, too, but I don't think his mother will be sleeping tonight anyway." Ever swallowed a mouthful of stew and paused.

"And Sister Flowers?" she asked quietly, keeping her eyes on her plate.

"Oh! Of course, dear, I plumb forgot!" Sister Hales' face went from morose to beatific in a blink. "It's the talk of the village! You passed out as soon as your hands left her head, but that girl got up with a rush as if she'd overslept! She walked out of here—not before I made her eat something, of course—less than an hour later and wouldn't stop until she'd told all of Bountiful what you'd done." Sister Hales shook her head in wonder.

"I've never seen anything like it," she said. "Oh, of course everyone knows you're gifted, child, but this... nothing like this has happened in years. Her skull was as solid as it was before she was struck, her heartbeat strong, the baby active and regular." Sister Hales reached over and cupped Ever's cheek affectionately. "You're a gift, Ever, a gift from our Father in Heaven."

Ever had known, she realized: she'd known since the moment she woke up that Sister Flowers was fine. But Sister Hales was right: she'd never done anything like this before. No one had, to her knowledge.

Ever Oaks had earned the title of Saint when she discovered, at a young age, that she had the gift of healing: she could cure minor ills with a touch, and speed recovery for any number of wounds or sicknesses. The kind of minor miracles that the Blessed expected of their Saints. But she had never thought that she had it in her to wipe away a fatal injury like chalk from a slate. She realized her hands were trembling and forced herself to eat some bread and cheese.

"Sister Flowers wanted to tend to you herself," Sister Hales went on, "but none of us would have it. It was bad enough that we couldn't get her to stay in bed. The other sisters made sure you were well cared for while I was busy with the other injuries."

"Was...did Erlan Ballard come to see me?" Ever asked. Focusing on comparatively mundane things like whether Erlan had cared enough to visit her was easier than contemplating working the power of God with her small hands.

"No, dear," said Sister Hales, "now that you mention it, I don't believe he did." She frowned in disapproval. "That boy needs to get his priorities in order, if you ask me. Which you didn't, so I'll mind my business. Just be sure you come to me if you ever need advice on getting him into line after the two of you are married."

Her round face brightened then.

"Jared Meacham did stop in, though," she said. "Just before your family left. He hadn't even heard what happened until we told him."

Jared. Two days ago she wouldn't have said more about Jared Meacham than that he was Erlan's friend, and entirely too sure of himself for his own good. How was it that everything had gotten so complicated in such a short amount of time?

Sister Hales chattered on as Ever finished her dinner—the honeyberry pie was particularly memorable—telling her all about the High Council meeting that followed the battle, and the way everyone in the village had horned in on it, and what Elder Betenson had said.

"Options?" Ever repeated. "What did he mean?"

"That's the question of the day, child," said Sister Hales. "You be sure to let me know if you figure it out." Looking at the clock on the mantle—the infirmary had one of the few working clocks in Bountiful—she dusted off her apron and rose, taking Ever's tray, now a wasteland of napkins and crockery scraped clean of food, with her.

"You can head home whenever you're ready, Ever," said Sister Hales. "There's not much left to be done here. I can manage on my own. Your parents will be wanting to see you."

Finding her strength much improved, Ever walked home slowly in the fading afternoon light. She passed the burnt shells of a number of cabins, some of them still smoldering; the smell of char was strong in the air, and would be for a long time. Aside from a number of enthusiastic waves and the occasional called out blessing, Ever made it across the village without much fanfare. She had just gotten to the mouth of the wooded lane that led to the Ortons' cabin when Sister Flowers suddenly appeared in front of her.

Before she knew it, the woman was pulling her into a fierce hug. Ever squeaked in surprise as she felt her ribs creak.

"Bless you, Ever Oaks," said Sister Flowers. "God bless you for saving my child." When she finally pulled away Ever saw that she had tears in her eyes, and from the redness of their rims, not for the first time that day, either.

"Sister—"

"Sessaly," said Sister Flowers intensely. "You will only ever call me Sessaly from now on, and we will be sisters forever." She hugged her again, kissing her cheek this time with lips wet with tears.

"If the baby's born a girl, her name will be Ever Aaron, and if it's a boy, he'll be Aaron Ever," Sessaly whispered, "and we shall be forever thankful that you were born into this world." And she kissed her again, and then suddenly she was gone, wiping her eyes and pulling her shawl close around her and hurrying off, as if she couldn't stand the emotion of being in Ever's presence for another moment.

When Ever got home her family greeted her with the same love and warmth that she had come to expect, and her father kissed her forehead and told her he was proud, and she sat with them and ate another dinner just to be near them. It was good, after everything that had happened, to be just Ever again, and to put everything out of her mind except her family and the meal that they shared.

Jared arrived home at the normal dinner hour to find two covered dishes on the Meachams' long wooden table, one at his usual place and one at his father's. His father walked in only moments later.

"Your mother and sister will be some hours yet. The Women's Society has a lot of work to do to feed the families who lost their homes and get them settled in with host families until the cabins can be rebuilt. They've left us dinner." Even girls as young as Airie would be put to work, Jared knew, carrying and fetching.

Jared sat down and began eating without prayer or preamble. After removing his weapon belt and leather vest, his father joined him. Neither spoke for some time.

"You acquitted yourself finely, Jared," his father said. "I'm proud of you. If half of our men were as good with a bow and disciplined as you, I don't think the Marmacks would have made it into the village today." Elder Meacham was not a hard man, but neither was he free with praise. Coming from him, such a compliment was not hyperbole. Somehow, it didn't make Jared feel much better, though.

"I'm here," his father said, as if sensing his feelings, "if you need to talk about anything that happened."

"Does it get any easier?" Jared asked.

"No," his father said. Neither Jared nor his father needed to clarify that they were talking about killing. After a few more minutes of quiet chewing—cold roasted chicken with potatoes and a salad of peppery greens—Elder Meacham changed the subject.

"You've been spending a lot of time with Sister Oaks, lately." It wasn't a question, and Jared knew better than to ask how his father knew so much about his comings and goings. He had probably seen them talking across the green. Jared considered pointing out that much of it had been by necessity, but didn't, knowing his father had brought it up for a reason.

"Erlan asked me to catch up to her when she went out to the Neck," Jared explained. "She's been through a lot since then. I felt like I should check up on her, at least."

"She's engaged to be married to Erlan, isn't she?" His father knew quite well that Ever was indeed engaged to Erlan. Swallowing a mouthful of potato and taking a sip of water, Jared put his knife and fork down on the tabletop.

"What exactly are you driving at, Father?" he asked. Elder Meacham smiled.

"There was a time when you would never have dared talk to me like that."

"I'm sorry, I—"

"No, no," said his father, waving off his apology with a bite of chicken speared on his fork. "I'm glad of it. You're not a boy any longer, Jared, and there's no reason we should dance around difficult subjects as if you are.

"What I'm getting at," he said, "is that you have to be careful how you deal with another man's wife."

"She's not his wife yet," said Jared, surprised at the way his mouth twisted when he said it.

"No, but betrothed amounts to the same thing as far as other suitors are concerned," said Elder Meacham. "All I'm saying is that you need to think about what your priorities are. Older and better friendships than yours and Erlan's have been destroyed by the type of problems that arise when two men compete for the same woman."

Jared looked at his father in surprise.

"I'm not competing for her," he said.

"Then you should take care that your behavior doesn't indicate otherwise," said his father, finishing his water.

"And if you *are* competing for her," Elder Meacham continued, just when Jared thought he was finished, "you must realize that there are no half measures in this game."

Despite feeling as if he was walking on thin ice, even with his own father, Jared was intrigued.

"What do you mean?" he asked.

"I mean that Ever isn't going to wait forever," said his father. They both smiled at the unintended pun. "If you love her, if you want to be more to her than her husband's childhood friend, then you have to *act*, and act quickly. You're not eighteen for another nine months. Ever and Erlan are to be married this coming Spring. Your time is running out, son. If you want her, you have to say something."

His father's words made his cheeks burn, but he also felt oddly grateful for them, and closer to his father than he had felt in a long time. As surprising (and worrisome) as it was to discover his father kept such a close watch over his affairs, it was also comforting. Jared didn't say anything to confirm or deny his father's suppositions. The two men finished their meal in companionable silence.

As they rose to clear, Elder Meacham sighed quietly.

"Speaking of not being of age," he said, "there's something else I should tell you." Jared's father poured himself a mug of cider from the jug in the cold cupboard and waved at Jared to follow him into the small sitting area at the center of their cabin. The cider was slightly hard, Jared knew, a small liberty the older men of the village took with the commandments on occasion. *Not a few of them will be tapping their cider kegs tonight*, he thought.

Sitting across the heart from his father in the second of two padded chairs, Jared poked the fire alight and put on a fresh log. Elder Meacham sipped his cider and thought.

"The Bishopric intends to call a special meeting of the Elders' Council tomorrow," he said at last. "The agenda will be short."

"What for?"

His father took another drink of cider.

"To discuss what to do when Elder Haglund's mission fails to return."

"Then you don't think they're coming back either," Jared said. He'd suspected as much—certainly that the Bishopric knew something the rest of Bountiful didn't about the Haglund group—but he hadn't know any details. Until now.

"Not only do I know they're not coming back," said Elder Meacham, meeting his son's eyes across the warm glow of the hearth fire, "I know they never went where everyone thought they did in the first place."

Jared stayed silent, his hands clenching the arms of his chair, strangely nervous that his father would suddenly decide not to confide in him after all.

"Elder Haglund didn't lead a group of boys to Serai to find wives and trade handiworks," explained his father. "He led a group of rangers north to scout out possible resettlement locations."

"Resettlement…of what?" asked Jared.

"Bountiful," said his father. "The Bishopric—and certain members of the High Council—have known more about the Marmacks' movements than we've let on. We've known for years that they were becoming more aggressive, and almost two years ago we resolved to make…arrangements…for certain worst case scenarios."

"You're saying you knew we can't beat them. That we'd have to leave," said Jared. Elder Meacham nodded.

"When it became clear to us that Bountiful couldn't survive in the long term if we stayed here, we tasked Elder Haglund with investigating alternative sites. You might remember, he was something of a historian and a map-maker. He turned out to be the perfect man for the job. Or so we thought.

"You see," Jared's father continued, "at first those of us who knew argued about what to do. One or two of us thought we should stay put, improve our fortifications, and focus on increasing our population size and toughing it out. Make ourselves more of a force to be reckoned with.

"Even if that were possible, the more information we got about what our enemies were up to, the more certain we were that we didn't have a lot of time. Certainly not enough time to build the kind of force or the kind of fortress some of us wanted. So we decided it had to be a move."

"You said north," said Jared. "Where in the North?"

"Elder Haglund's ultimate destination was deep inside the Maine," said Elder Meacham. "He had a theory, and he could back it up to a certain extent. He thought that there were—installations, I think was the word he used—fortresses of the Old People, hidden deep in the mountains of the North. Bunkers, built to last. Something nobody else knows about anymore. Somewhere we could hole up and defend, really defend, if we had to. Anyway, it was the best idea that we had at the time. Elder Haglund was instructed to take a group of men and search out these fortresses, paying close attention to any other suitable spots along the way. We knew we had to go far, and the thought was that the Marmacks would be less likely to follow us such a long way, particularly into the ice of the Maine."

"There's a forest," Jared said, remembering stories he had heard when he was younger. He'd even looked at one of the ancient maps in the Bishop's office, once. "A huge forest...."

"The Great Northern Forest," his father said. "That's where they were headed."

"Why did you lie about it?" asked Jared.

"We didn't want to create a panic, not so early on. The people needed time to prepare, to accept the idea. And we didn't have a solid enough plan to go around making bold promises. So we sent Elder Haglund."

"How do you know they won't be back?"

"They left this time last year," said Elder Meacham. "The plan was for at least two of them to return within six months—more than enough time to make the journey there and back—and report to the Bishopric. The outer date—the date by which, we all agreed, if no one had come back, it would mean they weren't coming. The point of no return, so to speak. It would mean they'd failed—that they were dead. Well, that date is this weekend, just before the Sabbath, and somehow I don't expect them to suddenly appear in their Sunday finest to attend church."

Elder Meacham finished his cider with a long slug and placed the mug on the floor.

"Not that I'm complaining," said Jared, "but why are you telling me this, Father?"

"Because you're my son, and I trust you," he said. "And because you'd find out tomorrow anyway. And because I know you'll be disappointed when you find out you can't go."

"Go where?" Jared asked, confused.

"With the second expedition. We're sending another group north. It's our only choice, now, and we might already be too late."

7

A few minutes later, Jared stepped out of his family's cabin and set off through the woods. His father had let him go with a small smile, as if he knew perfectly well where Jared was headed, but Jared didn't care whether he did or not. He needed to talk to somebody about everything he'd just heard, secret or no secret, someone who would listen to him until he was finished talking and have a real response, and there was only one person in Bountiful who fit that description.

He found her where he expected to: behind the Orton family cabin, her arms wrapped around her body, looking out through the pinewoods over the wall at the crashing water far below.

"I did it," said Ever, without looking around. Jared stopped abruptly and cleared his throat. He hadn't deliberately made any noise; somehow, she'd known he'd was there.

"Did what?" Jared asked, though he thought he knew what she was referring to. He had had ample time to listen to village rumor between the council meeting and coming home.

"I saved her," she said. "Sister Flowers. She was... Sister Hales says she was as good as dead, and the baby too. But it worked." She turned and looked at him.

"I've healed wounds, even a broken bone once, but I've never done anything like this. I wasn't sure I could. I'm not sure I even..."

"What?" Jared asked.

"I'm not sure I even believed it, really. Believed that it was *me* doing it. That I had any...power...to do anything. Laying your hands on injured rabbits and flesh wounds...it's not the same thing. Not like this."

"Tell me," he said, unsure of what else to say. And she told him: Ever described seeing Sister Flowers, seeing the awful damage to her head and the silent swell of her belly, and the anger she felt. She described how everything got warm, and then went black.

"And then I woke up in a bed myself," she finished. Ever laughed quietly. "I'll never be much use in the field if I pass out every time I use it."

"Ever..." Jared began, the right words seeming just out of reach, "what you've done—"

"Please don't say it's a miracle," she said. "I'm not sure I could handle it. Not from you. I've heard it enough times today already. I don't want to feel like a...like some kind of...like something not human."

"I was going to say it's something no one else can do," said Jared. "But if it helps, I think what you do is...

very human." He wasn't precisely sure what he meant even as he spoke, but the words suddenly seemed right.

"What do you mean?" Ever asked. She looked scared and hopeful and skeptical all at once.

"I mean, the way you described it," he said. "The anger...the way you felt when it happened. Wherever this ability comes from, the way you use it doesn't seem anything like...." He struggled for the right analogy.

"Like the Savior resurrecting the blind man?" Ever said.

"Exactly," said Jared. "That's it exactly. You use it the way a human—a person who isn't a god—would use it. There's no white light and angels and all that. Just an emotion, and then something happens."

The moon had risen some time before, and now Jared saw Ever smile in the faint light it cast down among the trees. It struck him suddenly that she was beautiful—not merely pretty, but beautiful. Her hair was the color the women called strawberry blonde, her eyes were the green of lake water, and her cheeks had a softness that somehow only accentuated the strength that Jared saw in her face.

"Something happened, all right," she said.

"Saint is just a word, Ever," said Jared. "It doesn't have to mean you're set apart. It doesn't have to mean you're different, or better, or—"

"You don't think I'm better?" she said, raising an eyebrow.

"I—I didn't mean..." He trailed off and made a hopeless gesture.

"Jared Meacham, lost for words," said Ever. "Now I've seen everything."

Jared favored her with what he hoped was a stern glare.

"My father told me a secret tonight," he said, changing the subject.

"Since I'm not going to let you tell me you know a secret without sharing it, you might as well get right to it," she said.

"Actually," Jared replied, "he didn't even tell me not to say anything." Although, thinking about it now, Jared wasn't sure whether it was because everyone was going to find out tomorrow anyway, or because he preferred not to ask his son to make a promise he had every intention of breaking.

"Elder Haglund's mission…wasn't a mission," he said.

"What?"

"I mean, it wasn't what we thought it was. They didn't go to Serai to make love matches. They went to the North. To look for alternate sites."

"Alternate sites for what?" Ever asked.

"Bountiful," Jared said. He repeated what his father had told him as faithfully as he could remember, then watched Ever's face closely to see how she took it.

"And they don't know what happened," she said. Jared shook his head.

"They never received any communication from them. Not a word. The Elders are presuming they're dead."

Ever looked more intrigued than troubled by this announcement.

"So what are they going to do?" she asked.

"They're sending another expedition. Apparently the Marmack threat is worse than they've let on. They don't think we can survive here, long term."

"How could they keep this from us?"

"How couldn't they?" Jared said, with more conviction in his voice than he expected. It just made sense to him, perhaps for the first time in this very moment, why the High Council had decided to keep it a secret. "How could everyone go on living their lives, knowing that it might all end any day? Any minute? How productive, let alone happy, could Bountiful be?"

"We don't know that anyone would have panicked. Maybe a little, at first, but—"

"It might've been different if they had a plan, Ever," explained Jared, as much to himself as to her. "But they didn't know what to do. They were uncertain, scared even. And they were, and are, responsible for the lives of every man, woman, and child in this community. How could they come to the people and admit that they, their supposed leaders, didn't have any idea of what to do next?"

He shook his head, convincing himself, if not Ever.

"No, they needed more information. They needed something positive, something more than determination, something more than faith, even. They wanted to tell everyone when they had an answer to the first question they know everyone will have."

"Which is?" Ever asked.

" 'What do we do now?' " said Jared.

"And what would the answer have been, if Elder Haglund came back and told them what they wanted to hear? That we run? Move north? Jared, that's how Bountiful came to be in the first place. We were running from apostates. Running from our enemies. At what point do we decide we've had enough?"

"What if deciding we've had enough means we all die?" asked Jared. "I don't know. I don't have the answers. But I know my father well enough to know there's more to this. He didn't tell me everything. He admitted the only reason he was telling me at all was because…because I couldn't go."

"Couldn't go where? On this new mission?" Jared nodded.

"Why not?" asked Ever.

"It's to be limited to unmarried Elders," he explained. Jared himself wouldn't receive the high priesthood until he turned eighteen, almost a year away. He wasn't as bitter about it as he'd thought he would be: it was true that this was exactly the type of task he would be the first to volunteer for, but instead of juvenile frustration he felt only disappointment that he wouldn't be able to help.

"I'm sorry," she said.

"Don't be," Jared said. "Though they might not get lost this time if they had me with them." Ever smiled again.

"Everything's happening so fast," she said. Jared silently agreed.

"I guess we'll find out tomorrow. I should go. And I'm sure you need to rest," he said. "You know…"

"What is it?" asked Ever, turning to look at him.

"You've got pretty eyes, Ever Oaks," he said. "Pretty as pond water."

"Oh?" she said, with a surprised giggle. "You mean brackish and stagnant?" Jared grinned.

"No," he said. "Sometimes, in the right pond, on an especially clear day, you can see all the way down to the bottom and the water is a beautiful clear green."

He didn't wait for her to respond. He took the expression on her face, half blush and half concern, as answer enough, and left.

The morning after the battle dawned cool and clear, the first true autumn-like day they'd had since Bounty Month ended. Ever woke up feeling remarkably refreshed, as if the trials of the day before had been somehow bracing, like a walk after dinner. *You've got pretty eyes, Ever Oaks.*

She was glad Jared hadn't given her a chance to reply, last night. She was afraid of what she might have said. At the time, she'd simply been struck dumb, though she blushed to admit it. Now, in hindsight, the options arrayed themselves before her like twisting, fragile branches. *You mind your velvet tongue, Jared Meacham. Oh? Have you told that to Erlan? Thank you, Jared, I appreciate the compliment. So do you, Jared, deep and blue and eager.... Thank you, Jared, but I should get to bed. Thank you, Jared; now kiss me.*

She sat upright in bed as if she'd been sleeping on a wasp. Airie and Dallin were still asleep. The light was dim and gray through their small, square window. It was barely past dawn.

To get her mind off of the worrisome thoughts she was having, Ever rose, washed her face at the washstand in the corner of the room, dressed, and was in the process of starting breakfast cooking over the hearth in the kitchen when she heard the rest of the family rousing. Her father, wearing his favorite woolen wrapper against the chill of the morning, came out of his bedroom yawning.

"You're up early," he said, but seemed pleased.

A knock came at the front door just as she was about to reply. Elder Orton walked across the room and opened it. A boy, wearing the waistcoat and breeches of a Deacon, stood outside with his hands clasped behind his back officially.

"Yes?" said Elder Orton. The boy cleared his throat.

"All Elders are called to council today at half ten," the boy said importantly. "A special closed session will be held. Have a good day." With that he nodded abruptly, spun on his heel, and took off down the lane towards the next house.

Ever's father sighed and shut the door.

"I was hoping to actually get something done today," he said, sitting down at the plain pine table between the kitchen and the family area. Ever put a steaming mug down in front of him.

Elder Orton was a cabinetmaker by trade, a calling that suited him perfectly. He was meticulous and patient, and always careful. The small workshop that connected to the cabin by a covered walkway was a tidy nest of industry, its surfaces covered with sweet-smelling sawdust and carefully arranged hand tools. Like every other man in Bountiful, three quarters of the work he produced went to the community to be divided according to need. Unlike every other man, Elder Orton loved his calling, but the work never stopped coming.

"Hot coffee?" he asked, and Ever laughed.

"Nobody's seen coffee in a hundred years," she said, "and you couldn't drink it even if we had it. Enjoy your cider."

To her parents' shared delight, she cooked and served breakfast singlehandedly, then cleaned up the plates and pots afterward. She saw her father to the door and left behind him, headed for the infirmary. She couldn't wait around her cabin for word of what happened at the council meeting; she'd rather have something to do than sit and worry, unlike her foster mother, who seemed determined to make a career out of it.

There was already a crowd of younger men and a few women loitering around the council building when Ever crossed the village green to reach the infirmary. She had half a mind to join them, but there were wardens posted outside the building itself to ensure that only Elders entered. Not boys either, but full Elders, who knew better than to be tricked or persuaded by such as Ever Oaks. Or anyone else lingering around outside, for that matter. Shaking her head, she enjoyed the bright sun on the green grass for the few moments she had it, then pushed open the doors to the infirmary.

Sister Hales was scrubbing the floors when she entered, humming contentedly to herself as she scrubbed the wide plank flooring with a large, wet brick. The infirmary, like all of the public buildings surrounding the Bountiful village common, saw a lot of foot traffic, and its floors showed it. The wood needed to be smoothed often, scoured and sanded and scrubbed to keep them free of splinters and defects.

Ever waved and went directly into the apothecary pantry, set on reorganizing the jars of herbs and powdered compounds into a more logical system. It had been on her list of things to do for some time, and it was perfect for today: the type of repetitive activity that was detailed enough to be absorbing without being too challenging for a distracted mind. Ever smiled to herself. That was almost Bountiful's motto: proper work for every hand.

By luncheon she had the pantry looking neat and new. Sister Hales had scrubbed the blond wood of the floors down to a soft, white finish, and Ever had put fresh linens on every cot in the ward. The two women shared a simple lunch of cheese and apples and brown bread, Ever eating quietly while Sister Hales regaled her with the latest village gossip, including everything from the rumors about what the Elders were up to—"a major attack on the Marmack stronghold!"—to which of the Elders Sister Tingey, one of the few younger widows in Bountiful who had refused to take a second husband, was most recently seen walking in the woods with—"it's only been Elder Winterton lately, the lucky devil."

You wouldn't have known that only hours before the community had been afire and under attack, women and children screaming in its lanes. But then, that was how it was supposed to be, wasn't it? The Blessed had faith, and kept a positive outlook. No matter what. That morning, Ever found the thought vaguely discomforting.

The afternoon was consumed with more chores and the occasional villager needing treatment for something. One of the Higbee brothers came in with a large splinter of wood embedded deep in his palm, requiring no small amount of cutting by Sister Hales and squirming by the patient. He left with a sullen expression on his face and his hand expertly poulticed and wrapped.

Sister Talbot arrived after lunch under the pretense of bringing them a basket of shortcakes but in fact seeking advice over troublesome feminine issues. Sister Hales talked to her in private and then asked Ever to prepare an herbal infusion, sending her off smiling with instructions to get more exercise and draw a hot bath.

Later on there was a stubborn cold, a woodsman with muscle aches, and a young man with an infection of the eyelids. Before Ever knew it the sun was low in the sky, bathing the green in hazy golden light, and Sister Hales was preparing to close up shop.

"It isn't closing time yet, is it Sister?" asked Ever. The clock read half three; the infirmary was usually open until past dinner time, at which point Ever and Sister Hales often alternated schedules.

"We'll be closing early today, dear," she said. "Whatever's going on over yonder"—she nodded toward the council building—"my husband tells me every Elder in the village will have news for his family over supper tonight. It sounds important. I'll leave a note on the door letting any latecomers know to stop at my house should they need something." Ever nodded, suddenly worried. She'd managed to avoid thinking about the council meeting for most of the day. Jared's advance warning aside, she found herself dreading whatever news her father would share when he came home tonight. Maybe it was a fear of the unknown, maybe a simple fear of hearing openly what she already knew in secret.

She walked home slowly, in no rush to sit and watch her mother's nervous fretting, but soon found herself opening the front door of the Orton cabin and stepping inside. Sister Orton was indeed fretting, though doing so in a somewhat useful manner, as she was darning a basket of socks by the fireplace when Ever got home.

"He isn't back yet," she said.

"I'm sure he'll be home soon," Ever reassured her. Sister Orton was a good mother to Airie and Dallin; she was always able to keep them entertained and distracted, keep their list of chores up to date and make sure they were fed and clothed and happy, but it seemed to Ever that after a person reached a certain age her foster mother simply ceased being able to relate to them maternally and began to play the part of a concerned child. She loved her for all that, nurturing as she had been when Ever, a horrified girl of eight, had been brought wrapped in a blanket to the Orton family's door after the death of her birth parents.

Ever put herself to work starting a soup over the fire, which was almost finished by the time her Elder Orton came through the front door of their cabin followed by a skirl of chilly air.

"The weather's certainly turned," he said, closing the door firmly and removing the light jacket he wore. "Is dinner ready?"

"It is, though the bread's not warmed," said Ever, carrying in an earthenware tureen from the small kitchen and placing it on the center of the table.

"Let's eat, then," said Elder Orton, taking his usual seat. "Cold bread will do us no harm. I've got a lot to tell you." After her mother herded Airie away from her dollhouse in the bedroom and Dallin into the house from the back yard, Elder Orton blessed the food and waited for everyone to begin eating before he spoke.

"I spent a full day sitting on a hard bench listening to a large group of quarrelsome men, so my memory might not be perfect, but I'll try to tell you everything," he said. "The Council has ordered all of us to take this news to our families. They thought it best to do it this way, rather than have the news announced all at once to the whole village." Sighing, he dipped a slice of bread into his soup—a simple broth filled with autumn vegetables and what herbs they had in the back garden—and chewed it thoughtfully.

His comments about memory aside, her father relayed to the family what she already knew in what sounded suspiciously like a rehearsed summary: that what most of Bountiful knew as Elder Haglund's mission to the Blessed community at Serai for the purposes of trade and social intermingling had been nothing of the sort; that it had in fact been an expedition deep into the heart of the Maine in search of a new site for the relocation of Bountiful; that the Bishopric and selected members of the High Council had sent Elder Haglund north because of the alarming resurgence of the Marmack apostates in the area; that Bountiful's leaders had concealed their knowledge of the dangers to the community; and that they now presumed the entire party permanently missing or dead.

He also revealed a few details that Jared had neglected to mention to Ever the night before.

"Elder Haglund had long made a study of the Old People and their civilization," Elder Orton explained. "He was fascinated by them, and in particular by the heights of their power just before the Fall—"

"Not an appropriate fascination," interjected Sister Orton, looking at the younger children. "The Old People were destroyed because they lived in sin and invited a new Apostasy. Not something to be studied, but something to be forgotten—except as a cautionary tale."

Ever could see that her mother was trying her best to hold it together, but the news Elder Orton had brought home with him had clearly affected her. She often got like this when she was nervous: short and unfocused, prone to interrupt, as if her perception had narrowed.

"Most of the Elders' Council would agree with you, my dear," said Elder Orton gently. "Elder Haglund's interests were well known to us, but we tolerated them for years because they seemed harmless. And when they actually became useful to our cause, the Bishop and his advisors put them to use.

"The Fall was not completely unforeseen by the Old People. Some factions other than our ancestors saw its shadow on the horizon and made great efforts to prepare for it. Unfortunately, they put their trust in technology rather than the Word, and they were not saved. But the things they built—great structures, underground fortresses, and storehouses impenetrable to time and corrosion—likely still stand. Or so Elder Haglund maintained."

Elder Orton cleared his throat and refilled his wooden water cup from the pitcher on the table. After drinking deeply, he continued.

"Not all of the Elders who were informed of this plan were convinced by it; some saw it as ungodly, relying on the preparations of apostates; others simply thought it impractical. Elder Haglund's group was tasked with finding these hidden havens if at all possible, but if not, with finding another suitable location for Bountiful."

"So small a group?" Ever asked. "How did they expect to make it so far?"

"The thinking was that a smaller party could pass unnoticed through places where a larger force would draw unwanted attention," her father said. "They also sent a Saint with them."

This was news to Ever, and to everyone; Jared certainly hadn't known. She knew he would have mentioned it if he had.

"Who?" she asked.

"Elder Bastian," said her father. "Apparently his Sainthood only manifested itself shortly before the expedition left, and as he was already on the short list of candidates to go north, the Bishopric instructed him to keep it quiet. They thought revealing it would only raise too many questions. A boon to the quest, they called it."

It was unusual for Saints to discover their powers past puberty, but it wasn't unheard of. Elder Bastian, if she remembered correctly, had just turned 18 when he left, a year before.

"How…what were his gifts?" she asked.

"According to the Bishopric," said Elder Orton, "he possessed enhanced strength and agility, as well as supernatural speed and vision."

It made sense to Ever why the Bishopric would want that kept a secret. Such traits were rare even among Saints. Most of the Blessed who manifested divine powers did so in less dramatic ways: enhanced empathy, the ability to speak with animals, or limited foresight. Ever's healing powers were considered equally rare. If the whole of Bountiful had known that Elder Haglund was leaving with a Saint like Elder Bastian, whose abilities might have been used to protect the village, there certainly would have been trouble.

"In any case," her father said, "the point by which the Bishopric expected to hear back from Elder Haglund has long passed. This coming Sunday—one day from now—marks the one year anniversary of their departure, and the official date by which their party would be deemed lost if no communication had been established."

"Perhaps it's for the best," Ever's mother said. She hadn't touched her soup since her husband began speaking, Ever noticed, and she held her hands out of sight in her lap. "We must trust in our Father in heaven to keep us safe. Not the works of a vanished race."

"I've been listening to the same argument all day," said Elder Orton. "Why do you think it took us so long? There was a lot of dissension, about the fact that so much was kept from the Council at large, and about what to do now that everyone knows."

"What was decided?" Ever asked, already knowing the answer.

"They're to send another expedition," Elder Orton said. "Slightly larger, most likely, and better outfitted."

"With what goal?" asked Ever's mother. Her thin face was drawn into a mask of anxiety. She was a pretty woman when she smiled, but these days especially she seemed to exist in a perpetual state of fear.

"First, to follow the route Elder Haglund's group planned to take and locate them, if possible, and if not, to finish what they started."

Ever's parents continued discussing the matter further while she listened silently. Airie, who had eaten her soup with gusto and was now on her second serving, appeared all but oblivious to what was going on, while Dallin had eaten sparingly. Her younger brother appeared to barely be restraining his excitement. Eventually, however, he couldn't hold back anymore.

"Who's going, Papa?" he asked. He was seated directly across the table from Ever; she could feel his right knee bobbing up and down in animatedly. Her father merely smiled.

"Not you, son," he said, not unkindly. "The one thing that the Council could agree on, almost unanimously, was that only unmarried men who had reached the appropriate age and been ordained Elders could go. As for the specifics, that's yet to be decided. I believe the Bishopric already has some ideas, but they've also asked that any volunteers present themselves on the morrow. No one will be forced to go who doesn't want to."

Ever was pleased that Dallin had asked the question first. It was the only piece of information Ever still needed, and now that she had it she stayed silent and began clearing plates when everyone had finished—or in her mother's case, when it became clear she had no intention of eating.

Her father reassured everyone that all would be well, despite what Ever thought was fairly discouraging news about the actual capabilities of the Marmacks. He was only mildly successful. Sister Orton appeared somewhat broken, and spent the rest of the evening looking like a little girl who hadn't gotten her way. The family went to bed even earlier than usual.

In the bedroom they shared, Dallin and Airie were asleep in moments. Dallin snored softly most nights, but that wasn't what kept Ever awake. She thought of the dream she had had, only the night before, and she thought of Erlan. After an hour or more of thinking, she squeezed her eyes shut and asked for help.

8

Shortly after breakfast the following morning, which she had forced herself to eat despite an unsettled stomach, Ever left the house under the pretense of making an early start at the infirmary. She presented herself at the door to Bishop Royce's private office in the new wing of the Council building. The Bishop opened the door himself only moments after she knocked. His eyes widened when he saw her.

"Sister Oaks," he said, showing her in and offering her a seat in front of the large, heavy table that seemed to serve as both desk and meeting table. "What can I do for you this morning? I should say that I'm expecting at least a few appointments this morning, given the Council's announcements yesterday, so you'll forgive me if I have to cut this short at some point."

Bishop Royce was a polite, stocky man with thinning brown hair and a trustworthy face. He'd been a popular Bishop for all of his tenure, and Ever liked him. She cleared her throat nervously.

"If I take your meaning correctly, Bishop," she said, "I believe I am one of those appointments."

"What do you mean, sister?" he asked. The look of confusion on his face made Ever want to giggle. She stifled the feeling quickly. The last thing she needed was the Bishop thinking that she made this request lightly.

"I want to join the second expedition north," said Ever.

To his credit, Bishop Royce appeared to take her request entirely seriously. Less than ten minutes later Ever walked out of his office with an appointment to meet again later that day with her foster father present. A line of young men had formed outside the Bishop's door, all of them members of the high priesthood—Elders—and all of them buzzing with the same nervous excitement that Ever had seen on Dallin's face just last night.

She had known the Bishop would want to consult with Elder Orton, if he even gave her request real consideration, but it still irked her. She was a grown woman. Why should a man have to speak for her? The customs of Bountiful were set, however, and unmarried women under the age of twenty-five were technically still wards of their fathers. Ever had thought it important that she appear herself, without the benefit of a guardian, to make her plea before Bishop Royce, the same as all of the other candidates. How could he believe she was capable of making the long journey to the

Maine, sure to be fraught with dangers and hardships, if she couldn't even stand up on her own and ask for it?

The morning was cool, the first true stirrings of autumn were on the wind that gusted through the pines. With winter less than two months away, it was hardly the best time of year to be leaving on a long journey north, but the timing was unavoidable. Ever was in the middle of making a mental inventory of the clothes she would need when she remembered that the Council hadn't given her permission to go yet. She couldn't tell if her easy certainty was due to her prayers last night or simply to her own stubborn refusal to admit that it could happen without her.

Trying to keep the confident state of mind she felt when she woke up that morning, Ever made her way to her father's workshop and knocked on the door.

Several hours later, Ever sat before Bishop Royce again, in the same chair she had sat in that morning, with Elder Orton beside her. This time, however, the other two members of the Bishopric were present: Elder Meacham sat to the Bishop's right, Elder Cardon to his left. Jared's father was a comfort, as she knew he would treat her fairly, but Ever could have done without Elder Cardon's critical stare. *I suppose I should just be grateful they took me seriously enough to show up.*

"I've informed my counselors of your request, Sister Oaks," said Bishop Royce, gesturing at the two men flanking him behind his work table, "and I thank you,

Elder Orton, for agreeing to meet with us here this afternoon. These are most…unusual circumstances, and I thought it would be best if we discussed it both officially and…informally."

In other words, thought Ever, *you didn't want to create an uproar by bringing this before the High Council, but neither did you want to dismiss my request all on your own—just in case it seemed somehow below board.* Ever couldn't let the fact that she found Bishop Royce likable to get in the way of the fact that he had an undeniable skill with politics.

Her father had responded as she expected him to, after he got over his surprise: taking her hands in his own before the hearth in his warm workshop, he had told her how proud he was of her bravery and encouraged her to apply that same sense of duty and courage to her work in Bountiful. It had been a dismissal, if a kind one. Elder Orton was a fair and agreeable man, however, and he had consented to accompany her to meet with the Bishop so that she could at least make her case. He had not promised to give his blessing, however.

The result was that Ever, sitting primly in her chair before Bountiful's leader, felt both incredibly alone and even more determined than ever to prove that she was right. She had not come unprepared. She only hoped that what she was about to share with them would be convincing.

"I hope you know, Sister Oaks," said Elder Cardon, "that the only reason you're sitting here is because of your status as a Saint." The skinny man looked like he had bitten into something sour.

"What Elder Cardon means to say, Ever," said Elder Meacham, glancing sidelong at his colleague, "is that you are special. You've been given a gift by God, and because of that fact we must consider your request, as we consider all the words and actions of the Saints, in the serious light which its source merits."

"Elder Orton," said Bishop Royce, "it's your right to speak first, if you want to. Ever Oaks is your responsibility and your child under the law. What are your thoughts about this matter?"

"I defer to my daughter, Bishop," said Ever's father. "I'm here at her request today. I'll be happy to give you my opinion after she has had the chance to speak her peace."

The Bishop nodded and looked at Ever. Ever took a deep breath and swallowed. This was it. The one chance she had, the only chance to—*No. No. Say what you came to say. Don't think about how they'll hear it; concentrate on telling it.*

"Two nights ago I had a dream," Ever began, folding her hands in her lap and looking at each of the men in front of her in turn. She described the visions she had seen: the mountain, the strange girl, the torn web, all of it. Elder Meacham paled noticeably when she described seeing Jared in pain. She finished by describing the part of her dream where she had seen her siblings and the other children of Bountiful alone in the forest, and Bountiful itself on fire. She talked until she had gotten out every detail that she could remember.

When she was done all of the men were visibly shaken. Her father had put a hand over his mouth—whether in consternation or nausea, she couldn't tell—when she had talked about Dallin and Airie and the children. She had told him she'd been inspired by dream and by prayer, but she had not told him the details.

"This," said Elder Cardon, his face twisting in restrained anger, "is an outrage. You would use our worst fears for your own—"

"Be quiet, Brigham," said the Bishop. Ever had never heard him speak so curtly before. Massaging his temples with the thumb and middle finger of his right hand, he closed his eyes and seemed to think for a moment. *Or is he praying?* When he opened them again he had regained his composure.

"I won't insult your intelligence or your character by explaining how serious a situation this is, Ever," said the Bishop. "The visions you've described are…disturbing. Very disturbing. Please forgive me for what I'm about to ask." He looked at her right in the eye, then, his own eyes narrowing in an expression of hawk-like scrutiny.

"Do you, Sister Ever Oaks, in the Presence of God, the Savior, and the Ghost, swear on your soul that what you have told us here is true?"

"How could she know whether it's true?" spat Elder Cardon. The Bishop held up a finger. The air seemed to fall silent and still; despite the heavy feeling she had, Ever couldn't help but feel like laughing—at the way the Bishop controlled Elder Cardon like an unruly child; at the bitter look on Elder Cardon's face; at the simple fact that she was sitting where she was sitting, having the conversation she was having.

"I do, Bishop; Elder Meacham, Elder Cardon—Father," said Ever. "Elder Cardon is right to question, I think—I can only tell you what I saw. Everything I said to you here is true, as best I can remember it—it's what I saw in my dream. But I can't tell you whether it's true in the larger sense. I don't know whether it's a divine vision or...or just a nightmare. But I prayed on it, and I believe that what I saw is the future, or a possible future."

"You see?" said Elder Cardon. "She admits herself that she doesn't know. The girl had a dream, Bishop. Nothing was revealed to her: she had an unpleasant dream. Should we now send an unprepared girl out into the wilderness to endanger the lives of her companions because of a dream?"

"Saints have been known to foretell future events," said Elder Meacham.

"But that is not her Gift," said Elder Cardon. "She's a healer."

"Saintly Gifts have been known to develop and change," said Elder Meacham. "Consider Elder Bastian: his gift only revealed itself last year. How can we know what's possible and what's not?"

"We can't," said the Bishop. "It is certainly not for us to understand the workings of the Godhead. Nor should we presume that we know how God would choose to give the gift of prescience, or how He would choose to communicate at all—not every message comes in the form of a burning bush, my brothers."

"I would not have come to you just because of a troublesome dream," said Ever. "I asked for guidance—I knelt at my bed and asked God to tell me what to do. I prayed for hours. No answer came, not directly, not right then; but when I woke up the next morning, and heard screaming, and knew that we were under attack, I knew that what I saw was no normal dream.

"And when my father told me that the Council was sending men north," finished Ever, "I knew—not guessed, not thought—I *knew* what I had to do. I have to go on this journey, Bishop. I have to go into the North. I'm afraid of what will happen if I don't."

"You're a woman," said Elder Cardon. *Thank you for noticing*, thought Ever.

"Yes, I am," she said.

"Even presuming we are to believe what you say, how can we send a woman out...out *there*, where there are Apostates, and Damned, and..."

"I'm not unfamiliar with woodcraft," said Ever. "You forget, Elder Cardon, that I travel outside of Bountiful regularly to treat the Blessed that choose to live outside our walls."

"And look what happened last time you did that," he said, almost snarling. "You would be a liability to the men who went with you. What if you were captured; what if they were forced to choose between saving you and completing the task we set for them? It isn't a fair thing to ask."

"I can defend myself," said Ever. Her voice was rising. She could feel heat in her cheeks. Her father put his hand on her arm gently.

"My biggest concern," said Elder Meacham, "aside from everything else, is the danger of sending one of our most powerful Saints away from our people. Ever is vital to the health of this community—and her powers are still growing. Look what she did for Sister Flowers. Even if we wanted to, the people would never support it. For this and other reasons."

Elder Cardon continued with his interrogation as if Elder Meacham had not spoken. Ever began to feel overwhelmed.

Bishop Royce, who had remained in silent thought during her back and forth with Elder Cardon, held up both hands, palms out, and stood.

"Clearly there is a great deal of emotion and belief weighing on this issue," he said. "It will certainly require careful consideration. We'll recess for now." Looking at Elder Orton, he began instructing him to keep the matter secret for the time being, and on when to expect a summons from him to return.

Elder Meacham was engaged in whispered conversation with Elder Cardon behind the Bishop; he seemed to be trying to calm the older man down.

Ever stopped paying attention. It wasn't enough. They had listened, better than she had expected them to, but they had not *heard*. It was strange: she felt certain, now, that she had had a revelation from God, but that certainty hadn't come all at once like she would have expected it. There had been very little magic involved. She hadn't been visited by an angel; God hadn't appeared to her in the woods. She had a dream—which was just a bunch of thoughts and images—and then she prayed, and soon afterward she knew that what she had seen was true. As simple as that.

The anger Elder Cardon had aroused in her began to change into something else. She felt the heat in her cheeks again, but it was both gentler and scarier—a turning anxiety that begged to be let loose. Her palms started to tingle like they did when she healed someone, but aside from that similarity this was quite different. The room before her seemed to grow brighter and slow down, as if every detail was more crystalline and perfect; she could see the dust on Bishop Royce's table, feel the imperfections in the floor beneath her feet, and hear every word the Elders spoke as if it had been spoken directly into her ear.

She found that she could focus this new perception like a lens. Moving it from Elders Cardon and Meacham, she turned to her father and Bishop Royce. The Bishop had sat down, and her father had taken her gently by the elbow to help her rise. Her perspective shifted dizzily when she moved her eyes, as if someone else was turning her head for her.

Ever felt separate from herself, as if she were only a passenger in her own body. Something or someone else was directing her actions. She could hear her heart beating in her chest like a slow drumbeat. The world moved around her, at once unreal and yet more real than she had ever suspected. She heard a sound like calm breath, not her own, and then she was rising.

Bishop Royce was speaking to her, smiling kindly and saying goodbye. She reached across the table, easily pulling free from her father's surprised grip, and took the Bishop's head in her hands. She gripped the sides of his head with her palms and looked into his eyes and his expression of surprise faded into oneness and acceptance.

They were one then, if only for a few moments, and then something bent from her mind into his, like a shaft of light directed through a prism.

Ever wasn't entirely certain what she was sharing with him. She was far from being in control of the process. She knew that Bishop Royce would now see her vision as she had seen it; she knew that he would feel the things she had felt when it played through her mind; she knew that he would feel the surety that prayer had brought to her.

It took only a moment: one perfect moment of shared, crystal time. Ever was already falling back ungracefully into her chair when Elder Meacham reached out to pull them apart. She shivered as if with cold, and the world returned to normal. Aside from a sudden exhaustion, like she hadn't slept all night, she was herself again.

Bishop Royce had barely moved. He still sat at his desk in the same position in which Ever had left him. His short, curling brown hair was mussed from her hands, but his eyes were open and staring, as if he was seeing something that wasn't there—which, perhaps he was.

When next he spoke, Ever relaxed. She had done it. The need to convince these men had been gnawing at her, perhaps more strongly than she had even realized—until that need suddenly disappeared. All would be well.

Elder Orton had taken her face in his hand and was peering down at her worriedly. Beyond her father's face Ever could see Elder Meacham doing much the same to Bishop Royce. When the Bishop didn't respond right away, Jared's father shouted for the Priests that worked as scribes in the adjoining offices. One of them opened the door, glancing around with wide eyes.

"Send for Sister Hales," said Elder Meacham.

"No," said Bishop Royce, shaking off his apparent daze and raising a hand to his forehead. "No. I'm fine. I—I'll be fine." At a nod from the Bishop, the frightened clerk disappeared behind the door again, and they were alone.

"I've seen—what I've seen…" Bishop Royce said, then cleared his throat and visibly collected himself. "I've been shown something. Ever is telling the truth. The matter before us is the least of our coming troubles, I think, yet something tells me it's very important. Sister Oaks will go north. May God protect her, and us all."

9

It wasn't that simple, of course, but Ever hadn't expected it to be. Bishop Royce curtailed the discussion relatively soon after his revelation, withdrawing to discuss the matter further with his advisors and leaving Ever to explain to her father what had just happened as best she could. Their walk home was awkward; she could see that her foster father was concerned by what had happened and she wasn't sure how to make him feel better—or if she even could. She tried to explain what she had felt when she laid her hands on the Bishop and what had happened when she did. She was shaken herself, however, and her descriptive powers were not at their best. In the end, she supposed, it came down to faith.

Taking his hands before the door to their cabin, as he had taken hers only hours before, Ever looked up at Elder Orton and smiled. She hoped her smile was reassuring.

"Do you remember when I was ten and I asked you how you knew God was real?" Ever asked him. "Do you remember your answer?"

"I said that I didn't know, not in the way that I know that pine is softer than oak, or that any board will warp if left in the rain for too long, no matter what kind of wood it is. But I felt it. I believed. And that was enough."

Once he was able to wrap Ever's experiences inside the folds of his faith he seemed satisfied, for the moment at least. Her father was the least of her problems, however.

When the High Council announced Ever's name among the list of young men traveling into the Maine, all of Bountiful twisted itself into a genuine uproar. Some were shocked, some outraged—mostly older men and boys too young to join the party themselves—and some unexpectedly supportive: the Women's Society in particular took Ever's inclusion as a sign from on high that the women of Bountiful were just as important to the fight for the community's survival as the men that manned its walls. Ever wasn't sure that any reasonable member of the Blessed actually disagreed with that idea, but nonetheless, her sisters seemed to make an unspoken decision to elect Ever their official figurehead overnight.

Elder Cardon was openly critical and more than willing to say so whenever given the slightest opportunity. Not in front of Sister Hales, of course, or Sister

Flowers, or any other female of Bountiful, for that matter, but his attempts to sow discord did seem to take root among the older members of the High Council.

Bishop Royce's declaration was sufficient for most of the community, but Ever was not blind enough to the ways of the Elders' Council to miss the fact that he had lost some support over it.

Then there was Ever's mother, who seemed to have decided that Ever going on a journey was a sign of the arrival of the end of days. Elder Orton was remarkably helpful in dealing with her, however, and Sister Orton's doomsaying lightened up remarkably after an incident on the village green involving one of Elder Cardon's devotees and a rotten pumpkin.

Ever hadn't asked any questions, but the story came to her through the rumor mill regardless. One Elder Harward, a crotchety old spindle of a man who was known to indulge in the smoking of certain medicinal plants in the woods behind his cabin, made the mistake of implying that Ever, in going north with the men, had lost favor in God's eyes—for surely no woman beloved of the Lord would find herself tramping across hard country in the company of unmarried men when she could be happily wedded and pregnant at home. Ever's mother, whose fatalism apparently did not extend to brooking external criticism of her children, had responded memorably. Versions of her verbal response varied, though most included the words "imbecile," "sinful," and "backwards," as well as the phrases "mad as a dog in heat," "the Devil's weed," and "your rotten brain."

Everyone agreed, however, that Sister Orton had punctuated her retort by hurling a small, convenient pumpkin at Elder Harward's head and conveying with equal eloquence what would happen should he "presume to spread his putrid slander" about members of her family again. All present agreed that the fact that the pumpkin turned out to be quite rotten was an indication of Heaven's actual feelings about Elder Harward's assertions.

Having the opportunity to vent her fears in the form of uncontrolled anger seemed to help Sister Orton, who almost immediately calmed down to a more manageable level. She was still clingier than usual—when she was at home Ever was often afraid her foster mother would try to follow her into the outhouse. Considering the outhouse was located in a closet behind the cabin barely big enough for one person to sit down in, this would have been a fairly difficult and embarrassing proposition for both women.

For Ever, the next few days alternately involved long periods of relative boredom followed by flurries of furious activity. The Bishopric had announced the make-up of the Northern Expedition—as it was being called—without particular fanfare and without taking a vote from the Elders Council or the High Council. This was narrowly within the Bishop's authority, given that the matter was one of Bountiful's security and well-being, but many of the men of Bountiful were still heard to grumble about "not being consulted."

She had barely seen either Jared or Erlan since her meeting with the Bishop. Jared, at least, had the excuse of being busy helping his father with preparations for supplying the party with the appropriate arms and other materiel they would need for their journey. He had waved a few times from across the common, but the pace Elder Meacham set appeared to be running his son ragged. Ever suspected Erlan, on the other hand, was simply avoiding her.

She had no doubt that the initiative she'd taken in approaching the Bishop about going had made him feel insecure or uncomfortable, if not outright embarrassed. Erlan's ego had a fragility to it that made Ever anxious to avoid conflict with him.

Erlan ended his silence on the Sabbath, the day that the people of Bountiful had believed Elder Haglund's mission was due to return.

Ever was winding clean white strips of freshly woven bandage cloth into neat bundles to be stored on the shelves of the infirmary's now-meticulous supply pantry when Dallin came in. Sister Hales was out doing home visits, seeing to patients too ill, too old, or too stubborn to come into the infirmary on their own.

"Ever," said Dallin, rapping softly on the wooden doorjamb. She hadn't heard him come in. Ever had found, in the last few days in particular, that her absorption in the more menial tasks of her duties to the infirmary was almost complete. Sister Hales had threatened to install a bell at the greeting counter if she couldn't be made to pay attention.

All the same, Dallin's sudden appearance in the pantry didn't startle her. Nothing much startled her these days; she had lived in a kind of dreamy bubble of comforting confusion since sharing her mind with Bishop Royce.

"Yes?" she asked, looking up. She was squatting on the floor of the pantry with several piles of bandage cloth, organized by size, shape, and application.

"Father wants to see you," said Dallin. "He's in the council building."

"Now?"

"He said it's important."

Ever knew without asking that her father wouldn't have summoned her like this if it could wait until she got home that evening. As much as she disliked leaving a mess behind her and the infirmary unattended, she knew at once that she had to go. Getting up and dusting off her apron—the pantry needed to be swept again—she followed Dallin into the infirmary's entrance room.

"Can you stay here and keep an eye on things for me?" Ever asked. "Sister Hales is out."

Dallin nodded.

"Father saw her on the green. He told me I should stay and watch the door if you wanted me to."

"Good," she said.

"Ever," Dallin said, as she was walking out the door.

"What?"

"Your hair," Dallin said, gesturing at her forehead. Ever frowned, stepped back inside, and fetched the polished silver plate that served the infirmary as a looking glass. Her hair was indeed something of a mess; several tendrils had crept out of the ponytail she kept it in and a halo of frizz floated above the crown of her head. How had it gotten such a mess? Moreover, why was her little brother, who cared as much about his sisters' hair as fish cared about the weather, remarking on it?

Ever sorted herself out, replaced the silver plate, and thanked Dallin, ruffling his own hair before ducking out of the infirmary. The council building was just across the green. She allowed herself a moment of curiosity about what her father was doing away from his workshop at this time of day, but in reality there were a number of reasons he might be in the village square, and an even greater number of reasons he might want to talk to her.

She pushed through the double doors, nodded to the Priest scribes bent over their desks, and made it almost to the door of the council chamber itself before she noticed Elder Orton waving to her from the other side of the large entrance hall that preceded the council chamber. With him were Erlan Ballard and his father.

Gripped by a sudden anxiety, Ever cleared her throat, waved back, and made her way with as much decorum as possible to where the three men stood. She nodded to Erlan and Elder Ballard politely and followed her father into one of the adjoining public sitting rooms. The sitting rooms were small and comfortable, if windowless, and served multiple purposes for Bountiful's public and the Elders alike. The Bishopric often received complaints from villagers there, and the Elders assigned to counsel members of the congregation with personal or spiritual concerns used them as a neutral meeting place.

"Good day, Ever," said Erlan. The room was sparsely but comfortably furnished. Four wooden armchairs supplied with a variety of lumpy cushions were arranged around a small, low table in the center of the room. A pitcher of water and four cups had been placed on a simple sideboard at the back.

"Good day, Erlan," said Ever. Elder Ballard had taken the chair next to his son. Ever sat down across from Erlan and, after shutting the sitting room's stout wooden door, Elder Orton sat next to her.

"You've certainly been busy, young lady," said Elder Ballard, peering at her over the thick, hand-ground lenses of his spectacles. Ever had once heard Elder Ballard described by one of the Women's Society sisters as "weedy," and the characterization still made her want to giggle. Erlan had a fleshy appearance, though he was not fat, but his father was a skinny man with a gleaming bald head. His arms and legs looked as if they had trouble supporting even his small weight.

"I suppose you could say that," Ever replied. She knew Elder Ballard and his wife, of course—she was technically engaged to their son, after all—but she didn't feel like she knew them well. They had no children other than Erlan and they kept mostly to themselves. Elder Ballard—whose first name she had heard so seldom that it was now escaping her—was quiet about his politics, though he was known to be a close confidant of Elder Cardon, and Sister Ballard rarely attended optional Women's Society gatherings or spoke up when she did.

Ever's father cleared his throat. It wasn't like Aethan Orton to appear nervous, but he seemed to be now.

"We're here," Elder Ballard said, as if realizing her father was about to speak and wanting to do so first, "because the Bishopric's decision to allow you—at your own request, I might add—to travel into the North affects our interests. Specifically, the promise you made to my son."

"I—I'm not sure I understand, Elder Ballard," said Ever. Which was at least half-true. She had feared, on some level, that Erlan would make trouble, but she hadn't allowed herself to think about it. The feeling that made her go to the Bishop had been too strong, and her feelings about Erlan not strong enough to stop her.

"It's simple, child: you are betrothed to my son," said Erlan's father. "You are to be married in the spring. Therefore, it certainly concerns us that you've decided to march into the frozen north with a group of unmarried men."

"I'm not sure I like what you're implying, Elder Ballard," said Elder Orton. "If you speak to the Bishop—"

"I meant no offense, Elder Orton," said Elder Ballard, adjusting his spectacles. "And I've spoken to the Bishop. As this meeting is clearly...uncomfortable for you and your daughter, however, allow me to get to the point."

Please do, thought Ever.

"Erlan and Ever have been promised for some years, at this point, and given both the timing and the nature of this journey she is about to undertake, it behooves us to make alternate arrangements for their marriage.

Simply put, Elder Orton, it would be inappropriate for Sister Oaks to go on this…mission…without the benefit of being wed. It would certainly save her from… any unfortunate presumptions others in the community might make about her character, as well as save my son from a long period of uncertainty about his future."

In other words, Ever thought, *it's bad enough that I'm running off into the woods like some hussy, but poor little Erlan would have to bear the terrible burden of waiting for me to return.*

"Surely you understand, my dear, that Erlan cannot simply *wait* for you to return? You may not return at all. And Erlan would then have wasted—what, months? A year?"

Did he really just say what I think he said? Did he really just say that it would be unfair to Erlan if I die in the wilderness because he'll miss out on opportunities to meet other girls?

Ever looked at her father, whose eyes had grown progressively narrower over the course of Elder Ballard's little speech. Elder Orton had been a strength to Ever for the past several days, but she also knew that there was a worry in him that he hadn't let out. It was difficult enough to trust the Spirit to guide you through your own life, let alone to trust it with your daughter's life.

"With that in mind," finished Erlan's father, who, oblivious to his audience, was now absently cleaning his spectacles with a scrap of cloth as if discussing the weather, "we think it would be preferable—*far* preferable—for all involved if they were to be wed before she leaves."

"I would think," said her father sharply, "that the most obvious course of action, in this case, would be to simply call off the betrothal altogether. That way your son"—he looked daggers at Erlan—"would be free to do as he wished without concern for his family's... *reputation*." This last came out as a growl. Ever had never seen her foster father speak with such hostility, but right now he seemed as if he wanted nothing more than to leap over the table and strangle Elder Ballard with his own cravat.

"That is precisely what I told my son," replied Elder Ballard, replacing his glasses, "but, alas, he is insistent on marrying Sister Oaks."

"Then maybe he should go with her," said Elder Orton. This got Elder Ballard's attention; the man met her father's eyes as if he'd suggested that Erlan put on a dress and dance about on the village green.

"Into the North? Preposterous," said Elder Ballard. "Erlan is needed here. I am grooming him to work with me in the Bishopric, and have no doubt that he will soon be called to duties befitting his abilities. Tramping through the woods hardly qualifies."

"I take it you don't agree with the Bishopric's decision to send another party, Elder Ballard?" asked Ever. She already knew the answer but couldn't help baiting him.

"No, Sister Oaks, I do not. This is a waste of valuable resources and manpower that Bountiful sorely needs. Bishop Royce, who is not immune from criticism, mind you, is paranoid. He has allowed his own fears to cloud his judgment."

Peering at Ever as if measuring as if measuring her for a shift, he leaned forward.

"Do you really think that Heavenly Father would allow a bunch of filthy savages to destroy his Chosen People? The mere notion of it is unthinkable!"

"They came pretty close the last time they tried," said Elder Orton, who had begun drumming his fingers on the arm of his chair.

"In the words of the Savior, 'Oh, ye of little faith!' " cried Elder Ballard, slapping his hand down on the table. "That is exactly the kind of thinking that endangers us all! The attack was a test of our faith in the Godhead. It is through obedience, prayer, and belief that we will be saved, not through mindless forays into the cursed ruins of a society long Damned."

Ever had so far managed to keep her own feelings about Elder Ballard's thoughtless words under control but something snapped when she heard him deride her father's faith.

"Don't you have anything to say, Erlan?" she asked. *Can't you speak for yourself?* Other than his cursory greeting to her when they sat down, he had yet to open his mouth.

"I still want to marry you, Ever," said Erlan, his voice cracking slightly from disuse. "I...regret not acting sooner. Perhaps if we were already wed, my opinion as your husband would have swayed the Bishopric's decision. I'm sorry for having failed you. I'm willing to wait…for you to come back, but only if we're married first."

"You'll pardon me if I don't swoon," she said. Elder Ballard narrowed his eyes in her direction.

"You made a promise to my son, a promise that—"

"That can be withdrawn if necessary," cut in Elder Orton. "You know as well as I do, Gage, that these types of betrothals aren't enforceable under normal circumstances."

The arrangement Ever and Erlan had was more based on custom than any real law. The tradition of promising children to each other young was becoming less and less common in Bountiful, but it still happened, particularly in circumstances like Ever's. Both because foster families who took in orphans wanted to provide for their new charges and because, depending on the child's age, it was often considered preferable to marry them off sooner rather than later, children like Ever who lost their parents usually found their future spouse chosen for them well ahead of time. Their consent was required, of course, and people did break off engagements. Sometimes.

"Enforceable?" said Elder Ballard quizzically. "No, I should think not. No, the young lady has agency in this matter, as do all young women. But as I said, I have spoken with the Bishopric. Once I made my case they came to share my concerns."

"What are you saying, Elder Ballard?" asked Ever, suddenly nervous.

"Simply this, child: should you refuse to marry Erlan before your departure, the Bishopric will be forced to reconsider your inclusion in the Northern Expedition."

· · ·

"I'm sorry, Ever," said her father as they walked across the village green. "That was an ambush. Elder Ballard led me to believe he simply wanted to discuss the betrothal, given that you may not be back by spring. I thought...I thought, to be honest, that they wanted out. Under the circumstances, I thought it might be the best thing." He sighed and shook his head. "I'm afraid I've let you down, daughter."

"No, Father," said Ever, with a conviction she didn't feel. "I should have seen this coming." And she should have, she realized. She should have known Erlan's silence meant something bad. She should have known that his ego would take over, that he would do something to try to control the situation. Erlan projected a quiet, unassuming nature, but there was a coldness to him that spoke of another person entirely hidden beneath that façade.

"You and Erlan haven't seemed very close these past few months," said Elder Orton. "I thought maybe you had reconsidered."

"I think...I've been distracted," Ever replied. "Getting married just hasn't seemed that important lately, and after what happened on Golden Neck, and the attack, and...what I saw in my dream, I just...put it to the side." They were walking across the green, now. The sun was high.

"Ever," said her father, taking her elbow and guiding her to one of the benches outside of the infirmary, "you don't have to go through with this. With any of it. You don't have to marry Erlan Ballard and you don't have to go on this journey. You can stay here and live your life the way you want. Marry who you want."

"I have to go, Father," said Ever. "That's one thing I'm sure of. Something bad will happen if I don't."

"What?"

"I don't know. The things I saw in the dream, maybe. It's just a feeling. But it's a true one."

Her father sighed through his nose, a sign of grudging acceptance he usually reserved for Dallin's boyish antics or Airie's temper tantrums.

"I could speak to the Bishop," he said at last. "I have no doubt that Gage...Elder Ballard exaggerated to some extent back there. Elder Cardon no doubt supports him, and he has the Bishop's ear, but I can't believe Bishop Royce would force you to—"

"No, Father," said Ever, smoothing her skirt and looking down at her folded hands. "I've been enough trouble. There's enough reason for the village to gossip as it is."

"This isn't making trouble, Ever. This is a decision that will affect the rest of your life."

Ever knew that only too well. When the Blessed married, they married for life, and beyond: she would be joined to Erlan for eternity—or so her people believed—if she knelt before the temple altar to be sealed with him.

As much as she hated to admit it, she knew what she had to do. It wasn't that she wanted to be with Erlan; it had become increasingly clear to her lately that they shared almost nothing in common. She certainly didn't feel anything for him that could be called love, although if she were honest with herself she wasn't sure what that felt like anyway. Love for friends, for parents, for siblings—that feeling she understood. The kind of love that flickered from her father's eyes to her mother's when they looked at each other eluded her, however.

She knew what to do because she knew that whatever decisions she made regarding Erlan, it didn't matter. The important thing was that she listen to the voice inside of her. It had led her to this point, after all. Everything else was secondary. Somehow, it seemed like the promises she made to Erlan here would matter little in the end. Not because she didn't expect to make it back—although that possibility occurred to her with increasing frequency—but because whatever the result of their journey, she knew her life would be irrevocably changed by it.

She said as much to her foster father, and after a few moments' serious thought, he nodded and embraced her.

Eventually she took her leave of him, quietly, and went back into the infirmary. Despite feeling like it had been hours, not much time had passed. Sister Hales hadn't returned. She looked at the jumble of supplies on the floor of the pantry for a moment, and, with a fraction of the concentration she had possessed earlier, she went back to arranging them on the shelves of the supply closet.

She took the long way home that evening, stopping at Erlan's door to knock. His mother opened it, and summoned her son without a word.

Standing up straight before him, Ever said what she had come to say.

10

Two days later, a small wedding party assembled at the front of Bountiful's chapel with little ceremony. Only the parents of the bride and groom filled the pews. At the couple's request, the Bishop had agreed to perform the joining in private. The excuse given to the rest of Bountiful was simply that Erlan and Ever wanted to wait until her return from the North to have their "real" wedding, but Jared was sure there had to be other reasons. Looking across the small aisle at Cambree Betenson, who had agreed to stand as Ever's witness, he wondered just how much of this business had been Ever's idea.

The news had come to him first through his father, who had told him with a tenderness Jared was unused to, and then through Erlan himself, who had asked him to stand up for him during the ceremony.

Jared remembered feeling his father's pity when like a tangible thing: the unspoken words—*you waited too long*—hung in the air between them. He had barely come to terms with the fact of Ever's departure, and now this...that night, Jared had lain awake for hours wondering how he had gotten himself so deeply involved in a situation like this.

Close to dawn, he had been forced to admit to himself that he had been avoiding Ever since he heard the news that she was to be part of the expedition party. Oh, he had waved to her and been friendly when their paths crossed in the village, but they hadn't spoken. He had convinced himself it had been coincidence, that his duties as a Scout and as his father's assistant had simply become overwhelming. *Really, though, you just didn't—still don't—have any idea what you would say to her when you saw her again.*

Accepting that he was too young to go on the mission himself had been one thing; there was simply no way around the age requirement. It made sense that the young men sent to the Maine should be Elders with the full authority of the higher priesthood. He had been disappointed but not truly upset.

This was different. Knowing that Ever Oaks would soon be leaving the comparative safety of Bountiful's walls to venture deep into the wilderness, a journey that would take her through apostate territories and expose her to attack by the Damned, weighed on him heavily. A gnawing feeling that had begun the moment he heard had only gotten worse with time.

Standing behind and to one side of Erlan in the awkward silence of the chapel—Ever had refused even a hymn to accompany the ordinance—Jared felt a feeling he could only describe as misery. It didn't make any sense. Only days before, he had been happy and self-assured. His life was simple and fulfilling. Then he had gone to Golden Neck with Ever and everything had changed. It couldn't have happened that quickly.

But it didn't, did it? You knew for a long time. Since your friend first noticed her. For years. You only started paying attention recently.

Bishop Royce appeared from a side door and took his place on the stage at the front of the chapel. Several long minutes later, punctuated only by an occasional cough or whisper, the doors to the chapel opened and Ever appeared on her father's arm. Giving the bride away was a custom too deeply ingrained in Blessed weddings for even this hasty ceremony to do away with it, but the bride and her father nevertheless wasted no time with pomp. Walking at a measured but efficient pace, they came up the aisle to where Erlan stood waiting, and Elder Orton handed his daughter off to the groom.

Was Jared imagining things, or had Elder Orton's expression been somewhat resigned? After he took his seat with Ever's mother, Jared was forced to look at the bride herself, whose eyes flickered to his briefly before focusing on the Bishop.

The gnawing became an emptiness that threatened to knock him over. Ever was dressed simply in a sky blue dress—the formal white temple garments were only worn inside the walls of the temple itself, the larger building next to the chapel where the most serious ordinances were performed. Her hair fell simply to her shoulders, its rosy-gold waves setting off her nervous green eyes.

This was it, then. *Is this what love feels like? Is that what this has been all this time?* Jared squeezed his eyes shut for a moment, fighting the urge to cry out and object to the marriage happening right in front of him with every ounce of his being.

He couldn't look at Ever, and looking at Erlan's back only made him feel like a turncoat. Choosing a point at random on the front wall of the chapel, Jared stared at it, letting the short ceremony wash over him like the calm waves that lapped the shores of the Sound.

Ten minutes later, it was done.

There was no party. Not even a dinner to celebrate their union. Ever had insisted, and Erlan had agreed. It was a half-wedding. Not something to be celebrated, merely a first step. That had been Bishop Royce's compromise. Her father had been right to suspect Elder Ballard of overstating his case, though not in the way he had presumed. The Bishop had bowed to Elder Cardon and Ballard's pressure in an unorthodox way: by reviving an all but forgotten technicality of church law.

Elder Orton had explained the matter to her after an extended discussion with the Bishop, some of which he refused to discuss. But he reassured Ever that the path the Bishop had settled on was the best for her, if she intended to marry Erlan.

Generations ago, before the Fall, her father had explained, the Blessed who had lived among the Old People had often gotten married in two steps. The first, the basic joining ceremony, wed them and brought them together as man and wife within the bounds of the world. The second was the temple sealing, which united their souls forever.

Some couples elected only to be married the first way, though their reasons for doing so were unclear to even the most knowledgeable of the Blessed's historians. They speculated, though. In order to enter the temple, both bride and groom, as well as all of the guests who wished to attend, were required to demonstrate their worthiness to do so. The ways of the world before the Fall being what they were, not all of the Blessed chose to maintain this level of religious devotion. They mixed with the Old People, and took the commandments lightly, and settled for the easier, more accessible ordinance of joining to represent their marriage.

For all intents and purposes, Elder Orton had said, *they were married, Ever, so far as the world was concerned. But without being sealed in the temple, they could not be an eternal family.* Which was apparently good enough for some people.

The realities of living in Bountiful and the remaining Blessed communities like Serai and far Camora required a more scrupulous attitude toward the commandments. The Blessed lived by the commandments because they made up the foundation of the faith that had saved them. The fact of living by the commandments had become so vital to their existence that it was almost assumed. To be unworthy was, in effect, to be outcast, though forgiveness was always there for those ready to receive it.

Bishop Royce is…leaving you options, Ever. No one's future should be controlled by circumstance, if we can help it.

Ever sensed there was more to what her father was telling her, a specific message she was intended to receive. But she found it difficult to focus on anything but the path that lay immediately before her. Erlan was a gate before that path, and the simplest way to open that gate was to go forward with the joining.

The chapel was almost chilly as Erlan placed a chaste kiss on her lips at the conclusion of the Bishop's prayers. The Month of Gold was coming to an end; Thanksgiving Month was almost upon them, with winter sure to follow.

They walked out together; Ever met no one's eyes but her father's as she left with her husband. Outside the chapel doors she embraced her parents, shook Erlan's parents hands dutifully, and was wondering what was supposed to happen next when Jared presented himself in front of her.

Cambree interrupted whatever Jared had been about to say, wrapping her arms around Ever and pushing a knit parcel into her hands. Ever had never had close friends the way some girls did, but of the friends she had Cambree Betenson was definitely the closest. They had drifted apart somewhat after Ever was called to the infirmary, but Cambree had agreed to stand up for her readily enough when Ever had asked.

"I wish you the best of luck, my sister," she said, kissing her on the cheek.

"What's this?" asked Ever.

"Just something to keep you warm of a night," said Cambree, giving her a final squeeze, then prancing away across the green without another word. Ever met Jared's eyes again and chewed her lip nervously.

"I—" Jared began, but it was too much. She couldn't listen. She didn't know what might happen if she let him finish.

Gripping his hand firmly with both of hers, Ever squeezed it and turned away, using the excuse of checking her hair in the reflection of the chapel windows to hide the tears in her eyes. Without looking back at Jared, she walked up to Erlan, who was speaking to his parents, put her hand on his shoulder, and smiled with as much passion as she could muster.

A few minutes later they were walking down the lane toward the empty cabin that had belonged to Ever's parents, a comfortable house on the western edge of Bountiful, overlooking the water through the trees, that had nonetheless remained vacant since their death. Sister Hales and Ever's mother had fixed it up and stocked it with linens and filled the larder with hard cheese and fresh bread. Her father had furnished the house with his own hands; the warm glow of newly polished pine and oak filled the cabin with the comforting smells of home.

After looking through the house, she came back to the main room and looked at her new husband, who for once looked as nervous as she felt. They were saved the greater awkwardness that newlyweds usually encountered at this point by Bishop Royce. At his "suggestion," they would wait to consummate—the word still made Ever blush fiercely—the marriage until her return from the North.

Knowing perfectly well that Erlan was having thoughts similar if not identical to her own, she went about preparing an early dinner. The joining had happened in the late afternoon, and evening was coming on quickly.

Erlan went to bed soon after the sun, silently folding himself into the single bed farthest from the window in their shared bedroom. Besides wishing her a civil goodnight, he said nothing to Ever, whether out of nerves, frustration, or both.

Ever wrapped her new shawl around her shoulders and went through the back door into the little yard cut out of the dense pine forest of Bountiful's northwestern edge. Over the top of the village wall, which was lower here and downslope from her, she could see the glimmer of moonlight on ocean water through the pines.

There was an old song fragment Ever knew from when she was a child. The festival musicians would often play it on guitars during the dancing at harvest time. She sang it softly to herself now, not entirely comfortable with how appropriate it seemed.

"You're gone for something and I know you won't be back," she sang, her confidence growing as the melody returned to her, "I know you're dying, baby, and I know you know it, too. I know you're dying, and I know you know it, too…" A lump rose in her throat and she trailed off.

Every time I see you, I just don't know what to do.

11

It was Sister Hales—good, dependable Sister Hales—who pointed out to the Bishop that the young people joining the expedition would miss the Feast of Thanksgiving and it was at her urging that he planned a banquet to celebrate their departure. Morale being what it was, Ever had no doubt that Bishop Royce had jumped at the opportunity to turn their leaving into something to celebrate. At the Bishopric's command, the long, wide storehouses nestled behind the green in the very center of Bountiful were thrown open and the precious foodstuffs, some of which had already gone toward preparing the company's food stores for the long journey north, were brought out for the whole village to share.

Ever remembered the first time her father—her birth father, whose face, to her shame, grew increasingly blurry with every passing year—took her to see the inside of the storehouses. Six stout log buildings built in a row, with stout doors almost as thick as Bountiful's main gates, all shelves from floor to ceiling, filled with airtight jars and canisters. All were marked by date and contents and all contained food. There were barrels of wheat along the walls, grown in the small fields the Blessed tended at the mouth of the peninsula, jars of pickled vegetables picked at the peak of ripeness in the gardens of Bountiful's villagers, jams, jellies, dried fruit, salted and cured meats, jerky, any number of different grains and cereals grown and stored over the years. One building was nothing but massive water tanks, cleaned and changed periodically.

Every villager in Bountiful paid a tithe of food or supplies to contribute to the community storehouses. They were, in a way, the foundation of their community, and perhaps of the Blessed as a whole. The faith that led them to store the necessities of life and to prepare for the worst had helped them survive the Fall when others did not. They still lived a civilized, godly life because of the storehouses. Each year, after the harvest, they celebrated the feast of Thanksgiving to give thanks to the Godhead for its love in giving them life.

The storehouses were life, but they were also a danger: it was the food and supplies the Blessed put up against disaster that drew their enemies to them, looking to take by violence what others had produced by honest labor.

Ever was slicing bread for Erlan's luncheon the second morning of their marriage when it occurred to her that there was something wrong in that thought. It was a small, niggling thought that wouldn't go away, and after a few moments of frustration Ever consciously put it aside.

The 21st day of the Month of Gold was set aside for the feast. Ever woke that morning feeling oddly hollow. It took her several long minutes to realize that the anxiety that had crouched in her chest like a predator stalking prey since the day of the attack—the day she woke up from her dream and knew she had to leave—was gone. The feeling was more resignation than happiness: the die was cast. They were leaving tomorrow at dawn. There was no going back. She had no more difficult decisions to make and no more loved ones and neighbors to worry about. Her only concern was the road ahead of her.

It's relief, not resignation, she realized. As dangerous as the journey ahead was likely to be, at the moment she felt mostly excitement at being relieved of the burdens of life in Bountiful. Compared to the hard choices of the last few days, the road was escape—the road was independence. For the first time in her life, she was her own mistress. It felt good.

It was only an hour or two after sunup when a knock on the door produced an uncertain looking Jared Meacham, dressed for ranging. His bow was strung and slung over his shoulder and his quiver was full.

"Good morning," she said.

"Good morning, Ever," said Jared, looking around nervously. "Is—"

"Erlan already left. The Bishopric is meeting this morning to go over last minute arrangements for our party."

"Oh," said Jared. "Well…good, actually. I came to see you."

"Why?" she asked.

Don't do this to me. I've finally started to accept everything that's happening…don't make it harder now.

"I wanted to give you something. A…gift. And show you something, if you're willing."

"A gift? Gift first, then."

Reaching behind him, Jared pulled an oblong parcel wrapped in dark cloth out of his belt.

"I was kidding, Jared," said Ever. "I'm not that grasping, am I? Do you want to come in?"

He looked at her like she had invited him to jump off of a cliff. After a moment, he shook his head.

"No, ahh…I wanted…It's silly I guess," he said. "I wanted to…"

Realizing that Jared was having an even harder time of things than she was, Ever stepped outside, closed the door, and then shoved him hard.

"Stop acting so stupid!" she said fiercely. "I got married—well, half-married. I didn't grow another head."

Jared barked a surprised laugh, scratched his head in confusion, and finally seemed to calm down.

"Will you come to the northern wall with me? It's not far from here."

"Yes," said Ever, "but if you're thinking of pushing me off, you should know that the wall isn't as high on this side. The fall probably wouldn't kill me."

• • •

Ever had to tie her skirts in a knot above her knees in order to get up the tree. The Women's Society would have been scandalized at the idea of a woman of Ever's age showing her bare legs to a man who wasn't her husband, but there was no one else out on the northeastern point of Bountiful's peninsula today. *Not to mention that you're enjoying what it's doing to Jared.* After seeing what she intended on doing, Jared had blushed and quickly started climbing the tree ahead of her.

They had come down a ladder Jared had leaned up against Bountiful's back wall, walked a short distance through the woods on one of the paths that the Scouts kept in good repair, and were now standing at the edge of the woods where an ancient cliff—that looked manmade, now that she thought about it—fell directly down into the crashing water below.

Ever had followed without comment. She hadn't complained about the danger inherent in what they were doing: aside from the fact that being needlessly outside the walls at all was a bad idea this soon after a Marmack attack, climbing a tall tree over a high cliff was just not good common sense. But it seemed important to Jared, and as difficult as it was to interact with him now—a feeling she chose not to explore further—she didn't want to disappoint him.

The tree Jared had chosen was a maple, tall and wide and multi-trunked—a good climbing tree. No child who grew up in Bountiful was a stranger to climbing trees, though doing so at Ever's age was certainly a bit out of the ordinary.

The sun was halfway to its meridian when they reached the highest stable crotch of the maple. Jared steadied her on a wide limb and offered her his water skin when she was settled. She took it and drank deeply. He had filled it recently; the water was still cold and refreshing as it streamed out of the leather.

Her thirst quenched, she handed the skin back to Jared and waited. Tossing the skin back to the forest floor, Jared inched farther out on the limb to the point where a number of branches obscured their view. He unsheathed the large knife at his belt and carefully cut a branch away, revealing a perfect window of light and sky in the tree's heavy canopy. Looking more closely, Ever saw other fresh cuts—several other branches had already been removed before they arrived.

He planned this. He came here and cut a little viewing window and left one branch to remove in front of me for show. Ever couldn't help but smile. She hadn't known Jared had a flair for the dramatic, even a slight one.

Dropping the branch and sheathing his knife, he moved closer to her again. He'd arranged it so they had a perfect seat together, looking through the hole he'd cut in the leaves.

"What do you see?" he asked.

Ever looked and saw the strip of gold and crimson that was Golden Neck across the rippling gray-green water of Marvel Sound. She saw the rowboat bobbing at its dock far below and to the right of them on Brokeneck Beach. She saw the remains of the ancient causeway where it crumbled into the sea. And beyond, small and clear in the distance, she saw the tarnished mirrors of the once great city of the Old People that lay miles to the south.

Well past the southern limit of the Blessed of Bountiful's domain, past Red Rocks and the ruined towns, past a wide stretch of the shorter of two murky rivers that emptied into the Great Bay, stood the jagged, dead towers of Bostonia.

It was a beautiful sight, Ever had to admit: damaged as they were, the morning sun caught the sides of the towers and made them shine. The Blessed didn't venture far from Bountiful unless traveling to one of the other holdfasts of the faithful, but even when they did they never passed through the ruins of the city. It was inhabited now only by ghosts and the Damned.

"The stories say the tallest ones used to reach so high that you couldn't breathe the air," said Jared. "They were built to sway with the wind." The height of the distant towers was impressive, but nowhere near so tall as that—which meant either Jared had succumbed to the stories that old Elders told their grandchildren, or the buildings of the ruined city had lost much of their height in the centuries since the Fall.

"Yes," said Ever, reaching past Jared to point to the right of the city, where a solitary stump-like mass jutted out of the earth. "And there was the great port where their ships flew into the heavens." She had grown up hearing the same stories—as happy as the Blessed were to have survived the decadence that led to the Fall, they still told stories about the Old People and the great works they did to turn the world to their use.

"They're not just stories, Ever," Jared said. "There's truth in them. Whether or not you believe man once flew to the moon on a pillar of fire or walked on other worlds, the Old People did great things."

"You admire them," said Ever, looking at Jared's face. He turned in surprise.

"I...suppose, in a way, I do," he said, as if admitting a mistake. "I know they caused the Fall...but they were a great people. Seeing the ruins of what they built... there must have been some good in them. Why would God allow them such powers if He knew they would use them for evil?"

"You know the answer as well as I do," said Ever.

"Yes, yes, *agency*," said Jared, waving a hand vaguely. "Free will. All that." They were both silent for a moment.

"Why did you bring me here, Jared?" asked Ever. "I'm pretty sure it wasn't to discuss the finer points of church doctrine."

He smiled sheepishly.

"It's just that...you're going out there, into that world. Part of me wonders whether it's as horrible as we think, or whether it's just...different. I envy you. I wish I was going with you...you shouldn't be going alone."

"I won't be alone, Jared," Ever said, unable to keep a small smile from her mouth.

"You know what I—you shouldn't be going out there without someone who...."

"Cares about me?"

He looked at her sharply, hesitant, then nodded.

What *had* he brought her out here for? This was an odd goodbye, perhaps even an inappropriate one—most of Bountiful would certainly think so. Had he said everything he meant to say, or was he holding back?

Reaching out, she squeezed his arm reassuringly.

"I'll be all right."

They climbed down from the tree without speaking further. The silence held until they had mounted the wall again. After Jared had pulled up the ladder, he took the cloth-wrapped parcel out of his belt again and handed it to her.

It was heavier than she'd thought it would be, and when she unwrapped it she discovered a sheathed knife, as long as her forearm and broad of blade. The grip was wrapped with leather cord and capped with a silver orb scribed with decorative engravings to match the small silver hilt. Ever pulled it from the supple chestnut leather sheath and admired the hand-forged steel blade. Etched into the beautiful stain finish were the sun, moon, and stars of the Blessed.

"Elder Betenson's been busy," Ever remarked, testing the edge of the blade with her thumb.

"Careful," said Jared. "It's sharp. Normally I'd owe him a summer's worth of work for something like this, but when he heard it was for you we settled on a couple of weeks of forge-tending and metal scavenging."

It was a Scout blade, albeit a fancy one, and as impressive as it was it was smaller than those the men carried.

"You had this made for me?"

"Your hands are smaller...I thought this would suit them better."

"It's beautiful," Ever said.

"The steel is special," Jared explained. "I found it in the ruins outside of the city. Much stronger than anything we can make. It'll take a lot of hard use before you'll need to sharpen it."

The knife's blade was sharpened along all of one edge and on the swedge that met the belly to form a wicked looking tip.

"Beautiful and dangerous," said Ever.

Jared winked.

"Just...be safe, Ever."

He hugged her once and walked away quickly without looking back, leaving her holding his gift atop the wall, wondering what had just happened.

Thanksgiving was a whirling rush of prayer, food, emotion, wood smoke, and the sharp chill of the autumn air. When Ever recalled it much later, she could remember only snippets and flashes: enjoying a bite of roast turkey until she remembered the Damned creature on the beach; the way her mother clung to her throughout the evening, as if afraid she might disappear without saying goodbye; the almost desperate edge to the laughter and festivities.

The children of Bountiful ran and screamed and wrestled as if the Savior had returned while the adults feasted and danced and sang. If there had been strong liquor in any great amount in Bountiful, no doubt it would have been broken out, regardless of the commandments.

The broad oaken tables, laden heavily with colorful gourds and squashes and fowl and bitter berry chutney and all the other fruits of the harvest, had been laid out on the green. Villagers mingled as they ate, standing up or sitting down as the conversation required; no particular etiquette was observed.

Ever remembered the odd dichotomy of the merry feast taking place on the green and the burnt, blackened shells of the cabins destroyed in the Marmack attack dotted around it. Most of the damage had been relegated to an area south of the green between the gates and the council building, but a few stray fire arrows had caused havoc even this far into Bountiful.

She would remember all of the moments she looked up to discover Jared Meacham watching her from afar and the way he held her eyes when she did. She would remember the boisterous prayers to the Godhead that were shouted by exuberant Elders moved to near religious ecstasy in the tumult of the celebration. She would remember dancing with her father as the bandleader scraped out a sad old tune on his sad old fiddle.

She remembered being lined up with her companions—with Chy Bingham, Acel Higbee, and Rolan Belnap—and presented to the people of Bountiful, who hailed them as brave and holy, even those who hadn't agreed with sending the expedition in the first place.

It seemed strange, but she'd barely spoken to the three young men whom she would be spending the better part of a year with since being accepted as part of the company. She knew them, of course, but all but Rolan Belnap were a year or two older than she was and she knew none of them well. For their part they seemed pleased to have her along, though she suspected that had as much to do with the fact that she was a Saint as it did with Ever herself.

Erlan neither spoke to her nor asked her to dance. On the contrary, he expressed his desire to go home shortly after they had both finished their dinner. Ever, too distracted to truly enjoy the merrymaking, saw no reason to disagree. She gave up trying to make small talk after the third or fourth one-word answer. If only to avoid the other potential topics that were swirling around in her head, she settled on trying to remember what she could about the three young men she would be spending the better part of a year with. Though the Bishop and his supporters had wanted to send a larger group, the strong opposition to the idea of sending anyone at all resulted in a compromise: only three boys, plus Ever, would go.

Acel Higbee was popular and good-looking, considered perhaps the most eligible bachelor in Bountiful by more than a few girls Ever's age. He, like Jared, was a Scout; he wasn't as gifted with a bow as Jared was—though few were, Ever reminded herself—but he made up for it in sheer physical prowess. He was tall and broad-shouldered, with a head of dark sandy hair that framed a strong-jawed face. Chy and Rolan had already begun deferring to him when questions related to their departure arose. It made sense, she supposed. He was well liked by Elder Betenson and Elder Meacham and had an easy way with the other boys that made them want to obey him.

Chy Bingham was of a height with Acel but broader of body. He'd been a chubby little boy, Ever remembered, often getting in trouble for stealing maple sweets from the Society kitchens. With manhood had come real growth, however, and what was once fat was now muscle. Chy was a farmer. He lived with his family on the southern side of Bountiful and ventured outside the holdfast each morning to tend the small fields farther down the peninsula. If Acel had been chosen for his obvious leadership qualities, Chy was clearly a solid workhorse of a man, intelligent enough to handle whatever was put in front of him but in no way rebellious. Chy would do as he was told and carry out his orders if he had to walk through fire to do it.

Rolan Belnap, on the other hand, was something of a mystery to Ever. He was smart and kind and quiet; he worked for the Elders' Council as a scribe. In comparison to young men like Acel, Rolan Belnap seemed almost meek, which had led a lot of Bountiful's marriageable females to dismiss him as a potential mate. Ever wasn't so sure, however. Rolan had an air about him that wasn't meekness. His was the kind of confidence that only came out when provoked. Her foster father would probably say that he had an "economical character," meaning he didn't waste effort on meaningless things like appearances. Nonetheless, he had only the basic skills in woodcraft and combat that every adult man in Bountiful had, which hardly made him an ideal candidate for this kind of journey.

Aren't you forgetting someone? A blush rose to her cheeks. Here she was judging people like horseflesh. *Many in Bountiful are doubtless asking the same questions about you.* But she was a Saint, a healer. And she was no slouch when it came to traveling in hard country, or so she told herself. You couldn't be an effective healer if you weren't willing to brave the woods for supplies, or to help someone in need. Her Gift could be miraculous, at times, but she wasn't always able to call it up at need.

Her reverie was interrupted by their arrival at their new cabin—the same cabin Ever had been born in.

It was hard enough pretending to be married to Erlan without the added pressure of her looming departure. *But then, you wouldn't be pretending if you weren't departing, would you?* She wished she could shake out the jumble of thoughts in her mind.

He began rebuilding the smoldering remnants of the fire he'd built in the hearth that afternoon. Ever picked up her shawl from her chair near the fireplace and wrapped it around herself. She waited, looking into the coals as Erlan stirred them alight, to see if he would say anything. After adding a couple of logs, he hung the old iron poker back on its hook and folded his arms around his body, closing his eyes. After a long moment Ever realized he was saying his nightly prayers and she felt an unexpected rush of disappointment.

There were so many things she wanted to say at that moment that in the end she could say none of them. *I'm your wife (or will be)—talk to me—look at me—who are you—why are you doing this to me—please just leave me—*

She opened the back door and went out to look at the pines and the stars glowing between them. A few minutes later Erlan joined her. He put his hand on her shoulder and spoke. She had to think back, later on, to remember all of what he said. The only thing that stood out was:

"I'll wait for you, Ever."

She didn't respond. She didn't move until several long minutes had passed. The thought that she held in her mind was both shocking and deeply familiar. *I'll wait for you, Ever. I'll wait for you forever.*

For the first time, Ever admitted to herself that she didn't want him to.

She waited a long time before going back into the house. She wanted to make sure he was asleep. When she heard soft snoring from their bedroom, Ever dragged the large, heavy pack that stood in the corner of the cabin in front of her chair and sat down. Her parents had helped her pack for the journey, using their own judgment and hers to augment the necessities the Bishopric had outlined for them.

On top of the pack, which had multiple compartments and pockets of heavy canvas on a rigid wooden frame, Ever had a bedroll, a spare blanket, and an oilcloth poncho for heavy rain. On the sides were strapped a small hatchet, a large water skin, and a coil of rope. Inside she had every necessity she could think of, and then some. Several complete sets of clothing and soap for washing—both herself and her attire. A basic medic's kit. A metal flask of oil for making torches. Spare stockings and a long woolen scarf. A pair of odd goggles made of brass and smoked glass for use against snow glare and sun.

Her clothing, at her own request, consisted of breeches, men's shirts, a leather waistcoat, and tall leather hunting boots. Not the most traditional of female attire, perhaps, but far more practical for running around in the woods than the full-length skirts and woolen bodices that most women of Bountiful wore. A small, secret part of her looked forward to the freedom of men's clothing—to discarding her petticoats and shifts for something more utilitarian.

Ever found herself checking each and every thing she would carry, physically when possible and mentally when removing it meant disturbing the packing job. Even as she was doing it she realized that she was channeling some emotion into busy work that she didn't feel capable of expressing otherwise. It was a trait she had developed quite recently and one that disturbed her more than a little. She had always felt at home with her thoughts and feelings, always able to say what was going on in her head. But over the past few days, it hadn't been that easy. She had gone through her packing three times when she realized it was almost midnight.

She slept poorly, vacillating between feeling wide awake and fitful periods of half-sleep. At one point, her thoughts racing so badly that she would have talked to Elder Cardon if he had presented himself, she almost woke Erlan, but when she saw how peacefully he was sleeping she let him lie.

She was awake when the first gray tendrils of dawn's light crept through her small window. Giving up her sleep for lost, she rose, dressed herself in a simple woolen dress—she would have to wait to don her traveling attire until they had left the holdfast, if only to spare the delicate sensibilities of some of Bountiful's older ladies. She opened the front door of the cabin and walked a few steps into the lane, down the length of which she could see the slow flicker of life coming into the village as the early-risers lit lamps and candles in hand-glazed windows hoary with autumn frost.

The land sloped downward toward Bountiful's center from their cabin. The pines and scattered hardwoods formed a cozy tunnel leading into the village, opening up just as the lane entered the green. Standing in the center of the lane, she could just see the council building and the blurry line of the main gates beyond. It was a pleasant view of her home and Ever silently said a prayer of thanks for being able to see it.

She breathed the chill air and saw her breath mist in front of her. All was quiet, except for the occasional yammering of morning birdsong and the creak of a cabin door here or there. She closed her eyes and tried to center herself, letting the quiet sounds of Bountiful waking wash over her.

She opened them when she heard the first shuddering boom. The peace she had found drained out of her when she saw the first missiles arcing over the walls. New blossoms of orange fire found fuel in Bountiful's rooftops as she stood in fixed shock. For the second time in two weeks, Bountiful was under attack.

Erlan wandered out of their bedroom as she reached her pack.

"What's happening?" he asked, scrubbing at his eyes with one knuckle.

"I have to go," Ever said, swinging her the heavy pack over her shoulders. For the span of a heartbeat she met Erlan's eyes. They widened slightly, but he didn't speak. Ever didn't spare him a second thought; moments later she was out the door and heading down the lane towards the green.

The booming continued in a slow, staccato rhythm. They were at the gates again with a ram—a better one this time, from the sound of it. She trotted as fast as she could under the weight of the pack, trying to control her breathing. Another volley of fire arrows launched over the walls ahead of her.

Men were running across the green toward the walls as she arrived. Elder Betenson had already appeared at the far end of the green and was calling orders to the frenzied troops forming up haphazardly under his watchful eyes. She looked about, momentarily torn about where to go.

The plan had been to meet at Storehouse 7 just after dawn, where the packhorses would be loaded down. Elder Meacham's riflemen would then escort them through the gates to the Southwestern tip of Bountiful's peninsula, where it met the mainland. From there they would part ways with their comrades and begin their trek north.

Ever felt a hand grab her arm and she looked up to find her father staring down at her.

"I have to go," she said, feeling silly even as the words left her mouth. If he even understood what she was talking about, her father would no doubt tell her to get back to the cabin, or to the infirmary, where she would be safe and could be of some use.

"Yes, you do," said Elder Orton, pulling her after him as he strode toward the storehouses. Surprised, Ever followed after him quickly, and soon they were running.

Her father led her behind Storehouse 1, giving them some cover from the arrows. They ran until they reached the back of building seven, on the western side of the green. Peering through the narrow alley between Storehouses 6 and 7, Ever could hear commotion and arguing, followed by the distinct snort of a horse. Her father led her down the dark passage and they emerged into the sunshine just in time to see that two of her party were already there. Elders Higbee and Belnap appeared to be having a disagreement over the small packhorse standing nervously between them. Elder Higbee had a rifle strapped to his pack, by the look of it one of the refurbished antiques Elder Betenson hoarded so closely.

"Where's Bingham?" barked Elder Orton.

"Haven't seen him," Elder Higbee said and returned to lashing a sack to the back of the horse. Elder Belnap frowned, but didn't say anything further.

"The main gates are under attack," said Ever's father. "You can't leave that way."

Elder Higbee nodded.

"We'll have to take one of the Scout passages," he said. Just then Elder Bingham jogged up from behind Rolan and Acel. Panting, he bent over to catch his breath. Like Elder Higbee, he also carried a rifle strapped to his pack.

"You'll have to leave the horses," said Elder Orton.

"We can get them through," said Higbee, reaching for another sack of flour from the pile at his feet. "The tunnels are narrow, but if we pack them right—"

"Don't be foolish. There's no—"

The rest of her father's sentence was cut off as the world exploded.

One moment Ever was catching her breath, listening to the men bicker, and the next a blind force as heavy and powerful as an ocean wave drove her into her father's back. It seemed silent at first, until she raised her face from the hard-packed dirt in front of the storehouse doors and heard a faint, distinctive ringing in her ears. Her father was the first one back on his feet, and his lips were moving as he hauled her to her own. Sound came back slowly and after a few panicked breaths she realized he was asking if she was hurt. She shook her head. She didn't feel hurt, only dazed. She stared blankly at her father's face for a moment, letting the world come back into focus.

Behind him, Storehouse 6 was burning. Its roof had fallen in and the corner closest to Storehouse 7 was almost gone. Her father took her hand and pointed at her forearm. Ever looked down to see a large spike of wood, some of it still bearing the forest green paint of the storehouse, emerging from the fleshy part of her arm. Whatever had hit the storehouse had missed her by a matter of feet. She pulled the shard of wood from her arm, feeling nothing as she did so, and turned to look at the others.

The horse was screaming shrilly. One of its forelegs was bent at an impossible angle and a wet, white length of bone protruded from the place where its knee should have been. The Elders seemed to have avoided major injury as well; Elder Higbee was helping Elder Belnap up off the ground.

"What—"

"Catapults," said her father. "They're using catapults." As he spoke, a cabin three houses down the green exploded in a smoky blaze. The second packhorse, a bay mare who had presumably been tied up inside Storehouse 7 until now, burst out of the double doors dragging a snapped lead behind her. The Elders barely got out of the way in time.

"That solves that problem," said Elder Belnap, who had an ugly scrape on one cheek and a red mark on his forehead that looked like it would be a nasty bruise before long.

A deep cracking noise split the air over the green and Elder Orton looked toward the main gates in surprised distress. For one brief moment, Ever saw a look on his face she had never seen before: total and utter despair, unmitigated by any façade of parental strength. It was gone in an instant, however, and he turned his eyes on Elder Higbee with a look of dire seriousness.

"You know the northernmost scout tunnel?"

Elder Higbee nodded. "Through the Bringhursts' root cellar. I've never used it. It doesn't go anywhere but north, to the water."

"You'll need the key," said Ever's father, fishing a leather thong out of the collar of his shirt. Ever had never noticed it before. On the end of it was tied a small iron key. He pulled the thong over his head and handed to Elder Higbee. "It's an older tunnel; the newer skeleton keys won't work."

"There's a small, shallow cove right before you get to Salem Point," said Elder Orton. "There are longboats stored there, above the beachhead, just inside the treeline. Under tarps. Use one of them to cross Jerusalem Sound. *Don't* go by land."

"You mean over the Sunken City?" Elder Higbee looked alarmed. "Wouldn't it be easier—"

"Don't question. Just go."

Elder Orton, apparently considering the matter closed, turned to Ever. He smiled sadly, placed a hand on her head softly for a moment, then kissed her forehead.

"Go with God, daughter," he said.

"I love you, Father," said Ever. She hugged him fiercely and wiped a tear from her eye.

"Tell Mother—and Airie and Dallin—"

"I'll tell them," he said.

Another deep, wrenching crack echoed over Bountiful.

"*Go*," said her father. And then they were running—between the storehouses, up the northern lane, past the frightened eyes of women and children peering from cabin windows.

Ever's heavy pack was already uncomfortable by the time they reached the rear wall of the holdfast. She was glad for the moment of rest she got when Elder Higbee stopped to fiddle with the wooden bulkhead at the back of the Bringhursts' pretty cottage. Tearing it open, he waved Ever, Chy, and Rolan down. They had to remove their packs to fit down the narrow stone steps.

The root cellar was dark and close. Elder Bingham lit a small torch and handed it to Elder Higbee, who was searching the old wooden shelves hung from the stout oak bracings of the cellar. Finding whatever it was he was looking for, he engaged something with a metallic click, and seconds later the shelves swung out of the wall. A door, Ever realized. This wall was made of wooden planks, unlike the rest of the cellar, which had natural dirt walls.

They were looking into a narrow earthen tunnel, supported much like the root cellar with thick oaken beams and joists. Elder Higbee led the way, brushing aside years' worth of cobwebs before descending a short set of wooden steps leading them even deeper into the ground. The air was stale and damp, but breathable. They were forced to walk single file, with Ever between Elders Bingham and Belnap, who took up the rear. She kept her eyes on the fierce orange glow of the torch ahead of her and tried to avoid thinking about the twenty-or-so feet of earth between them and the sky. And spiders. She hoped there wouldn't be spiders.

The Bringhursts' house wasn't far from her own. It undoubtedly sat empty now; Erlan must have gone off to find his father when he realized they were again under attack. She supposed she should feel sad to be leaving it, and Erlan, but the only people she was thinking of right now were her foster parents and Dallin and Airie, who must be terrified. *Dallin's probably excited*, she corrected herself, managing a small smile. *It's Mother and Airie who will be terrified.* She hoped they were all right. She hoped that Elder Betenson would be able to repel the Marmacks again, that they wouldn't enter Bountiful again, that they wouldn't hurt anyone, or—

Ever stopped herself before her thoughts ran away from her, and made herself focus on the torchlight. *Be here and now*, she told herself. She looked at the outline of Elder Bingham's wide shoulders against the light and concerned herself with not tripping over the loose stones and roots that lined the uneven floor of the tunnel.

The tunnel, which had been gradually descending, Ever now noticed, began sloping upward again. She began to see thick roots lining the walls and twisting out of the ceiling. A few moments later they stopped, she heard the squeal of a key in a rusty lock followed by a dull thunk, and then daylight was spilling into the tunnel.

Her happiness at being in the free air again disappeared when she turned around. They had come out of the bolthole on a downward slope; she could see Bountiful's walls up the slope above them.

She couldn't see any of the village itself from where they stood, but high above the trees black smoke was rising from the south.

Elder Bingham pulled the dun-colored tarp off of the longboat with a dusty flourish. They had found the boats, after a short search, just where Ever's father had promised they'd be, in a small clearing just inside the tree line at the top of the beachhead. Under a layer of cut pine branches and the tarps, they were surprisingly well camouflaged. Elder Higbee had been almost on top of them before spotting their large bulk amidst the trees, high above the rocky beach.

After emerging from the Scout tunnel, they had pressed on quickly and, to Ever's confused relief, mostly silently. The only words spoken among the four of them were simple warnings to take care over a rocky area or while crossing a stream.

The boats were stored upside down, keels to the sky. Rolan helped Chy flip over the one they'd uncovered. Once righted, they found a set of oars, a simple, removable mast, and a small square sail lashed to the inside of the hull. The boat was solid and well made, like most goods that came out of Bountiful. Polished benches to seat a dozen large men or twice that number of children ran from bow to stern.

"They really were preparing for the worst," said Elder Higbee, shaking his head in disbelief.

Aside from Acel's comment, the uncomfortable silence that had pervaded since leaving the village less than an hour before continued as the four of them stood around the craft.

"No use wasting any time," Ever said finally, with more enthusiasm than she felt. Rolan and Chy, at least, seemed to be sharing the same kind of thoughts she was: their minds were back in Bountiful, with their loved ones and families, where another brutal Marmack attack was well under way. At least, she presumed it was Marmacks. Who else would it be? It took great effort on Ever's part to stay focused and keep moving forward with that in mind. She supposed it was even worse for the boys—*men*, she reminded herself. Turning their backs on the defense of their home must have felt like—

"I feel like we're running away," said Chy, his thick fingers hooked in his belt. "Who knows what's happening back there by now. That cracking noise…"

"The main gates," said Rolan, a haunted look on his face. "They were coming through the gates."

"What if—" began Chy, cutting off in frustration as either emotion or confusion got the better of him. "What if they got through? We just…left. We don't know what happened."

"This wasn't the way it was supposed to be," said Acel, who had kept silent until now. "Not that we've come to it, I don't know that we should go on."

"We already made the decision to go," said Ever. "We're here. It's a little late now to start having doubts. My father told us to go. It was the right thing to do."

"How can we know that?" asked Acel. Elder Higbee's face bore an expression of cold disapproval. He seemed to lack the obvious emotion Ever and the other boys were dealing with. "I left because Elder Orton ordered me to, but now that I've had a chance to think about it, I don't think we can go further without knowing what's happened."

"There's still smoke to the southeast," said Ever, pointing to the thin columns rising above the trees. She eased her pack off of her shoulders as she spoke. Twin bands of sweat darkened the thin wool of her dress where they had lain. Rolan followed her lead, taking his pack off and putting it into the boat.

"We have to go back," said Acel. "They might need our help. We didn't expect to be leaving in the middle of a battle—I doubt the High Council would have approved that if they'd had a chance to think about it." He projected confidence, but there was a whiteness to his knuckles where his hands gripped the straps of his pack that belied it.

Chy Bingham was nodding along.

"That's right," said Chy. "We were supposed to leave this morning, but nobody said anything about leaving in the middle of an attack. They need us. We're supposed to be looking for a safer place to move Bountiful. What's the point of that if there's nothing left to move?"

"The Elders didn't go to all this effort over us just to have us turn around at the first sign of trouble," said Ever. The decision was obvious: they had to go on. What other choice was there? If they didn't see it, she'd make them.

"Ever," said Acel, shaking his head, "these are our families we're talking about. They need us now a lot more than they need us going off into the Desolation to find a better location for the village. We can't just abandon them."

"We're *not* abandoning them, Acel," said Ever. "Don't you think I'm feeling the same things you are? Don't you think I feel guilty, walking away from a fight like this? It feels like we're leaving them to die." Chy didn't appear to be listening any longer. He was tightening his pack straps and counting the arrows in the quiver at his waist. Elder Bingham would go along with whatever Acel decided, Ever knew.

"You don't understand, Ever. It's not the same for you. You're—"

"Just a woman?" Ever snapped. "Yes, I'm just a woman, Acel Higbee, which means I don't have the burden of male pride to deal with. If you'll use your swollen head to think, for a moment, instead of rushing off to try and kill something, maybe you'll learn a thing or two." Her voice had risen with each word; she could feel heat in her cheeks. Rolan was looking at her like she had grown wings and might start flying.

Acel and Chy were startled by the emotion in her voice as well. Chy's mouth drooped in an 'O' shape. He was staring at her like a simpleton. Acel recovered first.

"What would you have me do, Sister Oaks?" he asked. Ever noted with satisfaction that rosy blooms of embarrassment had appeared on his cheeks.

"I'd have you answer a question," she said. "What's the difference?"

"Between what?" asked Acel.

"Between leaving while Bountiful's under attack and leaving any other day?"

"Ever, what are you talking about?"

"We knew when we chose to do this that Bountiful might be attacked again. In fact, we knew it was almost inevitable—that's the whole point! Our home is in danger, so we have to find a new one. When the Bishop chose you to go on this mission, did he tell you to turn back if you heard Bountiful was under attack? You knew when you volunteered that anything could happen while you're gone. What's different about today?"

She wasn't sure if she was making her point. It felt to Ever like explaining that the sky was blue. How could he not see it?

"Ever's right," said Rolan, speaking up suddenly. Chy and Acel looked at him. "This is why we're here. This is God, or whoever, telling us that what we're doing is important. What we're doing is more important than being another bowman on the walls, Acel."

"Why do you think my father ordered us to go?" pleaded Ever. "He knew this was more important. Even if we fight off this attack, there'll be another one, and another, until they get what they want. Until there's nothing left."

Acel looked at Ever hard, then looked at Rolan. Chy looked at Acel like an expectant hound. Setting his jaw, Acel shrugged his pack higher onto his shoulders and started back the way they came. Before he'd gone two steps, he let out a growl of frustration, turned around, and faced his three companions. Unbuckling the chest strap of his heavy pack, he swung it down next to Ever and Rolan's in the boat.

Ever bit her lip. As well-meaning as Elder Higbee undoubtedly was, he looked like a spoiled little boy reluctantly doing as he was told.

"You're right," he said. "I'm sorry—I wasn't thinking." Chy looked from Acel to Ever and back again, and then also took his pack off and put it in the boat.

"Now that that's settled," Ever said, "I need you boys to give me a few minutes of privacy." The three of them looked at each other suspiciously, but they trudged out of the trees and several yards down the beach without a word.

When Ever called them back a few minutes later, she was dressed in breeches, shirt and waistcoat, and the high hunting boots she'd packed to wear once they left the holdfast. The breeches were tight but heavy and durable. She'd tailored all the clothes herself so they fit her perfectly, out of wool dyed in brown and dark gray and forest green. Aside from the obvious practicality of wearing pants while hiking in the wilderness, she had also thought that looking more like a boy might make Acel, Chy, and Rolan treat her more like one of their own and less like a delicate flower they had to keep from getting crushed.

Judging by the looks on their faces when they returned to the clearing, she may have made an error in judgment. The breeches *were* rather form fitting, she supposed. Elder Bingham was again making his simpleton face and Rolan's cheeks were scarlet. Acel, on the other hand, cracked a wide smile, made a show of looking her up and down, and shoved Chy to make him stop staring.

"Well," said Acel, "I guess we know who wears the pants on this mission."

13

Ever sat in the prow of the longboat, enjoying the feel of the cold ocean spray on her face as the craft scudded along the gentle waves of Jerusalem Sound. In the middle distance the water was a sheet of hammered gold in the sunlight. The day had grown warmer since morning. Rolan sat behind her, scribbling into a journal, as Chy and Acel manned two sets of long oars. The rhythmic splash-sweep of the oar-blades churning the dark water around their boat joined the high calling of gulls in a sort of nautical harmony. If she ignored the fact that they were fleeing for their lives and leaving their families to defend their homes against their mortal enemies, it was almost pleasant.

Their conversation in the clearing had helped break the tension they were all feeling. For a time Acel and Chy had seemed almost merry, taking to the oars of the boat eagerly and commenting on what a blessing the calm sea and beautiful weather was. Rolan had taken the opportunity to make notes in his diary, claiming he wanted to document it while the events of the morning—had they only left Bountiful that morning?—were still fresh in his mind. It was all a façade, of course; they had made the decision to go on and now had to live with it. It was the right one, Ever knew, but that didn't mean they would ever feel good about making it.

Ever, having nothing to do in the boat, sat in the bow and tried to avoid speculating about the fate of everyone and everything she cared about in the world.

She sighed, shading her eyes against the sunlight and turning back to look at her companions.

"That's the Sunken City ahead, isn't it?"

In the midst of Jerusalem Sound, jutting haphazardly out of the water like a set of broken teeth, were the ruins of a settlement of the Old People so luxurious that it made the crumbling foundations of the mansions that once adorned Golden Neck look small and poor in comparison.

" 'So great did their pride and avarice grow, that they built houses that walked upon the waves, in mimicry of the Savior,' " quoted Rolan, closing his journal and slipping it into the top of his pack.

"Let's hope we fare better than they did," grunted Acel over his shoulder.

Only God knew what the true name of the floating city had been; the Blessed knew it as nothing but a long-abandoned ruin. The people of Bountiful had long ago dubbed it the Sunken City, for that was what it was: a grand grouping of once-beautiful palaces that had fallen beneath the waves.

It hadn't floated, exactly: you could still see the remains of graceful pylons arching brokenly out of the water. They had once held massive leaf-shaped platforms dozens of feet above the Sound. On those platforms were built immense structures of fantastical design: leaping arches and high towers, all in beautiful shades of white and ivory and celadon and coral. All of it was shattered and drowned, now, the blade-like tips of the platforms jutting out of the water at every angle, the domes and towers no more than barnacle-encrusted hulks that breathed and swam with the changing of the tides.

"They used to move," Rolan said.

"What did?"

"The platforms. They were mechanized, somehow; built on struts anchored in the seafloor, but they could move around, change position."

"Why?" asked Ever.

"The better for the lords and ladies of the Old People to enjoy their views," said Rolan, nodding to the east, where the Marvel Sound joined Jerusalem Sound and flowed into the wide Atlantic.

"I overheard Elder Betenson talking about it once," Rolan explained. "My father told me he was as keen on the relics of the Old People as Elder Haglund when he was younger."

The children of Bountiful—the boys, mostly—had all grown up telling stories about the Sunken City. How it was filled with mermaids, and sea monsters, and gigantic crabs that would as soon eat you as look at you. Some were stories of adventure, but most were stories made up to help young boys frighten the wits out of each other when they were up past their bedtime.

"Only the richest of the rich lived there," said Acel. "The most powerful of the Old People, before the Fall. They built it to show how God-like they were. Look at it now."

Ever remembered the look on Acel's face when her foster father had told him to take one of the longboats across the Sound. He'd looked concerned, scared even—what was he worried about?

"Why don't we just go around, Acel?" Ever asked, but Acel shook his head reluctantly.

"Your father was right to tell us to go straight across. The Sunken City may be bad, but the ruins take up most of the center of the Sound. The alternative is to pass close by the old Jerusalem wharves, and there will likely be Marmacks nearby."

No craft significantly larger than their boat could have passed through the ruins safely. The jagged remains of the structures, steel and stone and more exotic materials, often lurked just below the surface, waiting to tear up the hull of the unwary sailor. The Blessed rarely sailed larger craft—where would they go?—and the longboats had shallow enough drafts to coast safely through most of the detritus.

Jerusalem Sound was less than two miles across at its narrowest point. They were almost halfway across now, well within the outer boundaries of the ruins. Rolan offered to take over for either Acel or Chy, but both shook their heads. Ever had to admit to a growing feeling of unease as they drew into the most concentrated part of the ruins. The platform sections, many of them jutting almost vertically out of the water, loomed over their boat as the boys guided it through. Ever didn't blame them for preferring to have something to do other than look around.

The water grew choppier as they drifted into the more crowded center of the ruins, green waves slapping hollowly against the tilted platform fragments and jostling their boat. *Much longer in this kind of chop and we'll all be hanging over the sides*, thought Ever. The strangeness of their surroundings did nothing to help her roiling stomach.

"Do you feel it?" Acel said suddenly. He slowed his rowing for a moment and Ever saw the back of his head move slowly from side to side. She knew at once that he wasn't talking about seasickness.

"Yes," said Ever, at the same time that Rolan and Chy did. Chy and Acel turned around, stopping the oars completely, and all four of them stared at each other in surprise.

"It's like there's something—" said Rolan.

"Wrong," finished Chy, licking his lips nervously. The boat bobbed on the water, its prow drifting slowly out of course with no oars to guide it.

"We should keep going," said Ever. Acel nodded heartily in agreement and he and Chy began rowing again with new vigor.

The feeling was subtle, like the first, nagging tingle of illness that reveals its true nature only after a high fever has blossomed in your head, and it was growing. The four companions didn't need to talk about it to know they all wanted to get out of the Sunken City as soon as they could.

Ever turned back to resume her watch from the prow. They had just passed beneath the underside of a tall, twisted shard of stone and metal when she saw it.

Perched at the edge of a pearlescent, leaf-shaped platform tip that jutted out of the water a few short yards in front of them was a creature unlike any she had ever seen. She hadn't noticed it at first because it was completely still and had skin of a bluish gray that blended in very well with the soft colors of the ruins and the cloudy blue sky. It had a slick appearance, like its skin was wet.

Ever froze. She must have given herself away, because the creature moved suddenly, unfolding itself from the strange crouch it had been in and standing—*how can it stand? What is it?*

Before Ever had a chance to warn anyone, she heard Rolan cry out in shock.

"What's that?" he yelled. Acel and Chy spun in their seats to look.

Silhouetted more clearly against the sky now, Ever could see that it had a vaguely human form, though its limbs were oddly shaped and it seemed to have a heavy tail that dragged behind it on the smooth, sun-beaten surface of the crooked platform. Apparently hearing Rolan's outburst, the creature opened its beak-like maw and let out a high-pitched, clicking cry.

Ever put her hands over her ears. A chorus of like noises from around their boat answered the creature's call. The creature loped strangely up to the tip of the leaf-shaped platform it was on and dove smoothly off, entering the water with a small splash off their port bow.

"Surrounded," barked Acel.

"What?" yelled Ever.

"They've got us surrounded."

"Father in heaven," Rolan murmured, closing his eyes.

Acel jerked his head sharply at Chy and they began rowing faster.

"What are they?"

"The things that live here," he said.

"I only saw the one!" shouted Ever. No more of the creatures had appeared, but the chirping, bark-like calls still repeated at various points around them.

"Trust me, there's more of them," said Acel, concentrating on rowing the boat. "We have to get out of here, as quickly as we can."

Hearing a sudden plop and a splash from beyond the starboard rail, Ever looked over to find the creature poking its shiny, domed head above the water. It chattered at her. She let out a short screech before clapping a hand over her mouth and staring at the thing that seemed to be looking at her.

Its eyes were on the sides of its head, deep, large, and black; its head was cocked to the right, one round eye squinting out of its slippery gray face to examine her.

"Ever!" Acel yelled, struggling to turn the boat away from it.

It opened its beak again, silently this time. If she didn't know better she might have thought it was grinning at her. It had a single row of cone-like white teeth lining the inside of its silvery lips; a pointed pink tongue curled languidly in its mouth. The creature opened and closed its mouth several times in a row.

Ever maintained eye contact with the creature—it was almost as if it wanted her to, though she knew how crazy that idea was. She heard Acel passing off his oars to Rolan and then he was at her side, pulling her away from the gunwale. When she refused to take her eyes off the creature, Elder Higbee gave her a gentle shake.

"Ever!" he said. "Sister Ballard!"

Ever looked at him dazedly, shaking her head and blinking her eyes to clear the growing lightheadedness she was feeling.

"I think...it's okay," she said. "I don't think it wants to hurt us."

"It's not okay," said Acel firmly, sitting her down next to him. "Rolan, Chy: row. Now."

"What is it?" asked Ever again.

"It's one of the Damned," said Acel.

"But it didn't seem...." She trailed off, looking past Acel to where the creature's head bobbed above the choppy water. They had begun to pull away from it, but when Ever met its eye again it continued to keep pace with them, swimming smoothly and easily alongside the longboat. It was clearly a smart animal: it was careful to stay just outside of the sweep of the oars, and it occasionally looked at Chy, Rolan, and Acel, as if to make sure they weren't making any threatening movements.

Ever felt a warm feeling in her skull, almost like a mild headache. It wasn't just physical, however—it was a sensation she'd had before. It was like—*like an arithmetic problem you can't solve*, she thought, *or the feeling of untangling one of Elder Betenson's iron puzzles.* She felt convinced there was something just beyond thought that she couldn't quite grasp. It was like forgetting something, or like having a word on the tip of your tongue that you just couldn't remember.

"It won't leave," said Rolan.

"Row harder," said Chy, grunting with effort as he heaved his considerable bulk against the wooden oars. Acel was fiddling with something on his pack by Ever's side but she was too distracted by the strange spell the Damned had put her under to see what.

A small part of Ever's mind rebelled at what she was doing. She couldn't help but try to reason through what was happening; it felt right. Squinting in concentration, her hands clenched in fists, she focused all her thought on the wet, black eye. She tried to swim into it, as if it were a small ocean itself, dark and warm and comforting. It wouldn't hurt her. It was an invitation. Ever reached out to it—

"Ever, watch out," she heard Acel say. Then he was standing, blocking her view, and she could see the butt of his rifle against his shoulder.

"No!" she screamed, rising. She got her hand under the stock of the rifle just in time to send the shot high and wide, unintentionally pushing Acel over the bench into Rolan's back as she did so. There was cursing and yelling, but just then something *popped* in Ever's mind: all other noise ceased. She heard a distant voice, as if overhearing a conversation in another room. It grew louder.

…are you…

You? She responded instinctually, not with her voice but with her mind, speaking to the voice in her head as if with a new organ of speech she didn't even know she had.

…Who are…

Who am I?

Acel had struggled to his feet between Chy and Rolan. Before she could stop him, he shouldered his rifle again and fired another shot. It cracked loud in the ocean air and hit the water with a whispered splash. He didn't seem to be trying to hit the creature this time, but he was definitely trying to scare it away. It disappeared under the water and Ever panicked. What was this? What had happened? If it left, how would she—

…you.

She looked aft and saw that it had appeared again, surfacing for a moment in the gentle wake left by the longboat, just long enough to look at her one last time. Dropping into her seat, suddenly tired, Ever looked down at her hands and saw that her fingernails had bitten deeply into her palms. There were half-moon shaped marks on her skin, one of which was oozing blood.

Acel came forward to where she was sitting and bent over to look into her eyes the way Sister Hales might peer into the eyes of a person with a head injury. Sitting down next to her again, he dabbed at her hand with a scrap of bandage then passed her his water skin. He stayed next to her for the rest of the ride across the Sound. She didn't object; she didn't speak at all. She was completely overwhelmed by what had just happened and right then she wanted nothing more than to be left alone.

Moments later they sailed out of the Sunken City into calmer, open waters. Ever drifted off, feeling as if she were floating outside her body, bobbing and flowing in the cold water below the boat.

She came back to herself when she felt the keel of the boat scrape against sand. They had come to the far side of Jerusalem Sound. Their crossing had taken a couple of hours, and only that long because of the delays in the Sunken City. Looking up at the sun's position in the sky, Ever could tell that it was only mid-morning. *Then why does it feel like I've been awake for days?*

Elder Higbee insisted on making a fire and preparing a hot meal.

"There's no sense wasting the opportunity while we have it," he explained. "We ought to keep fires to a minimum until we get out of Marmack territory anyway." Nonetheless, he had Chy keep the fire small. Sound enough reasoning, Ever supposed, but she knew perfectly well that what he was really worried about was her.

The sacks of kindling and small boxes of fatwood had been lost with the packhorses, but there was plenty of dry wood on the beach and Elder Bingham built a fire quickly with flint and steel and various sizes of kindling he chopped out of the driftwood with his knife. He dug a pit in the sand first and built the fire at the bottom to hide the flames.

"It's too bad we didn't put a baited line in the water while we crossed," said Elder Bingham, adding driftwood to the flames. "Some fish would go over nice right now."

Elder Belnap looked at him like he'd lost control of his senses.

"Beans are fine for me," said Rolan, his arms wrapped around his knees. "I'd just as soon avoid fish for a while." No one had to ask what he meant.

"There'll be plenty of opportunities to hunt and fish," Acel said. "We left a good deal of our food back in Bountiful. We'll be foraging a lot sooner than we planned as it is. And look at it this way: the more of our stores we eat, the lighter our packs get." *And the emptier our bellies get, too,* thought Ever.

Chy and Acel were seasoned hunters, good with rifle and bow, and everyone raised in Bountiful knew from childhood how to identify more than a dozen edible plants that grew in the wild. Experienced or not, though, it was always risky to rely on hunting and foraging to feed yourself, a risk the Blessed as a whole refused to take. Their storehouses, chock full of preserved food, were testament enough to that. *They're also what make the apostates want to attack us.*

But then, if that were the case, why had the Marmacks bombarded them so haphazardly? She chewed her food slowly and worried.

They ate beans and brown bread and jam. Rolan pointed across the Sound at one point and commented that smoke no longer rose over Bountiful. Ever allowed herself a moment of hope that the Blessed had fought off the attackers again and kept the village safe. Ever giggled when she saw that Chy, who had decided to finish off the last of the jam with nothing but his fingers and enthusiasm, had a broad, berry-colored smear across his face.

"What?" he said. Acel shoved him good-naturedly and tossed him a rag.

Ever decided to take the opportunity to pry whatever it was Elder Higbee knew about the Sunken City out of him while she had the chance.

"So what aren't you telling us, Acel?" she asked.

He looked at her sharply across the fire pit.

"What do you mean?"

"You know something about those things we saw back there. You knew to avoid them—you'd rather kill one than let me near it. And you weren't too pleased when my father told you to go this way."

Acel looked distinctly uncomfortable, but he didn't pretend ignorance.

"When I was a boy, Coll Hamblin and I borrowed his father's boat to go fishing in the Sound," he said, idly breaking up a twig and tossing it into the fire. "The biggest fish are farther out from shore. You can't catch them from the beach."

"Borrowed?" asked Chy, cracking a smile. "Did Elder Hamblin happen to know you borrowed it?"

"*Borrowed*," affirmed Acel, throwing a twig at him. "Anyway, we started in Marvel Sound and caught one or two, but after a while they just weren't biting. We rowed out to the big Sound, in sight of the ruins, and Coll started talking about how we should try fishing the Sunken City itself."

Rolan gave a soft whistle of surprise and shared a look with Elder Bingham, who raised his eyebrows.

"What?" asked Ever. "Clearly something astounding and boyish has just been uttered."

"Can't fish the Sunken City," said Chy. "You're not supposed to go out there at all."

"Everyone knows that," said Ever. Back before the Marmack attacks started coming again, when children of a certain age were allowed to go outside the holdfast, were prohibited from exploring it. The debris was dangerous.

"But what you don't know is what the Elders threatened every boy in Bountiful with if they broke that rule," said Rolan. Chy and Acel nodded.

"Any boy caught in or around the Sunken City would be banned from applying for the Scouts for two years," explained Acel.

"To this day I don't know why, but eventually I agreed we'd try it," he continued. "Just row inside the outer perimeter, see if the fish were biting. Of course, it turned into a stupid kid's game, each of us daring the other to go farther and farther in, the sort of thing boys do." Rolan and Chy nodded sagely. Ever rolled her eyes.

"So we get in there, near the center, and suddenly we start getting this feeling—the feeling you all felt earlier," Acel said.

Suddenly the humor was leached out of all of them; Ever felt the seriousness of their situation and the story Acel was telling sink back in. It was a discomforting feeling.

"Then we saw one—peering at us from a piece of wreckage. We screamed and Coll started trying to back water. We didn't have bows with us, nothing but our knives. That...awful screeching began, and then more of them started appearing, pulling themselves out of the water onto platforms and struts..."

Acel swallowed drily.

"One of them came out of the water right by the rail, wrapped its claws over the gunwale near the oarlock. Coll was face to face with it for a second or two. He screamed again and swung an oar at it, but awkwardly—they're too heavy to swing like that with one arm. He almost lost the oar overboard. I pushed him out of the way and started rowing like mad.

"We got out of there as quick as we could. I swear I didn't take a breath until we were past the last of the ruins—and even then I was terrified. They were perched there, watching us leave, until we were out of sight. I've never been so afraid in my life."

"Well you made the Scouts at eighteen," said Rolan, "so obviously nobody found out."

"I almost wish we'd admitted it," said Acel, shaking his head. "We were so stupid…we deserved to wait another two years. I swear that's why Coll never wanted to be a Scout, though he wouldn't admit it when I asked him."

"What are they?" asked Ever. "I mean, did you ever find out anything else about them?"

"No. I'm sure the Elders know, because otherwise why the ban? But we never told anyone we were there. It seemed too risky to go around asking questions. Speaking of which," he said, "what happened to *you* back there, Ever?"

She'd been afraid of this question since they'd gotten to shore. It seemed like the subject everyone was avoiding.

"I—need some time to think about it," she said. "I just—I'm still trying to figure it out myself." It wasn't a lie, but it wasn't the whole truth, either. The truth was that Ever had indeed begun to suspect what had happened between her and the creature they'd encountered out on the water, but the implications of it were still too overwhelming to put into words.

"We'll hold you to that," said Acel. A few moments later, when everyone had finished eating, he dusted off his hands. "Time to get moving."

They buried the remains of their fire and left the beach. They'd made land at a small point and they forged their way through an overgrown stand of hardwoods to find a narrow old road leading roughly north.

Less than a quarter of a mile inland the trees gave way to a flat, open space paved in the crumbling dark material the Old People used for their roads. Tall weeds and a few small trees had grown through the surface, but the remains of painted lines and a few lonely, rusted out hulks of metal made clear that it had been a storage lot for their powered vehicles.

Useful things could often be found locked in compartments of the ancient engines—the metal itself had proved useful, long ago, when the Blessed had first cleared the northern half of Bountiful's peninsula—but Ever and her companions had no opportunity to start looking.

Sitting in the shade of a tree atop one of the old cars, directly in their path, was a man. He was reclining comfortably, eating an apple, as if he hadn't a care in the world. Acel stopped short as soon as he noticed him, motioning the others to do the same and unslinging his rifle from his shoulder.

"No need for that," said the man, walking toward them. He finished the apple in two large bites, wiping his mouth with the back of his hand and tossing the core off behind him. His cloth was fine—relatively clean and whole—he wore a neatly trimmed beard, and his dark hair was tied back in a neat ponytail with a bit of leather thong. "Just set them on the ground and we'll be happy to relieve you of all of your heavy burdens, those fine rifles included."

Acel looked back at them with the beginnings of a confused smile on his face. Rolan—who didn't have a rifle but had pulled his long knife—and Chy stepped out to flank Acel, keeping Ever at the rear. She pulled her own knife hastily.

"We mean you no harm, sir," said Acel cautiously, holding his rifle pointed low but at the ready. "We'll just be going on our way. I suggest you go on yours."

"You Saints," the man said, grinning widely. "Always so polite."

Ever heard booted footsteps behind her and whirled just in time to see the face of the man who grabbed her. He caught her wrist easily when she slashed at him and took the big knife out of her hand as easily as Ever would retrieve a stick from the hands of a misbehaving child. He bent her arm behind her back until she gasped in pain, turning her around in the process.

Other men were appearing around them, rushing in from the trees and rising up from behind rusted cars. Rolan cut the arm of his attacker before being knocked to the ground and disarmed almost as easily as Ever had been. Acel was already on the ground. The man who had been eating the apple stood over him, examining his rifle. Bingham got off a single, wild shot that caromed off the pavement uselessly before being relieved of his own weapon. As she watched, a large man hit him savagely across the face with the rifle's butt, knocking him to ground. He collapsed bonelessly and Ever cried out.

"Don't fret, sweet thing," said the man with the ponytail. "You wouldn't begrudge us a bit of salvage, after that fine meal you had on the beach. It's not often we get to outfit ourselves with the goods of the Chosen People *and* enjoy the company of one of their pretty young maidens." He grinned lasciviously and stroked Ever's cheek with one scarred knuckle; she heard the brute holding her chuckle evilly.

"Don't touch her," said Acel hoarsely. Ever counted eight men surrounding them, one of whom was holding Acel up. Ever didn't think he'd been hit as hard as Chy; the bright red splotches on his cheeks were marks of shame, not injury.

"Oh ho," said Ponytail, turning in Acel's direction. "Is she spoken for then, Blondie? Perhaps you and I can have a round in the circle to see who gets her then, eh? First round's to me." Acel looked at him fiercely, struggling against the man who held him until he got a punch to his kidney for his trouble.

"Which clan are you from then?" asked Acel. "Brown River? Cabot's Mill? You're a long way from home."

Ever's heart sank, hearing Acel speak. Those were Marmack clans, albeit not ones she was very familiar with. She had held out hope that they might have run into a group of simple bandits, men who might be reasoned with... But Acel was a Scout, and Bountiful's Scouts were trained to know Marmacks on sight, even to differentiate between clans. Looking for closely, Ever saw that all of them were wearing some item of red clothing, be it a dingy neckerchief or an armband. It wasn't as obvious a marker as she'd imagined apostate sashes to be, but Acel seemed convinced. How he could tell their clans from any of it, she had no idea.

"Clever little Blessed," said the man. "But not clever enough. We're from all clans, and none. We serve the

Prophet. The Prophet unites all." Acel looked disgusted, but said nothing.

"Just get it over with," he said. "Kill us and be done with it."

"What in God's name are you saying, Acel?" yelled Rolan. The Marmack guarding him, a short man who nonetheless looked dangerous enough, hit him hard in the mouth.

The man with the ponytail was smiling.

"No lad, no such luck," he said. "Standing orders, you see. As much as I might like to have the boys here gut you and leave you all for the wolves—well, three of you, at least"—here he winked at Ever—"standing orders say otherwise. All Holy Folk to be brought to Salem for inspection."

"But where are my manners?" he exclaimed, clapping his hands. "I promised you we'd lighten your burdens. Kindly relieve these gentlefolk of anything worth taking, boys. Oh, and Piker? No marks on the pretty one this time, eh?"

4

Jared jerked the tip of the Marmack's knife away from his face for a second time and felt his left arm start to tremble. His strength was fading. The apostate was stronger than he was and they'd been wrestling on the narrow walkway atop Bountiful's southern wall for what seemed like hours already. He'd been trying to reach his own knife for some time now but the man had his right arm pinned.

After letting Bountiful's defenders waste arrows and stones on ill-equipped cannon fodder, the Marmacks' elite troops had come over the wall like dogs on a bone. The fact that a good part of the Blessed's fighting force was struggling to contain the destruction caused by the Marmacks' catapults meant that the walls weren't as fully manned as they might have been. Whoever was leading the Marmacks knew their business.

The man on top of Jared grinned, displaying twisted teeth the color of mud, and suddenly doubled his efforts. Just as his arm was ready to buckle and Jared was beginning to realize that this might really be the end, the Marmack shifted his weight onto his left knee, freeing Jared's left leg. Acting more on instinct than rational thought, Jared brought his knee up between the man's legs as hard as he could. The man let out a feral squeal of pain, blowing spittle and rank breath into Jared's face. Suddenly the worst of the apostate's strength was off of him and Jared flipped him onto his back, unsheathing his own knife in the process and ramming it deep between the Marmack's ribs. He twisted the hilt and pushed up; the man died with a wet gurgle; dark blood stained his greasy beard.

Pulling his blade free, Jared stared lightheadedly down at the man he'd just killed and took several slow breaths. If there had been any other enemies nearby he would surely have been killed, but when he shook off his shock a moment later and looked around, he saw that he was the only person left alive for at least thirty feet in either direction. The ramparts were thick with the bodies of Marmacks and Blessed alike; many of the raiders had come over the wall without stopping, leaping off into the village below, intent on stirring up violence inside Bountiful itself.

The horrible cracking noises had ceased, for the moment anyway. Peering over the battlements to make certain his section was truly still for the moment, Jared found the nearest ladder leading down and made his way to the gates.

Elder Betenson was yelling at a group of men bracing the great oaken doors with timber. They'd managed to stop the battering ram for the moment then. Jared had to stop and catch his breath before attempting to speak.

"What's happened?" Jared croaked. Elder Betenson, momentarily satisfied with the reinforcements to the gates, looked at him with bloodshot gray eyes.

"What're you doing off the wall, boy?"

"They've retreated from the southeastern corner," Jared said.

"Who's left in your unit?"

Jared only shook his head. Elder Betenson grimaced.

"Good you came to me then," he said, turning to call out orders. "Hamblin! Bennion! Cluff! The southeastern corner needs reinforcements!"

Reinforcements doesn't quite cover it. Maybe he's trying to be encouraging.

Elder Hamlin, who had a nasty looking gash running down his cheek, called back in frustrated defeat.

"Where am I supposed to find the men for that?"

"Send half of the riflemen up," yelled Elder Betenson. Elder Hamlin looked as if he might argue further, then shut his mouth, nodded, and turned away, beginning to bark orders himself. Elder Betenson always held the riflemen in strict reserve; they were meant to be a last line of defense. If he was using them now….

"Is it that bad?" Jared asked. Elder Betenson nodded grimly.

"We bloodied them well enough, but we lost half of our men doing it," he said.

Jared swallowed and felt panic grow in his chest. He forced himself to avoid asking about friends and family, of either of them—he didn't want to know. Not yet.

"They've pulled back," Elder Betenson said, "but they'll come again soon. They've got the numbers."

Jared couldn't help but breathe a sharp sigh of relief when he saw his father running down the gate lane to them. Elder Meacham clapped his son on the shoulder and spared him a small smile, but then got directly to business.

"One of the Scouts just reported in," said Elder Meacham. Aside from being dirty and smoke-charred, Jared's father looked in one piece.

"Which one?" asked Elder Betenson.

"Cragun."

"What about Holdaway?"

"No one else has come back," said Elder Meacham. "Cragun says the bottom of the peninsula's swarming with Marmacks, Glade. The force they've got here is just a fraction of them."

"That's it then," said Elder Betenson. "Come with me."

Jared followed his father and the master at arms, not knowing what else to do at the moment. Elder Betenson led them to the Council building.

When they entered, Bishop Royce was standing in the main entryway instructing a group of Deacons, who were obviously being used as messengers. Jared saw Dallin Orton among them.

"A word, Bishop," said Elder Betenson. Bishop Royce dispatched his young pages and joined them. No one told Jared to leave, so he stayed.

"How's it going?" asked Bishop Royce. "Last update said that—"

"In short, not well," said Elder Betenson. "I'm sorry to be curt, Farren, but we don't have much time. Where's the prisoner?"

The conversation Jared heard over the next few minutes made the blood leave his face.

Apparently a small group of raiders that had gotten over the western wall at the beginning of the attack, while the catapults were still active, included a somewhat high-ranking Marmack clan leader. A bowman had recognized the complicated combination of Marmack markings that indicated his rank and knocked him out with a blunt arrow once he was inside the walls. Elder Betenson had ordered him chained and held. The Marmack had so far responded to all attempts to question him with filth and violence.

It was the means of said questioning that Jared found shocking. Elder Betenson did not mince words when he described his intentions. A few minutes later the Bishop led them to Storehouse 2, which served Bountiful as an armory. The Marmack was shackled and shut up in one of the small, locking, windowless rooms that served as safe repositories for dangerous weapons and substances. After collecting a few implements from an adjoining room, Elder Betenson entered the room himself, asking them to wait for him outside and fetch him if any reports of Marmack movements came in.

The next ten or so minutes were tense for Jared and, he thought, his father and the Bishop as well. No one spoke; Jared's father looked bleak. Bishop Royce was clearly praying. There was shouting from within the room, which stopped quickly. A few minutes later a scream, then silence; then shrieking like Jared had never heard from a man's mouth that trailed off only after a full minute had passed. There was some muffled conversation then, and more yelling that cut off suddenly, with ominous finality.

Elder Betenson emerged from the little room a few moments, wiping his hands on a rag. Jared felt his own hands trembling and clasped them together to make it less obvious.

I don't know what's worse, he thought: *the fact that Elder Betenson just tortured a man to death or the fact that my father and the Bishop just stood and listened to it happen.* He shivered involuntarily and felt sick. *And so did you*, he reminded himself.

When Bishop Royce opened his eyes, they were wet with tears.

"There are over three thousand Marmacks on the peninsula," said Elder Betenson, without preamble or prevarication. "Bishop Royce, my official recommendation is that we begin evacuating Bountiful at once."

Neither of the other two men argued. Jared knew perfectly well why they didn't, too: there were around 300 people in Bountiful, only 120 of whom were legitimate fighting men, and a solid half of those were now dead or wounded. Even counting women and children, they were outnumbered ten to one.

"We may still have a chance if we use the northern Scout tunnels," Jared's father said. "The Marmack presence at the tip of the peninsula has been minimal."

"See to it, please, Elder Meacham," said Bishop Royce. "I'll join you momentarily."

"What of the storehouses?" asked Jared's father.

The Bishop spent a moment in thought.

"Every family in Bountiful should have emergency supplies prepared, Bishop," said Elder Betenson. "We cannot take all of our provisions with us. As of now they can only aid our enemy."

"Fire them," said Bishop Royce. The two words seemed to have cost him something, just by saying them. They hit Jared hard as well, though for a different reason. The idea of destroying the storehouses reminded him of something, he just couldn't think of what. It didn't matter now.

Elder Betenson turned to Jared's father.

"Tell Hamblin and Higbee to use the oil reserves," he said. "They'll burn faster, and hotter."

Elder Meacham nodded.

"What about Ever's party?" asked Jared suddenly. "If we leave…they'll have no idea what happened to us. If they come back, and we're not here—"

"I'm afraid we can't worry about that right now, Jared," said his father. "We'll be lucky to get out of here alive as it is."

"I'll go," Jared said. He said it without thinking. Either that, or he'd been thinking about nothing else since the attack had begun. Since he found out Ever was going north, maybe. The three older men shared a look, but none spoke. Jared took this as encouragement.

"I can track them easily enough," he explained. "Catch up with them, let them know what's happened."

"Which only means they'll know where we're not," said Elder Betenson, "if and when they ever get back here. How will you find us?"

Jared's father was nodding in agreement.

"Better to wait until we have some idea of where we're headed, at least," he said. "Then we can send someone out—"

"No," said Jared, surprising himself as much as Elder Meacham. Jared never interrupted his father, let alone disagreed with him publicly on so important an issue. "If there are that many Marmacks on our peninsula, there's no way of knowing how many more of them might be in the region. We know they've been scouting us for months, and we know they've come by boat to Red Rocks and the Neck. As far as we know, they're based out of Jerusalem, right?"

Elder Betenson nodded, his face unreadable.

"Then it would stand to reason that they've at least scouted the land to the northeast. I talked to Elder Orton. He sent Ever and the others across Jerusalem Sound this morning." It was hard to admit to himself that she was gone. He'd been so busy staying alive that he had barely had time to think about it.

"You think they're walking into a trap," said Bishop Royce.

"If not a trap, then at least a more dangerous situation than they anticipated. There's just…" he began, not sure how to say what he was trying to say.

"What is it, son?" asked his father.

"Take your time, lad," said Elder Betenson, as calm as if the entire village wasn't coming down around their ears.

"This is *it*, isn't it?" Jared said. "Bountiful's done for. If we can get out, we'll be taking hundreds of women and children into Marmack occupied territory, hoping against hope we can get some of them away.

"Ever—the party going north is our last hope," he finished. "Wherever we go from here, if they can't find what they're looking for, there may be nothing left for us."

Bishop Royce looked at him carefully, then put his hand on Jared's shoulder.

"I gave up trying to predict Heavenly Father's plan for us a long time ago. I say we let him go," he said, looking at Elder Meacham. "That is, if you can bear it."

Jared's father was looking at him strangely and Elder Betenson, of all things, was chuckling.

"I figured the boy'd find a way to go after that girl, Barek," said Elder Betenson, clapping Jared's father on the back. "I'm surprised he didn't manage it sooner." Elder Meacham frowned at Elder Betenson, then looked back to Jared.

"Someone has to do it, Father. It might as well be me."

After a moment, Elder Meacham nodded. He was nothing if not decisive.

"Ready your things, then. Say goodbye to your mother. I'll meet you at the Bringhurst Scout tunnel."

Jared stared at the full scout pack propped against the headboard of his bed. It was smaller than the heavy, framed trekking packs Ever and Acel and the rest had gone off with; Scout packs were designed for speed and stealth. It contained only the most basic necessities for surviving in the wild, plus a few extra items Jared had added, just in case. It was made of leather and oiled canvas. Its straps and buckles were adjustable and detachable, for use as slings or splint bindings, if necessary.

It hadn't taken him any time at all to get it ready. It had been packed for days.

He had started packing the night he found out Ever had been chosen to go north. She hadn't had time to seek him out, then, and he wasn't ready to talk to her yet in any case. The idea of her leaving was still too fresh. But that night, after his parents and his younger sister were asleep, Jared took the pack down off the wall and began filling it with gear. He'd added a few things each night since, finishing last night before going to bed with his eyes wide open.

It was as if there was a veil carefully placed between the part of Jared's mind that openly accepted the fact that Ever Oaks was leaving on a journey from which she might not return and another, less accessible part that nonetheless acted of its own volition. He hadn't allowed himself to pierce that veil. It was in that other, secret part of himself that Jared found the determination to pack his things for a departure he hadn't yet accepted as inevitable. And it was in that same corner of himself that the feelings that buzzed in the presence of Ever herself secretly lived and grew.

He left his house quickly and found his mother and sister helping with the fire-fighting crews. He knew as soon as he laid eyes on them that his father had already been there. His mother's face was blackened with soot, if also fierce with determination; his sister looked tired and scared. He hugged them viciously and didn't stay long enough to crack the brave façade he knew they were all putting on. When he left tears had made narrow, clear pathways through the grime on his mother's face.

Then Jared made another decision that he had, he realized, also been coming to for days: he sought out Erlan Ballard.

He found him shadowing his father, Elder Ballard, in precisely the same way that his father shadowed Elder Cardon. The three of them formed a strange little procession wherever they appeared across Bountiful; Jared could have found them by the villager's complaints alone. Apparently both Elders Ballard and Cardon, and by extension Erlan, felt it beneath their dignity to join the bucket brigades that were still at work putting out the worst of the catapult fires.

Jared had to pull Erlan away—literally—but eventually he managed to get him alone. The nearest private space was the council building, which was full of the Bishop's pages and scribes, who were frantically carrying out a variety of orders related to the evacuation of Bountiful. The quietest place in the building turned out to be the council chamber itself.

The room was dark and empty, but the sunlight that shot through the high, narrow windows in broad beams gave it a peaceful atmosphere at odds with the chaos that reigned outside.

"Well? What is it?" asked Erlan. "What was so important that it couldn't wait?"

"They're evacuating the holdfast, Erlan," said Jared. Erlan raised his chin a fraction upward.

"I already know that," he said. "My father and Elder Cardon were in the middle of discussing the matter when you showed up. I hope you didn't drag me in here just to tell me something I already—"

"Just shut up and listen," Jared said. His patience with the boy in front of him—who despite being the elder of the two of them Jared nonetheless thought of as a boy—had officially been exhausted. "Ever's gone. She left with Acel and Rolan and Chy when the attack broke out."

"What?" said Erlan, angrily. "No one told me—how can they just leave?"

"I told you to shut up. Elder Orton got them out as soon as the Marmacks arrived at the gates, and the

Bishop backed up his decision. The point is they're gone. They're headed north."

"*Three* elders abandoning Bountiful at a time like this?"

"Come on, Erlan," said Jared, "you know as well as I do that if this attack didn't break us, the next one would. We can't stay here. We've got to find someplace else to go."

"I do *not* know that, Jared," said Erlan. "What I know is that Bishop Royce made a decision to abandon our home without a vote of the council—and without the advice and consent of his first advisor, I might add. Elder Cardon is furious. The fact that Royce and Meacham are cowards doesn't—"

"What'd you say?" Jared's voice was eerily calm. He stepped closer. "Say it again, Erlan."

His friend—was he really his friend anymore? Had he ever been?—swallowed visibly, his face slackening.

"I didn't...I may have spoken too qui—"

"I'm only going to say this once, Elder Ballard, so listen close. You're entitled to think whatever you want. You're entitled to say whatever you want, no matter how much of a damned fool it makes you look like. But one thing you never seem to have learned is that everything has *consequences*. There will be some if you go on talking like that."

Erlan didn't respond; Jared couldn't read his face. Was he angry? Afraid? Both? It didn't matter, he supposed.

"Look, Erlan," he said, "I don't have time for this. That's not why I'm here. I'm here because I'm going after her. After them. Someone needs to let them know what's happening, and they could use the extra man anyway. I'm here to ask you to come with me."

In any other situation, the look on Erlan's face would have made Jared laugh. He looked like Jared had just asked him to turn apostate and take a Damned wolf for a pet. Given the current circumstances, however, all Jared felt was disgust.

"Are you—are you serious?" said Erlan. "That's the most—why would I...?"

"Damn it, Erlan, *she's your wife!*"

Erlan laughed. He actually laughed.

"My wife? In some technical way, I suppose, but really, Jared..."

"In *some technical way*?" Jared repeated, incredulous. Was he actually hearing this?

"—you're being a bit dramatic, don't you think?" Erlan finished, a strange smirk on his face.

Jared paused, staring over Erlan's shoulder into a high shaft of sunlight.

"I can't believe we were ever friends," he said.

"Is that supposed to mean we're not, anymore?" Erlan said.

"I just...I can't believe you, Erlan. I can't believe this is the man you've become."

"Who the hell are you, anyway?" Erlan snarled, his anger sudden and vicious. "You think because you're popular and good with a bow—th-that...th-that makes you better than me?" He was stuttering. Erlan had stammered as a little boy; his parents had thought it incurable until he suddenly got over it when he got his growth. It only came out now when he was very upset.

"No, Erlan."

"Some friend you are," he continued, his eyes shining with something like hate. "Some friend who has d-d-dalliances in the w-woods with the girl promised to his best friend. You think I don't know? You think I don't hear what people say?"

"I don't know what people say, Erlan," said Jared. As little as he wanted to be having this conversation right now, he found Erlan's anger refreshing. He'd been beginning to think his old friend didn't care about anything or anyone at all.

"No, of course you don't, because Jared Meacham doesn't care what anyone thinks. Jared Meacham's above all that. Jared Meacham does whatever he wants. *Jared Meacham*—"

"Come with me, Erlan," Jared said, trying one last time. "We'll go after her together. We'll make sure she's all right. You and I can work all this out—"

"Hah!" barked Erlan. Jared stopped talking and watched as Erlan seemed to get ahold of himself. When he spoke again, he had his voice under control; he was the same, emotionless Erlan again.

"If you care about her so much, you go after her. You two deserve each other. She's a—"

Jared glanced at him almost lazily.

"Think about it," Jared said.

Erlan held his tongue.

"Goodbye, Erlan," Jared said. "God be with you."

• • •

His father, stolid, unimpeachable, and ever-present, was waiting for him outside the Bringhursts' cellar. Something must have shown on Jared's face, because his father began to look concerned. Thankfully, he misinterpreted what it was.

"They'll be all right," Elder Meacham said. His mother and sister. That's why his father thought he was upset. Jared just nodded.

"Here," his father said, pushing something heavy into his hands. Jared looked down, felt cold metal and oiled leather.

"A pistol?" he asked, wonderingly. His father had given him a gunbelt, complete with a tooled leather holster for the heavy firearm. It was a blued steel revolver with a polished wooden grip and a six-inch barrel. Its lines alone, precision engineered, revealed it as a relic of another age. His father nodded.

"I had Elder Betenson touch up the bluing. Two rifles were as many as we could spare, and we gave them to Acel and Chy," he explained. "We'll need the rest if we're going to get everyone out of here in one piece. But this...this is only useful in close quarters. You'll get more use out of it."

The Blessed had few firearms, and most of those were rifles, which were more useful for hunting and defense—at least the type of defense the people of Bountiful, who put their faith in strong walls and a low profile, were likely to need. Pistols were even rarer, especially antiques like this, but due to whatever technological magic the Old People had mastered, they were still functional if you cared for them right.

"Thank you," Jared said, buckling the belt around his waist and tying down the thin strap that kept the holster stable on his thigh. It was a large caliber; the rounds stored on the gunbelt were long and thick.

"If I find them—"

"Then you'll do what you think is right. Just as you are now."

"Where will you go?" Jared asked.

"Initially, to sea," said Elder Meacham. "We'll get as many women and children and others into the longboats as we possibly can and put out into the Sound. From there, I don't know. Away from here. North, most likely. We may very well end up following a similar path. Have faith. You'll find us, when it's time."

Jared paused, looking out at Bountiful stretching away to the south. Seeing the columns of smoke in the air, something clicked in his mind.

"They're burning the storehouses," Jared said. His father squinted in confusion.

"The Marmacks," Jared continued. "Why would they destroy the storehouses unless…"

"Unless they're here for something besides our food," finished Elder Meacham, a new understanding in his kind eyes. He pressed his lips together. "At Elder Barrus's cabin—you said—"

"They didn't take any of his stores," said Jared. That had been the feeling he'd had, the one he couldn't shake: the Marmacks weren't here for the storehouses. Or at least, they weren't their first priority. Elder Meacham looked haunted for a moment.

"Who knows why men do the things they do. Does it even matter?"

His father put his hands on Jared's head then, murmured a short blessing, and took his son by the shoulders.

"I believe in you, Jared," he said. "Now go."

Then Jared was moving, ducking into the dark cellar and opening the hidden door to the tunnel that led out of Bountiful—away from his home. He spared a moment to wonder if he'd ever see it again, then dispelled the thought as quickly as he'd had it. He stopped only to light a small lantern he'd brought just for that purpose, then trotted down the tunnel as quickly as he could.

He didn't think about the fact that thousands of Marmack apostates were converging on Bountiful. He didn't think about the incredible difficulty and the slim chance of success his father and the Bishop and the rest of the Elders would have in moving the entire village off of the peninsula and away from the Marmacks safely. He didn't think about the distinct possibility that he would never see his family, or anyone else he knew, for that matter, ever again. He thought about the path in front of him, and the person he was going to find, and what lay ahead. When he came out into the light under the wall, Jared started running.

15

Ever woke up coughing. The right side of her neck was stiff and sore and her hair had come loose from its braid where her head rested against the cold, damp wall. Her throat was dry and swollen. The walls of their dank prison were moldy, and she knew from experience in the infirmary what breathing in too much of the stuff could do to a person.

Acel was still asleep in the adjacent corner of the small cell, his chin on his chest. They had both gotten as far away from the grimy iron bars as they could, for whatever good it would do them. The cellblock was small, a short hallway with two holding cells on either side. She could see the dark shapes of Rolan and Chy in the cell across from them. The only light came from a narrow, barred window at the end of the hall.

From what she had seen of Jerusalem on the way in, the ruined city had become a hive of Marmack activity, though her first glimpse of an apostate stronghold wasn't quite what she expected. The people she saw were rundown and dissolute, certainly, and the general atmosphere felt hostile, but there was an ordinariness to the daily life she'd seen that had surprised her. For every leering raider with rotting teeth there was a mother carrying a squalling child; for every man wearing a jagged sword there was one stirring stew over a campfire.

What did you expect? A pack of wolves, fighting over bones? Men and women rutting in the streets? Ever massaged her neck and swallowed a few times to ease the soreness in her throat.

The Marmack with the ponytail, whose name turned out to be Vost, had led them at a fast walk west along Jerusalem Sound, crossing into the old city by a ruined northern bridge. Despite some resentful grumbling from the group of raiders he led, who seemed to think there were better uses for Ever and her companions, all of the men followed Vost's lead without question. Their complaints were quiet and more in the vein of idle chatter than true insubordination. Acel commented quietly to Ever during the two-mile march that they obviously feared Vost for some reason.

The Blessed were allowed little to no conversation amongst themselves, however, so for the most part the four of them walked along in silence. The Marmacks carried their packs for them. Ever had presumed they would divvy up the contents amongst themselves, but in her sight they had only hauled them, untouched.

The Marmacks led them to a great stone building, the massive columns that once supported its entrance mostly intact. Once inside they were funneled down a set of stairs into the dank set of cells they now enjoyed. That had been at least three hours ago. After a short, heated, and ultimately useless discussion of what they should do, Ever and the three boys had given up and tried to get some rest.

Ever heard a squeal and a bang from the heavy door at the end of the hall. Scrambling to her feet, she shook Acel awake. His eyes opened immediately.

"What is it?"

"The door."

Her heart sank when she saw Piker stroll into view.

"Well, well, children," he said, leaning against Ever and Acel's bars, "taking a little nap, are we?" His voice was a lewd, husky drawl. Words dripped from his mouth like sinister oil. Ever had feared him immediately, more so than any of the others that had kidnapped them. Piker reminded her of a dog with brain madness. She wondered idly if he was Damned to some extent—a deformation of the brain, maybe—and decided it didn't matter. He was an animal kept on a short leash by someone; Ever only hoped they'd never have to see him off it.

"You can't keep us here like animals," said Acel, rising from the back of the cell.

"Oh, can't I?" said Piker, sneering.

"We need food and water," Acel continued, "and the chance to use the toilet."

"All in good time, my son."

"I'm not your son," Acel said.

"Acel..." Ever said, cautiously. It wouldn't take much to provoke a man like Piker into violence.

"They can't keep us here forever," said Acel. "You kept us alive for a reason. Where's this prophet of yours?"

"You'll meet him soon enough, boy. If I were you I wouldn't be so eager. He's busy with your kin up north'ard. I don't think anyone'll mind if I have a bit of fun in the meantime, will they?" Piker grinned his delirious grin and Ever felt her stomach churn. She could see Chy and Rolan stirring in their cell across the hall.

"Vost will mind," said Ever, hoping to at least delay whatever foul tricks Piker was planning. The list running through her mind was increasingly frightening, each imagined act more horrible than the last. "And your...prophet will mind, too, I think. He's the one who wanted us alive."

"Oh, but precious," said Piker, moving along the bars until he was standing directly in front of Ever, "there's *so* many wonderful things we can do that don't involve killin' nothin'."

"You won't touch any of us without a fight," said Acel. Ever appreciated his loyalty, but she didn't think he was helping matters. There was likely only one thing on Piker's mind, and she was fairly sure that it would primarily involve her. She was thinking of what to say next when the door down the hall banged open again. Piker looked sharply to the left and the smile left his face.

"Out," said Vost, his voice clear and commanding. Piker grimaced but moved away from Ever's cell, sparing her one last, lingering glance.

"Now, Piker," warned Vost.

"A'right, a'right," whined Piker, saluting dramatically. "Later, kiddies." Ever could hear him giggling to himself until well after he left the cellblock. Vost stepped into view and addressed her and Acel.

"There'll be food and water if you listen close," said Vost, his arms crossed. The evil wit he'd shown when they were captured was gone now, replaced by a strange, familiar sternness she couldn't quite place. "Prophet wants to see you, true enough, and you'll stay alive till he says otherwise. It's best you don't take that for more than it's worth, though: what he wants with you is his business, and you might not like it much.

"There's two things to remember. The first is answer every question he asks you. There'll be consequences if you don't."

"And the second?" Acel asked, walking closer to the bars.

"Don't lie," Vost answered. "He'll know it if you do."

"When will we see him?"

"When he's fugging ready, boy," said Vost. "He's busy at the moment. Keep quiet till then or I'll send Piker back in here to entertain you."

"What about a toilet?" called Ever, as Vost began to walk away.

"In the corner," he grunted, and walked out.

Acel stood stiffly for a moment, then sat down on the cold floor again.

"We're never going to leave this place," said Rolan. "What could they possibly want us for that's good?" Ever could see his eyes glinting dimly in the soft light from the window. Even from where she stood he looked afraid.

"Shut up, Rolan," said Chy.

"Both of you shut up," said Acel. "Right now the plan's the same as it was. Get some sleep if you can."

"Should we eat what they bring us?" said Rolan.

"They didn't bring us all this way just to poison us," said Ever. Having nothing else constructive to add at the moment, she searched the back of the darkened cell until her boot hit something metal in a pile of filthy straw. The bucket was small and dented, and from the weight of it not entirely empty. It sloshed when she kicked it again.

Ever sat back down on the floor across from Acel and tried her best to ignore the black thoughts growing at the back of her mind.

She woke feeling sicker and more tired than she had the day before. The dank, airless cell was doing nothing for anyone's health. She could hear Rolan coughing across the hall. Acel, though he'd never admit it, looked stiff and exhausted. Only Chy seemed relatively normal. He'd taken to pacing around the cell he shared with Rolan, much to Rolan's annoyance. He had little to say, but the exercise was obviously keeping him alert.

The food Vost had sent them was poor fare: hardtack biscuits, hard wedges of moldering cheese, and a potful of unidentifiable gray meat that only Acel and Chy were brave enough to eat. The water tasted hard and flat, as if they'd collected it off the wall of a damp basement. All of it had been pushed through a small, locking slot in the bars by a pair of mute, bored-looking Marmacks who looked at them with less interest than a Bountiful farmer would show their livestock.

Their cellblock seemed to face in a westerly direction, so they got very little light in the morning through the single, small window. The dim light was bright enough now to indicate that it might be late morning. None of them had slept well; besides the uncomfortable accommodations, Marmack-occupied Jerusalem only seemed to grow louder as night fell. Noise trickled in through the thin windowpanes at the end of the hall. Aside from the recognizable sounds of carousing and what sounded like competitive brawling in the large square outside of the building they were being held in, Ever heard the tramping of hoof beats. Several large groups of mounted men had passed through the city throughout the night. Acel had listened carefully and tried to estimate their numbers from the sounds, but eventually he had given up and lapsed into the grim half-sleep that seemed to be their new status quo.

From time to time, one of them would try to stimulate a conversation, but most of these efforts either ended in apathetic failure or resulted in a renewed argument about the best way to handle their current situation. Acel and Rolan argued about the likelihood of being able to overpower their guards and escape the prison, and even Chy, whose stolid good nature was normally a boon, was pessimistic about the chances of getting out of Jerusalem alive.

It was all academic, of course, as Ever usually had to remind them: any escape plan would necessitate them getting out of the cells, which didn't seem likely to happen. The Marmacks would only release them to introduce them to something worse, and they had as much chance of escaping the concrete and iron cells without tools as they did of flying.

It was lucky that they had decided to ration the food they got the night before, because they received no breakfast or lunch. The only thing that happened during the hours between waking and late afternoon was another visit from Piker, who came into the cellblock to leer silently at them for a little while. Ever made a point of turning her back to him and looking at the wall. After a few minutes she heard him chuckle to himself and leave, slamming the door behind him.

The afternoon sunlight was streaming through the ground level window at hall's end in bright yellow bars when they heard the door open a second time. Vost appeared carrying a simple wooden chair. He said nothing to them, only set the chair down facing Ever and Acel's cell and left again. The door closed behind him. A few minutes passed. Acel was rubbing his eyes and peering at the chair as if it had appeared there of its own volition. She could see Chy and Rolan moving across the hall. Several minutes passed. Just as Ever began to think that no one would ever appear and that the chair had been placed there by Vost as some sort of mind game, the door scraped open again.

The footsteps approaching were different from either Vost's or Piker's; these were sharper, as if the wearer wore hard-heeled shoes, and their rhythm was strangely syncopated.

The man that limped into view was surprisingly tall, though much of his height was hidden in the vulturine way he carried himself: his shoulders were wide and round, but hunched, and his head thrust forward as if peering at something unseen. He was bearded and wore a long coat similar to the frock coats the Blessed wore for temple weddings but made of rough leather; his clothing beneath was dark, and he wore a bright red neckcloth at his throat. He was indeed wearing tall, heeled boots of shiny black leather.

Oddest of all, he had a pair of darkened spectacles perched on his nose that concealed his eyes entirely.

"Good morrow, Sister Oaks," the man intoned in a deep voice. Ever stiffened. How could he possibly know her name?

"And Elders," he said, turning about to address Chy and Rolan as well as Acel, "how *blessed* we are to have holders of the priesthood in our humble chambers."

His voice seemed to carry layers of meaning: sarcasm over authenticity over something else entirely. From the moment he began speaking, Ever found herself working hard to figure out what he was actually saying. At times it felt almost like hearing two or more voices speaking over each other, as if his physical voice was merely an echo of something else.

"You're the Prophet, then?" said Acel, standing with his arms crossed several feet back from the bars.

"So I am called by my people, yes," the Prophet said. "And you must be Acel Higbee." Acel seemed as taken aback as she by the Prophet knowing their names. The man turned again to Chy and Rolan and addressed them as Elder Bingham and Elder Belnap. The two boys looked hopelessly at Ever and Acel, saying nothing.

"I understand that you are the leader of this little band," the Prophet said to Acel.

"We don't really have a leader," Acel said hesitantly. "We make decisions together—"

"Come now," the Prophet said. "You don't really believe that. You're being modest. Or am I talking to the wrong person?" He shifted his eyes to Ever, whose hands were working against each other nervously at her waist. "That's an interesting outfit you're wearing, Sister."

Ever fought the urge to blush and held her chin level. She wouldn't give this man the satisfaction of seeing her react to his barbs.

"Acel's right," said Ever. "We do things together, or not at all." The Prophet raised an eyebrow but didn't argue further.

"Very well," he said, seating himself in the wooden chair. "Even so, I hope Elders Bingham and Belnap aren't too insulted if I sit with my back to them. The chair's already facing this way, you see."

The small wooden chair only accentuated his height; folded up in it with one long leg crossed over the other, he looked a little like a predator taking its ease.

"I see that your accommodations are subpar. Forgive me for that. I've only just arrived in Salem. I'll have Vost see to making you more comfortable after we chat."

"What is it that you want from us?" Acel asked. "Why are you holding us here? We carry nothing of value."

"Right to the point," the Prophet said. "I like that, Elder Higbee. You may be surprised to learn what I consider to be of value. But first things first: I know you, as you can see, but you do not yet know me. So allow me to introduce myself.

"My name is Azariah Thayne. I am chief and Prophet of the tribe you know as the Marmacks."

Thayne is a Blessed name, thought Ever, looking at the Prophet with new eyes, *and Azariah is from the Scriptures....*

"And the man who ordered the attack on Bountiful," Rolan said from behind him.

"Just so," said Thayne, turning his head slightly.

"What's happening there?" demanded Chy, coming up to the bars of their cell. "How goes the battle?"

"Chy," Ever said sharply. The questions all of them most wanted the answers to were whether Bountiful still stood, whether their families were alive, whether they were free or in bondage; but appearing desperate would get them nowhere. Thayne was chuckling quietly.

"Yes, Elder Bingham," said Thayne, "listen to Sister Oaks. Don't reveal too much too quickly. Don't show your hand, as the Old People used to say. Even in these latter days, information does not come without cost. Not to put too fine a point on it, but none of you are in any situation to demand anything of me. That said, rest assured that I will get to the fate of your compatriots in time. But I am not here to answer your questions so much as you are here to answer mine."

"You speak as one of the Blessed," Ever said.

"Do I?" asked Thayne. "I will take that as a compliment. It is said that the speech of the Blessed comes closest to the speech of the Old People. But you mustn't judge all my people by the pidgin that passes for language among the rabble. This tribe—this growing nation, I should say—runs the intellectual gamut from top to bottom. My efforts to instill some form of education have proven quite effective, but there is some use to be had yet out of the...beastlier elements, I'm afraid."

"Why have you attacked Bountiful?" asked Acel.

"I thought we established that I would ask the questions, Elder Higbee," said Thayne, turning sharply to peer through his lenses at Acel. He had a way of swiveling his head independently of the rest of his body that completed the image of him as a carrion bird in Ever's mind.

"I'll answer your question, however, because it serves as an apt segue into our next topic. I attacked your village for a variety of reasons, some of which I will keep to myself for the time being, but one of which is only too obvious if you've met any of my men."

Thayne leaned forward, his elbows propped on the arms of the wooden chair.

"My people grow *hungry*, Elder Higbee, and they look to me to sate them."

"So much for the fruit of your labors, huh?" said Acel. Thayne smirked.

"Uneasy lies the head that wears the crown, Elder. But as you said, you're not a leader, are you?"

Thayne's emphasis on the word *hungry* was what made the realization click in Ever's mind. That was the thought that had nagged at her mind. She had begun realizing it the day of the feast, but even before then the thought had been there. Elder Betenson had said as much to the Elders' Council the day she eavesdropped from the balcony. It was commonly accepted that the wealth of food the Blessed worked so hard to produce and store was the primary motivation behind the Marmacks' aggression.

But that isn't it at all, is it? It went back to Elder Barrus. The Marmacks that murdered him hadn't even touched his provisions.

"If your people are so hungry, why leave a cabin full of food out on Golden Neck after you murdered its owner? Why try and burn down Bountiful with your fire arrows?"

Thayne smiled and winked, as if she had won a point.

"I think you know the type of hunger I'm talking about; not a craving for food and drink, though that is there, but a hunger for darkness that fills the souls of lesser men. I'm talking about pillage, rapine—*violence*. I've found that allowing a controlled amount of it makes them easier to control the rest of the time. Sort of like letting a child get its energy out before bed. I must drive them toward some purpose, or it all falls apart.

"Which brings me to the meat of this little interview," said Thayne. "Where are you headed, and why?"

"Why would we tell you anything?" Acel asked, echoing Ever's thoughts exactly.

"Why wouldn't you?" asked Thayne, spreading his long arms. "What have you got to lose?"

"Everything," said Ever. Thayne smiled at her again.

"It's true," he said. "I am your enemy. I command the largest group of apostates your holdfast has ever encountered. I have launched an attack against your very home. I won't even tell you whether that attack has succeeded. And, of course, I'm holding you against your will."

"That about sums it up," said Ever.

"You want us to cooperate," said Acel. "A show of good faith from you would go a long way."

"Yes, you're absolutely right," said Thayne, rising from his chair in one sudden, fluid motion. He stood beside it, holding the back of it with one hand. He placed the other, quite precisely, on the frame of his eyeglasses, and removed them slowly.

His eyes were now directly in the dim light of the window down the hall. As the rectangular black lenses came away, Ever gasped. Acel took a short step backward before catching himself.

Thayne's eyes had no whites, no pupils, none of the normal structures of the human eye. Each of them was instead an uninterrupted field of mottled sky blue. The blue appeared to reach back far behind his lids. He opened them wider and they caught the ambient light and shone softly. As Ever overcame her initial shock and peered closer, she saw that the surface seemed to swim with movement, as if clouds of brilliant azure gas were trapped in crystal orbs set in his sockets.

"Have faith in this, then," he said. "I have razed Bountiful to the ground. Your people are dead. We took no prisoners. They were shown no mercy. Those who resisted were cut down and left for the crows. For all I know you four are the last. And you have precisely two options: give me what I want, or die in these cells."

Squinting against the morning sun, Jared peered into the jumble of brick, concrete, and twisted metal that was Salem and wished he had one of Elder Betenson's field glasses. The old man would probably have given him one if he'd asked, precious as they were, but Jared hadn't had time to think of every last item he might need. His eyes were sharp, though, and they would have to do.

He was lying prone on top of a massive steel structure that looked as if it had once been some kind of storage silo for water, or maybe the oil that powered the motorized cars of the Old People. The morning was warm and beneath the flaking paint of the silo's domed top the metal was growing uncomfortably hot. Scanning the monotone sprawl of crumbling buildings one last time, Jared frowned and began creeping backwards toward the ladder rungs bolted into the silo's side.

It was a risk, perhaps a foolish one, exposing himself this way: even prone, any Marmack with sharp eyes looking in this direction would have no trouble spotting the small irregularity his body made in the silo's profile. The sky was clear and blue. *Perfect for picking out trespassing Blessed spies.*

Thankfully the ladder to the top was on the far side of the structure. Jared went down it quickly, then ducked into a stalker's crouch and made his way back out the crumbling concrete wharf toward the Sound. His pack and other gear were hidden in a broad rift in the cement near the water. He squatted down out of sight and took a sip of water from his skin. His stomach grumbled unpleasantly, reminding him that he hadn't eaten since before leaving Bountiful.

He'd wrapped some fresh meatloaf in a thin towel and stuffed it in the top of his pack before he left. He was well provisioned with trail food, dried meats and beans and the dense, honeyed grain bars that packed a lot of energy into a small form, but fresh food always lifted the spirits more. His mother's meatloaf usually cheered him, but at the moment its flavor seemed muted.

He'd expected to catch up with Ever, Acel, Chy, and Rolan quickly. They only had a few hours' head start and he was faster than any of them in the field. He'd expected them to be across the Sound and maybe a few miles inland by the time he made it to the boats stowed at the northwestern beach.

Knowing that Ever's father had instructed the group to do so, Jared also crossed through the center of the Sunken City. The crossing was slow and eerie, but he saw nothing out of the ordinary. He'd heard stories over the years—a lot of Bountiful's children had—about strange occurrences and stranger creatures. Children's fantasies, obviously. He glided through the jumble of barnacle-encrusted ruins without difficulty.

When he beached the boat on the other side the sun was setting. He found the their boat at the top of the beach a short walk from his own. He shook his head when he saw it: they hadn't even bothered to conceal it. They should have taken the time to cut pine boughs or cover it in detritus from the forest floor, but pulling it into the trees would have been better than nothing. Ever and Rolan might have an excuse for overlooking it, but Acel and Chy should have known better.

Locating their tracks leading away from the boat into the woods wasn't difficult, but by that time it was almost dark. He was sorely tempted to keep going, with a torch if need be. He could surprise them at their dinner fire, maybe; after seeing the mess they'd left with the boat Jared had no doubt Acel would allow a campfire. He smiled at the thought, but after a moment reluctantly decided against it. There was too great a chance he'd lose the trail in the dark. There was no particular hurry; better to be cautious and smart.

Wedged into his crack at the end of the wharf, Jared swallowed another tasteless lump of meatloaf and grimaced at the thought. *Stupid. You should have kept going.*

He'd camped just inside the tree line, rolling himself in a blanket under a bushy pine tree after a small, cold dinner. He woke before the sun and was already hiking north, following their trail, when the first light of morning brightened the sky.

He found the clearing less than half an hour later. After several long minutes examining the ground, the essentials of what happened became clear to him.

The tracks of the four Blessed led out of the woods from the old deer run they'd followed up from the sand and stopped in the midst of a large confusion of churned earth, perhaps fifty feet into the clearing. The area had once been a motor engine storage area for the Old People; the tarry substance they paved their roads with showed in many places under the centuries of mud, weeds, and debris. There was plenty of soft ground to read signs from, however, and Jared did so with an increasingly sick feeling in his stomach.

He saw where men—heavy, booted—had crept from the woods into the clearing behind Ever and the boys. He saw where one of them, the leader, he presumed, had jumped down off a rusting car and walked up to confront them. There were at least eight of them, perhaps as many as ten.

The trampled spot where the tracks all met was where the struggle had happened; Jared swallowed a throatful of fear when he saw a dark spot in the pale, sandy soil that looked like drying blood. There would have been a lot more if anyone had been seriously injured, though. They'd obviously been captured, but they were alive, at least until they left the clearing in the custody of the men.

It could only have been Marmacks. The tracks he found leading away to the west, toward Salem, had only confirmed it.

Jared finished the last of the hunk of meatloaf, rolled the towel up, and packed it back into his bag.

He'd followed their trail as quickly as circumstances allowed, but less than a mile after the clearing the tracks broke out of the woods onto a main road. Shortly thereafter he began to see other tracks, presumably Marmack bands moving back and forth from Salem, some of them lonely tracks that looked like scouts. It was late afternoon by the time Jared was able to confirm that Ever's captors had traveled directly along the main route leading into Salem.

He made his way through the ruins of an adjacent town, avoiding the main road when at all possible, checking both sides to see if any markings indicated the group had turned at any point. When he came to the bridge he stopped and waited for night.

At full dark Jared had crossed, scuttling over the broad, divided roadway scattered with derelict vehicles. The span was a wide divided road supported from below by massive pylons. It crossed one of the deep inlets of Salem Sound and on the southern end met a narrower road leading directly into the ruined center of the city the Blessed called Jerusalem. He followed it for more than a quarter of a mile along another narrow inlet bare of water at low tide, a long tidal flat glimmering faintly in the moonlight.

Twin watchfires burned at either side of the roadway where it entered the city proper, clearly manned by Marmack guards. Jared crept as far as he could before disappearing into the rubble off the side of roadway and heading east, skirting around the city center.

He'd found the abandoned wharf, thin and crumbling and slick with kelp in the shadow of the water tank, and squeezed himself into the crack for the night, his mind churning anxiously over what to do next.

He was stalling, he realized: the truth was he had no idea what to do next. He was stuck on the outskirts of the largest gathering of Marmacks the area had ever seen and his friends were being held somewhere in the middle of it.

His biggest problem was that he didn't know exactly where Ever and the other Blessed were. He presumed they were somewhere in Salem, but for all he knew the Marmacks had walked them through the city and out the other side. They could be anywhere by now.

You're being paranoid, overthinking it. Calm down and think through it logically.

The Marmacks had no reason to think that Ever and the three boys were being followed, therefore it was safe to assume that they'd take the most direct route to get where they were going. Marmack power was obviously concentrated in the ruins of Salem; it stood to reason that any prisoners they took would be transported there. Such a quick assumption, there: only weeks ago, the knowledge that there were Marmacks in the ruins of Salem would have set Bountiful afire with panic.

Why didn't they just kill them? The thought was sudden and disturbing. The Marmack attack on Bountiful was ongoing when Ever had been caught. The raiders Jared had fought on the walls certain weren't interested in taking prisoners. They wouldn't walk them all the way into the city just to kill them there—would they?

It was pointless to speculate. *You know they took them captive; you read the signs. Stop obsessing about what you don't know and focus on what you do. If they're keeping them in Jerusalem, which is the only thing that makes sense, they'd need somewhere to put them.*

The ancient city of Salem wasn't a large one, by the standards of the Old People, but the central district the Marmacks had turned into their home base held a variety of large, stone buildings, many of which were still standing. *They must have had jails*, Jared thought; even the Blessed had holding cells for the rare occasion that someone committed a crime, an enemy was captured, or a villager suffered from a brain sickness.

Still, his logic seemed…thin. *What would Elder Betenson say?*

Suddenly Jared laughed.

" 'Damned feeble, boy,' " Jared said aloud, mimicking the old man's gravelly voice. " 'You're a Scout. Go scout something.' "

His friends could be locked up in any one of thousands of rooms in the ruins or lashed to a peg in the city square, for all he knew. The only way to find out… *is to find out.*

He'd have to go in there blind; scout out the area, listen to whatever he overheard, find out where they were. He momentarily considered trying to hold up a Marmack straggler and steal his clothes, but decided against it just as quickly. It wasn't worth the risk—the risk that the man he robbed would raise the alarm or the risk that Jared's ignorance of Marmack customs would give him away. Best to rely on the skills he knew he had. And he could sneak around with the best of them.

His course of action decided, he stowed his pack deep inside the crevice. He hoped he'd have the chance to come back for it. He hoped his decision not to wait until nightfall didn't get him captured before the morning was out. He'd considered it, but in the end haste had seemed more important than caution. *I hope I don't end up regretting that.*

That was the thing about hope: it was, by definition, the absence of knowledge. It was faith. Taking only his gunbelt and his knife, he crept toward the looming, broken skyline of Jerusalem.

16

Ever cried for what seemed like hours. All of the pent up emotion—all of the anxiety, the fear, the anger, the sorrow, the guilt—all of it seemed to flow out with her tears. When she was finished she felt hollow, but she knew that no more tears would come for Bountiful now. It felt like being sick, when your stomach finally emptied itself and the heaving stopped. The boys betrayed few tears; Acel in particular had simply shut down. He hadn't spoken a word since the Prophet left, nor had he offered any comfort to Ever or the others.

Rolan and Chy were talking quietly across the way. She had heard what sounded like crying coming from one of them but, like Acel, neither had spoken. *Neither have you*, she reminded herself. *You sit here judging them when you've done nothing but weep.*

Wiping her nose on her sleeve, she swallowed the last of the salty river that flowed over her cheeks and lips and into her mouth. There would be plenty of time for crying later. For now they still had the Prophet to deal with.

"We don't know for certain that he's telling the truth," Ever said. Her voice sounded thunderous after the long silence.

"Yes, he could be lying," said Rolan. "I only wish I believed it."

There was another long silence, and then Acel finally spoke.

"It doesn't matter," he said. "No use thinking one way or the other about it, and there's certainly no use debating it. Either they're gone or…or they're not. We don't know, and we won't, until—"

"There's something he's not telling us," she continued. "Why would he destroy everything and everyone and keep us alive? It doesn't make sense."

"For his sick amusement, probably. We'll never know," said Chy. She couldn't see his face. "They're not going to let us live, Ever. Only Heavenly Father knows what he wants from us—it's not as if he's said, is it? But either way, do you really see us walking out of here? Do you really *see* that happening? We've all known the truth since they captured us. It's over. It's over for Bountiful—"

"Shut up," said Rolan.

"Or what, Rolan?" Chy said, turning to look at his smaller cellmate.

"Stop it," Ever said, her whisper a shout.

"Just shut up, Chy," growled Rolan. "Everyone likes it better when you just shut up. That's what you're good at. Be a good boy and let Acel do your talking for you, like he always does."

The ire in Rolan's voice shocked Ever. Was this really happening? After all they'd just heard, now they were turning on themselves?

"Big words," said Chy. "Big words, Rolan. Bigger than you. What are you even doing here? How'd you get chosen? You've got a smart mouth, that's all. Can't fight, can't shoot. Can't get a girl to look at you crosswise. I'd blacken your eye if it wouldn't be like beating a wounded lamb."

"That's it, Chy," said Rolan quietly. "You pound me. You break my face. You hit me till it doesn't hurt anymore. It's all you're good for."

Ever heard a shuffle and saw Chy rise up.

"You *fuggin'*—"

"You know what you two remind me of?" asked Acel. He didn't raise his voice. He barely looked up. He kept his seat on the cell floor, his arms wrapped around his knees, his blond hair lank and dirty, and looked out at Chy and Rolan like he'd never seen them before. The sheer placidity of his question interrupted the argument more effectively than a shout ever could. Chy was standing dumbly over Rolan, fist cocked, and Rolan was hunched beneath him, squinting suspiciously across at Acel.

"A couple of Marmacks," said Acel. "A pair of dirty, squabbling apostates. Two men barely worthy of the name who've never heard of the commandments, let alone forgotten them."

"Acel..." said Ever. The whole situation felt like a barrel of Elder Betenson's gunpowder placed too close to a campfire.

Acel only looked at her and cracked a morbid grin.

"But I'm no better," he said. "At least you two have a response. Even if it's a useless, violent one. I'm sitting here and I keep going over it in my head, every moment since we walked out of there and left them all behind, and I live through it again and again and I'm still not sure if any of it made any sense. And now there's nothing, and maybe we're the only ones left, and maybe we're going to die in these cells."

"Acel, are you—"

"Where's God, I wonder? In all of this, where is He? Has He gone?"

Ever didn't know what to say. Apparently neither did Chy or Rolan, because all three of them were sitting in their respective cold, dark spots with their eyes locked on Acel. It was disconcerting, to say the least, to see him this way. He seemed on the verge of giving up.

"Oh, ye of little faith!"

Ever snapped her head toward the empty hallway so hard she felt a muscle spasm, only to find that the hallway between their cells was no longer empty. The Prophet's voice was warm and paternal, at odds with his looming appearance.

"I'm sorry," said Thayne, stepping fully into view. He had apparently been lurking just outside their view. "It was not my intention to frighten you."

Acel, who hadn't revealed any surprise at Thayne's sudden appearance, got slowly to his feet.

"It seems to me that's exactly your intention," he said.

"Yes, well…" Thayne disappeared from view for a moment and returned with the wooden armchair in hand. He set it down across from their cell again. "I came here, in part, to apologize for my harsh words this morning. Not to recant them, you understand, but to convey my regret at my…unsympathetic delivery."

"If what you said is true," Ever said, "we have nothing left to talk about."

"The truth is," Thayne said, folding himself into the old wooden chair with an easy creak, "you are wise not to trust me. You would be even wiser not to trust anyone, in this age. But I have not come to talk about Bountiful. I've come to tell you a story."

"You want us to listen to you tell us a story," Ever said, "after you've just told us not to trust you."

"Listening doesn't require trust, my dear," said Thayne. "It merely requires silence."

Ever felt heat growing in her face; her anger at this man felt like a powder keg near a camp fire. As if sensing she was about to retort, Thayne held up one long index finger.

"Number the stars beneath the moon," he intoned. Ever felt her breath catch in her throat upon hearing the words.

"Three, for the stakes surviving doom," she finished. It was automatic; she couldn't help it. Looking at Acel, hearing the boys across the way murmuring to themselves, she knew they were thinking the same thing she was.

"The sickle moon in dark of night," continued the Prophet, then stopped, as if waiting for a response.

"Faintly illumes our secret flight," said Rolan softly. Thayne smiled.

"Need I continue?" he asked. "Or can we agree that these words have only ever been spoken by the Blessed?"

"I knew I recognized your last name," said Ever. "I thought it was a coincidence."

"Belief in coincidence is a luxury for the Damned," said Thayne.

The lines they had exchanged were from a longer poem, known to the Blessed as a passverse, written in the days just after the Fall to serve as both guidebook and passphrase:

> Number the stars beneath the moon: Three, for the stakes surviving doom.
>
> The sickle moon in dark of night Faintly illumes our secret flight.
>
> The East kindles sun's morning rays, Our compass true in latter days.
>
> An exodus our forebears made; From East to West their path was laid.

> Our own is laid to East from West May
> saints in grace be ever blest.

Every Bountiful child learned in primary school the history of the Fall and the great second exodus of their people. The wide land that became the Great Desolation was in chaos after the Fall. In the earliest days it was enough for the Blessed's distant ancestors simply to survive. When the worst of the destruction was over, and the Old People's civilization had fallen, a new violence had settled over the land. Raiders and looters and cannibals roamed the wilderness and the broken ruins, killing and defiling all in their path.

The remnants of the Saints, as their faith had been known before they became the Blessed, gathered into groups that became nomadic communities. Their options were to flee or die, and in the face of overwhelming odds they kept their faith and determined to move east, to the lands surrounding the remains of many of the great cities, the coastal population centers that had suffered the worst attacks of the Fall.

It was thought that traveling into the areas hit hardest by the destruction would put enemies off their trail. In the midst of all of the chaos, it became necessary to hide their purpose from plain sight and hearing, and to create a way to recognize each other in the case of separation and reunion with other potential members of the faith. Hence, the passverse. There was more to it, Ever thought, though she could never remember it all.

"That's right," said Rolan was saying, coming forward and gripping the bars of his cell, "Thayne. Thayne's a Blessed name."

"*Blessed*," said Thayne, making the word sound like a curse. He spat onto the floor in disgust. "It was only ever pride to call ourselves thus. 'Pride goeth before destruction, and an haughty spirit before the fall.' " The Prophet cackled strangely to himself.

"Yes, I am a Thayne, of the Thaynes that made the journey west from Illinois to settle around the Great Salt Lake, a thousand years ago or more. I am of the Thaynes that helped build the foundations of the great temple and who dwelt in the promised land, in the bright grace of God's desert sun. I am a Thayne of the Thaynes who made the second exodus in the wake of the Fall, wandering out of Deseret into the Desolation that man made out of God's sacred land.

"And I am the only Thayne who survives. The Azariah Thayne who was cast out of Ammon into the trackless waste to die for his people's fear. Because I was born with God's fire in my eyes. I am the Thayne who rose from the ashes. They called me Damned; they called me adversary; they called me devil. And under the lash of their judgment I became exile, wanderer, renunciate. With the light of revelation I became chieftain, bishop, Prophet. I am the only Thayne, now. I am their reckoning, and yours."

He cackled again, softly. Ever saw exhaustion and pain in his face, flickering, soon replaced by the arrogant calm that seemed to pervade the man. He adjusted his dark spectacles, massaging the bridge of his nose as if they pained him.

"It is...tiresome, my children. Tiresome to be Azariah Thayne. If you will listen, I will tell you my story."

They'd been captive for a day already, but Ever only now felt the true nature of their captivity. They had wandered into the web of some malignant spider, intent on toying with its food before it sucked them dry of all vitality for its own evil nourishment. Like a spider, though, she found it almost impossible to resist the stranger crouching before them. Ever felt empathy mixed with the beginnings of hatred; she wanted to scream and weep at the same time. She searched for God in the rubble of her mind and found only confusion and shadow.

She had been taught that God would always prepare a way for her, for any of His faithful, but in the presence of Azariah Thayne she found it almost impossible to remember what it felt like to believe that. In the Prophet's domain, the only way forward was the way he led. Mouth dry, Ever sat back and listened in silence.

Jared leapt the gap between two buildings and slipped in dirty gravel as he landed. He paused to listen in an awkward crouch, still as a frightened squirrel, hoping the crunching noise echoing into the alley below hadn't been overheard. After a slow count of thirty had elapsed, he eased himself back into the increasingly uncomfortable crouching position he'd been bent into for the better part of three hours. He'd lost track of how many rooftops he'd crossed since he scaled the twisted remains of a metal staircase late that morning.

Stealth was mostly a matter of enduring physical discomfort, in Jared's experience. He only hoped the reward was proportional to the pain. In this case moving slowly and carefully also had the benefit of avoiding weak spots in the aging structures. Some of the flat rooftops of the larger buildings were worse off than others: the ancient tar paper beneath the gravel gave way to rotting boards in some spots.

The Marmacks seemed to have little to no presence on Salem's rooftops. Jared had seen only one person, in the far distance, in his careful trek around the city's heights. He moved only when he had to; much of his day thus far had been spent searching out good vantage points and then sitting in them for long periods of time, watching the comings and goings of the apostates walking the streets below.

The activity he'd managed to observe so far had been fairly haphazard. Aside from the occasional guard watching the perimeter of the city center, most of the Marmacks Jared saw on the street appeared to be wandering about aimlessly. Some were working, but not in an organized manner. He saw several different blacksmiths hammering metal on crude anvils, but rather than grouping them together in a central forge they were scattered around, one in a blown out alcove here, another on a street corner there. Neither was their command structure immediately obvious; though he saw a number of fighting men wearing the bright sashes of raiders, he witnessed no clear exercise of authority over the sparse crowd filling Salem's streets and squares.

The wind had picked up as the sun rose in the sky, often thwarting his efforts to listen in on conversations happening below him. Being exposed to the brisk autumn wind was bad enough; feeling like he was stumbling around to no purpose was only making his bad mood worse.

It was just after noon and Jared was seriously considering doing something stupid—grabbing the nearest Marmack, sticking his pistol in his face, and forcing him to tell him where they were being held came to mind—when his luck turned.

He was in an exposed position, squatting at the corner of the roof of a tall, brick building looking down on a large square. There was little to no cover: the roof had a low concrete lip at its edge, but it barely concealed him lying prone. He'd reached it by hopping across from another building. There was no roof access from within, which gave him hope that nobody would expect to see a man crawling around on top of it. The square below seemed to be the epicenter of the Marmacks' activity in Salem. Most of the comings and goings he'd seen occurred there, and he could tell that several of the larger buildings far across it were inhabited up to at least the third or fourth floors.

An abrupt burst of laughter erupted behind him and Jared's blood ran cold. Snapping his head around and pulling his gun on instinct, he found himself aiming at an empty expanse of black rooftop. The laughter came again, a small chorus of coarse chuckling that could only be a small group of men. Shuffling on his belly over to the right edge of the roof, he looked down. A narrow alleyway separated his roof from the next, and by peering carefully over the lip Jared had a bird's eye view of the dark chasm between the buildings.

Not much light penetrated the alley, but Jared could make out two men, one taller than the other, walking through the alley toward the square. They weren't talking particularly loudly, but the narrow space had a way of throwing sound that explained his earlier confusion.

"Not if I can help it," the larger man was saying. "That one's sweet as cream, and just as pale." The smaller man laughed again, loping oddly beside him. Jared didn't like the sound of either of their voices. The big man in particular bothered him: he alternated between gruff threats and a tongue smooth as a devil's lure.

"Wut's Daddy gonna do with 'em?" the smaller man asked.

"You think old Blue Eyes just goes around tellin' me what he's thinkin'? How the shit should I know?"

"Wut abou' Vost? He—"

"He don't tell me shit neither," said the larger man. "But whatever it is Thayne's got planned for them, you can bet it'll be nice and unpleasant."

"Unpleasant for who?" said the smaller man. "You or them?"

"What, are you a funny man, now?" said the larger. "Stupid mutie. It'll be damned unpleasant for all concerned, that's what. What I had planned for them would've been pleasant for one of us, anyhow."

As they reached the near end of the alley Jared could see that the smaller man was deformed somehow—likely Damned. The Marmacks were known for keeping and recruiting Damned men if they were strong enough or vicious enough to be useful.

Many of the men and women he'd seen in the streets of Salem had seemed more…pathetic, somehow, than the raiders he had fought on Bountiful's walls, but these two curdled his blood.

"Daddy's leavin' again tonight, ain't he?" asked the smaller one, lurching beside the larger Marmack. "Why don' we have us some fun?"

"Who's us?" said the large one. "Why would I help your twisted ass do anything?"

The smaller one hung his head so pitifully that Jared almost felt sorry for him. After a moment, the little man looked up at his large companion again.

"Tell me how it is, then? After you done?"

"Tell you how what is? Vost ain't goin' nowhere. It's not like he's gonna let me do as I please. He and Thayne send me in to rile 'em up, when it suits their purposes, but that's all it is. Mind games. Always mind games with those two."

"Mind games?" asked the Damned man.

"Not something you'd understand," said the large man.

"So just go in when Vost ain't there. Might be there's a way. Might be Squeaker knows."

"I don't know why I ever opened my mouth in front of you," snarled the larger man, and pushed the twisted man hard into the wall of the alley. The little Damned gave a squealing cry and bounced off the wall of the alley into a pile of rubble. The large Marmack stood over him, pointing a thick finger down at him. Jared could see his face, now, dimly lit from the outside, a long, craggy slab with a permanent sneer attached.

"Man can't even comment on goods the Prophet brung in for the Prophet's own use without you sniveling in the background tryin'a get a piece. You listen good, you filthy mutt. I know better than you how things work around here, and how things work around here is, Thayne's business is Thayne's business. You stay out of that fuggin' courthouse or I'll open you a new mouth to squeal out of where your belly is now."

"But Piker, I—" The twisted little man was waving his limbs out of the detritus like a flipped turtle.

"Shut up," said Piker, snorting loudly and hawking a gob of phlegm down at the man who was apparently called Squeaker. "And stop following me around." With a last, booted kick to underscore his words, Piker strode out of the alleyway into the light of the square and stomped angrily across it. Squeaker was still whimpering faintly below, murmuring to himself in between hisses of pain.

Courthouse. Scrambling back to his corner perch, Jared peeked out over the square again and watched Piker walking away. The few Marmacks who passed him in the square gave him a wide berth. Diagonally across the square from where Jared sat, a cross street lined with huge old buildings began. He watched as Piker made his way in that direction and continued past the first two looming structures on that street.

Scrambling, Jared leaped the gap over the still-crying Squeaker and kept his eye on Piker, now quickly shrinking into the distance, as best he could. He quickly reached the last building on that side of the square, after which a thickly treed area gave way to the broken down structures along the narrow inlet he'd followed into the city. He could just see the dark splotch of Piker's heavy form taking the steps of a large, white stone building two at a time before disappearing inside.

It took Jared almost an hour to make his way clandestinely to a hiding spot closer to that building, picking his way carefully at ground level, staying to cover as much as possible, until he could mount another ruined building and regain the heights. He was perhaps a hundred feet from it when he stopped to catch his breath.

Closer up the building's stone was more of a dirty gray, its once-beautiful fluted columns gaping like a set of broken teeth. Two wings flanked the main section, one of which was almost entirely collapsed. Jared's eyes caught on the wide stone pediment above the remains of the columns. Carved in block letters into the stone were the words "TRY OF DEEDS AND PROBATE COURT." Much of the left side of the pediment had crumbled. Whatever the building's title had once been, some of it would remain a mystery. All Jared cared about was the fact that it was clearly some kind of courthouse.

Piker's words carried new meaning now that he'd thought them through. He'd been right in his speculations that morning: they had found a place with cells in it. Old courthouses had cells, didn't they?

Most of what the two unpleasant men had said in the alley had confused him—who was the Prophet? The word had ancient meaning for the Blessed, but their faith hadn't had a Prophet for centuries—but there would be time enough for thinking about that when he and his friends were safely out of Marmack prison cells. Maybe they'd met him. Maybe they would know.

Scuttling back from the edge of the roof he was on, Jared waited impatiently for nightfall.

17

"Three stars, three stakes, so the passverse claims," said Thayne, crossing one long leg over the other in his creaking wooden chair. Every now and again Ever saw a glint of his strange, frightening blue eyes, like a sliver of sky peeking out over the black glasses. "Three stakes remaining of the faith that became the Blessed people. But there was another."

Stake was an old word, rarely used anymore, for a large territory of the Church. After the Fall, when the Blessed had first fled the Desolation, they divided into stakes for protection and survival.

"There were only three," said Chy. "Everyone knows that."

"Everyone in Bountiful maybe," said Thayne. "Everyone in Camora and Serai too, most likely."

The fact that he knew the names of the other two Blessed communities was worrisome; they were even more clandestine than Bountiful was, being closer to apostate lands, and the faithful in those communities had hidden their holdfasts well.

Thayne leaned forward toward Ever and waggled his fingers upwards into the air as if traveling along a map.

"Far to the north and west, over the vast Desolation that is the remains of the American Empire, there was a territory known as Denali, which in even more ancient times was called Alaska. Great and beautiful it was, and wide and rugged and dangerous—a place of dreams and fantasy and, ultimately, death. Not a place for man."

"What's the point of this?" asked Acel. "Are we supposed to sit here and believe there were more of our people, hidden from us, all this time? Why should we believe anything you tell us?"

"As I've already explained, you shouldn't," said Thayne. "But as you are in my power, you will listen to what I have to say. Whether you decide to believe any of it is a different matter entirely."

Clearing his throat, he continued.

"But since you're all so intent on making this an interactive exercise, tell me, children: where was the Sundering? It's all right, you can tell me, I already know. I just want to know if you know. Let's see what they're teaching you these days in your little bubbles of paradise."

"A town called Lebanon," answered Rolan.

"That's right!" said the Prophet, brandishing his pointer finger in the air over his shoulder as if Rolan were a schoolchild who had solved a math problem.

The history of the Blessed had been passed down from father to son and mother to daughter since the first days after the Fall, though some said that the tale changed in the telling. Everyone knew the Sundering, however; it was, arguably, the most important part of the Blessed's exodus from the West.

"Lebanon, in Missouri," explained Thayne, "was announced, by whatever methods of communication the Old People had at the time, as a meeting place, a *rawndayvoo*, as they used to say. Those members of the Savior's Church were to meet there by a certain date so that the faithful who survived the Fall and the turmoil afterward would have a place to gather and decide on their next step."

"And so they gathered," said Ever, "four thousand of them, and a great conference was held, and the High Priests decided they would travel east—"

"Even into the very throat of the Fire," said Thayne. "Yes, yes, that's right. And so they split into different groups, to increase the chances that some of them would survive the journey, and traveled east. And thus were born the stakes of Camora, and Serai, and lastly Bountiful.

"But what your parents didn't add to your bedtime stories, my dears, because they didn't know—or didn't care—was that there were others, other faithful, who arrived too late." Thayne paused before continuing.

"And thus begins the story of Ammon."

Thayne touched his forehead, an odd, hesitant swipe, as if he felt ill.

"I was born in the cold, in the dark, where the sun shines at midnight and the moon graces the day. They were late, my ancestors, late in deciding to join the faithful at Lebanon, late in arriving there, late in deciding what to do when it became clear that the Church had moved on without them. Late, even, in finding their final home. The story of their struggle I'll spare you; suffice it to say that years later, a small group of stragglers arrived in the wet, ravaged northwest continued north into Denali. They thought to make their home in the south of that land, where the winters are milder and the fruit of the sea could support them, but they weren't so lucky.

"The land had already been claimed, by a vicious clan of apostates eager to dispatch contenders for their resources. They fought; some died. The survivors fled farther north, where it is not so easy to survive, and Ammon was born.

"I was raised on ice, and salmon and mountain berries, and in fear of the dangers of the wild, for despite being deep in the wilderness my people refused to admit belonging there. They never truly assimilated. They refused the help of the broad-faced natives who still dwell in the far places.

"The priesthood was…weak," continued Thayne, waggling his jaw. "They assumed that food and heat were the worst of their problems. They failed to account for the fact that Denali, too, had its Damned."

Ever heard a sharp scoff from behind Thayne. Chy, who had been pacing around his cell slowly while listening to the Prophet speak, came back to the bars.

"Poor little Prophet," he said. "Had to deal with some Damned. You and everyone else alive."

Thayne appeared to ignore the remark, but Ever thought she saw a twinge in the muscles of his face.

"The larger animals were the most destructive," Thayne said. "The ones that were already vicious became more so. When I was a boy a grizzly got through the gates in the middle of the night. Eight people died."

"You are known as a Saint, in Bountiful," he said, looking at Ever. It wasn't a question. Ever made no response. "I wasn't so lucky."

"The Ammonites grew steadily more fearful of the Damned, and in time they feared all changes brought on by the Fall—changes godly as well as ungodly."

Here Thayne grinned and removed his spectacles. His smile was almost as disconcerting as his eyes; he had a wide mouth full of yellow teeth.

"My eyes didn't change until puberty," he said. "Imagine waking up and having your sister scream at the sight of you. Imagine running to the water bucket, breaking the ice and seeing your reflection in the morning sunlight, an uneven cloud of milky blue obscuring your pupils. But your sight remained. And your family grew afraid, as over the ensuing days that cloud grew, covered your eyes, and you ceased being their child and became something…other.

"They cast me out. A boy, younger than all of you now, a boy without even his first growth of beard, alone in the trackless wild. I called to God, then—I asked the Savior why he and Heavenly Father had forsaken me—but no answer came. I was alone. Utterly, inarguably alone."

"Is this where we're supposed to feel sorry for you?" asked Acel. "Where the people whose families and friends you've just killed are supposed to hear about your terrible childhood and, what…pity you?"

Ever caught the same twinge in the Prophet's jaw, a slight flexing of the muscle at the corner of his cheek, but again he only grinned.

"I pitied myself enough for anyone," Thayne said. "And I soon found that I had…other faculties. I could feel the life around me—use it to my advantage, use it to survive. I had nothing but the clothes on my back and a small knife, but I drew the caribou to me, looked into its eyes. It gave me skins to warm me, meat to nourish me…."

He trailed off, his strange eyes swiveling in their sockets. The lack of pupils made it difficult to tell what he was looking at, even when he was looking straight at you.

"It's ironic, really," he said. "My exile began in the icy North. It was there that I stopped believing in God as you know Him. But it was there, also, that I had my first revelation. The skyfires appeared above me, a dragon of red and green flame writhing in the night sky. I saw them first with my old eyes, but after a few moments it was as if a new set of eyes opened up inside of me and I could see…everything.

"It was years before I completely understood what I was seeing, and that it was truth. The world and everything in it—and more importantly, everything beyond—was an infinity of points." Thayne quirked his head like a dog. "The universe spread out before my eyes and I saw my own place in it. It was both humbling and…empowering. It was difficult, at first, to control the scope of it. But I learned, children."

His eyes rolled smoothly in his head as he said this, sweeping around the room and over her and Acel's faces, but somehow Ever could tell that he wasn't looking at any of it. It was as if he saw beyond the hallway, and the cells, and the trapped young people inside. Azariah Thayne's unsettling eyes tracked something no one else could see, like a blind man finding the sun by its warmth.

"I saw something else that night," he said after a long pause. "Or rather, I felt it with some new organ I didn't know I possessed—can you imagine discovering a new sense? A flash of something, a pulsing light, far in the distance. And I thought, at the time, that it spoke to me…said something, a few words. I couldn't understand. But I felt a person behind it, trying to speak to me."

Thayne stopped again and cocked his head as if he'd heard something. His chin sunk slowly down onto his chest and his eyelids drifted almost shut. When a few breaths had passed and he hadn't moved, Ever looked at Acel worriedly. Thayne barely seemed to be breathing. Disturbed and uncertain, they waited, Ever and Acel standing shoulder to shoulder in the middle of their cell, Rolan and Chy gripping the bars of their own.

Four sets of young Blessed eyes mirroring fear and anxiety watched as Thayne sat, mute and still, his coat draped over the small wooden chair like the wings of a sleeping bat.

"What—" Chy clipped his teeth around the rest of whatever he'd been about to say as Thayne moved. A slight tremor seemed to run through his body; Ever could see a muscle in his angular cheek twitching rapidly.

When he spoke, it was in a voice not his own.

Thayne's own voice was deep and charismatic, the kind of confident baritone that made great Bishops at home in Bountiful. This was something quite different, low and soft, with a strange twang to it, almost feminine but for the very masculine malice Ever sensed underneath every word.

"They stoned us from the walls, darlings," he said. "Sharp rocks bit through the thin clothes they gave us and cut our skin. They shunned us, sent us packin'. Our own mother and sister high on the walls lookin' down as we scrambled off through the hip-deep snows into the endless woods."

Thayne raised his head slowly and looked directly at Ever, his milky blue eyes still and wide.

"And thus began my trial, darlin'. Like the prophets of old. 'They were stoned, they were sawn asunder, were tempted, were slain with the sword; they wandered about in sheepskins and goatskins; being destitute, afflicted, tormented; they wandered in deserts, and in mountains, and caves of the earth.'

"And I wandered, darlins, I wandered: from Denali's high tundra to the wet forests of the giants to the dry mountains and deserts. I wandered, and I sought, and I found."

His eyes flicked between her and Acel now, eager and conspiratorial.

"An' I learned—I picked my way through the ruins of the Old People, digging in the oldest libraries for the remains of the paper books they made before they brought their magic to bear on the word. I even found copies of Scripture—don't look so surprised, my darlins. You should know as well as I by this point that your fathers concealed the world from you as much as they did from me. Didn't you feel it, darlin', darlin' Ever, when you crossed the narrow water yonder and met the slippery denizens of that ruined city-on-the-waves?"

Ever's breath caught in her throat as she recalled the brief, harrowing journey through the Sunken City. What happened little more than a day before already felt like weeks ago. And could he be telling the truth? About any of it?

"All the written copies of Scripture were destroyed in the Purge," Ever said, suddenly uncertain. "Only those hoarded by the faithful escaped destruction for long enough to be…to be remembered, passed down, mouth to ear, from father to son and mother to daughter." The words felt rote on her tongue, the old childhood mantras swimming in her brain, exposed for the first time to uncertainty and question.

"So our fathers said, darlin'," said Thayne. "We Blessed have a better recollection of the Scriptures than most—you'd be shocked to hear how many people today don't even know they existed—but even the

Blessed don't got it perfect. Things change in the rememberin'. Words get lost; names get forgotten. Only the ideas remain, the message, the truth—so to speak. We hope. But I've seen the real thing. And it's so much less…inspirin'…when you can hold it in your hot little hands.

"I found God on my own, in my own way, in my own mind, stumbling through the cold darkness amidst the Damned, and I had an epiphany fit to make the Magi blush. A Great Revelation, my darlins."

"Your tongue is foul," said Acel.

"Truth is foul, boy," replied Thayne, an edge to the silky voice. "But it's the Truth that I'll share with you now. If there's a God, it's us; if there's a Prophet, it's me. And if there's any Truth in this world, it's that the strong take from the weak."

"Just as you took everything from Bountiful," said Ever.

"Bountiful received my righteous vengeance, just as Camora and Serai did before it," growled Thayne. " 'And my wrath shall wax hot, and I will kill you with the sword; and your wives shall be widows, and your children fatherless.' "

He came closer to the bars, then, and grasped them with long, thin fingers. Ever stepped back involuntarily. She felt a strange pressure in her skull.

"You're a monster," said Ever.

"No, child," said Thayne, standing abruptly. "I'm the monster's lord and master. I am the Second Coming. I am He who Sees beyond the veil. And you, Ever Oaks, my darlin', you'll be my bride."

The pressure seemed to burst in her brain and she heard words in her head that echoed and overlapped against the words Thayne spoke into the air: *You are my gift to me. Together we will number the stars.*

After Thayne left, Ever sat down on the stone floor of the cell and wondered whether she should feel scared or bewildered. She'd been afraid for long enough now that it was beginning to feel normal—what happened when fear became your default emotion? This was a new kind of fear, though, more subtle, less visceral. It was one thing to fear injury or death and quite another to contemplate the interminable emotional torture of marriage to Azariah Thayne.

"He can't be serious," she said, more to herself than anyone.

"He's obviously insane," said Rolan. Chy agreed heartily. The two young men looked at each other in surprise. After a moment Rolan put a hand on Chy's shoulder.

"I'm sorry. For earlier. It's just—"

"This place," said Chy, clapping Rolan on the back. "I'm sorry too. This place—that man—it's enough to make anyone lose it." Rolan nodded quietly.

"They're right," said Acel. "He's mad. Mad as Elder Hafen on Easter."

"Madder," said Chy.

Ever smiled weakly. Elder Hafen was the oldest living person in Bountiful. He'd been born with the mind of a child. Every Easter he would appear shirtless on the green during Sacrament and rave and trill and laugh at the Spring skies. The Bishopric had given up their attempts to stop it, as trying to restrain him only made it worse.

"The difference is," said Ever, "Elder Hafen was harmless. Azariah Thayne is anything but."

"We're going to get out of here," said Acel. "We just...we just have to be ready when the chance comes."

His voice, his manner, even his hands betrayed the first signs of determination he'd shown since they'd been thrown in the cells. Ever wished she could share it. Thayne's words had shaken her, though. He'd kept his eyes focused on her throughout most of the conversation. His growing obsession matched her growing dread note for note.

"I have to tell you something," Ever said. "Thayne—when he spoke to me—when he came close and looked at me with those eyes. I could hear him. I could hear his thoughts. It's like he was talking to me at the same time he was talking to all of us—a whole separate conversation."

"Ever..." said Acel, his face a mask of concern and poorly concealed disbelief, "this has been a...difficult time for all of us—"

"No, Acel," said Ever. "It was like a...a pressure in my head, that turned into words. We communicated. He spoke to me. It felt just like..."

"Like what?" Rolan prompted from across the hallway.

"Like what happened in the Sunken City," she finished.

"With the dolphin," Rolan said.

"The what?" asked Acel.

"That's what they are, those creatures—or what they were, any way," explained Rolan. "Some kind of big fish, like a leviathan—a whale, but smaller and smarter. The Fall affected them more than most creatures. Nearly all of them are Damned, and unlike most of the Damned that you find in the wild they're—"

"Rolan," said Acel.

"Oh, right. Well I didn't say anything because it's been kind of, you know, *hectic* since—"

"Rolan," said Acel.

"What?"

"Shut up."

"Oh."

Acel turned to Ever.

"Keep going," he said.

Ever only shook her head.

"The…dolphin said something to me too, but I didn't hear all of it." She was a silent for a beat. "I don't know what's happening to me."

"You're a Saint," Acel said after a long pause. "Who knows what abilities God gave you? Maybe you don't know what all of them are yet."

"What did he mean," said Rolan, "about making Ever his bride?"

"I think it's fairly obvious what he meant, Rolan," said Acel.

"He didn't make a lick of sense the whole time he was talking, if you ask me," said Chy.

"Could he have been telling the truth about Serai and Camora?" asked Ever. The others fell silent.

"How could they have fallen without us hearing anything?" asked Chy.

"Easily," said Acel. "Our Scouts only make the run to Serai once a season. To Camora even less frequently. And with the Marmacks getting aggressive...."

"We didn't send Scouts to the other communities this summer," said Chy. Acel nodded, his face stone.

"Thayne had months to attack Camora and Serai while we were busy skirmishing with his cannon fodder. I wouldn't be surprised if he planned it that way. In fact, the more I think about it, the more I'm sure of it."

"That means they didn't get even one Scout out, to send for help," said Rolan. "Or at least, that none of them reached us."

"They probably didn't even see the need," said Acel, pacing around their cell. Ever sat with her back to the wall, hugging her knees to her chest. "If he used the same tactics with them as he did with us, they wouldn't even have suspected the number of men he had until it was too late."

Acel sat down suddenly, across from Ever.

"This is all too much," he said. "I need time to think. But I think we can agree on a couple of things, at least."

"Such as?" asked Ever.

"First, that none of us is going to aid Azariah Thayne willingly. And second, that you, Sister Ballard, need to start being a lot more open about what's going on in your head."

• • •

Several turgid hours had passed and Ever was watching motes of dust floating in the late afternoon sunlight when the door at the end of the hallway scraped open again. Vost entered with Piker and a third Marmack she didn't recognize. Vost neither spoke nor looked at any of them, only approached Rolan and Chy's cell and put a key in the lock.

She saw Rolan and Chy get up and wait, still and nervous, as the lock's aged mechanism crunched and revolved.

Vost entered alone, the other two standing shoulder to shoulder outside the door. Ever grasped the bars of her own cell, her chest suddenly churning with anxiety.

Rolan started forward when Vost took Chy by one thick arm but backed off at a glare from the Marmack captain. Chy tensed at first, seemingly on the verge of struggling, but Vost leaned in and whispered something in his ear. Chy relaxed and his shoulders sagged, apathetic or defeated, and Vost pushed him forward out of the cell into the hands of Piker and the other man. Vost locked up Rolan's cell door as the other two Marmacks shackled Chy and led him out of the cellblock.

"Where are you taking him?" Acel demanded.

"Prophet wants him," Vost said flatly, finishing with the thick steel key and returning it to his pocket.

"For what?" asked Ever.

Vost turned to her and grinned.

"That all depends which one of him's come out to play, now, doesn't it?"

• • •

The Marmacks made sure they heard the screams clearly: the door to the cellblock was left open, and the room they took him to was just down the hall. Chy was gone almost an hour before they began. They were more squeals than screams: high-pitched, abrupt, almost feminine.

Ever gripped the bars of her cell again, the craggy layers of chipped paint digging into the pads of her fingers.

"What are they doing to him? What do they want?"

Acel only shook his head. Rolan had gone to the back of his cell and had his head between his knees.

They tortured him in short bursts, judging by his cries, and after a while the noise stopped altogether. The light from the window slot faded. At around the dinner hour Ever heard muted laughter then and footsteps in the hallway, heading in their direction.

Just outside the cellblock something happened. There was shuffling and grunting, then a Marmack—Piker, she thought, hollered down the far hallway for help.

Ever moved to the far side of their cell, nearest the door, and pressed her face between the bars to see if she could catch a glimpse of what was happening. The concrete block walls that framed the cell jutted out beyond the bars, however, and she couldn't see the door no matter how hard she strained.

She heard a deep growl that sounded like it came from Chy followed by a sound like a venison roast hitting a stone floor. Boots tramped down the hallway toward them and there was another scuffle of some kind, then an awful noise in Piker's voice: a whining roar, followed by a choking gasp from Chy.

Ever felt her eyes burning with tears when Piker and another man dragged Chy bodily back down the cellblock hallway. He seemed to be unconscious. A smear of dark blood followed his body along the floor, livid against the pale concrete in the light of the Marmacks' lanterns.

Rolan caught him when the Marmacks dropped him into the cell and slammed the steel door shut. He stumbled under Chy's weight but managed to lay him on the floor of the cell with an odd tenderness.

Vost entered again. The third Marmack, whom Ever didn't know, addressed him.

"Oughtn't we get him some help, sir?"

Piker snarled and slapped the boy in response.

"Got what he deserved. Big lad like him, shouldn't have any trouble from a little prick in the belly." Piker spat on the floor.

"He fought back," said Vost. "That's his own fault. Besides, Thayne says he's expendable."

Piker pushed the third man out the door. Vost followed after a moment, meeting Ever's eyes as he left.

When they were gone, Ever wasted no time.

"Chy!" she called. Rolan was leaning over him. "Where's he bleeding, Rolan?"

Rolan made an overwhelmed gesture and then started examining him.

"They did something to his fingers, but those are bandaged—most of them at least, though it looks like they could use a change."

"Check his torso," said Ever. "He bled all over the floor when they dragged him in, and Piker said...."

Rolan tugged at Chy's shirt and Chy finally grunted and swatted at Rolan's hand.

"He's got a wound in his stomach," Rolan said. "It looks bad."

"Is it still bleeding?"

"Yes."

"Then you need to put pressure on it," said Ever. "Wad up his shirt or yours and hold it down over the wound. Can you tell how deep it is?"

Chy murmured something and Rolan leaned in to listen.

"Stabbed me," Chy said, louder. "Evil bastard stabbed me. Own fault. Fought them."

Rolan tore the hem off of his own shirt and used it as a compress, pressing down on Chy's belly with both hands. Chy groaned. After a minute he seemed to become more animated.

"What did they want?" asked Rolan. "What did they ask you?"

Chy coughed wetly several times; it took Ever a minute to realize he was laughing.

"Nothing," he said. "They didn't ask me anything. Just taunted me for a while then left me alone. Then Piker came back in with a pair of pliers…"

Chy held up his hands to show Ever and Acel. His fingertips were shoddily bound in blood-soaked cloth.

"What…" said Acel.

"Fingernails," said Chy. Ever forced down nausea.

"None of this makes any sense," said Rolan, still pressing down on Chy's stomach. "Why…torture him for no reason?"

"Who says they don't have a reason?" said Acel, coming forward. "The Prophet's own sick amusement, most likely. Hang in there, Chy."

"Both of you shut up," snapped Ever. "Can you feel his pulse, Rolan?"

"Hold on—yes."

"Is it weak or strong?"

"I'm…I'm not sure. How do I tell?"

"Never mind. Describe to me exactly where the wound is on his belly."

"Level with his navel," said Rolan. "On the right side."

"His right or yours?"

"Mine."

"How big is the wound entrance? Don't look, just try and remember."

"Um…an inch and a half?"

"Alright," said Ever, biting her lower lip and thinking as quickly as possible. "Can you…do you smell anything?"

"Like what?" asked Rolan, obviously confused. It occurred to Ever that she might be the only one of them who understood the potential seriousness of Chy's situation.

"We need to know if his bowels were pierced," she explained.

"So how—oh," Rolan said, suddenly understanding. "No, nothing like that."

Chy himself hadn't spoken in a minute or two.

"Chy?" she called. "Chy, how do you feel?"

"Sleepy," he said after a long delay. "Hit my head pretty hard, too, on the door…" He trailed off.

Ever cursed quietly.

"Rolan," she said. "You can't let him fall asleep. Keep him conscious. Give him some water, if there's any left, and bind his wound around his stomach with whatever cloth you have—the cleaner the better. Tight, but not too tight. You should be able to get a finger under it."

While Rolan started gently slapping Chy's cheeks in an attempt to rouse him, Ever chewed her fingernails and looked at Acel.

"How bad is it?" he asked.

"Not as bad as it could be," she said, "but it's still bad. If he doesn't get help…my God, Acel."

Whether it was her demeanor, her voice, or the mild blasphemy, Acel obviously sensed that she was shaken. He took her gently by the shoulders and met her eyes.

"Can't you…" he suggested. She shook her head forcefully.

"I need to touch him," she said. "It only works if I can touch him." Her last words were mangled by a sob that she only barely suppressed. She hid her face and scrubbed at her eyes. The last thing Chy needed was the rest of them breaking down.

"Ever," said Acel. "Look at me."

She looked at him.

"Tell me what to do."

"I...I don't know," she said. "I don't know. Just let me...think. I need to think for a minute."

"Look," he said, whispering. "I know you're scared—"

"I'm not scared," Ever said, more forcefully than she intended. She repeated herself more civilly. "I'm not scared. I'm *angry*."

And she was. Her anger was like a campfire fed a feast of dry pine needles and firewater; it went from a quiet flame to an uncontrolled blaze in seconds. She was angry, furious, that she'd let herself get caught up in this situation. She was angry at herself that she couldn't reach Chy to help him. She was angry at Acel and Rolan for not knowing what to do when she didn't. And below all of that, consuming it like the white hot coals fueling the cooler flames of that campfire, was a growing hatred of Azariah Thayne that threatened to overwhelm her.

Ever knew in that moment that Acel was right about one thing: the Prophet hadn't done this without purpose. Whatever lunacy ran through his blood, everything he'd done and said to them since bringing them here was to a purpose. That purpose was no longer a mystery. Thayne had told them himself. It was Ever he wanted. Perhaps he knew she would never—what? Join him? Marry him?—willingly, and he'd gone directly to harming her friends to force her to action.

He either knew exactly what he was doing, or he had underestimated her severely. She knew without considering it consciously that she'd let all of them die horribly before she'd submit to Thayne—it was a gut reaction of the kind that she'd come to trust instinctively. It was the Spirit talking to her. *Fight*, it said, *fight to your last breath. Death is only a doorway.*

But Thayne would know that's what I'd say, she responded. As insane and unpredictable as he obviously was, the man wasn't stupid. So what did he want from her?

He wants you to reach out to him. He wants you to need him. He wants you to share yourself with him as he has invited you to do.

Thayne must have suspected that the most severe form of torture for her would be to watch her friend suffer without being able to help. Which meant that he knew that her Sainthood abilities included healing. Which meant that he knew even more about them than he'd been letting on.

"Fine, then," she said aloud.

"Fine, what?" said Acel, confused.

Ever only shook her head, seated herself cross-legged on the cell floor, and closed her eyes.

"I need some time," she said to Acel without opening her eyes. "Don't disturb me unless they come back or Chy gets worse."

• • •

With nightfall came Marmack bonfires, large, roaring blazes in the center of every square and at the major entrances to the center of Salem. Several large groups of armed men came into the city with the dusk, trooping down the streets in disorganized, milling crowds.

Two guards were posted outside the courthouse doors, but otherwise the street below the roof Jared was hiding on was empty. The majority of the apostates seemed to be congregating in the large square he had circumnavigated earlier in the day. From the sound of it, they were celebrating something. Jared smiled. It was a grim irony. The cause of their celebration was likely the downfall of his home, and yet the noise of their merrymaking would serve as cover. A horse in belled harness could sneak around undetected with the racket they were making. *Let the firewater flow,* he thought.

He'd had plenty of time to plan out his route while he sat waiting for the sun to set. It took him only minutes to descend to street level, cross, and disappear into an overgrown grassy area one building down from the courthouse. From there he snuck behind the adjacent building and came up on the courthouse's ruined west wing. There would be no point having guards on the front door if there were an easy way in through the ruined section, but he'd decided it was worth a try. The Marmacks' civil security hadn't impressed him so far; he could only hope they were as lax about their apparent headquarters as they were about Salem in general.

It wasn't as easy to move in the rubble as he'd hoped; for every block of granite or overgrown column section there was an equal amount of gravel and ancient broken glass that tinkled at the slightest touch. The back of the roof had collapsed more dramatically than the front, however, so his movements were concealed from the street side. Behind him there was only the uneven remains of a highway and an ancient, rusting rail yard half consumed by the briny water of the inlet he had passed on his way in.

Jared could smell roasting meat and, just underneath it, the pungent odor of the hemp blossoms they smoked out of crude pipes, all of it rising from the various bonfires into the crisp night air.

The central body of the courthouse extended farther back toward the water than Jared had initially thought, but the broken down wing still seemed the most likely entrance point.

He was scrambling down a tilted island of concrete, a shower of gravel preceding him, when he heard a low growl.

It was too late to arrest his slide. The dog came out of the shadows near the interior of the broken wing into a shaft of moonlight just as he reach the bottom of the slope. It was shorthaired, with a heavy, square head—nothing like the shepherd dogs the Blessed kept. And it was aggressive.

The animal wasted no time. As soon as Jared moved it lunged for him, its powerful chest muscles propelling it across the short distance even quicker than he would have imagined. His hand had barely reached the hilt of his hunting knife, sheathed at his hip, before it was on him.

It was smart and quick, planting its paws on his chest and snapping at his face before he was even able to rise. His knife, half out of its sheath, clattered to the ground. Jared wrapped his hands around the dog's thick neck in a feeble attempt to keep its maw away from his face. Its strength was impressive; he wouldn't be able to hold it off for long. Its ears had been cut down to scarred nubs; there was no purchase to be had there. Getting one booted foot under himself, he heaved awkwardly, managing to unbalance the beast on its hind legs, then twisted and rolled hard to the right.

Glass, twisted metal, and concrete debris dug into his shoulders and sides as he rolled. The dog had already righted itself and leapt toward him again with a coughing growl. He scuttled backwards, kicking rubble at it. He couldn't see what was behind him and he wasn't surprised when his left hand came down hard on a shard of glass. Jared hissed in pain and kicked clumsily at the dog's face. He managed to clip it on the nose, which only seemed to enrage it.

It snapped and got hold of his right ankle before he could move out of the way. The pain was instant and incredible. Its jaws were like a vise; he could feel the bones in his ankle straining under the pressure.

Frantic, he grabbed the nearest object he could find—an arm's length of light metal framework—and brought it down as hard as he could on the animal's flat head. It yelped pathetically, sounding for a split second like a kicked puppy, and let go, ducking its head and turning away from him.

Jared tried to jump to his feet but only made it as far as his knees; his movement aggravated the fresh wound to his ankle, sending thrumming spikes of pain up his leg. Flopping painfully across the ruined scree toward his knife, he caught grip and rolled over just in time to catch the dog as it pounced on him again.

This time he brought the knife upward into the animal's ribcage with all his remaining strength, grinning when he heard its breath hiss sharply inwards. He guarded his face with his left forearm, feeling the jaws bite down weakly, then drove the blade home again and again until the dog's muscles went slack.

Rolling it off himself with no small effort, he lay for a moment looking up at the night sky. The stars were remarkably clear from within the darkened ruin, glittering points of gold on a midnight blue canvas.

The dog whimpered and went still next to him, one thick leg draped across his chest. When he'd caught his breath, Jared propped himself up with his uninjured hand, still gripping his knife, and got painfully to his feet.

Jared looked down at the dead dog with growing alarm. It had attacked him so quickly he'd barely gotten a look at it, and he'd been too concerned with staying alive during the struggle to note its more unusual features.

The thing was enormous—easily twice the size of any dog he'd ever seen in Bountiful. Looking closer, he could see that it was no ordinary dog, either. *Damned,* he thought, looking at its lumpy, misshapen face. Its musculature was exaggerated, too, and its teeth were crooked and large. The ears had clearly been docked.

Most Damned animals he'd encountered, while often more aggressive than their healthy counterparts, were severely handicapped by the desecration God had wrought upon them. A snarling, feral mountain cat with no bones in its hind legs, for example, or a vicious boar blind as a bat. This thing had all the aggression with none of the damage, vicious and cunning and granted powerful, unholy strength. It almost seemed as if it had been—*are they breeding them?*

It shouldn't have been possible. Most, if not all of the Damned were supposed to be sterile, or so Jared had been taught. The Word promised swift retribution on those who meddled with the creatures God had chosen to punish with defects of mind and body. *But if it was possible....* If it was, then any Marmack with half a brain could breed dogs strategically until he'd gotten a pup with increased strength and aggressiveness and no major health problems. He'd seen shepherds do it with livestock.

It occurred far less often among the Blessed than outside their communities, in the Desolation, but occasionally a Damned animal was born to Blessed stock. The shepherd or farmer would put it down, as a mercy, and to prevent it from passing on its curse to future generations, as the Word mandated.

He shivered at the thought that the Marmacks had fallen so low. Crossing Damned with pure animals? He wiped his bloody blade on the dog's fur and sheathed it.

He was considering whether or not to hide the body when he heard voices and the crunch of footsteps.

Silently cursing himself for a fool, Jared limped as quickly as he could behind the same slanted wall of concrete he'd come in on and tried to make himself as small and quiet as possible.

He could tell there were more than two voices, but not what they were saying. As they grew louder and closer, Jared prayed these Marmacks would be idiots. So far this day he'd underestimated them. He had charged into a Marmack stronghold on the presumption that it was completely unguarded, only to find out the hard way—the very hard way—that it was merely unguarded by *men*.

He heard the curses and alarm that went up when they found the dog's body; he heard booted feet crunching on glass and gravel.

"These are knife wounds," someone said. The voices were close and clear now. "Fan out. Search the area."

Gritting his teeth, Jared tried to ignore the growing pain in his ankle and quietly eased his pistol from its holster.

18

With her hands palm down on her knees, Ever tried to focus on her breathing. She had no idea what she was doing, but it felt somehow right. As if taking a moment to seek calm and peace amidst chaos was part of some plan she could only feel but not yet see.

If Thayne wanted to talk to her this way, then she'd oblige him. If the Prophet didn't like what Ever Oaks—*Ever Ballard*, she reminded herself—had to say, well, that was on him.

Focusing was difficult. When she first closed her eyes there was only confusion and anxiety. After a few minutes, she relaxed enough that her other senses began to compensate for her lack of sight. Her environment became distracting. She could hear Acel moving, shuffling, hear him wipe his nose and draw breath. She could hear Rolan quietly comforting Chy across the way, and the slow drip of water somewhere down the hall. She could smell the rank odor from the bucket in the corner of their cell and the scent of fire and smoke. She could hear distant noise outside the building, a clamoring noise like a gathering or a party. She could feel every pebble and crack beneath her bottom and the scratchiness at the back of her throat from the mold.

And she could hear her heartbeat, feel it pounding in her chest, pulsing in her wrists and ankles and throat. She heard her lungs filling and emptying, and the soft creak of her body as it settled and shifted.

When she finally found stillness, the world of her prison cell shattered and she was somewhere else entirely.

Or at least part of her was: her senses still operated. She could still feel and smell and hear everything, but from farther away, as if her body was in the next room from her mind.

The place she had traveled to was not a place of the senses; she could no more describe it than she could describe God or the feeling of joy. It was *other*, entirely and completely, and Ever felt utterly lost inside of it. It felt long, and broad, and deep—infinite, if she were being honest. It felt infinite. She was both afraid and excited, as if she were perched on the edge of a high cliff, looking down at sparkling waters below. Something begged her to jump.

She could have spent hours, days, even, familiarizing herself with this place of infinite nothing, but only moments after she had fully immersed herself in its substance something *popped*. Like everything else about the place it was not a feeling she could describe in the context of the five human senses, but the word felt right nonetheless. Regardless of its nature, Ever knew instantly that she was no longer alone.

I have waited...so long...to find you here.

The voice—voice wasn't the right word, but it was the closest she had—undeniably belonged to Azariah Thayne. It dripped with his essence.

Every word that comes out of your mouth is a lie, she responded.

Not every one, my dear, said Thayne.

Their conversation took place on a plane she couldn't describe, in a not-language that had more to do with thought and image and feeling than words— Ever could feel her brain translating the impressions Thayne was sending her into the nearest approximate verbal translation.

What do you want from us?

What I have always wanted.

I don't know you. I've never met you before. You attacked my people without provocation or reason. Why do you now pretend to know me?

I have always known you, Ever, in some form. I felt the moment of your birth, when I was freezing on the tundra—you were mine even then, as you are mine now. Soon you will be mine in heart as well as in body.

I'll never be yours, said Ever, trying to transmit all of the disgust and revulsion she felt for the man through the bond they shared. She felt him smile.

You've already taken the first step, he said. *The rest is inevitable. Our paths are intertwined, Ever Oaks—God has chosen us to be his Saviors on Earth.*

Don't blaspheme, she commanded.

How could I commit blasphemy against my own name? Humanity had its beginning. I am its end. Together we will make a new world in our own image. And our kingdom will outlast the stars.

I don't believe anything you're saying, Ever said hopelessly. What *was* he saying? Did this man truly believe he was a prophet, or a god, or the God? His delusions seemed to know no bounds. She could tread water indefinitely here, getting nothing but Thayne's vague hallucinations in response to her questions.

My friend is dying, she said, trying a different tack.

All men die, Thayne replied.

He will die soon if you don't let me help him.

So help him.

I can't help him from where I am, she explained impatiently. *If you…if you want me to consider any of what you're saying*—her sense of revulsion returned as she said this, but she did her best to conceal it, not sending it through the strange ethereal link—*then you must let me into his cell. I need to touch him.*

There was a moment of silence; if they had been conversing in real life, Ever might have thought Thayne was considering what she had said.

I…I know why you had to hurt him, she said. Back in the cell, she felt her stomach turn at the thought.

You do? Thayne responded.

Yes. I know that you needed to...to get through to me, somehow. You've made your point. Let me help him. Let me help him and let the others go and I'll stay here with you. A very real feeling of nausea rolled through Ever's stomach, momentarily jarring her.

You will learn, Ever, as we begin on our path together, that what you can say to me, in this realm or in person, will always be constrained by my ability to see through you, said Thayne. *You're a glass vase, my darling, a crystal figurine with a mind and a soul flickering inside. I can see the thoughts crossing that internal landscape as easily as you can see an expression of pity or revulsion on the face of another. Do not test me.*

Then you'll never have me, said Ever, her thought the equivalent of a scream. *I won't play your game anymore. Help me or I'll oppose you at every turn.*

But it's not a game, my darling, said Thayne. She could sense the mocking in his sending. *A game implies two players, matched against one another. This is more like...a test. An obstacle on the path that leads you to me. You overcame the first obstacle valiantly—the destruction of your home has not slowed you.*

This second, he continued, *will determine whether you are ready to recognize the true power you are capable of. Only then, when you have transformed into the being you will become, will you be ready to join with me. Enjoy the warmth of your cocoon, little pupa. Cold reality awaits, but there is beauty there too...*

Ever screamed, a long, frustrated wail that sent ripples through her mind and into Thayne's. She broke off in surprise; her shout had rattled the whole of the place they inhabited, as if its very fabric had been warped. She felt Thayne's amusement and her anger quickly returned.

Then she felt him pulling away: his presence receded, as if he were walking into the distance. She tried to follow but she couldn't even tell if she was moving—or if movement was even a thing, here. The distance between them did not lessen.

Thayne's presence was growing smaller and smaller; it threated to wink out of existence with every passing moment. He was leaving. He had taunted her, and tempted her, and now he was leaving, without any explanation or response. Anger and confusion churned inside of her; the scream she had let out a moment before was only the beginning of her fury.

Her emotions seemed somehow…tangible, in this place, floating masses and fields of energy that swam in the same medium as Ever herself. Her confusion was a skittering spark, reeling through her mind; her anger was a shuddering mass of white fire. She reached out with her will and *grasped* it.

It was difficult to hold, a fuzzy ball of power that wanted more than anything to be released. Ever held onto it with all of her will for as long as she could, then suddenly let it go. It was like releasing a fox hound: all that pent up energy suddenly burst forth in one great surge and Ever found herself launched toward her target.

She reached out and pursued Thayne, drawing close to his presence in one sudden swoop of mental energy. He was almost gone from this place; the felt him only weakly. But when she touched his presence with her own, there was a reaction.

She felt surprise—Thayne's; an unfiltered sensation of masculine shock coming through their bond. Ever *pushed*, exerting her own will over his, and for a moment she was somewhere else.

She saw daylight, felt a horse beneath her body, heard the Marmacks around her talking amongst themselves. Raising her—Thayne's, she realized suddenly—head, Ever looked around. They—he—was traveling on a forested road. The experience took all of two seconds, a brief flash of reality intruding on the strange, dreamlike plane she and Thayne had entered together.

Then the Prophet was back. She felt him like a quick welling of anger, a surge of power so strong that if she had breath in this place it would have been knocked out of her, and suddenly she was thrown free, backwards, away.

When Ever opened her eyes there were tears running down her cheeks. She could taste the salt of them, running into the corners of her mouth. Acel was hunched across from her wide-eyed, his right hand stretched halfway between them.

Taking a deep, wracking breath, Ever met his eyes with a grim smile on her face.

"It was my fault," she said. "All of it. They came because of me."

• • •

Jared saw the raider's booted foot long before the rest of him came into view. He was crouched under the ramp he had come in on, knife and pistol to the ready, waiting for the nearest man to come within his reach around the slab. He wasted no time, stabbing downward with his hunting knife, feeling boot leather and flesh and bone part like a wrapped roast before its finely honed edge. The Marmack's scream was instant and bloodcurdling. He fell forward, reaching vainly for his injured foot, and smacked his head soundly on a chunk of stone. His scream cut out as suddenly as it began. Jared couldn't tell if he was dead, but he didn't stop to check.

The others would rush directly to the source of the scream. He had decided against stealth. There were four of them and they had inadvertently blocked all his available exits. There was no getting around them. He'd be lucky to survive it at all, let alone get through four men without raising an alarm.

Creeping as quietly as possible in the opposite direction, Jared waited until he heard them find the man's body and then squeezed himself out from behind the slab on the other side. He saw two backs bent over the first raider's body. He raised his gun.

"Hey," he said, just loudly enough to be heard. When they turned he fired twice, putting a bullet into the chest of one and the shoulder of the other. He didn't want to resort to shooting men in the back if he could avoid it, but neither was he going to give them the chance to kill him.

The pistol had a manageable recoil; he watched the whisper of smoke trail off the barrel for a moment. Oddly enough, despite knowing it was two rounds lighter, the gun felt heavier in his hand.

He must have paused longer than he realized, because just as he remembered there was a fourth Marmack somewhere near him Jared felt something heavy hit him across the shoulders. He fell to the ground, the pistol flying free to bounce heavily over the scattered concrete and twisted metal. For a moment there was blackness, but he rolled hard to the left quickly enough to avoid the raider's next swing.

The last man was short but powerfully built. He held a long, flat wooden club wrapped at the narrow end with some sort of hide. He had been lucky to get it across the shoulders: a hit to the head would have killed him. However strong the Marmack was, he wasn't that bright. Stomping over as Jared scrambled to his feet, he raised the club high over his head for a massive finishing blow.

Jared surprised him with a handful of gravel and broken glass to the face, kicked him hard in the side of the knee, then put his knife into the man's chest to the hilt. The Marmack fell and Jared finished him off with his own club, dropping it in exhaustion after the man stopped breathing.

The strength seemed to leach out of his bones. He retrieved the pistol, bending over with a groan to pick it out of the sharp scree and holster it. He had no time to be tired. It would take only moments for the other Marmacks in the building and nearby to find the source of the gunfire and the screaming. The one he'd hit in the shoulder was probably still alive. He was surprised they hadn't shown up already, in fact—

The blow to the back of his head was quick and hard. Before he had even seen his attacker, everything went black.

"What do you mean it's your fault?" Acel asked.

Ever wiped the tears from her cheeks, succeeding only in smearing the dirt on them around in streaks.

"Thayne," she said. "He attacked Bountiful because of me."

"That makes no sense," he said. "How do you know that?" She shook her head.

"He wants me because I'm a Saint. Because of my powers."

"That might be why he's keeping us here, Ever," said Acel, "but you have no way of knowing that had anything to do with Bountiful."

"He told me," she said.

"What? How?"

"Just now. I can...I spoke to him."

Rolan, who had been listening, his palms still on Chy's wound, spoke calmly.

"What do you mean, Ever?" he asked.

I told you I could hear him," Ever explained. "Talking to me. In my head. Just like the...the dolphin. This time I talked first." She left it at that. Ever wasn't entirely sure she had the vocabulary to explain her experience; nor was she convinced she wanted to even if she could.

Her Sainthood had been unexpected but comparatively easy to understand when it was merely the gift of healing—no one could deny that such a gift was God-sent. And it fit so naturally into her own goals and desires that she had never seriously questioned it. But this...this was something else.

How could she share something this important with a man like Azariah Thayne? Her people's greatest enemy had always been the Marmacks, and now the Marmack tribe was personified for Ever in its leader, its Prophet. Thayne was an evil man, a deceptive man. She was nothing like him.

"It doesn't matter," Ever said, clearing her throat and rising. "How's Chy, Rolan?"

"I'm still here," Chy said, his voice ragged and weak. Rolan shared a long look with her across the dim hallway. He shook his head slowly. Every squeezed her eyes shut.

"Thayne's not here," she said suddenly, turning to Acel. "I saw—I could tell where he was, when I...He's on horseback, heading away from Salem. If we can do anything to escape, now would be the time."

"I'm with you, but what could we do?" Acel said. He gripped one of the thick cell bars. "We're not breaking out of here."

"Then we have to get them to open the door," said Ever. Acel was already shaking his head.

"There're too many of them, Ever," he said. "They took our weapons. Chy's injured. Trying to fight our way out of here would be suicide."

"What's the alternative?" said Ever, her voice a hoarse whisper. "Sit in here until we rot or Thayne thinks up another sadistic game to play?"

Several sudden, dim popping sounds interrupted their conversation. Rolan stood up across the hall.

"What was that?" he asked. "It sounded like gunfire."

"Probably was," Acel said. "The Marmacks do have some guns, though they're not very reliable. Old, unmaintained, filled with ancient ammunition. Just as likely to blow up in your hand as shoot right. Probably some drunken raider firing shots into the air."

To Ever, Acel looked frustrated but defeated. She could tell that he didn't want to give up, but he couldn't see a way forward. Neither could she, for that matter; there was no reason to take it out on him.

"I'm sorry," she said. "I just—I'm so *angry*."

"You can't believe him, Ever," Acel said, kneeling down beside her. "You can't believe anything he says. He lies. He's…of the Adversary."

It wasn't often that one of the Blessed mentioned the Adversary, the fallen angel cast out of God's kingdom before the creation of the world. The Adversary was behind the Fall; he had spent centuries tempting and inspiring humanity to make decisions that would ultimately lead to its destruction. People were gifted with agency from Heavenly Father, but just as He invited them to choose the right, the Adversary tempted them toward evil.

"I know," said Ever. "I know it. But for whatever reason, he thinks I'm something special—"

She cut off, her eyes widening.

"What is it?" Acel asked.

"I've got an idea," said Ever.

Jared regained consciousness just as someone finished tying his wrists together behind his back. His face was pressed painfully against the broken concrete, bits of glass biting into his cheek. The cord binding him was thick and rough, tied tight enough to restrict blood flow to his fingers. He wouldn't have feeling in his hands for long bound like this. He gasped in pain as whoever had hit him dragged him roughly to his feet by his elbows.

The pain in the back of his head was spreading into a pounding headache; he closed his eyes for a moment to fight back a wave of nausea.

"Move," growled the man behind him. Jared had yet to see his face.

"Who are you?" he croaked.

"That's rich," said the man. "Sneak in here, kill four of my men, and you're the one asking questions. Just be happy Thayne hasn't revoked his order to round up Blessed fugitives, otherwise you never would have woken up."

Whoever he was, the Marmack didn't seem particularly concerned about his dead comrades. If anything, he sounded more annoyed than angry.

"Haven't seen one of these in a long time," the man said. Jared heard the click of his pistol's hammer behind him. "Now move."

There was indeed an entrance into the courthouse through the ruined wing. The Marmack prodded him past a line of broken support pylons and through a blown out archway, where Jared saw a set of crude wooden doors that had been fitted roughly into an old doorway.

Gripping Jared's left arm securely above his elbow, the Marmack came abreast of him and knocked hard with the butt of the pistol before pointing it at Jared.

"No more trouble now," he said. There was a shuffling behind the doors as someone lifted a bar. The man wore his hair long, tied back at the nape of his neck. He was sharp-nosed and looked to be perhaps five years older than Jared. Suddenly realizing that the man spoke well for a Marmack, Jared spoke up.

"You're a...captain?" he asked. "What clan?"

The Marmack grinned.

"Why is it you're all so interested in that? Think you know something about us, do you? If you knew half as much about us as we knew about you, you might not be standing here."

The door opened and a shorter, grizzled man held it for them.

"Call the others back," said Jared's captor. "And send someone out there to deal with the bodies."

The other man ducked his head silently and scurried off, pausing to secure the door again before he went. Jared found himself propelled out of the ruined hallway the doors opened into and into a broad stone lobby, its steps and high ceilings in remarkably good repair given the state of the rest of the building. A group of Marmacks, these wearing bright red sashes and various clan markings, were walking towards them across the dusty marble floor.

"Vost," called the one in the lead. "Wut the fug's goin' on?"

"What's going on is this one just killed Duboy and three others," Vost answered, pushing Jared forward until he met the rock solid arm of the approaching raider.

"Bring him down to Room 2. Just leave him, for now. Thayne will want to talk to him when he gets back."

Sticking Jared's gun into his belt next to Jared's knife, Vost turned on his heel and walked up one of the broad staircases that bracketed the back of the lobby.

The man Jared had been passed off to treated him more roughly, sneering and shoving him down a small, close staircase into the building's basement. Jared tripped and hit the floor at the end of the stairs and the man casually kicked him in the ribs, forcing the air out of his lungs in a painful rush. Jared struggled to get up, his already bleeding face pressed against the cracked flooring. The Marmack grasped the ropes between his wrists and hauled him up one-handed, ignoring Jared's croak of pain.

Luckily their destination was nearby, a few yards down the hall. The Marmack opened a thick, windowless door, giving Jared a brief glimpse of an empty, equally windowless room before shoving him inside. He hit the floor and rolled, trying to save his face and shoulders from further damage.

The raider grabbed the doorknob and swung the door towards him. Jared clambered to his knees, realizing with sudden panic that when the door closed he would be in complete darkness. The door stopped, halfway closed. Jared could see just enough of the man through the opening that remained to tell that he had turned to look farther down the hallway, almost as if he were listening to something.

A loud crack, unmistakably a gunshot, rattled and reverberated down the hallway and the Marmack's hand dropped away as he started shouting up the hall. Jared, on his feet now, was moving forward before he realized what he was doing. *Sometimes*, Elder Betenson had once told him, *survival means leaping before you look*.

He clipped his right shoulder on the edge of the door as he rushed through it, but the majority of Jared's mass hit the Marmack, whose gaze was still on the far end of the corridor, directly in the chest.

Jared bulled through him as if he weren't there, knocking the larger man to the floor of the hallway. The Marmack's head hit the floor as he landed, not hard enough to knock him out. Jared, his arms numb and useless behind his back, smashed his forehead into the Marmack's nose.

There was blood, then, after a sick, crunching noise. The hallway disappeared as Jared smashed his head into the man's face a second time. The Marmack went slack, his nose gushing bright red blood all over his face and the floor. Jared thought he'd killed him until he heard a slow, moist wheezing begin a moment later. Just unconscious.

Hoping he hadn't broken his own skull, Jared struggled upright and scanned both ends of the corridor. His head felt like it had been inflated and his balance was off, but the emptiness of the hallway still surprised him. He could hear banging noises down the hallway and around a bend, but for the moment he was alone.

It took most of his concentration just to avoid passing out. Quietly thanking God for making him long of limb, he sat down, rolled over onto his back, and forced his bound arms up behind his legs, pulling his boots through the closed circle of his arms.

Freeing the Marmack's belt knife from its sheath was no simple matter, given that his fingers were almost entirely numb, but after several tries he managed it. First he tried gripping the knife with his hands and sawing backwards, but its weight quickly dropped from his useless fingers. Clenching it in his teeth didn't work either: the handle was too large and thick. In the end he was forced to wedge it between his knees, creating a sort of vise with his legs to hold the blade while he sawed the bonds downward against it. This particular Marmack apparently believed in keeping his weapons sharp, however, and after a dozen or so seconds of frantic, dangerous cutting the rope parted and his hands were free.

Jared looked up and down the corridor again, still not quite believing his luck, and rubbed some of the feeling back into his hands before hauling the raider's body through the door into the cell.

Moments later he was wearing the raider's sash and tunic, knife tucked in his belt, walking quickly down the hallway toward the source of the commotion, hoping against hope that he was heading in the right direction.

19

The Marmack they had left on the cellblock door—a toothless, low-ranking boy who didn't appear to be able to speak—came in the moment Acel started yelling.

"Go!" Acel yelled. "Get help! There's something wrong with her! She won't wake up!" The boy, barely Acel's younger brother Darl's age—14, maybe 15—gaped comically when he saw Ever's limp form lying across the floor of their cell.

"Get Vost, damn it!" Acel shouted, coming to the bars. The Marmack boy looked at him, made an uncertain noise, and then started running when Acel yelled at him again.

Several long minutes passed before Acel heard boots in the hallway again. Vost stormed in, flanked by Piker, the boy, and another Marmack he thought was called Dereg.

"What now, godammit?" snapped Vost, his eyes taking in the situation in Acel's cell quickly. They widened for a moment when they saw Ever, but narrowed again just as quickly.

"What's this, then?"

"She just collapsed," Acel said, trying his best to sound panicked. "I'm not sure if she's breathing." He crouched over her for effect, placing his hand gently on Ever's throat.

"Just collapsed, eh?" said Vost, raising an eyebrow. "How convenient. I suppose you'd like me to let you out of your cell, maybe get her a nice feather bed and a cool cloth for her forehead." Vost shook his head and turned to leave.

"No, I'm telling you," said Acel, pleading. "She was—she said something about Thayne, and reaching out to him, and then she sat down and started talking—almost like she was having a conversation with someone who wasn't there."

Vost stopped. He looked at Acel sidelong, then down to Ever, then back to Acel, considering.

"Open the gate and take her out," he said after a moment. "Just her. Find that old crone that mixes herbs and bring her to me."

"Prophet won't like that," Piker said, not moving. "Said he doesn't want anyone—"

"I don't remember asking for your opinion," interrupted Vost. "Just do it. Thayne will like it even less if she dies." Piker gestured to Dereg, who produced a ring of large keys and approached the cell door.

"If you're lying to me, boy," Vost said in a low voice, "I'll cut off your virgin balls."

Dereg swung the door open just enough for Piker to slip in.

"Back against the wall, sweetie," Piker said, grinning his rotten grin. When Acel had backed against the cell wall, sharing a worried glance with Rolan, who was watching from his own cell, Piker squatted beside Ever and prodded her roughly with one finger. She was lying with her right side toward the front of the cell, her body partially on top of her left arm. When she didn't respond to his poking, Piker leaned in closer, putting his dirty ear near her mouth.

Acel drew in one long, quiet breath and time seemed almost to slow down. When Ever brought the chunk of concrete out from under herself and smashed it into Piker's right temple, Acel pushed off the wall and leapt toward the cell door.

The hallways of the courthouse basement seemed to form a rectangle running around the central wing with rooms on either side. Jared turned the corner at the end of the hallway and saw a Marmack emerge from a narrow staircase up ahead and run in the direction of the commotion. He didn't look in Jared's direction.

He could see a doorway up ahead. The raider ahead of him seemed to be making for it. There was a growling coming from the darkened area beyond it. He let the raider get there first, watched him pull his own blade, then rushed him from behind, burying his knife to the hilt in the man's back while wrapping a hand over his mouth.

His stealth was hardly necessary. The scene in the cellblock before him was a grisly one, and no one involved was paying any attention to the door.

Piker collapsed on top of Ever as Acel crashed into the cell door. She reacted instinctively, smashing the concrete chunk into the same side of his head over and over again until he tumbled off her limply and she was able to pull herself out from beneath his bulk.

Acel's wild rush had forced the barred door outward into Dereg, knocking the man off his feet onto the floor. Acel had slammed Vost up against the bars of Rolan and Chy's cell. Ever saw that Vost was carrying a pistol—had she seen him with that before? She couldn't remember. Acel was struggling with him violently, trying to force Vost's gun hand up against the bars.

Hurrying up to Dereg, who was gripping his head in one hand and trying to prop himself up with the other, Ever kicked him in the ribs. She aimed a second kick at his head, hoping to knock him out, and shrieked when he caught her foot. Dereg looked up at her for a split second, eyes bloodshot, mouth bloody, wheezing, and then wrenched her legs out from under her with one savage tug. Ever fell backwards and landed on her elbows, seeing stars at the sudden spikes of pain in her arms, and then Dereg was on her.

She fought him violently, trying in vain to remember anything she had learned during Elder Betenson's regular self-defense lessons. She recalled only that he had once said there wasn't any such thing as a fair fight. *You fight to survive, to live, sometimes at any cost.* Ever dug her thumb into Dereg's right eye. He pulled away before she could do serious damage, but when he got his hand over her face she bit it, hard.

The Marmack screamed and Ever felt hot blood running into her mouth and down her chin. Dereg clubbed her in the head with his other fist and she fell back, dazed. For a short moment she lay on the floor of the cellblock clutching her head. She could see Vost and Acel's legs intertwined as they struggled against the bars of Rolan's cell. Rolan had reached through and grabbed Vost's throat; they seemed about to overpower him. She only had to wait another moment and they'd help....

Dereg's hands clamped around her throat, slick with his own blood. Ever let out a choking gasp and then her airway was cut off. The man was straddling her now, squeezing harder each moment. Ever lost the strength to do anything but claw at his fingers, which felt like iron. Pressure built in her head; it felt like her eyeballs were about to explode. She felt her body weakening. Dereg's face was a dark grimace above hers, his crooked teeth exposed in a vicious rictus. She tried pathetically to speak, to whisper anything, to try and make him stop, but his eyes were glazed and far away. A line of drool fell from his lips onto her cheek.

She stopped prying at his hands when a dark halo started to encircle her vision. There were black spots floating across her eyes. Ever pawed at Dereg, almost gently, her strength gone.

She was on the brink of losing consciousness when she felt it: a rough wooden handle sticking out of the man's belt. Her fingers felt like floating sausages but she managed to wrap them around it and pull.

Her first stab was shallow and weak, almost useless, but it was enough to loosen his grip momentarily. Dereg cursed and as the blood rushed back into her head Ever rammed the knife blindly into his side. His eyes went from narrow and far away to wide and close. Ever's arm worked harder, plunging the blade in and out of his flesh in a repetitive motion until she could no longer even feel her arm. She could have been stabbing herself, for all she knew, for all she could feel.

The only thought in her mind was air, and survival, and not letting this stinking beast get the best of her. Someone was screaming hoarsely; after a moment she recognized her own voice. She realized then that Dereg had been dead for several seconds and shoved him off of her, coughing and choking. She breathed in, savoring the moldy air of the cellblock as if it were a fresh ocean breeze.

She was halfway to her feet when another Marmack appeared in the doorway. Ever sobbed in defeat. The fingers of the hand holding her knife were tingling and numb. She couldn't fight any longer. She was on the verge of throwing down the knife and pleading for mercy when the man let out a curious grunt. He breathed in once and his knees gave out, revealing another man behind him.

He was dressed in Marmack clothing, but she would have recognized his face anywhere.

"Jared Meacham," she said, staring.

"At your service," he quipped, sketching a little bow.

Stifling her amazement, Ever turned and found that Acel had Vost pinned at gunpoint.

"Jared?" Acel said, not taking his eyes off of Vost. Rolan was gaping openly.

"I heard that shot from the other end of the building," Jared said, stepping into the cellblock and helping Ever up. She stared for a moment at her right arm, which was slick with Dereg's blood. "Others will have heard it too. Most of them are celebrating around the fires, but there are still some in the building—what?"

Vost was laughing, grimly and quietly.

"You think you'll actually make it out of Salem alive?" he asked. "You're bigger fools than I thought. We hold this city. Our patrols range out to five miles in all directions. You'll be lucky to make it out of this building."

"If I were you," said Ever, stepping closer, "I'd do everything in my power to make sure we *do* make it out. Your master won't be very happy with you if I die. In fact, I'm willing to bet you'd rather Acel just shoot you right here than face telling Azariah Thayne that you let anything happen to his future bride."

But Vost kept grinning.

"Jared," Acel said. "Open the cell."

"The keys?"

"On that one," Acel said, nodding towards Dereg's corpse. Jared fumbled at the man's belt for a moment, finally finding the ring of keys several feet away. Acel moved Vost aside as he tried keys in the cell door. It opened with a squealing click on the second try.

"What happened?" Jared asked as he saw Rolan bending to help Chy to his feet.

"Knife to the belly," Chy answered weakly. "What're you doing here, Jared?"

"Rescuing you," he said. "Though I'm not sure you needed the help."

"That remains to be seen," Rolan said.

"Where are our packs?" Acel asked Vost.

"First door on the left," said Vost.

"Can you walk?" Jared asked Chy.

"I can try," he said. Rolan got an arm under the larger boy and they moved out of the door. The look on Chy's face was blank and grim. Ever didn't like how pale his skin was.

Jared got underneath Chy's other arm when it became clear that Rolan couldn't support his weight on his own. Ever looked back at Acel to see him raise the pistol over Vost.

"No!" said Jared, but it was too late: Vost didn't get his hands up in time to block Acel's blow and collapsed like a sack of grain as the pistol butt hit his skull. "We could have made him walk us out," he finished.

Acel spared a glance for the man the shook his head.

"Too late now," he said. "Too risky anyway."

"Here," said Jared as Acel came over to him. "Take Chy. I'll take my gun back."

"Your—"

"I'll explain later," Jared said, taking the gun from Acel and holstering it at his hip. He bent over Vost's body and retrieved a hunting knife as well. Acel had hit Vost hard, but the man appeared to be breathing. Just knocked out.

"Lay Chy back down so I can try to help him," Ever said. She'd never used her Gift in such a stressful situation before, and certainly not when she felt as weak as she did. She only hoped it would come when called.

"No," said Chy, his voice tight with pain. "We have to get out of here. It can wait."

"He's right, Ever," Acel said. "We've got a couple of minutes at best. We don't even know that he'd be conscious afterwards. We can't carry him and escape."

Ever clenched her teeth and nodded once, then followed Jared out of the cellblock. They found their packs and weapons in a small adjacent room. Jared opened the lock with one of Dereg's keys.

Ever surveyed their things quickly and was surprised to see that they seemed relatively undisturbed. Something was sticking out of the top of her own pack, a yellowed square. She loosened the drawstring quickly to tuck it back in and found that it was a sealed envelope. The paper was thick and rough, either ancient or very crudely made. Her first name was written across the front. She squinted at it, but stuffed it back into the pack quickly. They didn't have time to dawdle. Likely her father had written her a letter and hidden it in her pack before she left. The Marmacks must have rifled through the bag and disturbed it.

"Why would they—" But she broke off, shaking her head. It didn't matter right now. Swinging her pack over her shoulder, she picked up the knife Jared had given her—*Jared Meacham came to rescue me*, she thought suddenly—and stuck it through her belt.

Why would they go through our bags but leave everything there? The thought wouldn't leave her mind.

"Where to now, Jared?" Acel asked. "You got in here. Get us out."

"This way," said Jared, leading them down the hallway to the left toward the back of the building.

They turned right at the end of the long corridor and found themselves in an unlit hallway at the back of the building. Ever looked back at Acel and Rolan, supporting a floundering Chy between them. They weren't moving fast enough, Ever realized. They were barely a hundred feet from the cellblock. It was only a matter of time until they were found. They had to get out of the building.

Jared put a finger over his lips and approached a wide metal doorway. A sign next to it, miraculously legible after centuries of decay, read "Stairway." There was a narrow window above the door's handle. Its thick glass was long since busted out; only a warped wire mesh remained. Jared peered through it cautiously, then opened the door and ushered them through.

The two flights to the main level were agony for Chy, who grimaced with each step. Jared again took the lead, staying a few feet ahead at all times. Ever followed at the rear.

When they reached the lobby level they waited for a few moments to give Chy a chance to recover from the climb. After the injured boy nodded, Jared took a quick look through the archway leading out of the stairwell and gestured them through.

They emerged into high-ceilinged room that seemed to be a library of some sort: tall shelves held hundreds of thick, moldering volumes with matching spines. Some of the shelves had been tipped over; there were piles of books in places, most of which were swollen with rot and half-eaten by rodents.

In the center of the room, an arrangement of long tables held a series of strange frames—blank, black rectangles on stands perched over smaller devices and strange gridworks of labeled buttons. Many of them were knocked over.

"Computers, I think," Rolan said. "Calculating machines. The Old People could make them do miraculous things—"

"Hush, Rolan," chastised Acel. Rolan shut up with an abashed look on his face.

Jared, who had rushed off to inspect the back of the library as soon as they entered, returned with a frown on his face.

"There aren't any doors or windows leading out the back," he said. "We're going to have to go forward to get out."

Acel nodded without speaking and followed Jared to a set of double doors that seemed to be the library's main entrance and exit. There were windows in them, glazed in frosted glass, miraculous intact after centuries. Jared tried his hand on the brass handle and turned it slowly.

"Be ready for anything," he said, sliding his pistol out of its holster. "I don't know exactly where this comes out. But there are definitely exits along the sides of the main wing. It shouldn't be far to find one."

Ever saw the shadow darken the frosted glass before Jared did, but her squeak of warning was too late to help.

The doors burst inwards as if a horse had charged them, knocking Jared to the side like a rag doll in a shower of glass.

The figure that came through the door paused only long enough to lock eyes with her and then charge forward again. The Marmack had his hands on her before she realized it was Piker. His right eye was solid red and swimming oddly in its socket; the hair on the right side of his head was matted with blood.

"I've got 'em here!" he shouted just before Acel's arm wrapped around his throat, choking him off. Bootsteps echoed in the hallway outside and then everything started happening at once.

The door exploded into him and Jared found himself thrown to the hard marble floor, showered in slivers of broken glass. He twisted when he was thrown, landing on his shoulder, but the wind was still knocked out of him. Brushing at his face before opening his eyes to clear any glass away from them, he pulled his gun while still prone and aimed over the iron sights.

A large man with matted long hair and one eye swimming in blood had his hands around Ever's throat. Too close. They were too close. *No shot*. Then Acel was there, pulling the Marmack off of Ever in a chokehold. Jared got to his feet just as another three men came through the double doorway.

He squeezed the trigger once, twice, three times: his first shot hit the raider closest to him in the head. The second went through the same man's throat and he collapsed in a spray of arterial blood. The third hit the far Marmack in the cheek and then the pistol started clicking.

Empty, he realized, surprised. The pistol was a revolver; it only held six shots. He'd used two getting in, and someone had shot off another in the fight downstairs. In the chaos since being attacked and captured, Jared had forgotten to reload.

Acel was still struggling with the large man; two of the three who had followed were down and the third, the middle one, had cowered and shuffled backwards through the doorway. Before he could decide whether to pull his knife or load the pistol from the rounds on his belt, Ever stalked through the doors after him, her knife drawn.

Jared followed, his throat a bulge of worry. Drawing his own blade, he came through the doors and watched her kick the man, still scrambling backwards on all fours, hard between the legs. He whimpered and curled up, protecting himself.

"Ever," Jared said, as she sheathed her knife in the man's side, calm as a butcher. The Marmack gasped harshly and she stabbed him again, this time in the heart. He stopped moving immediately. Ever turned and looked at Jared. Neither of them spoke. The deafening crack of a rifle shot at close range filled the air and they turned back to the library as one.

Rolan stood in the doorway, the butt of Chy's rifle still pressed to his shoulder. Acel's struggle with the large man had suddenly gone silent. Jared ran to them, rolling the large raider off of Acel with no small effort—the man easily weighed more than 200 pounds. The rifle shot had gone through his back—not through the heart, unfortunately, as the man still lived, though he breathed shallowly and with great difficulty.

Acel Higbee was so still, his stare so wide and blank, that at first Jared thought he was dead. Then he coughed and blinked. Jared saw the entrance wound at his shoulder; he put pressure on it immediately and felt around on Acel's back to see if the bullet had gone through.

"You've got an exit wound just above your shoulder blade," Jared explained calmly. The bullet had gone into the stone flooring beneath him.

"What?" Rolan said, walking up behind them. Jared turned to look at him, seeing that Chy was propping himself up against the wall just inside the doorway.

"You shot him," Jared said. "The bullet's lodged in the floor beneath him."

"But—"

"You shot him at close range," said Jared. "That's a large bore rifle. Elder Betenson designed it to stop a man from the walls. You can't use it that close if there's anything on the other side of what you're shooting." He nodded at the wheezing Marmack off to the side. "That round would have gone through a brick wall at that distance."

Which is why Acel didn't use it to get the raider off of Ever, Jared thought. It was difficult to keep down his irritation. Rolan Belnap, like every other Blessed in the room, was a year older than Jared, but he knew about as much about guns and scouting as Ever. *Less*, Jared corrected. Ever had clearly demonstrated that she knew how to take care of herself.

Tearing a long strip from his stolen Marmack tunic, he quickly bound Acel's shoulder in a makeshift field dressing.

"The cloth's dirty," he said, helping Acel sit up, "and it won't hold for long, but it's better than nothing." Wiping his hands on his clothing, Jared quickly reloaded his gun, swinging out the cylinder, plucking rounds from the loops on his gunbelt, and slotting them in as quickly as possibly.

"We need to move," he said, swinging the cylinder back into the pistol with a click and holstering it.

"Acel, I'm—"

Whatever Rolan, who was now as white as a ghost, had begun to say was lost in a sudden, searing roar.

• • •

The glass bottle—she thought it had been a bottle—shattered against the doorframe, which was what saved Ever's life. The fireball that erupted from it mostly hit outside the library, torching the outer wall above the double doors and pouring black smoke and heat into the library itself. Ever lurched forward in surprise, inadvertently breathing in a lungful of the greasy smoke. Then she was coughing, hacking like she was being strangled.

Something heavy and moving fast knocked her sprawling. She scrambled frantically and twisted around, trying to see through the thick smoke. A group of men, how many she couldn't say, were moving toward them in the confusion.

As the worst of it started to clear, Jared started firing his gun again, each whipcrack shot finding its mark in the flesh of a Marmack. Seeing more shadowy forms tramping in the hallway outside of the library, her heart sank. They weren't going to get out alive, she realized. There were too many of the Marmacks and they had already made too much noise, caused too much commotion. And with Chy and Acel both hurt….

Ever tightened her grip on her knife and set her jaw. The least she could do is make them pay for it before she went. *Make sure they can't take you alive again.* Somehow she didn't think the Marmacks would show the same restraint they had before, after the mess they'd caused.

She had come as close to accepting her fate as she could. Jared was reloading again next to her. The flames from the explosive they'd thrown still burned on the floor and doorjambs; thankfully—or not so thankfully, she supposed—there was little wood inside this building. The fire would soon consume whatever fueled it and burn itself out. She took a step toward the door.

"Ever," she heard someone say. She turned to look at the three men behind her: Jared was still focused on the gun, and Rolan was supporting Acel. "Ever."

It was Chy. Leaning heavily against the wall, closer to the doorway now, he had drawn two knives from his belt.

"Get them ready to run," he said. His voice was tight; he sounded winded even though he wasn't moving. "I can buy you a minute or two."

"What—" Then she understood. "Chy, no." He only shook his head.

"I'm done. I can't run any farther. Let me do this. It's what I can do. All I can do, now." The look on his face was so sad, so determined, that she swallowed whatever plea she had been about to make. The smoky room seemed to swirl around her—whatever strength and focus she'd found in the grip of fear and necessity was fading into unreality. She found herself nodding. She looked at the others; Jared looked back at her. He'd overheard some of it, then. He nodded back. They waited. Chy drew in three or four deep breaths, then pushed off the wall and launched himself through the dying flames with a bellow.

The smoke had cleared enough for Ever to see four men in the broad hallway outside, huddled to the left near an archway leading farther into the building. What speed Chy had managed to coax out of his failing body was apparently enough: she saw them draw back in surprise as the large boy leaped towards them, blades drawn.

Jared grabbed her by the shoulder harshly and pushed her forward, dragging Acel and Rolan behind him.

"Run," he shouted hoarsely, coughing through the remaining smoke.

They pushed out of the library into the hall. Ever caught a quick flash of Chy kicking and slashing; two of the raiders were bleeding, but the other two were flanking him as she watched. She hesitated and felt Jared's hands on her again.

"Don't you dare stop," he growled.

They passed them, hearing one of the Marmacks call out as they did so. Chy responded with a scream, a war cry, really. Ever looked back once to see him tackle one of them, and then the other three were pulling him off. The man beneath him, at least, looked dead, but the others had weapons of their own. She looked away as they started stabbing him. Looked forward.

Jared led them through a small room off the hall and into a larger one—a room with windows. Most of the glass was gone, but he still had to knock out ancient mullions and weather worn shards of glazing to make a large enough hole. Rolan went through first and reached back up to help Acel out; the drop was only five or six feet to the ground. She went through, and then Jared.

And suddenly Ever was in the cool night air, and the stars shone above, and Jared was telling her to run,

run toward the water. They ran along the building, the sounds of distant Marmack merrymaking still at a high chorus.

The chaos of the library already seemed far away as she ran. The tears on her cheeks were for Chy and from the smoke and for the guilty, massive feeling of relief in her heart at escaping the grinding hell of that building. No one pursued them. Perhaps Chy had done more damage to that last group of men than she'd thought. She smiled briefly at the thought.

They followed the water, a great inlet like a river, north out of the city and into the dark night.

20

My dearest Ever,

My deepest apologies for the pain and suffering you were made to endure in Salem. Believe me when I say that I would sooner cut off my own hand than see you harmed, physically or spiritually. But Heavenly Father sometimes tests the strength of our faith—it is in the darkest of times that we must strive the hardest toward the light.

My counterpart and I have very different methods. We share the same goal, but we rarely see eye to eye on how to reach it. I can only apologize, once again, for his behavior. You would be well within your rights to hate me, though I hope you do not. I would have spared you and all of your friends the slightest discomfort were I able, but tragically my hand was forced.

It is too much to hope that you can ever love me as I love you—you were the beacon that led me out of darkness into the light of knowledge, the knowledge of my destiny and yours—but, for now, I will settle for your hatred. For hatred is a passion like unto love, and the line between them is thin. In time, I hope I can convince you to cross over.

Thus we have had our first meeting, and our first parting; I can promise you that neither will be our last. As you will learn, however, if you haven't already, physical distance is meaningless for such as us: our souls are connected. Spiritually, we will never be far from one another.

The next part of your journey, however, is yours to make alone. I am needed elsewhere. I Saw your escape plainly, just as I saw that I could not prevent it. I've learned to trust to the hand of fate in these matters. I'll make sure they don't follow, at least not right away. I can hide it from him for a little while. We will meet again when fate's plan demands it.

I will make him see that my way is best. He seeks chaos, but chaos only begets chaos—there must be some order, some reason, if we're to make it to the end.

My entire life, Ever, has been prologue to meeting you. As it says in Job, "Behold, I cry out of wrong, but I am not heard: I cry aloud, but there is no judgment. He hath fenced up my way that I cannot pass, and he hath set darkness in my paths. He hath stripped me of my glory, and taken the crown from my head."

There was a time, my love, when I despaired, when I shared Job's hopelessness. But it is my privilege to have foreseen the path that you and I must follow, the path on which glory shall return for all, under our dominion.

You will lead me to it, and then I will lead us all to salvation.

Go with God, my love, and know that I watch over you, whatever path you walk. There is no escape for us.

> Yours Always,
>
> *Azariah Thayne*

• • •

Ever read the letter one more time before dropping it into the campfire. She took perverse pleasure in watching the paper curl and blacken in the flames. She imagined it was him, Thayne, that she watched. She imagined his skin crackling, peeling off his flesh as he screamed, and screamed, and screamed....

"Absolutely, utterly, fantastically insane," said Rolan. "It's enough to make you believe there is an Adversary, like they teach in Primary—if anyone's a servant of evil...." He trailed off and stared into the fire like the rest of them as night fell. There had been a lot of false starts and half-hearted attempts at conversation over the last day. None of them wanted to talk, it seemed.

Acel stirred the rabbit stew in their one pot—most of their cooking supplies had been with the packhorses, who hadn't even made it out of Bountiful with them. They had both of the rifles, though. Rolan had still had Chy's when Chy—she tried not to think of that. They'd barely mentioned it since the night before last. She'd said enough to confirm that he couldn't have survived.

They had followed Jared out onto some kind of pier at the northern edge of the city, where he'd collected his own, smaller pack and his bow and quiver. From there they scavenged an ancient metal rowboat and crossed Salem Sound for the second time in three days. They had still presumed the Marmacks would chase them, at that point. They had all still thought that the apostates—even their touched leader—must follow some kind of logic, however gruesome.

They stopped long enough on the northern shore for Ever to force Acel onto the sand and heal him. Drawing on her Gift hadn't been difficult with all of the emotions swirling around in her head. She had no shortage of fuel to feed that fire. *Can I still call it a gift, after all of this? Can I still consider myself a Saint? What true servant of God would draw such a creature as Thayne from across the world?*

Even with his strength and youth, Acel's healing had cost them almost two hours of travel time, hiding in the woods until the two of them could recover. The power simply took too much out of the patient—and the healer. Ever knew she ought to feel mollified at this renewed evidence that she couldn't have possibly helped poor Chy, but she only felt worse. A real Saint would have known how to help him. A real Saint's powers wouldn't be so limited.

She remembered the letter when she opened her pack to find something to eat. She'd forgotten all about it in the harried escape from Salem. Upon closer examination, it obviously wasn't from her father. The handwriting was spidery and strange.

Ever knew who its author was as soon as she read the salutation, but by the end of the letter Thayne's signature still stood out like a brand. It was sharply inscribed on the thick paper. She knew it would be a long time before she could get its haunting words out of her head. He had engraved his words and his name on her soul, and worse, he knew it.

The company—still a quartet, but newly composed—were forced to consider the ramifications of the fact that Azariah Thayne claimed to, and in fact seemed able to, see the future to some extent. Ever and Acel told Jared about her strange mental contact with Thayne, what had been done to Chy, and everything since leaving Bountiful, for that matter. They all believed that Ever had spoken to Thayne, though both Jared and Rolan offered alternative theories to how and why Thayne had left that letter.

"You don't know that he didn't place the image of him leaving Salem in your head on purpose," Rolan had said. "It could have been his plan all along: string us along, act crazy, make us believe he was some kind of oracle. Maybe he was sitting in a room in that courthouse the whole time, knowing we'd escape."

Jared had pointed out the flaws in this argument—the Marmacks that had fought them had hardly been faking it, and they would hardly have gone to their deaths just as a diversion—would they?

But they were undeniably not being chased. They had argued, off and on, always to no avail and in fits and starts, the whole previous day as they trekked north.

"If they wanted to catch us," Jared was saying, "they could have caught us by now. They have the manpower.

Even if every Marmack in Salem got so drunk last night they couldn't stand until noontime, they'd still have been on us by now. They let us go. Or Thayne did, anyway. He obviously hadn't told Vost about his little scheme, but he must have contacted him somehow, afterwards—told him not to follow us. Whether that means Thayne can see the future, who knows—who cares. He's obviously crazy, and we know he's a liar. I say let's take the opportunity he gave us, if he really gave it to us, and get on with what we were supposed to be doing in the first place."

Was he a liar? Ever didn't know. Nothing made sense except the fact that Thayne was mad. If you took that as your first principle, then everything did make an insane sort of sense—precisely because it made *no* sense.

Acel and Rolan had smiled in relief when Jared told them that the Bishopric had been in the process of organizing a retreat through the Scout tunnels and off the peninsula when he left. Ever couldn't feel happy. Not after what had happened. And what had Thayne actually said?

I have razed Bountiful to the ground. Your people are dead. We took no prisoners. They were shown no mercy. Those who resisted were cut down and left for the crows. For all I know you four are the last.

He wasn't wrong. Even if some had escaped, their home, their way of life, was all but destroyed. He didn't seem to care if he'd been accurate regarding the loss of life. It wasn't his priority. Thayne had something much larger he was planning, and it had something to do with Ever. What was she supposed to lead him to? The chaotic cycle of her thoughts just kept repeating itself. *Chaos begets chaos.*

Tired of thinking, Ever hugged her knees to her chest and stared into the fire.

Jared watched Ever out of the corner of his eye as he helped Acel lay out and redistribute their supplies. Part of him still couldn't believe he was looking at her in the flesh. He really hadn't expected to see her again, he realized. Despite his half-conscious plan to follow her, when she had left Bountiful a few days before he'd thought it was the end—either for him, or for her, or for them both. He had never really believed that he'd see her again, this side of the veil.

She was staring into the campfire blankly. They had all been moody since escaping; leaving that courthouse had produced an anxiety that hung thick in the air between them. She was beautiful, her hair a mess, dirt and char on her cheeks. Her traveling outfit became her. Realizing suddenly that her eyes had refocused and were staring into his, Jared blushed and looked back down at their provisions.

"We needed that pack," Acel said.

They'd had to leave Chy's pack behind. Each of them had a pack of their own to carry, and Chy couldn't carry his.

"We were lucky to get out at all," Jared said. "Let's just be happy that we've got the clothes on our backs. Besides, this should be more than enough."

Rations and water were the main problems. Each of them had a small amount of emergency stores in their packs, but most of the food had been on the horses.

"How's that?" Acel asked. "And I thought we'd decided our escape was anything *but* luck."

"I can hunt," Jared said. "There's no shortage of game between here and the Maine."

"The Maine?" Rolan said. "What are you talking about? We can't…we can't go on. We have to find the survivors, tell the Bishop what's happened."

"Tell him what?" Jared asked. "That we've had a setback?"

"It's different now," Rolan insisted. "Chy's dead, and—"

"There was always the possibility that one or all of us could end up dead, Rolan," said Acel. "We've been over this. The situation now is no different than it was when we decided to go on outside of Bountiful."

"It's better, in fact," Ever said suddenly. "At least now we know that some of them might have survived. At least we know they had a plan. Jared brought us that much."

"So where are they going, Jared?" Rolan asked. "What's their plan? Would we even be able to meet up with them if we wanted to?"

"When I left," said Jared, beginning to re-stow items in some of the packs, "the plan was to get as many people as possible out through the Scout tunnels and into the emergency longboats hidden at the head of the peninsula. I didn't stay to watch."

"So you don't…you don't *know* anything!" said Rolan. "You're guessing. They could all be lying there dead right now—"

"I'm not guessing," said Jared, trying and failing to conceal his annoyance. "The Marmacks were massed around the main gates and at the western wall. Aside from diversionary tactics there was little to no activity on the other walls. There are plenty of Scout tunnels. Some of them got out. How many, I can't say. But Bishop Royce, my father, Elder Betenson—they got some of them out. I know it."

Jared forced down the niggling doubt that Rolan's comments had raised in his own mind. Rolan had a point, after all: he *didn't* know. Not for certain. Even if Elder Betenson and Jared's father and all the rest of the surviving Elders got the people moving through the tunnels, there was no guarantee they had made it before the Marmacks broke down the main gates and slaughtered the entire village. There was no guarantee, either, that they hadn't all been run down and killed after escaping. But in Jared's mind, there was no room for doubt. Not if they wanted to go on.

"There's no point in debating it," he said. "There *were* emergency longboats hidden at the top of the peninsula. That's where they were going. The Marmacks are incompetent sailors; my father and the Bishopric knew that. They could have headed for any of the offshore islands, or—"

"Or anywhere," Ever finished. "Jared's right. Some of them made it out. They might have surprised us, but the Bishopric knew this was coming. They weren't entirely unprepared. It's not our job to sit here thinking about every possibility and fearing every bad outcome. It's our job to do what we swore we'd do when this all started."

This seemed to sate Rolan's discontent, for the moment at least. Jared hadn't allowed himself to contemplate the possibility that everyone he loved had been killed. His last conversation with his father had been hurried, but hopeful. For some reason he couldn't entirely describe, he simply didn't believe they were gone.

"So we go on, then," said Acel. It was question, he realized. Jared smiled.

"Obviously I'm going with you," he said.

"I figured," Acel responded. "Not that I have the energy to try and dissuade you, anyways. What about you, Sister Ballard? Rolan?"

"Oaks," said Ever. "Sister Oaks."

Acel glanced at Jared and Rolan worriedly before continuing.

"But you're—"

"I'm Ever Oaks," she said. "And I'm going." Acel swallowed what he had been about to say.

Rolan, looking distinctly hunted, nodded dejectedly.

"The sun's almost down," Acel said. "We should get dinner going and get to sleep as early as we can. Jared, you can help me draw up a watch schedule…."

Jared listened with half an ear as Acel went on, looking again at Ever, whose eyes had returned to the fire. *Ever Oaks. Not Ever Ballard.* He couldn't share Rolan's despair—didn't, in fact, even understand it. There was hope everywhere.

• • •

Thayne was true to his word in one respect: they were not followed, that they could detect. Their path north seemed almost laid out for them, in fact. The coastline swept eastward north of Salem, jutting out into the cold, dark waters of the Atlantic in a vast cape several times the size of the one on which Bountiful was located. By common consent, relying upon Jared and Acel's scouting knowledge of the lands surrounding Bountiful, the company cut across country, heading directly north whenever possible, and found nothing but small scattered ruins and empty territory.

Rolan was surprisingly helpful in directing their route. His qualms about the continuation of their mission calmed after a few days and he began making an obvious effort to contribute to the group's efforts.

Ever worried at first that Jared's presence would pose a problem for Acel, who had been the de facto leader of the group to this point. Jared Meacham was nothing if not a strong personality. But the two young men worked together surprisingly well. Both displayed an unexpected humility in dealing with the other: Acel never hesitated to ask Jared for his advice, and Jared respectfully allowed Acel to take the lead as the older, more experienced Scout.

The land to the immediate north of Salem was a mixture of woodland, small meadowlands being reclaimed by the forest, and acres upon acres of salt marsh. They followed a crumbling main road from afar through scattered residential wreckage and ancient farmland. With Acel's injury healed, the four of them made good time, walking most days from dawn until shortly after dusk. The land provided a surprising yield of game, much of it unsullied by the effects of the Fall. The Damned creatures they saw were mostly benign: twisted, skulking animals that generally stayed to themselves.

After several days they could see from high points that the area began to be built up more to the west, the fields leading into tangled woodlands and overgrown communities that in turn grew into small cities. They avoided those areas, cutting a northwesterly line that stayed as much as possible to the wilder parts.

"No use tempting fate," Jared said, agreeing with Acel's intuition that it might be best to avoid large ruins. The Marmacks preferred buildings to bivouacs, and despite their luck so far, none of them was prepared to test Thayne's promise any further than necessary.

Soon they broke into thick, unending forest, the likes of which Rolan said they could expect for the foreseeable future. One morning after breakfast he surprised them all by producing an oiled vellum map wrapped in a leather roll.

"Acel and Jared might be familiar with the lands within ten miles of Bountiful from personal experience," Rolan explained, "but I'm just a pen-pusher. That said, I'm not without my uses."

They had all studied what maps the community had of the Northeast Kingdom, but past a certain point the Blessed's knowledge became conjecture. They rarely strayed far from home.

"The maps the Old People left are either disintegrating or out of date," Rolan said, spreading his map out on the grass and weighting it with small stones at the corners. "Apparently they had some other manner of navigation that had long taken the place of paper charts. The major routes, though, they stayed mostly the same.

"I looked at all the paper copies we had and combined them to make my own. These are the major arteries between here and the Maine. I figured we could use them as guides, even if we didn't travel on them directly."

Jared was nodding appreciatively, but Acel and Ever looked at Rolan as if he'd suddenly become a different person. Which, in a way, she supposed he had.

"What?" Rolan asked. He cracked a sudden smile. "You didn't think the Bishopric sent me along with you for my charming good looks, did you? That was my purpose. Acel and…and Chy were Scouts, skilled with weapons and all that, and Ever was a Saint…I guess something useful has to come from books eventually, right?"

Acel and Jared started including Rolan in their discussions more directly after that, frequently referring to his map. Only Ever remained mostly silent, a fact the three young men seemed to be, for the most part, ignoring. She supposed that she would do the same in their position—how was a simple man supposed to interpret the alien emotional needs of a moody girl? *Like trying to communicate with a lobster*, she thought, and smiled ruefully.

And so they went, a company of four, heading north ahead of the falling winter, weaving their way through forestland that was the very southern tip of a country of forests as old as the land itself. The weather grew colder by the day, which only encouraged them to walk faster to keep warm.

Ever knew there was something bubbling inside her head, but as she had no sound idea of what it was herself yet, she didn't think it wise to speak about it. She let the boys lead the way and kept her thoughts to herself. Let them focus on the moment. She would think about Azariah Thayne, and what lay ahead of them, and the dark powers swirling in her mind. Right now, it was enough that they were together, and safe. Let the journey be the destination, for the time being.

21

On Sunday, exactly one week since leaving Bountiful, they celebrated the Sabbath in a small clearing at mid-morning. The sun glanced in at head height as Acel blessed and broke biscuits of hardtack into bite-sized pieces and passed them around. Jared blessed a small cup of water poured from his water bottle and passed it. His eyes fixed on Ever's hands, the fingers fidgeting nervously, as he said the prayer.

The terrain was growing increasingly hilly, and after half a day's walk they finally broke out into a wide clearing sparsely populated with medium-sized pines.

"This is it," Rolan said suddenly, taking out his rolled up map. They gathered around as he traced a thick line in the center of the map with one dirty fingernail. He smiled. "Interstate Route 93. Look at what you're standing on."

Jared looked to his feet and realized that beneath a thin layer of humus and pine needles was the roughened surface of an ancient road. He scraped at it with his boot to make sure. Looking northward, he could see now that the clearing was in fact an overgrown corridor running through the forest. The remains of one of the Old People's enormous roadways. This one was even more overgrown than most.

Rolan trotted forward, looking from side to side.

"There should be—a-hah!" Crouching down, he started tugging at something large in a tangle of branches and dead wood. After a moment he raised something as tall as he was: a rusted metal strut with a metal sign attached. The face of the sign was rusted and peeling, but Jared could just make out most of a "9" and half of a "3."

"We can follow this north for—oh, I'd say another two or three days at least," explained Rolan.

Acel took the map from him for a moment and studied it.

"This road runs almost due north to south. We could cross the old border into the Maine sooner if we went northeast," he said.

Rolan nodded.

"That's true, but as I see it that presents two problems. One, we'd be hiking through mostly virgin forest. It might end up taking us twice as long. And two, we want to stay as far away from the coast as we can."

"Marmacks?" Acel asked, glancing up at Rolan. Rolan shook his head. Swinging his pack off, he dug around in it for a moment and finally pulled out another sheaf of papers and seated himself on the ground. After a moment, Jared sighed softly and sat down with him, followed by Ever and Acel.

"I'm beginning to think," Ever said, "that we should have spent more time planning our route before we left Bountiful."

"Understatement of the age," said Jared. Acel smiled grimly.

"It's my fault," Rolan said, pausing. "I was supposed to—there wasn't enough time, you see, and I hadn't quite finished all of the work—"

"You were supposed to what, Rolan?" asked Acel gently.

"Bishop Royce asked me to research the best route and keep all of you informed, involve you in the process. I got distracted, and then the attacks started—"

Jared noticed a tremble in Rolan's hand.

"It's okay, Rolan," he said. "Everyone did the best they could. Just tell us now." Ever met his eyes briefly. Her look was unreadable.

"Well," he said, returning to shuffling maps and charts, "the problem is that there's a site along the coast somewhere that was…disproportionately affected by the events of the Fall. A power station of some sort. Somehow when the Fall happened, something about that place increased its effects…"

"How do you know this?" Ever asked.

"Scout reports, mostly. One or two ancient documents Elder Haglund had, talking about the power station. A few old periodicals from just before the

Fall that talked about American defense efforts. What scouting parties have gone that far north have reported a greater than average number of Damned. Lots of human Damned too, aggressive ones."

"So we stay on this road, then," said Jared.

"It seems right," said Ever. Rolan smiled gratefully at her.

They covered more than a dozen miles that way, stopping only briefly for water and food. The weather stayed clear, though the air seemed to grow colder by the mile.

That night they camped in the middle of the road. It had been so long since they had seen another person that the idea of sleeping in the tangled woods when they could sleep under the stars seemed unnecessarily paranoid. Acel even permitted a large fire, and Rolan tootled on a wooden flute he'd produced from his pack as they cooked a dinner of fresh rabbit.

Something about finding the road had lightened the atmosphere among them, Jared thought, as if, in leaving the dark confines of the forest, they had left behind some of their dark thoughts, as well. The rabbit had helped. He'd taken to setting at least a couple of wire snares over likely nearby game trails before bed each night, hoping to get a head start on the next day's dinner. So far he'd snared two rabbits and a couple of squirrels.

Hunting and trapping were becoming more and more important as their meager stores ran low. What they carried was designed to maximize nutrition while minimizing weight and pack space—dried beans and grains and meats—but the packhorses they'd been forced to leave behind in Bountiful were a sore loss. He didn't mind the time alone in the woods. He'd done a lot of thinking over the past week, and he found that no matter how they started, his thoughts almost always came back around to the same subject.

When Ever rose after dinner that night and strolled up the road a ways, looking at the sky, Jared followed.

He approached her quietly, as always, and he didn't know whether she even knew he was there until she spoke.

"The North Star," she said, pointing straight up. "It lights our way."

"You've been quiet," Jared said. She turned her head to look at him.

"What is there to say?" she asked, looking back at the night sky.

"You've got me there," he said, finally. He'd been waiting for a chance to speak to her alone, but now that he had it, he had no idea what he wanted to say. Duty struggled with desire struggled with fear. In the end, duty won.

"Ever," he said, "there's something I should tell you. About Erlan."

"Is he alive?" she asked, not lowering her eyes.

"He was when I left him," said Jared. "Before I left to come after you, I—we had words, Erlan and I."

"I don't want to know." The look in her eyes when they met his was fierce. Something must have shown in his own face, because she quickly went on.

"Not because I miss him. Because I don't miss him. Because he doesn't matter. He's not here."

"But you're ma—" She cut him off, not ungently.

"I did what I had to do, Jared," Ever said. "They wouldn't have let me go otherwise. I needed to be here, to come on this journey. If Erlan Ballard was the price, then it was one I was willing to pay. I don't know what happens from here on. I don't know if any of us will come back alive. All I know is, my life is my own, and he's not here. I'm not going to live like I'm married to someone I don't love when night is falling and he couldn't be bothered to follow me into the dark."

Jared, tongue-tied, only nodded. How was she able to confound him like this? It was only around Ever Oaks that he ever found himself so hopelessly stymied.

"Are you scared?" she asked suddenly.

"Yes," he admitted. "But…at least we can be scared together."

She hugged him then, suddenly and tightly, and kissed him on the cheek before walking back to the warm glow of the fire. It had grown colder. No less confused, Jared watched her go. After a moment he felt a small smile grow on his face, and he followed her back to their friends.

Overgrown and uneven as it was, they still made far better time along the road than they had tramping through fields and woods and marsh. There were comparatively few of the Old People's derelict cars on it;

certainly not enough to slow them down. They walked in the center of the roadway for the most part, particularly when they passed ramp-ways exiting the road into the ruins of the surrounding communities.

Water became more of a problem than food. Deer, turkeys, and all manner of smaller animals preferred the roadway as well, grazing on the tall grasses that grew in thick stripes webbed across the cracked pavement, but they had to be careful with the streams and brooks they crossed, testing the water carefully for taste and effect before drinking. Jared was often able to scout ahead and make a kill with his bow, resulting in at least a night or two of fresh meat. He mourned the lack of time to stop and smoke the meat, but Acel was intent on pushing forward as fast as possible. Ever agreed.

The road widened and narrowed depending on how close they were to ancient settlements, but after another handful of days' travel it narrowed to a 40-foot corridor and stayed that way. Once they saw a hulking shadow atop a rise, silhouetted against the morning sun. Jared said it was a moose. Few of them were seen south of the Maine.

Ever's legs had hardened from the walking; she tired less quickly and breathed easier even after long hours and longer miles. She was surprised to realize that, if anything, their progress was speeding up. It seemed all of them were reaping the benefits of such constant exercise.

By Acel's estimate, they had walked almost ninety miles in a week, always staying to the road, through close forest and over questionable bridges through small, crumbling cities, where they stayed to the middle of the roadway. The closest they came to human contact was sighting a column of smoke far to the east in one of the more populated areas; they sped up until they left it far behind them.

Mountains loomed in the distance, growing closer every day.

It was when the road narrowed for the final time and continued roughly straight for miles through woodlands that they first heard the howling of wolves. Ever's heart froze when the first howl cut through the cold air, miles away but at the same time sickeningly close. It was as if some deeply ingrained part of her knew to heed that warning and fear it; an insistent part of brain urged her to *run, flee, hide.* Jared seemed concerned as well, which only heightened her anxiety.

That night, a light snow fell, floating around their fire in big, fat flakes. Acel had them build it up higher than usual, until they had a roaring blaze that was so hot they had to sit several feet away from it.

"Wolves don't like fire," Jared explained bluntly. Up until now only one of them had stayed awake to watch for danger as the other three slept, waking the next person in the watch rotation after his or her hours were up. That night Acel and Jared took first watch together.

The wolves bayed sporadically throughout the night. Every time Ever began to fall asleep, it seemed, another would call out at the moon. She was glad to get up and take watch with Rolan when Jared and Acel grew tired; sitting with a pitch-coated wooden club at hand, ready to be set ablaze as a brand should wolves appear, was more comforting than trying to sleep through their howling.

They left the great road the next morning, climbing down the high berm on which it ran and hiking across a small, dew-damp field before again entering the woods. They found a lesser road to follow eastward, which wound through small, wild hills thickly forested with conifers. The mountains were an ever-present shadow to the north, hanging midway in the sky, far off and close at the same time.

They camped that night in the stone foundation of a cabin set up a steep trail off the road. Ever unrolled her blankets facing away from the fire, looking into the woods above.

Dinner was a quiet affair; the wolf howls had begun again as dark set in and all four of the Blessed were tired and anxious. Ever went to bed without a word and fell asleep only moments after wrapping herself in her blankets.

She knew she was dreaming when she woke up in her bedroom in Bountiful—the bedroom in her father's house, not the cabin she had shared briefly with Erlan. She was dressed in skirts and a warm woolen bodice, presumably against the cold air that drifted through the open window at the back of the room.

Ever closed the window, noting that Dallin's bed, which lay beneath it, was empty. Airie was also missing from her smaller cot, kitty corner from Dallin's bed. Her concern at seeing their empty beds clung to her mind for only a moment before blowing away like a leaf on the autumn wind.

Walking into the main room, she saw in the moonlight that a thick fog had risen, crouching about the house, claustrophobic and close. She stood for a minute, looking at the familiar room, unsure of what to do. Usually the dreams she had in which she knew she was dreaming were fast and unpleasant; it was mildly disconcerting to stand alone in an empty room and know that you were, in fact, asleep beneath the stars.

A scratching came at the back door. She turned to look, remembering only when she reached it that there was no window there. When the scratching came again she opened it and found nothing but the mossy backyard, empty of all but fog. She stepped outside and immediately knew something was wrong.

It took a moment to isolate it; there was something missing. Something that should have been there, that she unconsciously associated with this place. The distant crash of the ocean was missing.

Ever walked to the edge of the backyard clearing, to the spot where the land dropped to the beach below. When she stepped into the trees, however, the fog engulfed her entirely; she could see nothing, barely even her own hand held out in front of her face. She returned to the clearing to find that she was no longer alone.

A hulking shadow paced slowly out of the foggy tree line directly behind the cabin. When it strayed into the shaft of moonlight that reached the moss, she saw that it was a large dog—no, a wolf, padding silently toward her. She felt no fear, though she knew she should. There was only curiosity.

It stopped a few feet from her and sat on its haunches. The wolf was huge, a shaggy, black beast with slaver running from its jaws. It seemed to have its eyes closed, and sniffed the air as if scenting for prey.

It opened its eyes, and they were blue: large, milky, and lambent. The eyes of Azariah Thayne.

Ever woke up with a start, sweating beneath her heavy blanket. She jerked her body up, flinging it aside, only to find herself again face to face with the creature: it loomed over her bedroll, standing in the corner of the cabin ruin, its eyes boring into her head.

You can never escape me, no matter how far you run.

No, Ever said. *No.*

She felt frozen in place, as if she had suddenly lost power over her body. She could feel Thayne's presence near her like a hovering storm cloud; its pressure weighed on her, made it difficult to breathe. The darkness in him opened up, and it felt as if she could slide into it, body and soul—a black so deep it was almost comforting. Part of her—a not insignificant part of her—wanted to jump in. The same dark voice that whispered to anyone standing on a height whispered to Ever, coaxing. She felt herself, somehow, leaning forward—

If you do, you will fall forever. This was another voice, a very different voice, at once powerful and gentle, but lacking the sheer volume of Azariah Thayne's mental presence. *You need to come back. I will help you.*

There was a *stretching*; Ever could feel it, like tension on a rope, stretching and tightening until, all of a sudden, it snapped.

She could move again, and she threw off her blankets and opened her mouth to scream, backing away from the still present specter of the wolf.

As she watched, it vanished as quickly as it had appeared, blinking out of existence like a firefly. Ever got to her feet in a heart-pounding lurch.

She was alone. Thayne's presence was gone, as was the other. Was it just a dream—a dream followed by, what, a hallucination? She pressed at her temples. *I'm losing my mind.*

Then the wolves—the real wolves—started howling again, much louder than before.

They were up and moving in a few short minutes. The howling was incentive enough for speed.

"Are you sure we should leave the fire?" Ever asked. "Wouldn't it be better to stay here and build it up?"

"Ordinarily, maybe," said Jared. "But that's a large pack, by the sound of it. At least if we're moving we have a chance to stay ahead of them, find a better place to hole up."

"Besides," said Acel. "We don't even know that they know we're here, yet. If we get away now, maybe we can avoid them entirely."

Jared looked at Ever and saw the same doubt he felt reflected in her eyes. He couldn't have said why, but he was certain Acel was wrong. These wolves knew they were here—they were stalking them.

Each of them readied a torch, one of the thick, pitch-soaked brands of Bountiful make.

"We won't light them until we absolutely have to," said Acel.

"You should unsling that rifle, Rolan," said Jared. Rolan had it lashed to his pack frame, as he had since leaving Salem. "We might need it." Rolan swallowed noticeably and did as Jared suggested.

They descended to the secondary road beneath their campsite in the cabin ruins and walked east at an easy jog. After a quarter-hour of comparative silence, the howling began anew, closer, and the company started running.

Ever stopped, bent over, her hands on her knees, and panted.

"I'm so tired of running," she said, realizing the futility of the words even as she spoke them. The howling of the wolf pack was loud and hoarse and close, long bays mixed with shorter barks and growling whimpers. They had run for miles, and the wolves were only getting closer.

"We have to stand and fight," Acel said, sounding equally winded. "They're going to catch us. Better that we save some energy to fight." All four of them used the unexpected break to catch their breath; Jared paced around Ever, Acel, and Rolan, bow drawn, scanning the tree line. They were on an overgrown lane heading northeast.

"There's a town a few miles east of here," Rolan said, squinting at his maps in the torchlight. "If we could get there—there might be a house or a building. We could get inside, pick them off from the roof…"

"That's as good an idea as any," said Jared. "If we can make it to the town." He looked at Ever, and she stood up, nodding.

"Douse the torches," said Acel. "They're just destroying our night vision."

"I can manage a few more miles, I think," Ever said as Jared and Rolan snuffed the flames, and managed a shaky grin. The wolf dream still lingered in her mind. She hadn't mentioned it to the boys, fearing they'd think her insane, but she was having trouble shaking the idea that the dream and the very real animals now pursuing them were connected. How could they not be?

They had only gone a few hundred feet when a flash of light and a searing pain in her head brought her to a clumsy halt.

This isn't the way, little one.

The moonlit forest lane seemed veiled in the purple gray of storm clouds, and images flashed in her head in harsh contrast. She was vaguely aware that she had fallen to her knees, could see Jared and the others standing over her with frightened looks on their faces. She saw their lips moving but heard no words coming out. The only sound she heard was the *not*-sound of him speaking to her, the *not*-voice of Azariah Thayne.

Get out of my head, she said—too weakly. She could feel her lips moving, though the world was still muted. She pushed again, spoke the words with that other part of her, put the force behind them that she'd used to pursue him in the cell in Salem.

GET OUT OF MY HEAD.

That's it. You need anger behind it. She felt a ripple in the fabric of their connection—he was amused. The hate she felt roiled her stomach.

You're going the wrong way, said Thayne. *There will be time enough to go east. There's someplace else you need to go first. You know that. Be a good little girl and do as you're told. My pets won't hurt you if you stay on the path.*

He sent her an image, then, the grizzled black face of a huge wolf, the same she'd seen in her dream and in front of her at the cabin. Its face was scarred and it was too large, its body too muscular, and when it opened its eyes they glowed milky blue. The image became a moving picture; she watched as if hovering over the animal's shoulder as it coursed through the trees.

Look now, little one. Do you see that I can always watch over you?

The wolf was climbing, its powerful shoulders easily carrying it up the densely forested slope of a hill. It crested the rise and trotted out onto a shelf of rock. A break in the trees gave a clear view of the landscape below. It turned its terrible eyes on a black ribbon beneath it, a sinuous cut through the woods, the overhanging trees hiding its surface from the light of the full moon. A road.

Ever coughed and fell forward, feeling as if she'd been holding her breath. The night around her was clear again and she could hear Jared's voice.

"Ever, what—"

"*Run*, we have to run," she croaked. "They're here. He's driving them. Driving us."

"Who? What are you talking about?" asked Rolan, his face pale and slack in the dim light.

"Thayne," she said, getting to her feet. "The wolves are his—somehow. He's controlling them. Driving us in the direction he wants us to go."

"Where? What sense does that make? I thought he let us go?"

"I don't know," she said, "but not east. He said not east. The wolves are close, just above us. They'll attack if we keep heading east. The other one must be calling the shots, now."

Acel looked at the treed rise above them.

"Then I say we go east," he said.

"What? Why?" asked Rolan.

"Because Azariah Thayne can go to hell, that's why," said Acel.

Ever shook her head.

"These aren't normal wolves. They're Damned. Enormous. Vicious. And Thayne's done something to them. They see with his eyes. He's watching us."

"So our options are to go where a violent madman wants us to or face a murderous pack of wolves," said Jared.

"I for one am getting very tired of Azariah Thayne," said Acel between clenched teeth. He was quiet for a moment.

"I have no desire to go anywhere that man wants me to be," Acel said finally. "But we'll vote. This isn't a decision just one of us should make. I vote we keep going east, and to hell with Thayne and his dogs." The howling continued in the near distance; every moment they wasted talking gave the beasts a chance to overtake them.

Ever, who had regained some semblance of composure, nodded. She didn't relish the idea of confronting Thayne's twisted creatures face to face, but anything was preferable to letting him lead them into something worse. Acel turned to Jared.

"Does it really matter? Not much of a choice either way, if you ask me," Jared said. "But all things considered I'll take my chances with the wolves."

"That's a majority, but I'd just as soon have it be unanimous," said Acel, looking at Rolan.

"What the hell," Rolan said. "I'd rather be a wolf's dinner than let him win." Acel smiled, brought his rifle to his shoulder, and started walking east.

"We make for the town, then," he said over his shoulder. Rolan, Ever, and Jared followed.

By Jared's best estimate, they'd gotten almost a mile before the wolves were on them. He saw them first, loping shadows coming out of the trees into the broken road far behind them.

"Behind us," he yelled, "maybe a quarter of a mile, moving fast."

Acel whirled, bringing his rifle up to his shoulder.

"Go," he commanded, taking a knee in the middle of the roadway. "I'll be right behind you."

"I can—"

"Go, Jared." Jared went. Ever and Rolan followed close behind him.

"Spread out behind me, you two," said Jared. "One to either side." Drawing his revolver, he handed it to Ever. "Same principle as a rifle. Aim twice, shoot once." She accepted the pistol without comment, swinging out the cylinder to check that it was loaded. Every youth in Bountiful learned to fire a rifle, girls included, but pistols weren't common. Ever seemed confident enough with the gun in her hand, though.

Jared pulled an arrow from his quiver and fitted it to his bow, keeping a light tension on the string. Behind them, Acel fired his first shot. Jared smiled when he heard a distant whimper in response.

The road bent gently left a few yards ahead, hiding the road from view. Another rifle shot rang out behind them. They slowed approaching the bend, but Jared was still surprised by the animal that burst out of the woods at the top of the curve, shaggy and black, streaked with gray, its breath alone loud in the still, cold air. His shot went wide of the beast's chest, but its sheer size worked to his advantage and the arrow lodged in the wolf's hindquarter. The bolt barely slowed it down.

It was almost on top of him by the time he drew a second arrow and let fly, at the same time that Ever squeezed a round out of the revolver next to him. The wolf barreled into Jared's legs, its momentum carrying it forward even after his arrow and Ever's bullet had struck home. The wolf's furry mass hit him hard, carrying them both to the broken pavement in a tangle of limbs. The pain in his back was hard and immediate. Jared felt his bow clatter to the ground behind him; the wolf was still snarling weakly as its life's blood leaked out of its chest. He could feel the heat of its breath on his cheek. He was still struggling out from under its body when he heard, rather than saw, one of its pack mates attack Rolan, who got one futile shot off with his rifle before it too hit the ground.

By the time Jared got up and found his bow, another monster had Rolan pinned, slowly but surely pressing past his frantic defenses. Ever was aiming, looking for a safe shot, when Jared saw another one behind her, closing fast.

He screamed and pointed, saw her swing the gun around in time. Jared heard her fire twice, then ran to Rolan with his knife drawn, stabbing the wolf brutally and repeatedly in the side until it died. Heaving its corpse off of Rolan, Jared's heart sank when he saw the mess the wolf had made of his shoulder. Rolan already had a hand pressed to his belly. The shoulder wasn't the worst of it then.

"Can you get up?" he asked, even as he was hauling Rolan off the ground. He groaned weakly, most of his weight on Jared.

"Ever—"

But Ever was shooting again, aiming into the trees to their left flank. She squeezed the trigger until it clicked empty.

There was another rifle shot in the distance, and then Jared heard pounding toward them up the road. Jared was about to tell Ever to help him with Rolan—the town couldn't be that much farther; maybe they could make it if they pushed—when he saw another set of wolf eyes shining in the woods.

But they weren't the yellow eyes of natural wolves: these were blue, and seemed to glow faintly with their own light, and there was more than one set of them. As Jared looked, he saw dark, canine shapes moving in the shadows beneath the trees. Turning, he saw more on the other side of the road. *They see with his eyes.* He set Rolan down carefully and took the boy's rifle.

"Ever," he said, whispering. "In the trees." She nodded, looking at him hopelessly.

Jared held up a cautioning hand to slow Acel as he approached, and carefully turned to face the right shoulder of the road. It had all been a feint, then. The wolves were toying with them, daring them to go farther. A warning.

"There's too many of them," he whispered. Too many, but he supposed numbers didn't matter now. The sound Rolan's rifle made as Jared cleared the breach and slid the bolt home to chamber another round was deafening as all else grew still.

• • •

The wolf fell after the third shot, skidding to a stop on the road just in front of her boots, a thick streak of blood glimmering in the road behind it. The pistol was empty. Ever heard another gunshot and Acel running up, then Jared was warning her about the wolves in the trees. Her breath caught in her throat as set after set of milky blue eyes opened in the dark of the trees and shone into the night.

How far are you willing to go?

Thayne's not-voice boomed in her mind like a revelation. There was an edge to it, this time—the dangerous calm of the other Thayne.

I permitted him to let you go—against my better judgment. But there is a delicate balance to be maintained, in me. You'll understand someday. You shouldn't vex me, child, or I'll carve you like a turkey at Thanksgiving.

You won't kill me, Ever thought at him. *If you wanted to you would have done it already.*

Unfortunately, you're needed alive for the time being. But your friends aren't. It's nothing for me to hurt them, to kill them—less to me than killing a spider lurking in the eaves. And as for you... there are so many wonderful things that hurt far, far worse than death, my dear.

Ever squeezed her eyes shut, trying to control the storm inside her mind—anger warred with dread.

I hate you.

Laughter. *Oh, I am aware, child. Let us hope your hatred will be the key to unlocking what my... companion so lovingly calls our destiny. Now turn around, and walk north.*

Ever opened her eyes. She couldn't have had them closed for longer than a few seconds, but Acel and Jared were staring at her—whatever she had said or done, they knew what had happened.

"Thayne?" Jared asked grimly. She nodded.

Ever walked over to Jared and nodded at his belt.

"I need a reload."

Eyeing her uncertainly, he plucked six cartridges from the diminishing supply on his gunbelt and dumped them into her upturned palm. Ever didn't speak as she reloaded the gun.

"I'm going east," she said. Jared nodded slowly. Acel came up and helped Jared drag Rolan to his feet.

"That's it then," said Acel.

Ever walked forward, cocking the gun as she did so. The wolves started milling behind the trees again. *What are you doing?* she asked herself. Maybe Thayne and his creatures wouldn't kill her. *Why is he trying to drive me north?* Maybe they'd leave her alone entirely; maybe they'd just hurt her. But she was leading her friends to their deaths.

Ever stopped walking when the first wolf padded out in the road and stood opposite her. Its brothers and sisters encircled their little band, slavering and panting, blue eyes staring wildly.

If you won't kill me, she said to Thayne in her own not-voice, *then you've only given me another weapon to use against you.*

She raised the gun and started firing. Jared and Acel again helped Rolan to the ground, then raised their own weapons and fired alongside her. Between the distracting link to Thayne's mind and the fear and anger that coursed through her like blood, Ever lost track of how many shots were fired. The beasts started toward them as they began firing; at least three went down before any of the others reached them.

Her gun clicked empty again and she threw it at the nearest wolf in a rage, sobbing as it shot past her toward Jared.

Acel went down with one on top of him, and Jared was still firing—but there were too many. She could see it, clear as day, as the creatures, Damned and evil, closed in, more of them appearing out of the forest as she watched. Gripping her knife, Ever ran toward the wolf on top of Acel, tears streaming down her cheeks. She wasn't sure when exactly she'd begun crying, but now that the tears had started they wouldn't stop.

She was almost there, blade raised to plunge into its back, when a gunshot cracked in the air like thunder and the wolf rolled off of Acel like so much baggage. There was more gunfire, a caliber she didn't recognize; she couldn't even tell where it was coming from, but the wolves were dropping around them, suddenly, miraculously, as if Heavenly Father himself had descended to defend his children.

Then there were strangely dressed men running out of the woods with foreign looking weapons, rifles in black metal and strange field gear, clothing and accouterments like nothing Ever had ever seen in various shades of black and shifting green. She gaped, her knife held out in one hand, watching impotently as they killed.

Before the connection was broken she felt a spike of pain from Thayne—he could feel them dying. As each wolf's twisted life was snuffed out by a high-powered burst of fire from the shadowy warriors, she felt Thayne's essence grimace like he was being jabbed with a needle. There was a certain grim satisfaction in knowing someone had caused Azariah Thayne to suffer, however briefly.

Then the wolves were all dead, and Ever, Jared, and Acel stood in the middle of a growing circle of their dark saviors.

For the first time in many hours, the sound of wolves was completely gone from the night. One of the men—oddly slender in his strange clothes—walked up to Ever and raised his rifle, pointing it directly at her heart.

22

Ever blinked. The man pointing a gun at her had asked her a question. His voice was muffled by the odd mask he wore over his face, like a black scarf wrapped around a protruding assortment of lenses and armored plates. If she hadn't recognized the language, Ever might have thought him some kind of overgrown insect. The glass of the lenses over his eyes reflected the moonlight; Ever could see her own face in the reflection. It was finer work than she had ever seen in Bountiful.

"I'm...my name is Ever Oaks," she said, suddenly realizing she was still holding her knife as if she meant to use it. "I'm going to put this down now." The masked figure nodded.

Following her example, Jared and Acel also lowered their weapons carefully to the ground. The other men seemed to be waiting on the one in front of Ever—was he their leader, then?

A soft groan from behind her reminded Ever that Rolan was injured.

"Please," she said, in what she hoped was a humble and plaintive voice, "my friend is hurt. Please let me help him." The figure in black didn't respond immediately, but after a moment gestured slightly with her weapon. Ever, taking this as permission, moved slowly to Rolan's side and knelt down beside him. Jared, still standing above them, looked down worriedly.

"It mauled his neck and shoulder," Jared said, loudly enough to avoid any accusation of conspiracy from their—what were they, Ever wondered? Saviors? Captors? Killers? "But I think his belly's worse."

Ever stroked Rolan's face gently; the boy was obviously in pain—a great deal of it, now that she looked at him closely. He was conscious, but his eyes were pressed shut; his breathing was quick and shallow. His face had a clammy pallor she didn't like. Carefully, Ever comforted him and moved his hand away from his stomach.

As soon as she did so dark blood welled up and spread; she could see now that it had already soaked his body. Pulling up his torn shirt, she wiped some of the blood away and examined the wound. Her jaw tightened and she pressed her own hands down on top of it.

Jared had gotten to him just in time: another second, another bite, and the beast would have eviscerated him. As it was his wounds were deep—she thought she could see the blue gleam of an intestine inside one of the gashes—and he would soon die without aid. She looked up at Jared, then over at Acel, and finally to the masked leader.

"I need to heal him," she said. "Or he'll die." She didn't particularly care whether they understood what she meant, but she didn't want them to be entirely surprised by what was about to happen.

The leader exchanged a look with one of his men, but said nothing, continuing to watch. Ever turned back to Rolan, who seemed even less lucid than he had been.

Keeping one hand on the wound to his belly and placing her other on his forehead, she closed her eyes and hoped, as always, that the power would come when she called. She prepared herself, starting to gather the ball of emotion that she usually needed in order to summon the healing power.

Something felt different, however: she opened her eyes, looked down at Rolan, and felt the Gift rush out of her, flooding through her hands and into his wounded body. Rolan's eyes snapped open and he arched his back, gasping. In a moment it was done, and Ever sat back on her heels, tired but still awake, vaguely amazed at what had just happened.

Rolan's eyes had closed again, but after a few moments they opened, and he began, weakly, to sit up.

"You...you're both awake," said Jared. Ever could only nod. Every time she had used her gift before, it had exhausted both herself and her patient to the point of unconsciousness, which usually lasted for hours. This time, both she and Rolan were not only awake but only slightly tired. Jared helped him up and he blinked, pulling up the blood-soaked remnants of his linen shirt. Jared passed him his water bottle; Rolan drank from it, then poured some out into his palm and messily wiped his belly clean.

The men around them murmured in confused fascination, their exact words muffled by their masks. Guns lowered around them. Pushing herself to her feet with an effort, Ever turned back to the man in charge.

Slowly, the man lowered his gun and reached up to his face, undoing several strange clasps before pulling the thing off. Long, golden blonde hair fell out of the black fabric, and as the lenses came away from the man's eyes, Ever could see that he was not, in fact, a man at all. The woman who looked back at her was beautiful, though taller and wider of shoulder than Ever was used to. She blinked, her eyes a pale blue the color of morning sky.

"Tell me again who you are," she said. Her accent was slightly strange.

"I am Sister Ever Oaks," she said, "and these are Elders Acel Higbee, Rolan Belnap, and Brother Jared Meacham." She gestured at each young man in turn. "Late of Bountiful, holdfast and community of the Blessed."

The woman's eyes widened further, if such was possible, and Ever heard what seemed like a collective intake of breath from the rest of the woman's band of soldiers. To Ever's utter amazement, the woman put her weapon aside slowly, as if she was the one held at gunpoint, and dropped down to kneel before her on both knees. Her men followed suit, removing their own masks and lowering their weapons as they did so.

"My name is Sephine, Scion of the Valley, and I am yours to command, Sister Oaks."

A short time later, Ever found herself walking through the woods at the head of a column of heavily armed men who appeared to view her—and, to a lesser extent, her companions—as some kind of authority figure. Thus far Sephine—who walked next to her, rifle slung, and who appeared ready to throw her own body across a puddle should Ever disdain getting her boots wet—had respectfully avoided most questions Ever had asked regarding her origin and purpose. The woman acted as if it were perfectly natural that she and her band of intimidating fighting men should come across four teenagers in the woods and offer to serve them.

"You must be tired, Sister Oaks," Sephine had said, when Ever asked her to explain who she was. "First we must get you food, water, and shelter. All of your questions will be answered, but I'm sorry to say that I shouldn't be the one to answer them." Ever had thanked her, of course, and then, after several whispered conversations with Acel and Jared, she tried a different tack.

"You have to understand, Sephine," Ever said, trying to sound as authoritative as possible, "this is a very surprising set of circumstances for...me and my people. I need to make sure that wherever you are taking us is someplace we want to go." Sephine squinted at this, her look of confusion almost comical.

"You have us at something of a disadvantage," Ever added. "We are a small group, alone in a strange place, surrounded by strangers with guns." Sephine's eyes widened again, and she stopped suddenly, holding up a hand to the men behind her. They were on what appeared to be a well-maintained trail through the forest, heading almost due north, so far as Ever could tell.

Sephine looked at her boots for a moment, and then up at Ever.

"I never expected to find a Saint wandering in the mountain foothills," she said, "but it hadn't occurred to me that you might be just as surprised to find me." Taking her gun off her shoulder, she offered it to Ever, holding it out nonthreateningly in both hands. "This is yours, if you want it. We mean you no harm. Every man—and woman—here will happily hand you his weapon should you ask it. Use them against us, should you wish. Shoot me down where I stand. I will not resist. Certainly, you're free to go wherever you wish. We're your servants, not your enemies. That is all I can say—I lack the authority to say more; my oaths forbid it, even to one such as you."

Ever, staring at the woman for a long moment, shook her head at the gun. Sephine took it back and slung it on her shoulder again.

"If," she continued, "you're willing to come with me, maybe you'll find the answers you seek in the Valley. Someone waits for you there—someone who can tell you what I can't. If you can take that much on faith,

I'll be your guide and your protector until we reach the Valley, and beyond. If not, as I said, I am yours to command. I'll go where you wish.

"Although," she added, with a look of hesitation on her face, "it would be much simpler for all concerned if you just came with me. There would be fewer... complexities."

"If I could just have a moment with my companions," Ever said.

"Of course, Sister."

Ever gestured for Jared, Acel, and Rolan to follow her, and she walked a few dozen feet up the trail, still in sight of Sephine and her men, who made no move to follow.

"Am I the only one who thinks this is damned creepy?" Jared said, as soon as they were out of earshot.

"I'd have to agree," said Acel. "Until that little show with the gun back there, I assumed we were going with them whether we wanted to or not, whatever she said. These people...they seem a little—"

"Crazy," finished Jared. "The word you're looking for is crazy. Maybe not Azariah Thayne crazy, but crazy all the same. And I've never seen anything like these weapons they're carrying before. They're either something new, or something very old."

"What are our other options?" Ever asked.

"They did say they'd let us go," Acel said. "We could test that statement. They killed the wolves for us, and gave you a chance to heal Rolan...we could head east, like we planned. There's nothing stopping us now."

"And if they are crazy, like Jared said, and they're lying to us? Then what?" asked Ever.

"Then..." Acel shrugged. "Then I guess we find out."

"I don't know," said Ever. "I don't know what to believe. Did Thayne drive us here knowing we'd meet these people, or was he expecting something else?"

"Do we want to risk going with them if there's even the possibility that it's what Azariah Thayne wants?" Acel asked.

"When did we start assuming that Azariah Thayne can actually see the future?" said Jared. "I'm sure *he* thinks he can, but if he's...the way you say he is, then I'm not sure we want to indulge in the same delusion."

"If he can," Ever said, "and he did know we'd meet them, then we can't believe anything they say. We're just as trapped here as we thought we were."

"But that's not what you think," said Jared, looking at her face closely.

"No," said Ever, hesitantly. "No. This feels...right. Sephine isn't lying to us. I think I'd know." Acel looked skeptical.

"I think we should go with them, at least for now. We can always change our minds," Ever said.

"Until they get us to this Valley of theirs," said Acel, but with an air of defeat. "Or somewhere else we can't escape."

"What about you, Rolan?" Ever said. "You've been quiet." He'd been quiet the whole way, come to think of it. She wasn't sure she'd heard him utter a word since she had healed him back on the road.

"I'd just as soon be around people," Rolan said, "even strangers, than deal with any more of Thayne's…pets." There was a haunted look on his face that made Ever nervous. Perhaps her healing hadn't been complete….

"That's a good point," Jared said. "There's no way to be certain Thayne couldn't just call down another bunch of Damned on us, and then we'd be right back where we started."

Ever looked at her three friends. Jared seemed the most confident; Acel looked worried; Rolan stared into the underbrush, or at nothing at all.

"So we'll stay the course for now," said Ever. She waited for them all to agree, then walked back to face Sephine.

"Lead the way," she said.

Sephine's Valley turned out to be closer by than Jared had expected. The trail, which Sephine and her people obviously maintained with blade and shovel and axe, let out onto another road, three or so miles from where the four Blessed had stopped to discuss their options.

The road bore the same tarred, broken pavement as the one Sephine had found them on, but was far better taken care of. It was kept clear of trees, large brush, and tall grass—Jared could see where saplings had been sawn down and brush chopped away. The trail emerged from the woods just before the road crossed a marshy area, suggesting a more substantial wetland behind them, to the south.

The road ran along a narrow, lively river, crossing it at several points with simple, rusty steel bridges, some of which had been reinforced with beams smeared with black pine pitch. The road followed the river upstream, toward its source, cutting a corridor through the pine forests beneath a group of green mountains that dominated the Northern horizon.

The sun was well risen by the time they stopped to eat, illuminating the thick carpet of trees that covered the peaks, interspersed randomly with granite ledges and walls too sheer for trees to grow. Sephine's men passed out bars of a thick, chewy substance, composed mainly of dried berries and nuts and tasting faintly of animal fat and pine. They also supplied the Blessed, whose own skins were near dry, with fresh water from their own bottles, though most of the Valley people drank directly from the river.

"I wonder what those are?" murmured Jared around a mouthful of the stuff, standing next to Acel and looking up at a strange pattern of partially cleared areas on one of the nearby peaks.

It was Sephine who responded, following his gaze.

"Old alpine trails," she said. "This area was once part of a skiing resort. You can still see the remains of the old chairlift system. The forest never completely reclaimed the larger parts, at least not yet. Too cold and steep, I imagine."

"Skee-ing?" repeated Jared, swallowing another mouthful of their trail food to hide his ignorance. Sephine smiled.

"You slide down a snowy slope on planks attached to your boots," she explained, "and use poles to help navigate. The ancients did it for fun. We still do it in the winter, to patrol the trails. It's easier and faster than snow-shoeing."

They really are crazy, Jared thought.

"Interesting," was all he said, however.

It wasn't that Jared didn't share Acel's suspicion of Sephine and her rangers, as Jared thought of them—he was the one who had called them crazy, after all. But he trusted Ever's judgment that their intentions were peaceful—not to mention his own judgment that anyone who would offer to turn over her weapon and the weapons of all of her men to a complete stranger either was just as crazy as she seemed or, indeed, meant what she said.

Sephine seemed to have an amazing amount of knowledge of—and access to—the technology of the Old People. How had she known what skiing trails were? Did they have access to better records here than the Blessed did?

Their firearms in particular fascinated him. Dark slabs of metal and some other, softer substance, they had no discernible barrels or breeches, nor did they appear to eject any kind of shell casing when fired. What was their ammunition? They were lighter than they looked, given the way the rangers handled them. He wasn't quite bold enough yet to ask, though he was certain the suspense would drive him to it eventually. Good enough now to observe quietly. Maybe the answer would present itself. Maybe Sephine was telling the truth, and everything would be all right.

Maybe they were walking into a trap.

Jared finished the rest of his breakfast, hoping he'd be able to keep it down.

Sephine set an easy pace, perhaps out of consideration for the Blessed. Neither Ever nor any of her companions had slept in over a day. Sephine's men, on the other hand, looked as if they could easily walk another ten miles when the column finally reached the entrance proper to the Valley.

It was mid-morning, the sun glancing down from a clear sky, and the weather was crisp as Ever crossed a wooden bridge and walked out of the trees. The road ran directly out past a broad field, covered in knee-length grass, and she could see the entire, broad bowl of the Valley spread out before her.

"Tecumseh, Osceola, Kancamangus, Tripyramid," announced Sephine, pointing out peaks from west to east around the valley. "Those are the names on the old charts, at least. Tripyramid we call Three Peaks. And there, far in the grey north, is Washington, Father of Mountains. The ancients built a road leading to its summit. The view is...unbelievable."

Beyond the field was an oddly shaped structure, the rotted, fragile remains of some kind of lodging house, half a dozen wide towers connected in a sort of arc. Its skeleton still stood, concrete and steel, but the wooden fascia had long since fallen away, and Ever could see the sky through the squat, skeletal cones making up the tower roofs.

They followed the road past the wide field separating them from the towers. The land to their right was wooded, though not as heavily as what they'd seen on the way in, and Ever could see the remains of structures scattered in the trees there, as well. After a few moments a large pond came into view, nestled below the sheltering arc of the towered lodge and another set of more decayed buildings that seemed to rise out of the quiet water.

"The pond water rose when the dams broke," Sephine explained, "whenever that was. That used to a little square. The water's only two or three feet deep, there, under the buildings. The water level rises and falls with the weather."

Ever saw that the little river they'd followed into the valley flowed into the pond and out of it again. They crossed it for the last time at the eastern edge of the pond, where it flowed beneath them under another old metal bridge.

Behind the flooded square and its surrounding buildings there was a broad, open, paved area interspersed with treed islands—some kind of vast storage area, Ever supposed, or one of the lots the Old People had used for their vehicles. It was here Sephine led them, across the edge of the asphalt field—the trees had been allowed to grow through the pavement unmolested, here—and into the largest stand of trees. There was a narrow trail leading through it, which they followed for a few hundred feet before coming to a small clearing. In the center of the space, inside a perfect square of polished concrete dimly reflecting the morning sunlight, was a steel hatch that looked like it led directly into the ground.

Sephine approached the hatch and squatted down beside it. Ever looked back curiously at her friends, only to notice that a large number of the men who had been behind them had disappeared.

"They faded away a few at a time," Jared explained. "All different directions." He shook his head to indicate that he didn't understand it any better than she did.

The faint squeak of oiled metal drew her attention back to what was happening in front of her. Sephine had opened the hatch. One of her remaining men went in first, at her command, then Sephine invited them to follow.

Trying to ignore the sudden seizing of anxiety in her chest, Ever took a deep breath and approached the hatch. A ladder led straight down into darkness. As she watched, light appeared below.

"It's all right," said Sephine.

Climbing into the hatch, Ever put her foot on the first rung and hoped she was making the right decision. Descending into a hole in the ground...felt oddly symbolic, under the circumstances.

She put one foot beneath the other, her boots ringing faintly on the worn steel rungs, and soon found herself in an older, brighter world.

23

Almost two days later, Ever woke up slowly, a sense of panic building as she contemplated her surroundings with a rested mind. She knew, without having to ask, that she had slept a long time. If she had dreamed, she had no memory of it.

She had a dim memory of being led down a long, branching series of concrete tunnels, lit with dazzling electrical lights, after descending into the ground, but she must have been more exhausted after their flight from Thayne's wolves and her healing of Rolan than she had thought. She had no recollection whatsoever of how she had come to be in this room.

Moving with the pleasant stiffness only a long overdue night (and day) of sleep could bring, she slowly pushed off a blanket and sat up. The bed she lay on was built into the wall, formed out of the same polished concrete as the structure—fortress? Bunker?—itself.

The mattress was made out of a squishy material she didn't recognize.

She had apparently managed to get her boots off before falling into bed—they were propped against the wall—but otherwise she was fully dressed. She stood up, exploring the small room.

It was sparsely furnished; aside from the built-in cot, only a metal chair, a small steel table, and a strange, painted cabinet adorned the space. She slid her palm over the cabinet, steel painted in a garish red. Someone had stenciled stylized flowers onto the side of it—a long time ago now. The paint was chipped and fading. Everything seemed to be made of metal or stone, in this place.

The chair was pushed in politely beneath the table, on top of which was a neatly folded pile of clothing, a clear, capped pitcher of water, and a cup. She held up the top item: a simple shirt, made to be pulled on over the head, woven out of the strange, silky fibers Sephine and her rangers had been wearing.

Ever looked down at herself and realized she was filthy—her clothes were actually stiff with mud, grime, and perspiration, and from the feel of it alone her hair was an utter disaster. She could also smell herself, which was unsurprising since it had been over a week since her last proper bath. Thinking about it now, she was mortified to realize that Acel, Rolan, and Jared had likely smelled her too. Not that they smelled any better. As tempted as she was to disrobe right then and wash herself with the drinking water, if need be, she resisted.

First things first. She had no idea where Acel, Rolan, and Jared had gotten to, or if they were all right.

There were two doors in the room. The first led into a smaller room with a high ceiling. There were shelves cut into the walls, as well as a strange, covered seat built out from the back wall, and another closed door stood in the opposite wall. She stepped in hesitantly. The shelves were filled with folded fabric and small, translucent bricks. Picking one up, she sniffed it, then laughed. *Soap.* And the fabric must be toweling....

Looking up, Ever saw a set of perforated metal discs suspended from the ceiling on pipes. Was it possible Sephine's people had running water? Such a thing hadn't been heard of, by the Blessed, at least, since.... *since before the Fall.* There was no obvious way to control the flow of the water, however, so she stepped back into her bedroom and tried the other door. This one opened into a larger room with a sunken seating area and a large metal dining table surrounded by chairs.

Sitting on a cushion in the seating pit with his back to her was Jared Meacham. Sitting across from him was a petite woman dressed in clothing similar to the articles Ever had found on her own table. The woman, seeing her enter, rose.

"Jared," said Ever.

Jared craned his neck to look behind him, then climbed out of the pit by way of a shallow set of steps and hugged her briefly. He was also wearing the strange clothing, and looked—and smelled—as if he'd bathed.

"I'm glad you got some rest," he said. "You needed it. We all did."

Turning, he held his hand out toward the small woman.

"This is Sandrine," he said. "Sandrine, this is Sister Oaks."

The woman had risen as Jared presented Ever, and now she gave a slight bow and smiled.

"It is an honor, Sister Oaks," said Sandrine. "I will leave you in privacy, Brother Meacham."

"That's really not—" Jared began to say, but the woman had already left the room, opening another door that led out into one of the tunnels Ever vaguely remembered. He scoffed in frustration. "These people are slipperier than eels. I'd just gotten her to sit down."

"Do you think they're up to something?" she asked, the panic she'd felt upon waking returning in full.

"No. Yes," he said. Ever frowned. "I mean they're obviously up to *something*," he continued, "because they're not telling us anything yet, but if you mean am I worried we're in trouble—no. No more than before, anyway. All they'll say about anything important is that our questions will be answered. I managed to get her talking about the water, but that's all."

"Where are Acel and Rolan?" Ever asked.

"Still asleep, as far as I know." He gestured to two other doors. "They call this a pod. There are six bedrooms surrounding a common living area. I only woke up myself a little while ago."

"Do you have any idea what time it is? What day?" she asked. Even in the few minutes she'd been awake, Ever had already experienced the strange timelessness that came with living underground.

"It's morning," he said. "We slept a whole day and night."

Ever was silent for a moment, wrapping her arms around her body.

"So we're…" *Safe*, is what she wanted to say, but she trailed off.

"What?" he prompted. She shook her head.

After they decided jointly to wait for the others to wake up on their own before exploring further, Jared led Ever back into her own room and showed her how to use the water.

"They call it a shower," he said, pointing to a set of knobs at the back of the little room. Ever hadn't noticed them before. "The left one carries cold water, the right one hot."

"Hot?" Ever said, confused.

"The water's heated in big tanks somewhere, then piped into these rooms. Adjust the mixture till you get a temperature you like. Soap and towels on the shelves. They left you clothes, and they'll take yours and clean them when you're ready. They've got *electricity*, Ever. The lights in here…." Jared sounded amazed. Ever felt more overwhelmed.

"Another world," she said. Jared nodded in understanding.

"Where does that go?" Ever asked after a shared silence, indicating the other door in the shower room.

"Into one of the other bedrooms," Jared explained. "Two rooms share each shower, I guess."

"Don't worry," he said after a moment, when the obvious finally occurred to him. "There's no one living in that room. You've got this to yourself. And, um, I'm sure you can figure out what to do with this." He stepped over to the odd little seat she had seen earlier. The top of it turned out to be a lid, however, and when he lifted it up Ever realized what it was.

"Not quite an outhouse, huh?" Jared joked.

Ever wondered how the Valley people themselves dealt with bathing privacy, when the doors leading into the shower room didn't even have locks or latches of any kind. *Add it to the increasingly long list of things I don't understand*, she thought.

"Well, in that case..." she said, and smiled, gesturing to the room in general. Jared smiled back. "Um, I mean, I'd like to use this now, Jared."

"Oh. Oh!" Jared's face reddened. "Of course. I'll be out in the main room, then, when you're finished." He gave a kind of awkward nod, turned, and left hurriedly.

For the first time in as long as she could remember, Ever felt like laughing. She didn't, but wanting to felt almost as good. Then she remembered kissing Jared in the light of the campfire, only a few nights before, and felt heat rise to her cheeks. Even when she wasn't in fear for her life, everything seemed to happen too quickly to contemplate these days.

After removing her soiled clothing and spending several awkward, naked minutes fiddling with the water control knobs, Ever coaxed a hot rain to fall from the ceiling, filling the tall, narrow room with steam. Ever edged beneath it carefully at first, then with increasing pleasure, as her body grew acclimated to the temperature. It was very hot.

Now this *is amazing*. She worked up an impressive lather with a bar of the clear, amber soap and scrubbed her entire body. The hot, soapy water cascading over her skin felt sinfully wonderful; the lukewarm baths she had grown up with in Bountiful were crude puddles, by comparison. If Elder Cardon had appeared at that very moment to tell her that the Adversary himself heated the water with the fires of damnation, she wouldn't have cared.

Afterward, having toweled off and brushed out her clean, crackling hair, Ever put on the strange attire that had been left for her. The neat pile included undergarments, a tightly fitted base layer, and pants and a light jacket all made of similar fabric. For all its warmth it seemed to breathe, wicking away the moisture left on her skin from her shower. There were no shoes, so Ever put on her tall leather boots, which were in fine condition anyway.

She walked back into the common room to find Sandrine serving a hot breakfast to a freshly awakened Rolan and Acel. Jared came out of his own room and sat down as she did.

"That smells wonderful," said Ever. "Are those eggs?"

Sandrine nodded, setting a platter of freshly scrambled eggs down on the table. There was also a platter of bacon, fried potatoes, toasted bread with berry jam, and a bowl of fresh fruit the likes of which Ever had never seen. She picked up a large orange fruit with a tough rind.

"What is this?" she asked.

"An orange," Sandrine said. "We grow them under ultraviolet lights in a heated section of the nursery, along with lemons, limes, and bananas. It's worth the energy cost for the nutrients we get out of the fruit."

Ever merely nodded, unwilling to admit how little of the woman's words she'd actually understood. It seemed many things were possible here that were mere legends in Bountiful. She'd heard stories about all of the exotic foods the Old People had grown and eaten, of course, but in Bountiful the only fruit they grew were apples, pears, and berries. The Northeast Kingdom had short summers and shorter springs; it wasn't ideal for agriculture. They did have a few hothouses, but their bounty was limited by the seeds they had access to.

"Where did you get orange seeds?" Ever asked. Once in a great while, some enterprising Bountiful farmer would scavenge seeds from the ruins of an ancient building, but aside from a few false starts and sterile one-offs, nothing had come of it.

"From the seed vault," said Sandrine. She smiled when Ever only looked at her blankly. "All will be explained."

"I'm getting tired of hearing that," grumbled Acel, around a mouthful of eggs.

In addition to juice and water, Sandrine also poured them each a mug of a steaming dark liquid with a pungent, earthy aroma. She showed them how to mix milk and sugar into it, after realizing they were unfamiliar with the drink.

"It's coffee," she said. Ever, already mid-sip, paused.

"Coffee?" she repeated, looking at the others. There was an awkward silence, broken by a loud scoff by Jared, who rolled his eyes and took a hearty gulp from his cup. They laughed and the tension was broken.

"We don't have coffee, where we're from," Ever explained to Sandrine, who looked confused. "The stories say that before the Fall our people were not allowed to drink it."

"Why not?" Sandrine asked.

"I...have no idea," said Ever, then took another sip. "It's delicious." She felt strangely energetic; a heady buzz seemed to course through her veins. She kept this discovery to herself.

"There are certain items we ration, because our supply is limited, including coffee. But this is a special occasion," Sandrine said. "After you've finished here, I will bring you to meet Sephine. You have an appointment with Mother Greta."

"Who?" asked Jared. Sandrine, having finished laying out their meal, had folded her hands politely at her waist and seemed to be waiting for a chance to slip away.

"It will all—"

"—be explained," Jared and Ever finished, together. Sandrine blushed, gave one of her little bows, and again disappeared into the corridor.

The first ten minutes of breakfast consisted of a lot of eating and very little talking. After the worst of their hunger had been sated by eggs and baked goods and fruit, Ever and Jared spent the next half-hour telling

Rolan and Acel what they'd learned—very little—about the Valley and its incredible technological abilities.

"I think the main question we should be asking," said Rolan, who had begun to bob his knee compulsively beneath the table, "isn't *how* they managed all of this"—he paused to gesture expansively at their surroundings—"but *when*. As in, how long have they been this advanced? Is it their own accomplishment, or did they merely preserve something left over from before the Fall?"

No one had an answer, though Ever found the question inexplicably troubling.

When they had finished eating, she and Jared waited for Rolan and Acel to shower and change. Sephine arrived, as if summoned, just after the two boys had emerged, freshly scrubbed, from their rooms.

"I am to take you to Mother Greta," she announced. Sleep had done wonders for Ever's observational powers; with a clearer mind, she saw that Sephine was quite young, barely older than Acel, who was almost twenty. In the dark, armed and commanding, surrounded by fighting men, Sephine had seemed a good deal older. "I am permitted to answer any questions you may have about this facility along the way."

The tunnels were high and wide, far from the claustrophobic likes of the Scout tunnels beneath Bountiful. They were more dimly lit than he remembered from the walk in. Sephine set a brisk pace, leading them farther in to the facility, and Jared made sure to keep up, intent on hearing everything that was said.

"The lodge," Sephine was saying, "as we call it, is a system of connected bunkers and tunnels fifty feet beneath the Valley floor. On average, that is—some areas run deeper, of course. There are more than two hundred miles of tunnel, all told."

"How do you generate electricity?" asked Rolan.

"A combination of hydroelectric power and solar cells, mainly," said Sephine. "Water power and sunlight. We try to generate as much power as we can this way; the alternative is to rely on the reactor, which is no longer enough for our daily energy needs.

"Even so, we ration it closely. The lighting in your rooms, and the amount of light in these tunnels, is mainly for your benefit."

"Reactor…?" Rolan said, trying the word out. It wasn't one any of them were familiar with.

"That, I can't tell you much about," Sephine said, not breaking stride as she led them left down an intersecting tunnel.

"Will that be explained, too?" asked Jared. Sephine smiled.

"I wish someone would explain it. No, Brother Meacham, I can't explain the reactor to you because we don't understand it ourselves. It's almost entirely self-sufficient—a relic of the ancients, left here to power this place and preserve it for…well, for us, I suppose. For you."

Jared watched the woman—who was far from bad-looking, he had to admit, though perhaps a bit imperious for his tastes—carefully. She was getting close to why they were here, but he wanted to be careful not to press her too hard.

"How many of you are there?" he asked, changing the subject.

"Just over two hundred," said Sephine, glancing at him. "We have to...impose limits—on breeding. On how many children we have. To stay within our resources."

"You seem to have more than enough to go around," Ever commented. "And you are safe, here. I couldn't imagine any place safer."

"Perhaps not so safe as you think," Sephine responded. "We've only survived as long as we have by staying hidden, and guarding our borders fiercely. There are violent tribes in the region, many of them mutants—"

"Mutants?"

"Yes," Sephine said. "Surely you have them where you're from—those whose bloodlines remain damaged by the radiation. From the nuclear fallout. Many of them were harmless to begin with, dangerous only to themselves—at least, according to our oldest records. But there were aggressive mutations, too, after the worst cancers culled the herd, and they prospered in the aftermath. And they bred. And now we have their grandchildren's grandchildren to deal with, and they only seem to grow more hateful.

"There aren't as many here as farther south, near the cities, but that only seems to make them more desperate."

"But with all you do have here," said Acel, walking a few feet behind them, "you could help others—take in the peaceful ones, protect them."

"Do you?" Sephine asked.

"No, but—"

"You'll find, Elder Higbee," she said, "if you'll forgive my interruption, that what we have here is very limited, in its own way. Could we feed, house, and clothe a few hundred more people? Probably. But not without making our existence known. Not without alerting the worst of our enemies that there is something valuable here for the taking. Our mission here is, I'm sad to say, more important than that. But please don't think that makes it easy to stomach." She looked at him sharply, meeting Acel's eyes. He looked away first.

Jared cleared his throat uncomfortably.

"So...what *is* your mission, exactly?"

"That," she said, "is what you're about to find out."

They walked in silence for a few minutes then turned into a smaller tunnel. It ended a few hundred feet on; Jared realized as they approached the door at the end of it that they had been climbing gradually the whole way. Sephine touched something at the side of the door and it opened to reveal a concrete stairwell, leading up.

Jared was surprised at how good it felt to see the sun again. The natural light felt wonderful. He was glad to exchange the safety of the bunker—the lodge, he corrected himself—for a breath of fresh air.

The weather was unseasonably warm outside, a change from the brisk temperatures they'd had coming north. It had to be—*what, Thanksgiving Month?*

Well into the first week of it, at least. He'd lost track of the days.

The stairwell emerged into a forest clearing similar to the one they had come in on, and Sephine led them out of the trees soon thereafter, onto the remains of a roadway.

They were closer to the Valley's center, now, and Jared was somewhat surprised to see other people out and about. There were small, tilled fields to one side of the road; several people worked at weeding one of them—barley, by the look of it.

"Do you all live underground?" he asked Sephine.

"For the most part it is up to the individual to decide," Sephine explained. "As long as they stay within the Valley's bounds, the people are free to live above ground if they wish. There are several families who do, in cabins and repaired houses. But all have a place in the lodge during times of trouble, of course. And what government—what law we have, is conducted there."

"So this Mother Greta," Ever said, from the other side of Sephine. "She's your…leader?" Sephine smiled, warmly this time.

"Yes," she said. "And no." Acel rolled his eyes—out of view of Sephine, of course.

"She's our leader in every sense that matters," Sephine said, "though day to day, our people govern themselves, for the most part. The Scions have certain obligations that others do not, and of course we have a chain of command when it comes to military decisions."

The road rounded an easy bend, and Jared's next question escaped him as they arrived at a broad grassy space outside the crumbling foundation of a large building. In the middle of the small field was the first familiar structure Jared had seen since their arrival in this strange place.

"A gazebo!" said Ever, beating him to it. It was made of whitewashed wood, and a flowering vine crept around it in colorful, choking tendrils.

Inside the structure, seated at a round wooden table, was an old woman. She stood up as they approached.

"Welcome," said the old woman, "I am the one known as Mother Greta. A pseudonym, I can assure you, that was not chosen by me, nor by those of my ancestors who also bore it. I choose to look at it as a term of endearment, though some days, I wonder. Please, sit." She gestured to the empty chairs surrounding the broad wooden table.

"I often come here, on sunny days, to think. I find it peaceful. The tunnels below too often remind me of tombs. Sephine, would you be so good as to have someone bring us something to drink?" Sephine nodded and strode off in the opposite direction from which they'd come.

"Now," said Mother Greta, looking at Ever and taking both of her hands in her own, "you are Ever Oaks. It is truly an honor to meet you, my dear."

Mother Greta's hands were wrinkled but strong, and her eyes were clear and blue. Her hair, tied in a simple ponytail, was almost entirely white, but Ever could see that it had always been pale—probably blonde, just like Sephine's. She wore a knitted shawl of soft gray wool to keep off the chill, but underneath it she was dressed in a simpler version of the clothing everyone seemed to wear: fitted shirt and trousers, tucked into a soft pair of boots. Ever didn't quite know what to make of her; she seemed like a bizarre combination of one of Sephine's forest rangers and someone's grandmother. For some inexplicable reason, she couldn't help but feel that the old woman was...familiar, somehow.

"You're wondering what to make of me," said Mother Greta, her piercing blue eyes still on Ever's own. She smiled at Ever's surprise. "We have so much to talk about, Ever, and so very little time." Her smile faded as quickly as it appeared.

Acel, Jared, and Rolan were still standing somewhat awkwardly around the table, watching the two of them. Mother Greta turned to them now and gestured impatiently.

"Sit, sit! Don't stand on ceremony. I'm sorry, I'm being terribly rude. It's just that Ever and I have a... special connection. Now, the rest of you tell me your names. They haven't all come to me as clearly." She took the boys' hands warmly as they seated themselves, before lowering herself gracefully into her own chair. Jared's name she knew, and seemed to spare him a special smile before turning back to Ever. Acel and Rolan greeted her as they would the aforementioned grandmother, quietly and politely, their boyish confidence dimmed in the face of seasoned femininity.

"You must all call me Greta. Now. Where to start. I've thought of so many different ways to begin this conversation," said Mother Greta, "but perhaps the best would be to let you do it. I'm sure you have questions. Please, ask away." She settled back in the sturdy wooden chair, which was turned slightly toward Ever's, who sat next to her, folding her hands across her lap.

Ever looked nervously at her friends, who seemed just as bewildered as she. Where to start? Why did she feel like she was meant to be sitting here, for one thing? Who *were* these people?

"What am I doing here?" she blurted, finishing her thoughts aloud. "How do you know who we are?"

"Ah," said Mother Greta. "A very good question, which will require a longer answer than you think, I imagine. We were never aware of how much you would know when you came to us, or exactly what you would be like, but we knew you would come. So I will begin, as they say, at the beginning." She paused for a moment with a considering look on her face, then smiled widely. Her laugh was like crystal shattering on stone.

"But what is the beginning, really? To truly find the start of all of this, I suppose you'd have to go back to the *real* beginning—to the first human who looked up at the sky and saw stars, who thought of herself as an 'I,' who spoke and loved…. Or why not go back even further? To the first fish who crawled out of the ocean and onto land and said to himself, 'This is better.' Or to the spark that lit the universe, for that matter." Her chuckling continued. It was honest laughter, a relieved laughter. Nonetheless, Ever looked at her friends worriedly.

Wiping a tear from her eye, Mother Greta scanned the faces of her guests and raised her eyebrows.

"I assure you, I'm not crazy," she said. "At least, not very. It's just that I've waited my whole life to meet all of you, and now here you are. I'm a little overwhelmed myself, I suppose. So let's make it easier. Rather than beginning at the beginning, we will begin at the end. At the apocalypse, the devastation. The last of mankind's great wars."

"The Fall," Jared said.

"Is that what you call it?" she asked. "That makes sense. That suits it quite well, in fact. Yes, we will begin at the Fall."

"It wasn't a surprise, you know," she said, settling back into her chair once again. "A lot of people saw it coming. They wrote of it, talked about it, warned of it—but of course, no one listened. And soon it didn't matter who had seen it coming. The point is, before the bombs fell, people knew it was a possibility. They knew even when it became a probability. The vast majority of them did nothing, went on living their lives as if their world could survive forever, as if, somehow, they could ignore the end and make it go away. They knew, and they did nothing. They didn't prepare, they didn't try to stop it. And so, it happened, and here we are. Never underestimate humanity's ability to adapt to terror. Even the most horrifying truths grow mundane, given enough time.

"Some few did try to put something aside, to think beyond their comfortable existence and acknowledge the possibility that the world as they knew it was actually about to end. They died too. Their provisions were helpful to the survivors in the aftermath, I imagine. But they never took it seriously enough to actually survive themselves.

"It is both encouraging and depressing that the will to survive seems to grow to accommodate the threat presented," she said, tapping her finger on the table. "Like water taking the shape of its pitcher. For most creatures, survival is a struggle against nature. Eat, or be eaten. But for man...once nature proved incapable of destroying us, we happily took up the job for ourselves. We did such a good job of it, in fact, that we nearly succeeded. And yet, again, here we are. We few survive."

"To come to the point," said Mother Greta, "there were a very, very few who took the threat of the Fall seriously. One such man built what you see here." She raised her arms slightly, indicating their surroundings. "He and those who followed him built what lies beneath your feet. And he was not the only one. He was one of many, across the nation that this used to be, who saw what was coming and knew that, in order for anyone to survive, they would have to devote the rest of their lives to preparing for the end. He built the fortress beneath the Valley, and he and his compatriots built that which we are sworn to guard with our very lives."

"How do you know all of this?" asked Rolan, leaning forward. Even in the midst of Mother Greta's story,

Ever couldn't help but notice how pale and drawn he seemed. Rolan had been very quiet since they had arrived here. Something was wrong, though what form that something took, Ever had no idea.

"It is my job to know, you could say," said Greta. "The people you have met here are the descendants of those who first settled the lodge as the bombs came down."

Sephine appeared, carrying a tray with a pitcher and six glasses, which she placed in the center of the table before taking a seat at the table herself.

"Sephine is one of my granddaughters," Greta explained. "My favorite, as it were, though don't tell her I said so." She said this behind her hand, as if Sephine weren't sitting right across from her. "Being a Scion is sometimes a burden, but a necessary one. Sephine bears it well. But now, we hope, all of that is over."

"What do you mean by that title—Scion?" Ever asked.

"Just what it sounds like, essentially. A descendant. A child of an important line."

"Whose line?" asked Acel. "Your...founder's?"

"Oh no, dear," said Greta. "We don't even remember his name, sadly. Our records, being mainly oral, are spotty at best. The things I'm telling you were whispered in my ear as a child, and in my mother's before that, and in her father's before that. I suppose some of the knowledge was preserved physically at some point, but it was felt at the beginning, in the long term, that an oral history was better.

"No...a Scion of the Valley is anyone born with the Gift." At this she turned to look at Ever again, her eyes sparkling knowingly.

"The Gift?" Ever asked. It couldn't be chance, that they shared this word. Ever's own Gift had surprised Sephine and her men, but not as completely as she'd expected.

"A beneficial mutation," said Greta, "a rare positive result of the Fall, bestowing seemingly superhuman abilities upon an ordinary person. Like you. Like me. Like Sephine."

Sephine blushed, and tried to hide it by pouring glasses from the pitcher for everyone.

"I barely have it," she said, setting a glass in front of Ever. "Just enough to hear Mother Greta when she calls."

"It doesn't come as strongly in everyone, you see," said Greta.

"It was you," Ever said. "When Thayne...you helped me." The other voice she'd heard—felt—in her head, when she struggled with Azariah Thayne in their camp in the cabin ruins. "You saved me."

Greta's expression darkened, and she leaned back slightly, wrapping her shawl tighter around her body as if she'd caught a chill.

"I'd hoped," Greta said, "to avoid that particular discussion for a little while longer, but that's the coward in me talking, I think." She stared at the tabletop in front of her for a moment. When she looked up, it was she who asked the next question.

"What is his name, this...adversary of yours?"

"Azariah Thayne," said Ever, again wondering if it was coincidence or divine influence that made Greta name him *adversary*.

"Um, what exactly is it that we're talking about, here?" asked Acel. He, Jared, and Rolan all looked confused; only Sephine seemed unsurprised by the turn the conversation had taken.

"I had a ...dream," Ever explained. "And when I woke up...Thayne was speaking to me. In my head. Just like he did in Salem. Like he did on the road afterward, when the wolves had us. Except it was the... *other* Thayne, the bad one, and he did something. It felt like...like falling into a dark sky...." She trailed off, at a loss for words. The experience had been disturbing, and she found that even in the light of a sunny day she had no desire to revisit it.

"I am no great power," said Greta. "I only helped show you the way. Fighting off men like that... is beyond me, I'm afraid." She shook her head. "We knew, when you came to us, that evil would pursue you...but we didn't know what form it would take. Or how fearsome it would be. I felt the two of you struggling, from afar, and did what I could. But in that moment I also saw the extent of our enemy...it's hard, not to despair."

Greta's eyes were knowing. Ever wanted to believe in this woman, to trust her, but something held her back. She didn't know who she was, really, and despite their good treatment thus far, she still wasn't entirely sure whether Greta was friend or foe. They shared something, that much was certain—some emotional bond from the time in the dark of her mind. Was it only fear, or was there something else?

There was a little girl inside of her that wanted desperately to be taken care of again—to be reassured, to be told everything was going to be all right. To find the contentment she had known before her world ended. But there was also a slim core that fought against that child's instinct, a spine of steel running through her mind that refused to let her ignore the reality that she was on her own.

"You still haven't told us how you knew we were coming," she said, "or what it is you think I'm supposed to do here." She wasn't unkind, but nor did she feel that they owed these people any warmth—not yet.

Sephine seemed to be looking at her appraisingly, her eyes flickering between Ever and her grandmother. Jared, Acel, and Rolan looked anxious and uncomfortable. It really was a beautiful day: the sun was high and strong, taking some of the autumn chill out of the air; tiny birds chirped from a mulberry bush nearby; in the hazy distance, a handful of people worked in the surrounding countryside like worker bees gathering food for the hive. Their queen sat before her, fingering the woolen hem of her shawl, considering.

"On the summit of Tripyramid," Greta said, finally, pointing over Ever's shoulder to the three-peaked mountain behind her, "there is a…beacon, of sorts. This facility, the Valley, was built to protect it. To hide its location and guard it. It was one of many.

"Those who foresaw the Fall knew that the world would never be the same—they knew humanity would need help to survive, to rebuild. So they stored all of their knowledge, all of their resources, and equipment and machinery to reproduce it, in a safe place. The beacon will show you the way. Help you take the first step towards salvation, as it were."

"So why haven't you used it?" asked Jared. "And you said there were others—other beacons. What happened to them?"

"The beacon is guarded," said Greta. "The guardian waits for its chosen messenger. She has yet to select one." The old woman stood up and walked to the railing of the gazebo, looking out at the mountain. "The ancients had their own reasons for doing what they did. What they were, I couldn't begin to imagine. The Scions of the Valley are those with the Sight—those, like me, like Sephine, who are gifted with the ability to see glimpses of the future. Whether the ancients understood that this would happen or not, the foresight of the Scions is what kept the Valley alive. Many of my ancestors have seen visions of what might be. No one has ever been exactly alike, but the bones of the story are always the same.

"A young person will come, a woman, Gifted, with evil at her heels, and she would gain access to that which has been denied to all others who have tried. It was never perfectly clear that this person would come from outside, and so all young women born with the Gift, all Scions, make a pilgrimage when their powers manifest. To see if they are the one. Thus far, all have failed."

"I'm guessing this is where Ever comes in," said Jared.

"She fits the profile," Greta said.

Jared leaned forward, resting his arms on the table, and looked at Greta closely.

"So what's in this for you?"

"Salvation isn't enough?" Mother Greta said, raising an eyebrow at Jared. She seemed amused, but nervous—there was a strange edge to her voice. She turned back to the mountain, gazing out over the treetops to the three peaks, bright and clear in the morning sun.

"You seem rather...saved, already," said Jared.

"None of this can last forever," said Mother Greta. "It was always a losing battle, on a long enough timeline. Even now the solar panels corrode, the seeds in the seed vault begin to succumb to time and mold and pests. The hydroelectric turbines whine with the effort of turning for hundreds of years.

"We have neither the knowledge nor the materials to repair them. Their maintenance was our responsibility, but there was a limit to what the ancients could prepare for. We are not them, nor will we be.

"This place exists for Ever. Ever's coming will determine its end, for better or for worse.

"Please don't presume, Brother Meacham, that this is easy for me," Greta finished. "The four of you being here...is at once our beginning and our end. The end of everything my people have ever known."

Ever felt rooted to her chair. She could no more respond than leap up into the air and fly. This was all too much. She wasn't prepared for any of it. There was a burden settling across her shoulders she had never expected to feel. Who were these people, really? What did she owe them, if anything? How had this journey, which had started with such a simple goal, gotten so far off track?

"I don't...I need some time," she said, swallowing. She said it quietly, but everyone turned to look at her anyway. In her peripheral vision, she saw Mother Greta nod, still looking at the mountain. For a long moment, no one spoke, or moved. Acel and Jared exchanged looks; Rolan stared at nothing between his hands. Sephine's eyes moved worriedly between her grandmother and Ever. It was Greta who broke the silence.

" 'And Samuel answered Saul, and said, I am the seer: go up before me unto the high place; for ye shall eat with me to day, and to morrow I will let thee go, and will tell thee all that is in thine heart.' "

"You know the Scriptures," Ever said.

"Of course we do," said Sephine, suddenly. She looked surprised at having spoken.

"Go and have your time, Ever," said Greta, turning finally to face her again. "And when you're ready, come to me again, and I will send you up to the mountain, and we'll see what's in your heart."

29

The glade seemed to catch the midday sunlight and intensify it; the grass, clinging to its summer verdure, waved slightly in the breeze. The place was at once familiar and alien: birds sang in the treetops and wildflowers grew in the verge, but she didn't recognize the birds and the flowers were pretty but strange, little three-pointed stars in purple and blue that seemed to pop up everywhere.

She had asked to be alone. Sephine had pointed out the trailhead to her and told her it led to this place. A good spot for contemplation, she had explained. That was over an hour ago. She had thought to come here and sort through everything logically, but her mind kept drifting: to the brilliant colors of the autumn foliage around her, to the ever-present rush of upland streams, and more than anything else to the mountain before her. Its tripartite peak loomed above the glade, and even in the open space she felt hemmed in by it. It seemed to fill her vision and her mind, reminding her of the dream she had before leaving Bountiful.

Is this that mountain? Somehow, she didn't think that it was; it didn't seem right. The mountain from her dream had seemed farther away, in both place and time—that peak was still in her future. This was something unexpected, something her vision—if that's what it was—hadn't prepared her for.

When she forced herself to think through the problem that lay before her, reasons to be suspicious accumulated quickly. She didn't know these people, not really. She had no idea whether they spoke the truth, or if they had some ulterior motive they hadn't yet shared. More importantly, none of this was why she was out here. The mission she, Acel, Rolan—*poor Chy*—and now Jared had set out to accomplish was simple: find a new home for their people.

The fact that Azariah Thayne and his minions, human and inhuman alike, had driven them off course didn't change the fact that Ever had no business wasting time in a strange valley, not to mention sticking around long enough to fulfill some questionable prophecy.

She didn't even know what had happened to her family, to the people of Bountiful. Jared had brought news that they likely escaped the Marmack attack, but almost anything could have happened in the weeks since. They should already have been inside the Maine by now, well on their way to search for the abandoned facilities that Elder Haglund believed still existed there.

It didn't make any sense that she was even considering doing this, but she was. The voice inside of her, the one she'd listened to since she was a child, the one she associated with the Spirit, was talking again. Despite the various reasons not to walk into something she didn't fully understand, Ever was tempted to do just that. And if Greta was telling the truth, if this mountain did indeed offer some ancient salvation prepared by the Old People, then didn't she have an obligation to seek it out? Their mandate was to find a new home for the Blessed at all costs, even if it turned out to be somewhere unexpected.

She turned back toward the trail leading out of the woods and found herself face to face with Jared.

"You have a habit of sneaking up on me," said Ever.

"I'm sneaky," said Jared. Joking aside, he was making the squinting face that he and every other man Ever knew tended to make when they were worried about something.

"You're the making the concerned face," she said.

"You're making decisive face," he countered. "You've decided to go through with it." She nodded once, face serious, and he sighed.

"You don't have to do this, you know," he said.

"I know."

"It's probably a really bad idea."

"Probably."

"It's not our problem."

"I'm hoping it might be what we're looking for," said Ever. "Where are the others?"

"Waiting. I convinced them to let me come talk to you," Jared said, crossing his arms. "Now tell me why."

"Why, what?" said Ever, knowing perfectly well what he meant.

"Why are you doing this?"

"I—I don't know," she began, and then the thin veneer of determination she had summed up cracked. She hadn't realized, until that moment, just how fragile she felt. She felt her hand shaking, and she started breathing quickly, and all of a sudden her eyes were hot and then Jared was holding her. They came together hard, the embrace almost jarring, and Ever cried quietly into his shoulder for several long moments before pulling back and looking up at him.

"I'm sorry," she said, meaning it. "I don't know...I feel like I don't really know anything anymore. Nothing makes any sense. It's like the world's turned upside down."

He nodded.

"You're scared," he said. "I am too." Ever felt surprisingly safe in Jared's arms; looking up at him now, she began to see him differently. He seemed older, less the immature boy and more a confident young man—

Thought fled as he kissed her. His lips were warm and soft, but also urgent; he pressed her body into his with one hand at the small of her back, and then she felt the other sliding into her hair at the nape of her neck. Her eyes were open in surprise, at first, and she stiffened slightly, instinct screaming at her to pull away. Then she closed them, and her brief, confused resistance shattered, and she melted into him with a passion that matched his own.

She was never able to describe precisely what she felt during that first, brief embrace. Afterward she could only think of the romances the young women of Bountiful used to share at their weekly meetings—fanciful tales of love at first sight, and chaste passion first consummated with a kiss that set lovers' hearts afire, tales that were half fantasy and half infatuation on the part of the tellers. She remembered the stories the older girls told, of how a good kiss could make seconds seem like hours. She remembered disbelieving them, thinking to herself that such fanciful exaggeration was the natural result of insufficiently stimulated female minds. Invariably she would privately roll her eyes and return to the infirmary to roll bandages and prepare tinctures.

It was clear to her that time passed, but when at last she opened her eyes, taking his face in her hands and pulling back gently, she could not have reliably stated the season of the year, let alone the hour of the day.

"I'm s—" Jared began, but Ever laid her fingers over his lips, shushing him.

"Don't. Don't apologize." She kissed him again briefly for good measure, then broke their embrace, stepping back and fixing her hair, which had come loose from the simple ponytail she had tied it in that morning.

The moment was over, however long it had lasted, and part of her was glad. Whatever it had been, it was a distraction, and another distraction was the last thing she needed. Let it be what it was. Hopefully Jared could understand.

"I can't explain it," she said, continuing their conversation where they'd left off, as if nothing else had happened. Jared walked beside her as she made for the trail leading back into the open part of the Valley. "It just seems...right, somehow. Or maybe right's the wrong word: it fits. It just fits. Something drew us here, Jared. It's worth an extra day to see what that something might be."

"That's one way to put it," Jared responded. "Another way to put it would be to say that we were driven here. By Thayne."

Ever stopped, turning towards him in the middle of the trail. As selfish and inexplicable as she knew it was, she didn't want to have this conversation right now. She wanted him to trust her. She wanted him to know—to believe, as she believed, that she was acting as her conscience directed her. She opened her mouth to say—what? Just that? Believe me, because I told you to?

Jared spoke first.

"I don't mean to argue," he said. "Acel and Rolan and I talked about it. We're behind you, whatever your decision is. We're here, in large part, because of you. We trust you.

"But you know," he continued, his smile a small quirk of his lips, "you don't have to do it on their terms."

Jared continued talking as they walked through the well-lit wood together. Ever smiled after a moment, and slipped her hand through the crook of his elbow.

• • •

Mother Greta's eyes narrowed slightly as Ever spoke, and Jared imagined that he could see a mischievous glint in them as well. The old woman was craftier than she let on, he thought; the set to her face as she listened to Ever's terms revealed that she was not only unsurprised by their negotiating, but prepared to respond in turn. Like Acel and Rolan—or Acel, at least; Rolan had grown increasingly silent the more time they spent in the Valley—Jared didn't trust the Valley dwellers, Mother Greta least of all. But at the same time, he sensed no evil in her. *Though why I imagine I could sense it, I don't know.*

"I will go up the mountain," Ever was saying, "and I'll find what is to be found there. But I won't do it for free. And afterward, our part will be complete, and we'll go where we please. We won't be beholden to you beyond this one task."

"And what payment could we possibly offer you, child?" asked Greta, tapping one wizened finger on the railing of the gazebo. The others had roamed freely in the grassy field surrounding the gazebo as Ever, and then Jared, went off into the woods. Seeing he and Ever emerge from the little trailhead, Acel and Rolan had drifted toward them, all of them eventually ending up back at the gazebo. Mother Greta stepped down from it, and now they stood on the grass to have their little negotiation.

"Nothing too dear," Ever said. "Weapons and provisions for our journey into the Maine—or wherever we go from here. And an armed escort by Sephine's rangers, to the old border or a like distance." According to Rolan's maps, it was 20 miles as the crow flies to the ancient border of the Maine, and at least 30 on foot. They had worried that asking for a further escort would be both excessive and, perhaps, unnecessarily restrictive on their own movements.

"I've never said that you were not free to go, Ever," said Greta, her eyes considering. "Do you think that I would hold you against your will?" There was a tense pause, and after a beat Ever answered.

"I don't know," Ever said. "I don't know you, Greta, or your people. All I know about you is what I can see, and what I can see is a trained military force, obviously used to getting its way. I'm not a fool. We're at your mercy here. Should you choose to try and stop us, you could do it."

"Do you think I would do that?"

"I don't think so. But as I said, I really don't know you. In any case, those are our terms."

"You're forgetting one thing," said Mother Greta. "I would be lying if I told you that I knew exactly what you'd find atop that mountain, but what I do know is that the treasure it guards is a beginning, not an end. If my people are to survive, we may need you with us."

"We have our own people to consider," said Acel. His arms were folded across his chest and his face was stern and set. "Yours have shelter—an underground fortress—and technology and resources we've only heard about in stories of the Old People. Ours are on the run from a dangerous enemy who seems to want nothing more than to wipe them out."

"In short," Jared said, cutting in smoothly before Acel went from assertive to belligerent, "we've got our own problems. And the Blessed—our own people—need our help a lot more than yours do."

Greta wrapped her arms in her shawl and looked at them, one at time. They had explained the purpose of their journey to her before, in describing their flight from Thayne's wolves and the plan to head east into the Maine. While Ever thought, Greta, Acel, and Jared had continued to talk.

"It strikes me, Ever," said Greta, coming forward to put a hand on her shoulder, "that we have a common purpose. We're both looking for salvation, each in her own way." Her light blue eyes shifted, finding Sephine, who had come up to join them as well. "Perhaps instead of being adversaries, we should be partners.

"See what the mountain has to tell you. When you return, I will send Sephine and her best men to return to your home with you and find your people. They know how to maneuver in enemy territory—you might say it's their purpose, really. If—when you find them, bring them here. We will offer them shelter, a home, for as long as we are able. And then, if you succeed where the others have failed, perhaps a better place will be waiting for all of us."

Greta looked sincere; Sephine seemed, if anything, excited. Ever looked at her friends. Jared knew the answer that lay in his eyes. There was no guarantee of finding safety in the North. The quest to the Maine had always been uncertain at best. What Greta was offering them was security, safety, and more hope than they'd had for weeks. Ever didn't question their good fortune further. After a long moment, she clasped the old woman's hand in agreement. Jared felt an unexpected smile on his face, an expression at odds with the worry that still gnawed at his heart.

The path to the summit of Tripyramid, as it turned out, was fairly straightforward: there was a trail. The summit was known as North Peak, reached after climbing the Middle Peak and on up a vast slide of bare rock; Sephine said it was several hours' hike to the top. It wasn't a particularly dangerous or difficult climb in the summer, she had explained, but it was wise to start early and take it slow.

Despite this caution, under the circumstances both Sephine and Ever had wanted to make the climb immediately after she and Greta had reached their agreement, but the old woman had insisted that they wait until the following morning. The boys had mostly looked to Ever for guidance, though she wished that they would be more opinionated.

At some point she had apparently become something of a leader to their little company, much to her own dismay. She couldn't quite tell what had precipitated the change. As they approached the trailhead, she filed the subject away for future investigation and considered the mountain before her.

They had eaten a quiet dinner in their quarters—Sephine had seemed to think they would want to be alone, though Ever would have been just as happy to learn more about the Valley people. She had found herself shaking Mother Greta's hand happily, despite her fears, because of the convenient solution it offered: a place for the Blessed to go, where they would be safe, at least temporarily. Better than wandering blind into the Maine, especially when she didn't even know where the Bountiful residents had gone.

The four of them had discussed the matter in depth over a dinner of venison, sweet bread, fresh honey, and a curious cheese Sandrine, who had again appeared to wait on them, had explained was made by one of the farming families that lived above.

Acel had brought up the hasty discussion they'd had just outside of Bountiful, when they decided to go on despite the seriousness of the Marmack attack, and admitted that he had questioned that decision ever since he made it. He, too, saw Greta's offer as a welcome opportunity to forego traveling into the Maine wilderness and instead seek out their families and friends. What use was a new home, after all, if there was no one left alive to enjoy it?

The mood at the table was somewhat subdued; Acel was troubled by thoughts of home, Jared kept looking at her with that same concerned face she had seen in the forest clearing, and Rolan maintained the same sullen silence he had been lost in since they arrived in the Valley two days before. Under normal circumstances Ever would have tried to reach out to him and find out what was on his mind, but she was having enough trouble dealing with her own thoughts to help anyone else at the moment.

She slept fitfully for hours before subsiding into a dreamless unconsciousness. She woke up exhausted. For the first time, she was grateful for the pitcher of hot coffee Sandrine brought with breakfast, which, aside from its obvious properties as a stimulant, turned out to be quite tasty with the right combination of milk and sugar.

The sky was overcast when they first climbed out of the bunker, with a darker mass of storm clouds moving up from the south. By the time their group had reached the base of Three Peaks the sky was as dark as dusk.

"I was afraid of this," said Sephine. "Those clouds look ready to open. Are you sure you want to do this today? We can always try again tomorrow." Ever could tell that Sephine was suppressing her own enthusiasm out of concern for Ever's comfort, but she had no intention of wasting any more time. She shook her head.

"A little rain never hurt anyone," she said, favoring Sephine with a small smile. The trail was wide and gently sloping for the first mile, at which point it began climbing more steeply up the mountainside. Acel, Jared, and a predictably sullen Rolan were accompanying Ever, and Sephine had brought a small contingent of her rangers—four of them, Ever thought, though they stayed masked and faded in and out of the surrounding forest, moving silently and, for the most part, staying out of sight.

The climb was easy at first, a gently sloping trail mounting grassy foothills crowned with pines. Within an hour the path had steepened significantly; Ever often found herself grabbing onto saplings bordering the trail for purchase.

They stopped to rest at midday at a comparatively flat area near a stream that cascaded down the mountainside in a loud rush. Sephine handed out bread and cold meats wrapped in oiled paper and they sat on a massive, flat boulder that jutted out into the torrent, watching the whitewater churn beneath them as they ate. Even in the dark weather, the sight was a beautiful one. When Ever had finished eating, Sephine got something out of her pack and sat down on the stone beside her.

"I...have something for you," she said. She fidgeted with the item in her hands nervously for a moment and then thrust it at Ever abruptly. "I thought you'd like it."

The object was a small book, hand-bound and not dissimilar from the blank ledgers and journals Bountiful's bookbinders made to record important events. She accepted it reverently—paper was a scarce luxury, difficult to produce, and even the most banal book was a rich gift—running a hand over the scarred leather cover.

"What's this?" she asked. Rolan, sitting near by, leaned forward with grudging interest, the first positive sign she'd seen out of him in days.

"Open it," said Sephine. Ever did so, turning the first few, blank leaves over, and read the first lines written in neat script on creamy, thick paper. Three words in, she gasped, almost dropping the book over the edge into the water. Sephine reached out and caught it before it could tumble off, smiling crookedly.

"It's…how did you…?" Ever couldn't find the words. "I thought almost all copies were lost…?"

"Not all," explained Sephine. "And we have other resources, in the Valley. It's not complete—I don't think anyone could boast to having a complete copy—but much of it is there."

Jared, Acel, and Rolan gathered around, Acel still chewing his lunch, as Ever read the first few lines out loud.

" 'In the beginning God created the heaven and the earth. And the earth was without form, and void; and darkness was upon the face of the deep. And the Spirit of God moved upon the face of the waters….' " Acel, who apparently still hadn't realized what exactly was going on, began to choke on his food. Jared pounded him on the back until he could breathe again, and the boys moved in closer.

"How…where…?" murmured Jared. Ever was glad she wasn't the only one feeling flummoxed.

"We pieced it together," Sephine continued. "Bits and pieces, recovered over the centuries, both from the rotten remnants of hard copies and electronically stored data."

"Electronically stored?" repeated Ever, turning the phrase over in her mind. How did one store data with electricity?

"Computers," said Rolan suddenly. "You're talking about computers." Sephine nodded.

"The Valley compound still has working computers. The Valley founders stored a remarkable amount of information in their databanks before the Fall wiped everything else out."

"This is...incredible," said Ever. "Thank you, Sephine. I...really don't know what to say. This will mean so much to my people. To all people, I should hope. We keep the Word orally...there's always been resistance to writing it down, officially anyway, for fear of preserving an imperfect copy. We don't how accurate what we remember is."

Some of the more progressive of the Blessed had taken to copying down parts of the Scriptures, but conservatives like Elder Cardon considered it sacrilege.

"We're not your enemies, Ever," Sephine said, before squeezing her shoulder and getting up from the rock.

Ever passed the precious book around to the boys.

"Will you keep it for me, Rolan?" she asked, noting how he lingered over it. Maybe such a little act could help whatever he was going through, even if really helping him get through it would have to wait. "I don't want anything to happen to it."

He nodded slowly, but didn't speak, and after a moment went to sit by himself to pore over it.

Jared shook his head.

"I never thought I'd see a real copy of Scripture," he said.

"When did any of us think we'd see any of this?" she responded, her eyes on the rushing water.

They had packed their lunch away and gotten another quarter of a mile up the trail when the first rumbling of thunder rolled through the darkened sky. It was then, as the trail before them grew steeper and more wooded, that Ever began to see milky blue eyes opening in the distant darkness between the trees.

Greta could feel the long fingers of his influence reaching out toward her Valley as the first peals of thunder tore the sky. Part of her wanted to despair—the fool girl part that had hoped it wouldn't come to this, the part that had wished up to the last moment that she wouldn't be asked to go through with it—but she wrapped that weeping inner child in the folds of her long years as the Valley's Mother and focused on preparing her mind for the fight to come.

There was still time, yet—a calm before the storm, literally and figuratively. She smiled to herself. Her rooms belowground were comfortable, but she longed for the freedom of the open air, rain or no rain. Sephine had made her agree to stay inside before departing, of course, and she saw the wisdom in it even if she didn't like it.

As she ran her mind through the exercises that had become almost unconscious over the long years, Greta wandered through her apartments, eventually ending up precisely where she knew she would, where she always did: standing before the vestibule carved out of the back of her bedroom. Its screens were dark, as they almost always were these days; what engineers they had were almost as unfamiliar with the ancient technology as she was, but they could tell when a machine was on the verge of failing. The whole Valley was on the verge of it: the water wheels were warping on their axes, the wiring, designed to last even as it was, was steadily corroding in its sealed conduits beneath the ground, and the advanced weaponry that made their rangers a force to be reckoned with was largely beyond their abilities to repair when components failed.

The girl had come just in time, if she was, in fact, the one. Greta replayed her own Seeings in her mind, both those she had shared with Ever Oaks and those she had kept to herself, as well as the precisely memorized, recorded accounts of the visions of earlier seers. All the signs were right; the time was now. And though she had long ago learned to trust the strange precognition that was her birthright, the random genetic mutation caused by the Fall that they had so carefully preserved with selective breeding over the centuries, Greta couldn't help but feel afraid.

As she had many times before when this feeling settled in on her, she entered the vestibule and sat in the comfortable chair before the monitors, bringing them to life with the tap of a finger on the polished surface.

The familiar image flickered out of nothingness before her eyes, rising from the metal console before her: a woman's face, rendered in pale light, albeit incompletely, as if someone had taken an eraser to it. It alternately shuddered and froze and ran for moments of undisturbed, smooth play before finally regulating itself. It became understandable a few seconds in, the woman's voice surprisingly soft and distant, in stark contrast to the pale reality of her unfinished face. Greta had listened to the recording more times than she could count, but she always found herself coming back to it, always wanted more from it. She wanted to reach out to the ghostly image and pull this woman into her reality, her now, and ask her questions, so many questions. But she waited, and watched, as she had grown accustomed to doing.

"The guardian," said the woman, whom Greta had come to think of over the years as a distant relation, a great-great-great-great grandmother, perhaps, "is an utterly independent being. Such was the cost of its creation. The blocks and limitations we—" Here the recording cut off, the woman's pretty face freezing silently again for a long count of seconds.

"—must not think of it as a person," she said when she shuddered to life again. "Its will, methods, perhaps even its desires, are its own. In the time we had, we were forced to choose daring over caution. I only hope we haven't made a devil's bargain." The image froze again, the woman's face stuck for a moment in an expression of deep anxiety.

"—who will come will test it as much as it tests her," she continued. "But that is as far as we dare speculate, given the limitations of our projections." A garbled flicker, and then: "—are not certain about anything. We suspect—" More noise, along with a stuttered interference that slithered through the image. Then, "—the female line, due to a higher probability of—"

"—beneficial mutation will of course be subject to chaotic—"

Finally she came to the longest stretch of silence, a frozen, lost section of the recording that lasted almost a minute. When the woman's face animated again, it spoke finally, as if concluding.

"The optimists among us think that we are building an ark," she said, her mouth a grim line. "The pessimists say we're constructing a life raft, and a shoddy one at best. But I can't help but think that maybe we are only making things worse. That maybe this is a mistake. That our pride is still intruding on our judgment, and that it will be as dangerous to those who survive us as the Armageddon is to ourselves. We wanted to give them the stars. What if we're only giving them more death?"

The recording ended, the woman's face dissolving into the nothing from which it came, and Greta stepped back. She was unsettled, as she always was after watching it. But it was important, she had decided long ago, important to keep the truth alive, even if only in her mind.

The thunder cracked again, loud enough to penetrate even through the thick walls of the bunker—or maybe she was listening with her other ears. And after the thunder came the lightning, and riding on it was the blue-eyed man.

25

Later on, Jared couldn't remember what happened first: Ever letting out a choked yell, or one of Sephine's black-clad rangers being thrown—as easily as Jared might throw a toddler—out of the trees and into the company's path.

Sephine already had her gun out and was barking orders by the time the man's body stopped tumbling. No closer inspection was necessary to determine that he was dead. His throat had been hollowed out as thoroughly as a pumpkin on Hallows Night.

"Wolves?" asked Acel, his rifle at the ready as he scanned the trees. More and more glowing blue eyes were appearing in the middle distance, wavering as they encroached on the trail. The darkness of the morning was disturbing. He ignored the whisper in his mind that said that no storm could cause this unnatural gloaming.

"No," said Ever. "Something else." As she spoke the underbrush rustled near where the ranger's body had emerged and a decidedly man-shaped creature lurched out of the trees at a stumbling run.

Jared's gun cleared leather as quickly as he'd ever drawn it, but Sephine had already put two rounds in the man before he'd finished cocking.

"Take her forward," Sephine said, standing down the trail from him. Whatever surprise she felt was clothed in rigid determination. Acel was firing into the woods as Rolan struggled to clear the breach on Chy's old rifle. "We'll hold them here. It isn't much farther."

"No," said Ever. "We—"

"Go, Jared," said Sephine, looking at him. "Once she reaches the summit, she'll be safe." He nodded, taking Ever by the arm.

"You two, you're with me," yelled Sephine, pointing at Acel and Rolan. She whistled strangely to call in her remaining rangers—though the nearby stuttering of the strange rifles they carried indicated they might already be engaged—and then the things were on them. Jared saw Acel shoot one in the head before battering another with his rifle butt before he started dragging Ever up the trail.

"Jared, no," snapped Ever, but Jared ignored her and continued up the trail.

"They're Thayne's, right?" he said. "Chances are they'll follow us anyway. They're here for you, not the rest of us."

Ever stumbled reluctantly alongside him as they made their way up the trail. He could hear movement in the trees all around them, but for the moment the things seemed to be concentrating their attack on Sephine and the others; as he watched, two more rangers appeared out of the woods to join them.

"They're Damned," Ever said, beside him. "Damned men…Thayne's taken control of them…." They were monstrous, hulking creatures, shaggy with hair and thick with bloated muscle.

"Sephine said it's not far to the top," Jared responded. "Let's hope we make it that far."

Farther on the trail suddenly broke out of the trees into the middle of a massive rock slide; Jared remembered seeing it from the Valley below, a large, open slash of bare granite in the dense green of the pine trees. The grade was just forgiving enough that they could scramble up it on all fours.

"We're close," he said. "The summit's only a few hundred yards." A few hundred yards over a precarious granite rock field, angled steeply up the side of the mountain, with nothing to arrest their slide if they fell but the trees and rocks far below.

Holding Ever's hand, he led her out onto the rock face and they began climbing the messy scree side by side. They were three-quarters of the way up the slide when the first raindrops began to fall. Within minutes it was pouring, and both of them were soaked through.

"There," Ever said, pointing. Jared followed the line of her finger to the mouth of a trail that plunged back into the trees on the upper left side of the rockslide. They reached it, with difficulty, just as the thunder rolled again and the rain was starting to make the rock slippery and dangerous.

The storm clouds were so dark and heavy that day had almost become night; lightning split the air and for a brief moment the rockslide below was illuminated, which was the only reason Jared saw the blue-eyed Damned emerging from the trees onto the granite below them. He counted six of them before he turned and nudged Ever into a run.

The trail followed the curve of the mountain's slope instead of climbing directly to the peak, and so it was a much more merciful climb than the rockslide they'd just ascended. In other circumstances Ever would probably have been more than a little worried about running flat out on an uneven trail high on a mountainside, but since they'd left the group below a pressure had been building at her temples. She'd felt it before. Every time Azariah Thayne had touched her mind, she had felt the same pressure, sometimes verging on pain, in her head. He was here, somehow, here but not here; the storm bore his scent. *I'm smelling people who aren't here, now? What's happening to me?* She clenched her teeth and kept running.

Tripyramid's North Peak was wooded; she could see the summit up above them at times, a few hundred feet away, between the pines. The trail continued along the curve of the peak's broad cone, however, and they followed it.

Soon the trail leveled out and widened, and they picked up speed, their boots pounding the fragrant humus beneath them. Sephine had said they'd be safe, if only they could reach the summit.

The cliff appeared out of nowhere. With no warning the trees on the downslope side of the trail ended and Ever was running headlong at an unprotected curve, hurtling toward an unexpected, majestic view of the neighboring peaks. She felt air beneath one of her feet just before Jared threw an arm around her chest, hooking her painfully away from the edge. They slammed into the trunk of a tree hard before their momentum carried them to the ground.

Her scream was more of a short bark; she hadn't had time to be truly afraid. She lay in Jared's arms, feeling his heart pounding under her back, his breath hoarse in her ear. After a long moment of shock, she slowly extricated himself from him.

"Are you alright?" she said, still out of breath herself. He clambered stiffly to his feet, rubbing at one of his shoulders.

"I think so," said Jared. "My shoulder caught most of it—it'll be stiff tomorrow." He grinned sarcastically.

"I—thank you." Looking down now at the drop below them, Ever saw that she would have launched herself directly out into space and fallen almost a hundred feet before hitting rock and trees below.

"Maybe we should slow down," Jared said. "I think I'd rather those things catch up with us than fall off the edge of a cliff."

The point was almost moot, however, not only because they were both winded and hurt, but because the trail ended less than a hundred feet from where they stood.

They had traveled around the top of the mountain, putting a good chunk of North Peak's shoulder between them and their enemies. *And our friends*, Ever thought. The trail would be easy to follow, however; they had limited time.

The path ended on a broad, flat space open to the air on the left hand side. Too broad and too flat, Ever realized; counter-intuitively, the space extended from the edge of the cliff the trail ran along—*into* the mountain, forming a sort of wide, open ledge, a balcony, almost, overlooking the slopes below. The summit was just above, but the trees had been cleared around the edges of the space. A few tenacious, scraggly pines clung to the top of the artificial cliff wall rising from the back of the notch toward the summit.

Jared knelt briefly, running a palm along the smooth granite floor.

"This whole thing is manmade," he said. "It's like somebody...cut a platform right into the mountain top."

Ever nodded absently; her attention was on what lay in the middle of the notch, nestled against the raw, cut rock of the mountainside: a wide, raised dais in the shape of a circle, made of some featureless gray material with four wide crenellations forming a smaller circle within it. Around the whole structure was a larger circle of silvery metal embedded into the granite floor of the strange balcony, marked at four equidistant points with large stone and metal pylons the height and thickness of a large man.

No one had told her what to expect when she got here—for here was certainly her destination. Sephine was supposed to be her guide. Ever had expected to arrive here with her, and the Valley people were so silent and respectful of the "beacon" on the mountainside that she hadn't asked for more details. She looked at Jared.

"We don't have much time," he said.

"You have a talent for stating the obvious," said Ever, feeling at a loss. "Well, here goes nothing."

Taking a deep breath, she approached the silvery border and, after hesitating for a moment, stepped over it.

She felt nothing at first except a slight tingling; the hair on her arms and at the nape of her neck rose, and she felt goose bumps forming on her skin. Static crackled through her hair and then she heard a low droning, followed by a *shinging* sound that came out of the air nearby as clearly as if someone had rung a bell.

Then there was a flash of blue light, and she couldn't move, and she heard Jared screaming her name.

The metal strip surrounding the odd structure—which reminded Jared uncomfortably of an altar—suddenly rang like a bell and a field of blue light shot into the air around the entire dais, fading as quickly as it appeared. Ever stiffened, her back straightening, and she raised her arms outward as if petitioning heaven.

Jared shouted her name and hurtled across the metal circle—or, rather, he tried to. As soon as the first part of his body—his hand and part of his cheek—crossed the outer edge of the silver curve, a numbing pain ran from his fingertips all the way up his arm, and he was pushed back by some unseen force. Ignoring the sudden loss of feeling in his right arm, he backed up, giving himself space, then ran at the metal circle as hard as he could.

The air around it might as well have been made of stone. He hit it hard, and the air shimmered light blue again where he struck it, before rebounding him to the smooth granite floor of the balcony on the same shoulder he'd fallen on just minutes before. He groaned in pain, unable to speak, barely able to think, and lay for a moment where he had fallen.

He could see Ever's back, arms still raised, unnaturally still, from where his numb cheek pressed against the stone. He could have sworn her feet were no longer touching the ground.

He pushed himself up with considerable trouble; his right arm was still numb, though feeling was beginning to return in a rush of pins and needles. He grimaced and tried to climb to his feet several times before he succeeded.

He thought back to Sephine's words to them before they left the rest of the party back on the lower trail. *She'll* be safe once she reaches the summit, Sephine had said. Jared hadn't taken her literally at the time.

He could still hear occasional gunfire in the distance—both the *crack* of the Blessed's rifles and the odd stuttering of the Valley rangers' guns—behind the ominous rumbling in the heavens and the occasional outburst from a sheltering bird, but it was the sound of boots crunching on stone that made him turn around.

Across the broad balcony, a few dozen feet away, blue-eyed man-things were stalking wolf-like out of the trail's end.

The voice was cold, but its words were reassuring. It encouraged her to remain calm and not to struggle. Ever experienced the inexplicable feeling of anxiety unaccompanied by physical symptoms; she couldn't feel her body, let alone move any part of it. Her eyes were frozen open but they didn't dry out, even after long seconds had passed.

Finally, just as Ever really started to panic, the force holding her in place loosened and let go, setting her gently back on her heels and allowing her arms to drift back down to her sides.

She blinked, shaken, and looked around, gasping as she saw Jared pulling himself up off the ground, saw Thayne's Damned creep out of the trailhead onto the granite balcony. She called out, but Jared didn't turn, couldn't hear her. She approached the inscribed silver line again, meaning to cross over and help him, and the air above it suddenly clouded, quickly becoming opaque. The entire silver circle had created a blank gray barrier, a wall blocking out sight and sound. It extended well above her head, where she could still see the sky—except it wasn't the same sky. This sky was clear and blue, with fluffy white clouds scudding along its dome.

After a moment the gray wall dissolved again, extending the illusion: Ever saw the sun, high and small, and the green trees on far peaks. Sound returned, the cheerful chirping of birds, along with all of the other innocuous noises of life in the forest. The sound of thunder and gunfire and rain had completely vanished.

Jared was gone, as were the Damned; Ever was alone on the gray stone pad, staring out at a beautiful vista. And it was all an illusion.

"This simulation has been provided to facilitate this system's assessment of you," said a voice.

Ever whirled, and found herself looking at a slim, attractive woman standing in the center of the dais. She wore a fitted garment the same color gray as the walls had been. As Ever watched, her clothing flickered into a perfect copy of Ever's own—the Valley clothing complete with her own knee-high boots, albeit unstained by mud and sweat.

"You may call me Lia," said the woman, approaching. She appeared to walk, but when Ever looked closely at her feet she could see that there was a tiny gap between the soles of her boots and the gray stone—metal? She didn't really know what it was made of—of the dais. "Initial imaging indicates anomalous activity in your prefrontal cortex. If you will permit me, I will now move on to DNA analysis."

Ever was speechless; for a moment, all thought of Jared and the things filing onto the high platform left her mind. She felt a crawling sense of unease when she looked at the woman in front of her, only made worse by the fact that every so often a strange flicker seemed to pass through parts of her body, a faint ripple tinged in blue light. *I'm speaking with a ghost*, Ever thought. Her insight into her situation was entirely born of panic: the fact that what she was seeing wasn't real was based more on instinct than observation. The truth was, she found herself inexplicably horrified. She swallowed as Lia stopped in front of her and extended her hands.

"What are you?" Ever whispered.

"Please," said the ghost, "give me your hand. I mean you no harm." She held out her hand toward Ever and waited with a patient placidity that made Ever think of Sister Orton, waiting for a pie to finish baking before lifting it out of the hearth.

No, not a ghost; a person...an image made of light. Could the Old People could make such things?

"I need you to let me go. Send me back. Whatever. My friend is outside," said Ever, her voice shaking. Her mouth was dry. Of all the experiences she'd had since leaving Bountiful, none had been as unnerving as this.

"The simulation is secured until the authentication process is complete," said the specter, her outstretched hand unwavering. "Please present your hand for verification."

"You don't understand," Ever said, more firmly, backing away a few steps and squaring herself up. She would *not* quiver before an apparition, no matter how alien. "My friends are out there. People are being hurt. Someone…someone I care about very much is waiting for me, just outside of this…place."

There was a pause, and then Lia blinked.

"This installation is actively monitored. It will automatically defend itself against intruders."

Ever stared, her heart beginning to pound. Parsing each of this thing's sentences took all of her mental energy; it was bad enough that she was stuck in here, but the fact that she felt like Lia was speaking a different language only tightened the cord of anxiety wrapped around her chest.

"Jared's not an intruder. The rest of my friends aren't intruders. How will you even tell the difference?"

"The diagnostic protocols are designed to identify all human organisms not possessing a predefined set of genetic parameters as potentially hostile. These parameters were calibrated according to reliable projections of beneficial mutations likely to result from the effects of widespread nuclear fallout in the long term, particularly those capable of measurement by remote magnetic resonance imaging at the time an individual enters this installation. Should authentication prove successful, however, companions of the subject who remain non-hostile will not be harmed."

"I don't understand you." Jared was out there, with those things, and she was stuck in here, listening to this thing babble at her. She had understood perhaps one word out of three in its previous statement. "Just let me out."

Lia paused again, and then made a face that Ever eventually realized was intended to be an approximation of a regretful frown.

"This installation's iteration of my core programming has extremely limited personality modules. You are worried for your friend. If he is not hostile, or if he is like you, then he will not be harmed. In any case, the defense systems cannot be activated until authentication is complete."

"Like me?" repeated Ever. The woman's words were beginning to fade into babble as she frantically considered her options. Abruptly she turned and walked across the circular platform, approaching the silvery ring from another side. The view was pristine: the cut rock walls of the installation's notch, the radiant blue of the sky above, the verdant green carpet of trees covering the distant mountains. She touched the air over the ring again and felt firm resistance. Whatever the wall was made of, it was invisible; it yielded slightly under gentle pressure but became impenetrable when she pushed harder.

Ever tried to steady herself. In order to get out of here, she would have to know where here was. In order to do that, she'd have to talk to this woman-thing that seemed to speak in riddles.

"Difficulties in communication were to be expected," Lia said. Her slender form, rippling with that faint shimmer, had appeared close behind her. Ever hadn't seen her move. "I apologize for my limitations. I can assure you, however, that the only way to proceed from this point is to consent to genetic testing."

"Consent?" snapped Ever. "How is it consent if you're telling me I can't leave?"

The regretful frown returned.

"Such measures were deemed necessary. I am programmed to be as respectful as possible. The test will only take a moment. Please extend your hand."

Ever tapped her teeth together in nervous thought behind her closed lips. Finally, giving in more out of annoyance than defeat, she uncurled the fist she had made with her right hand and presented it, palm down. She was pleased to see that it only shook slightly when she held it out.

Lia's face returned to the maddening placidity that seemed to be its default expression, and she reached up and touched Ever on the fingertip. Ever felt a slight pinch, so quick that she wondered whether she had imagined it. Her eyes widened when she saw the tiny bead of blood well up on her fingertip, which Lia deftly swiped up with another of her own slightly spectral fingers. A slight heat, then, and her finger stopped bleeding. Lia lowered her own hand and blinked.

Ever was about to demand an explanation when Lia blinked again, and spoke.

"Genetic analysis complete. Redundancy tests confirm validity of initial sample." The woman looked at Ever strangely, then, more closely, as if she hadn't really looked at her at all until now, and gave a slight nod of her head. "Welcome, Alpha Scion."

The vast, beautiful mirage Lia had summoned faded, then, dissolving smoothly back into the charcoal gray sky under which Ever and Jared had arrived, and the sights and sounds of the outside world returned.

Ever felt a split second of relief as the images disappeared, which turned quickly into horror as the carnage outside Lia's tranquil oasis was fully revealed.

Jared shot his last arrow directly into the face of a rushing Damned, then drew his knife. The bow itself could be used as a blunt force weapon, of course, but Jared tried to avoid that except as a last resort. Too much risk of damaging the bow. He dropped it as gently as he could, holding his knife in a reverse grip, and met the walking nightmare head on. He was ready for this one, but the others would be on him soon enough. Plunging the blade deeply into the joint of neck and shoulder, he heaved forward, dragging it down into the Damned man's chest. There was no life in those milky blue eyes to speak of; this one had the powerful, curving limbs of one of the demon tribes, the vicious, animalistic predators that prowled the lands far to the West of Bountiful, beyond the edges of the Northeast Kingdom. He had never seen one, only heard them described by more experienced rangers. Its teeth were thick and yellow, more like a cat's teeth than a man's. Thayne's influence certainly hadn't made it any prettier. Jared shuddered in disgust, freeing his knife as quickly as possible.

It died with a gush of dark blood, still trying to grapple at him with its enormous arms. He gasped in relief as he saw Sephine, Acel, and two Valley rangers break through the trees at the trailhead. They came out shooting; Sephine took out two Damned within yards of Jared in quick succession, giving him a moment to catch his breath. He'd spent his pistol rounds in seconds and his arrows almost as quickly; more than half a dozen of them had barreled out of the trees in small groups, and it took more than one shot of pistol or bow to take each of them down.

"There are more behind—" Sephine didn't get a chance to finish her thought. Even as she and the others came up to him, another pair of Damned lurched into sight at the edge of the cliff.

This is bad. He had no remaining ammunition of any kind and he had to guess that Sephine and her rangers were also close to empty—though, if he was being honest, he had no idea what those guns of theirs shot, or if they were loaded with anything he would even understand. Ever was still behind the strange gray wall...*this is very bad*. And where was Rolan? Was he—*no. Not now. Later.*

"Where's Ever?" shouted Acel.

"She's—" *In there.*

But the gray barrier was fading, and he could see Ever running toward him, and then there was a high-pitched *scree* that pierced his ears like the call of a bird of prey.

26

Hatches, their edges barely perceptible when closed, opened in the featureless gray decking of Lia's platform as Ever ran toward her friends. Skeletal turrets in matte black metal rose out of them with a soft mechanical winding noise, topped with slim, threatening structures that folded outward like the pump handle of a well. Their lines were square and chunky, but she knew guns when she saw them. And they were aimed directly at Sephine, Jared, and Acel.

Her scream of warning was cut off by the high shriek of the weapons opening fire, and it felt almost as if her heart had stopped when the strafing ammunition cut through the small group of Blessed and Valley dwellers in burning lines of crackling white and blue.

But they didn't fall down. Ever saw Acel check himself after the initial burst of fire, feeling his chest and stomach and back in search of the horrible, gaping wounds the bullets had made. He found nothing. They stood there, in the line of fire, unharmed, for a brief, insane moment before ducking down below the deadly storm.

The guns were finding their marks in the remaining Damned, several dozen of whom were already lying dead all over the stone shelf. The weapons seemed to be aiming themselves, moving and whirring and adjusting with incredible speed and pinpoint accuracy, eating up the Damned like a fire burning through dry brush.

She realized suddenly that the bullets—or whatever they were—*had* gone through her friends, just not through their flesh. The machines had known, somehow, what to look for, aiming with superhuman precision around the innocent flesh of Ever's company while decimating the enemy.

Acel, Jared, Sephine, and the two rangers were pressed to the stone floor with their hands over their heads. The firing must have lasted for several minutes, at least, the streaming tracer shots lighting into the bubbling mass of Damned like red-hot cattle brands fired from a bow.

The quiet afterward was eerie and long; Ever could hear the innocuous scrapes and cloth sounds of her friends getting up and dusting themselves off across the stone of the platform.

When she turned back to the gray dais, Lia was standing there calmly, hands at her waist, back in her fitted gray outfit, and a circular shaft had opened in the center of the platform, its circumference lit faintly with white light.

Acel and Jared walked up; Jared took her hand quietly and squeezed it. She laid a hand on his chest, checking him for wounds, without even thinking about it. She blushed when she realized she was essentially caressing his chest and stomach in front of a group of people.

"I'm fine," said Jared, taking her other hand gently. Acel frowned and cleared his throat.

"The rest of us are fine, too, thanks for asking." Ever's blushed deepened and Sephine, of all things, laughed deeply as she walked up.

"We knew this place had defenses of some kind," she said, "but no one has ever seen them before. These make our weapons look like toys."

"I didn't know what to do," said Ever. "We didn't know—"

"I'm sorry," said Sephine. "I should have prepared you better. I thought I'd be here...no one expected... whatever this attack was."

"It's him," said Ever. "Azariah Thayne. I can feel him."

Sephine nodded slowly.

"I felt something too...a pressure—but I don't have much ability. Rest assured that Mother Greta will be watching, from below."

Ever wasn't sure how to feel about that; was she supposed to be comforted? Compared to Thayne, the old woman didn't seem particularly formidable. But then, she'd saved her once before.

"I'll take whatever help I can get," Ever said.

"In that case, she will guide you the rest of the way," said the blonde woman, nodding at Lia.

Sephine posted her remaining two rangers at the trailhead to watch for more Damned and joined them. Just as she was about to ask after him, Ever saw Rolan appear, scrambling down one of the cut rock faces where the walls of the notch sloped toward the edge of the cliff. The rangers tensed and aimed their weapons before recognizing him. He looked at them nervously and paused before continuing to where Ever and the others stood near Lia's placid projection.

"Rolan!" Acel shouted as he approached. "Where in damnation have you been?"

"I…I got pinned down," Rolan said, eyeing the strange ghost women before them anxiously. "Separated. It doesn't matter now. I'm sorry." He looked shaken, as defeated as Ever had seen him—which was saying a lot, given his demeanor over the past week.

"We lost track of him on that rockslide," explained Acel. "But then, everyone was pretty busy with other things at the time." Acel had the cuts and bruises to prove it. Aside from a number of small lacerations, there was a nasty looking bruise covering the side of his neck and jaw.

Jared was looking at Rolan oddly.

"There were so many of them…" Rolan said. "I got cut off from the rest of you." Jared nodded slowly, but his eyes lingered on the other boy for a moment before returning to Ever.

"Well, good to have you back then. Glad you're OK." said Acel, clapping him roughly on the shoulder. Rolan jumped as if he'd been struck.

Ever looked back at Lia, who stood to the side and gestured them forward. Ever started forward without speaking further, trusting her friends to either follow her or stay as they saw fit. It was past time to get this—whatever this was—over with.

The room they found themselves in had no edges. The virgin rock of the mountain had been scooped and shaped and smoothed as if by an enormous sanding block, coated in the same gray material the dais was made of. The walls were circular; the corners where the walls met the ceiling and the floor were radiused. Whoever—whatever—had constructed this place had possessed abilities the Blessed could only dream of. She didn't know why that was still surprising, after all they had seen, but it was.

A staircase had descended from Lia's dais into this strange vestibule, which appeared to be a kind of entrance hall; Ever could see where a round tunnel continued farther into the mountain at the back of the chamber.

Lia walked—a display obviously intended for their benefit, as it seemed she could appear anywhere within the facility at will—to the exact center of the room and faced them. She opened her mouth and froze, the first syllable of whatever word she had been about to say repeating in a stutter; more of the strange blue shudders disturbed her image, rippling through the smooth illusion of her quiet form.

It wasn't until she heard the strange cackling that Ever realized something was wrong. The air in the room seemed to grow even more chill. Lia's slender body seemed stuck, caught in some invisible web.

"I know that laugh," she said, and her heart seized in her chest as whatever energy made up Lia's ghostly person convulsed, shuddered, and began to coalesce into a different form entirely.

"*My children,*" said Azariah Thayne's voice, "*why do you run from me? Why do you flee your Prophet?*" Thayne's voice seemed to come from everywhere at once, as if the sound of it pervaded the very air of the room. It was pervasive and cutting, like the drone of cicadas on a summer day. His image was formed in blues and grays, a shifting kaleidoscope of muted light that stood where Lia had been, as if he had painted himself crudely out of the ruins of her. Ever could still see patches of what appeared to be Lia's clothing and features, rearranged in a crazy patchwork to make up the rudiments of Azariah Thayne.

"I don't know about the rest of you," muttered Jared, "but I'm getting really sick of this maniac."

"And his blasphemy," said Acel. He had readied his rifle—Ever would have been surprised if he had any ammunition left, but he held it at his shoulder just the same. "Who are you to call yourself Prophet?" he asked loudly. "That title is a gift, a blessing. Demon would be a better word for you. Or Adversary, though I think that's giving you too much credit."

Ever found herself saying a silent prayer of thanks for the bravery of her friends. An evil voice was speaking to them out of thin air, and they stood firm, rebuking it. She only wished she felt as confident.

The apparition cackled again, the motes of color dancing in the soft light of the chamber.

Thayne's form shuddered again, and Lia returned, flickering back into existence like a firefly winking into light.

"—experiencing unidentified interference," she was in the middle of saying, her words shaky and off key, slightly garbled. "Anomalous data signal breakthr—"

Then Thayne took control again, the bluish image reforming in his likeness like a thousand thousand shards of colored glass forming themselves into a sculpture.

Ever felt the pressure in her head again, but this time it was growing stronger with each passing moment. She clutched her temples with both hands; suddenly, the pain was so bad that her legs gave out. She felt someone catch her, faintly, but the world was growing dim and fuzzy: it kept getting farther away. She could hear somebody screaming. Only as the pain stopped and *he* was there did she realize that it had been her.

• • •

Jared caught her as she fell, easing her to the cold stone floor of the bunker. She was screaming as if someone was torturing her and clutching her head so tightly that he was afraid she would hurt herself. Acel helped him hold her down; Sephine bent over and peeled back one of her eyelids. Her eyes— green and fierce even now—were rolling wildly in their sockets. Jared felt tears building behind his eyes. The frustration—the *fury*—felt almost palpable. To watch her endure this—to watch her endure any pain—made him want to kill something, and the fact that her enemy wasn't there to be killed made him want to weep.

"It's okay, Ever," he said, stroking her hair as Acel and Sephine drew her arms away from her head with an effort. "It's all right. It will be all right." And he prayed, then, prayed as he never had before: prayed that whatever she was feeling might be transferred to him, laid on his own shoulders.

She gasped, suddenly, and then was still. Her screaming stopped, and for the moment she appeared almost peaceful, though she didn't wake up. Jared squeezed her hand firmly, as if he could press his help and anger and love—*love?*—into her very flesh.

"This place you've brought me to, child," said Thayne, his eyes closed in apparent rapture. "It's as if I've entered one of the kingdoms of heaven. The *power*...."

At first Ever could see nothing beyond his face—his real face, now, or a perfect image of it: the close-cropped beard, the raven black hair, the strong nose. Only his posture was different: instead of hunching, vulture-like, he stood easily, his shoulders wide and open, his face tilted upwards. *As if he's praying*, Ever thought. *Just like he's addressing the heavens.*

As she became more aware of her surroundings she realized that she was again in a version of the *not-place* where they had first encountered each other's minds. It was similar in that the very substance of it, the *feel* of the place, was somehow hazy, unreal, like a lucid dream. In every other way, however, it was different. Beyond Thayne a featureless gray void swept away. They cast no shadows. Looking down at her hands, she realized her body felt different; she could feel her hands, her legs, but they were fuzzy at first, prickling just on the edge of real pain, like waking limbs. It reminded her suddenly of the claims some Blessed scouts who had lost limbs in battle had made—that they could still feel their missing hand or leg, like a ghost of its presence.

The place lacked all sense of depth; though she and Thayne looked and felt real, their world was a featureless backdrop of gray. And yet there was something familiar about it...*Lia's clothes*. The color was the same: the neutral, medium gray that had clothed the strange woman-ghost who had brought led her here.

"Where are we?" she asked, not truly expecting an answer.

"Somewhere new," said Thayne, "and also someplace very old." He opened his milky blue eyes, meeting Ever's own, their endless, whitewashed cobalt depths wide and eager. "A place I've sought since I was alone and naked in the wilderness. One of the many keystones that will hold up the foundations of our future. And you have brought me here, Ever. You're fulfilling the destiny I foresaw for you—*our* destiny. This is the first step, the first milestone along the road."

"You can't hurt me here, Thayne," said Ever.

"Can't I?" he said, quirking his head like a dog. "That's what you don't understand, child. We're connected, you and I—joined together at some point long before now. Meant to lead our people forward to a new dawn—a new history."

"You're insane," said Ever. He sounded so *sure*, though; everything Thayne said, he said with the conviction of a prophet, as if he truly believed in his own moniker. She was sure he did.

Thayne didn't react, though she expected an outburst; he looked distracted, his eyes sweeping around the space as if he could see something she couldn't. She didn't have his complete attention, she realized. He was still caught up in whatever experience he was having.

Ever breathed in, slowly. There had to be something she could do. Some way to focus herself, to get out of here. But she had no idea where here was—the second time that dark morning that she had felt that way.

And then she thought of her family: of her parents—not her birth parents, but of Sister and Elder Orton, her real parents, the people who had raised her to adulthood. She thought of Dallin and timid little Aerie, and their cabin amid Bountiful's pines. She thought of her friends and their families, of Chy, dead so she could live, and all of the people she called her own, who called themselves Blessed, who were now scattered to the wind like so many hayseeds. If they were even still alive.

Ever realized with abrupt dismay that she hadn't even thought about them for days. They hadn't even *entered her mind*. She'd been so distracted with being held captive in Salem, with Thayne, with their journey North, that the people who were supposed to be the most important in the world to her had vanished from her thoughts.

The burning that came behind her eyes stung in a way it never had before. If she had been in the real world and not this un-place, she knew, she would already have felt hot tears on her cheeks. Here she only felt a tightness, and the surge of something familiar in her mind. It was the old familiar anger, the fury she felt when she healed someone, when her Saint's powers broke free from wherever they slept and changed reality to what she wanted it to be. It was that, but more: it felt colder, calmer. It was anger tempered by determination.

And that's when she knew she would fight him. *Let it be here, then*, she thought, collecting the ineffable energies that made up everything she was. She formed her cold rage into a focus of power and struck back at Thayne with everything she had, pushing him out with as much force as he had used to pull her in. Wherever, whatever this place was, she wanted him gone from it. Gone from the world, if possible, but gone from here, gone from her life. She put her will behind that thought with all the power of prayer.

The force of it hit Thayne like a thunderbolt: he screeched in pain, curling his body around himself and gripping his skull with long, pale fingers.

"Do I have your attention now?" Ever snarled.

There was a moment of perfect, eerie calm, a birds-stop-chirping-in-the-forest moment, and then Ever felt Thayne's response.

It was swift, and brutal, and it hit her like the ocean in storm. She realized several things in quick succession, then. The first: the only useful way to measure the abilities of a Saint—or, Ever supposed, anyone with Greta's "beneficial mutations"—was to compare them to another one. The second: compared to Azariah Thayne, she was a sparrow trying to outrun a hawk. No—a child fighting a hurricane. For that's what he was, she realized: Azariah Thayne was a storm, primal and unstoppable in its destructive fury.

At least, that's how it seemed when he caught her up in the grip of his will and smashed her with a numbing mental scream against the rocks of unconsciousness. The third thing Ever realized was that she was almost certainly about to die.

Thayne had been distracted, before, dazzled by whatever bright vision he had experienced upon coming to this…place. Now that she *did* have his attention, Ever was no longer sure that she wanted it.

The blue pools that were his eyes darkened, condensing into a deep cobalt, then a midnight blue darker than black, and then he struck again, and the fabric of the void wrinkled with tension.

• • •

Jared almost wasn't fast enough to catch Ever's body as it blew backwards toward the entrance to the antechamber. Only a slight twitch of her muscles gave him warning. She was light, however, and he got a shoulder between her and the wall before she could be carried farther. He was shocked at the force of the blow, particularly given that she hadn't been struck by anything he could see.

For the past minute and half, he, Acel, Sephine, and Rolan had watched dumbly, with increasing anxiety, as Ever struggled with whatever power the Thayne-ghost was throwing at her. He'd known something was happening when Ever's eyes rolled back in her head and she made fists the way she did when she was in the throes of her Gift.

Thayne's apparition had frozen when Ever did, though the strange blue aura still shimmered wildly from time to time.

"Ever," he said, easing her onto the floor. She struggled weakly, murmuring something incomprehensible, and was silent again. "Ever, wake up. Wake up. You have to—"

• • •

"—wake *up*, girl! This is it! This is the beginning of the end! You've led me right to it! I can feel her, feel her all around me. She's the key, this angel—this demon.

All the knowledge of the ancients is at my fingertips, mine to command with the merest thought...."

Thayne was rambling, badly, standing over her with his blue eyes again unfocused, staring into nothing. She groaned inwardly and passed a hand over her face; she was still in the not-place, but she could feel, even here, a dull pain thudding in her head.

She tried to get up, but couldn't. Her body felt weaker than it had when she was four years old and had scarlet fever—sensation remained, but she could barely lift her arm. Look past Thayne, she saw the gray void flicker, once, then again. For just a moment each time, the strange not-world disappeared and reality came back. She concentrated harder, focusing with what strength remained to her, willing the antechamber in Lia's bunker to materialize around her. The opaque gray became translucent, and suddenly she could feel hands on her—she could see the faces of her friends, gathered around her, leaning over—then Thayne looked at her again and grimaced. Their faces vanished and the pain in her head grew unbearable. She screamed.

And then someone else was there: not Lia, but a familiar presence—

Together, child, said Mother Greta, the shape of her mind clear and oddly comforting. Ever waited a beat, then felt Greta's presence entwine with her own, an uncanny sensation that felt like nothing so much as a joining of hands. She felt Greta's mind as Greta felt her own; it was as if their personalities shared a common body, or had become offshoots of some central consciousness that ultimately made them one.

Then they pushed, together, and Greta's light and will infused her own, and the gray world went white.

The not-place became suddenly clearer, as if she had opened her eyes wide instead of peering through lowered lids, and she felt, rather than saw, a much wider plain open around them. Unlike the not-place, this felt very *real*, an endless field of gentle amber shimmering with golden lights like stars.

Thayne was a dark lesion in it, a blot shadowing everything around him. He was close, and huge. In it were his eyes, the deep, disturbing blue eyes that had come to haunt her dreams. She saw-felt as Greta-Ever struck out, a bright slash like lightning, touching the Thayne-blot with power subtle but great, and one of the blue pools went dark.

She heard Azariah Thayne scream, a piercing, vulnerable sound. He lashed out, a counterstrike both terrifying and wild, its swing cutting a swath of nothing through the broad golden plain. Where the wave of his backlash cut, the golden stars went out—not in fiery bursts but in quiet blinks, as if Thayne's touch had simply reduced them to non-existence. The wave rushed toward them, swallowing light.

What strength Greta had granted Ever seemed to dissipate, then: she was again keenly aware of the weakness of her body and mind. The delicate Greta-Ever, Ever-Greta balance that they had maintained began to shift. She couldn't tell whether it was she, Ever, or she, Greta—which one of her pushed or pulled—but they separated enough for Ever to regain a sense of her own identity, and then the part of her that had been Greta changed again.

The crest of the Thayne-wave reached them and crashed: as it curled it ate the amber sky entirely, and Ever felt a sad, dull fear steal over her. There was no fighting this.

Just as the curl of Thayne's darkness swept over the huddled point of light that was Ever and Greta, the old woman separated entirely and seemed to surround Ever, squeezing her inside of her own light and rushing forward like a bulwark.

There was no explosion, no great catastrophe: only a split second of crackling rush, and then Ever opened her eyes.

In the quiet of her bedroom beneath the Valley floor, Mother Greta fell to the cold concrete floor, the pain in her head white and hot and final.

27

Jared was staring down at her, his brow wrinkled in dismay. She had never expected to open her eyes again, and she was looking into his. It was almost funny. He helped her sit up; the weakness she had felt had disappeared, though the pounding in her head was, if anything, worse.

Acel had an arm around Sephine, who was weeping openly.

"Greta?" Ever asked. Sephine shook her head.

"I felt her go," said the blonde woman, her eyes wet and wide. "I felt her go. She didn't even have a chance to say anything."

Ever got unsteadily to her feet and squeezed Sephine's shoulder, certain she should be feeling something more than what she was. Greta had undoubtedly saved her life. She should feel sad, or at least grateful. She felt only resigned determination. She'd come this far; the way was open. She couldn't stop to think of one old woman. She added Greta's name to the long list of people she would cry for later. If later ever came.

Lia had reformed at the center of the room, her expression as placid as ever. The ghost-woman managed to convey both patience and expectation, as if she would suffer Ever's human need to interact with her friends for as long as necessary, but clearly didn't think it relevant to the task at hand.

"Are you…you again?" Ever asked. She couldn't keep a bit of resentment out of her voice; they were putting so much trust in this thing, and it couldn't even defend itself?

"My systems encountered unexpected interference," Lia explained, as if it should be perfectly obvious. "I am unable to identify the source, though my systems are now beginning to identify several patterns in the data stream consistent with recorded neurological activity in your own cerebrum."

"What?"

"The intruder is likely another human with a mutation similar to yours. This person's ability to infiltrate my systems remotely is…unprecedented. A complete log of the incident has been added to the device for further analysis by my central node."

"Device?" said Rolan. Ever paid no attention.

"I know who it was. It wasn't unidentified. It was Azariah Thayne," said Ever, impatiently. "Who is he?" She didn't know why she expected Lia to have an answer, only that she was tired and hurt and anger and she wanted *someone* to have an answer.

"He appears to be a man. Nothing more."

"I'd say he's a little more than just a man," said Jared, behind her.

"Couldn't you see him?" Ever asked. "He took over your…your body."

"His ability to project a holographic image into this simulation is, as previously stated, unprecedented. But my systems were blocked from doing more than perceiving it at the time."

Ever stayed silent for a moment. There were so many questions she could ask—though if she were honest with herself, they were slipping away from her with each passing second.

"But we're safe, for now?" she asked.

"This system is once again secure," said Lia, "and improvised firewalls have been established to counteract the intrusion should further interference occur."

"Then show me what I'm here to see."

It began when she touched the device, a ball of curious workmanship ensconced in the top of a plain pedestal in an adjacent room. She touched it and saw the featureless gray void, but without the corruptive presence of Thayne.

Later, she would recognize the similarities between the images Lia showed her then and the dream she had the morning of the first Marmack attack on Bountiful, but as the information rolled before her eyes, she could think of little beyond the overwhelming rush of pure knowledge that seemed to flow into her mind like water into a cup.

The orb's surface was the same gray as everything else, with strange, minute designs seemingly scribed onto its surface; she was surprised to find it warm to the touch. The effect was instantaneous: one moment she was standing before the pedestal in the inner chamber, the next she was somewhere else. It was similar to the feeling of passing Lia's silver circle, but she was alone, and she could still feel the ball beneath her hand.

"The message was designed to be understood even if advanced verbal communication had been lost," she heard Lia saying, her voice omnipresent. "Your forebears could not predict how long it would take for a compatible mutation to emerge. Therefore, they prepared for the worst."

The gray void faded away and Ever found herself outside, atop Lia's dais. She was stationary for only a moment before rising. She gasped, looking down frantically as her feet left the ground. She was floating—*flying*. But she could still feel the ball beneath her hand. Another illusion, then. She was able to relax a little. Lia's voice accompanied her, narrating as she flew into the sky, Mount Tripyramid falling below her, the broad blue expanse of the earth's dome unbroken by a single cloud.

"This is a primer," Lia explained, though the word meant little to Ever. "An introduction, if you prefer. The device you hold is called Ora, and this information is stored in its memory. You will be able to access it at will. A copy of this iteration of my personality construct is also included, to serve as a guide until you reach my central node."

Ever remained silent, focusing on the exotic—and unexpectedly thrilling—feeling of soaring above the world like a bird on the wing. The air felt cool around her, and it rushed gently as they moved north from the mountain over the beautiful green carpet of the forest.

"You have reached the first milestone in a longer journey, Ever Oaks," said Lia. The rolling mountains below began to move by faster, an increasingly rapid stream of conifers reeling beneath her feet as Lia brought them North, and forward. "The Ora will serve as your compass. Keep it with you at all times."

"A compass to lead me where?"

"To safety."

"But safety where?"

"This simulation was designed to present information at a pace designed for easy consumption," said Lia, a chiding note in her tone. "Your questions will be answered in due time. Please cooperate with the—"

The rest of Lia's sentence was lost in a sudden rush of blood to Ever's head. She had had enough of this. She would not be treated like a child by a…a damned specter! Though on some level she realized that her anger was cumulative—the compounded result of weeks of turmoil and fear—and that Lia was not its cause, she couldn't have controlled herself if she'd wanted to. She lost it.

"*Stop*," she commanded. She stopped moving. "Enough. I'm done being led by the nose. I'm not a bull." The orb felt warm beneath her hand, which was comforting; she wasn't really floating above the mountains, she reminded herself, she was safe in a bunker, with her friends surrounding her. She didn't know if they could hear her voice or not. She hoped they could, but it didn't matter. If she was supposed to be so important, then people could start damn well paying attention to what she thought and wanted, instead of treating her like a frightened child.

"Make it so I can see you," she snapped. Lia appeared before her, the fact that she was floating in mid-air completely belied by her posture and demeanor, which remained calm and unaffected.

"What was it you called me?" Ever asked. "Up above, outside, when I passed your test."

"You are the Alpha Scion," Lia said.

"Does that mean that you have to do what I say?" she asked. She was reaching, she knew; it may very well not mean that at all. But Ever had to believe that all of this "specialness" had to include some level of authority—otherwise what was the point?

"I am programmed to follow your commands to the extent that they do not interfere with the ultimate goals of this enterprise."

Which is just another way of saying "If I feel like it."

"Then we're going to start doing things my way," said Ever, with a confidence she didn't feel. "I'm going to ask you questions, and you're going to answer them." She took a deep breath and tried to think.

"Who built this place…who made you?" she asked.

"Initial development of my core processes and construction of this and related facilities was financed by a private business entity called Deseret Technologies, Inc. Later phases of the enterprise required outside investments. I can list the investors in order of phase, investment group, liability, and security access, if you wish."

Deseret? But that's.... The name of the legendary home of the Blessed, when they were called Saints. It was supposedly far to the west, deep in the greater Desolation, long overrun by Damned and apostate tribes.

"No. Later. When did this all happen?" Ever asked. "When did the…enterprise begin?"

"The incorporation date of Deseret Technologies is recorded as June 24, 2167 CE," Lia said. As she spoke, she and Ever began moving again, albeit more slowly, heading in the same direction: north. She let it pass for the time being.

The year—she thought it was a year—Lia cited meant little to Ever; only the old name for the Month of Marriage, June, stood out. The Blessed kept a simple calendar of years, starting with the Saints' flight from Deseret after the Fall, but referred to them for the most part only for record-keeping purposes. One month, one day was the same as another in these latter days. The end times were come; why keep track of the year?

"And what was its purpose? Why am I here?" Ever asked.

Lia paused.

"Give me the short version."

"The salvation of the human race," said Lia.

Oh, is that all?

"You're a few centuries too late for that, I think."

"The nuclear destruction of 2217 was merely the beginning," said Lia. "The dangers posed by its aftermath, particularly the long term damage that fallout would do to the human genome, necessitated a long term solution. Thus, the enterprise's primary mission is to preserve *homo sapiens sapiens*, along with its benign evolutionary offspring."

"And how, exactly, do you plan on doing that?" Ever asked.

"By finding you a new home."

"That's what we set out to do," said Ever. "If you can help us, great—but why would we need to follow the instructions of people long dead in order to find a new place to live?"

"Your current technology level precludes interstellar travel without assistance from the enterprise."

"I don't understand."

"This simulation was intended to provide just such an understanding. If you will allow me to continue?" Ever nodded, hesitantly.

"As I previously noted," Lia said, whisking them forward once again, "this is merely a primer. You will be briefed and, where necessary, educated on the details of mission requirements over the coming months. For now, it is sufficient that you understand the following.

"Pre-war projections placed the likelihood of catastrophic genetic breakdown of the human race at 64.3 percent in the first millennium after a predefined set of ecological, biological, and infrastructural circumstances known collectively as total nuclear devastation, an extinction-level event. This was deemed to be far too high of a risk, and the enterprise was prepared in order to isolate and preserve modern human survivors as well as the likely genetic offshoots that met certain parameters—for example, you."

The landscape changed now as they began moving east; the mountains became hills and lowlands, increasingly speckled with lakes and rivers. She recognized the terrain as being part of the Maine, from the profusion of water alone.

"Upon confirmation of the existence of such survivors, I was programmed to provide guidance to the enterprise's main installation in order to begin launch preparations. Please stop me if you don't understand. I can return to the programmed orientation at any point."

The land beneath her accelerated until it stopped, without ceremony or rebound, on a mountain. Ever inhaled sharply as she recognized it.

It rose, its peak purple and white, into the sky, a vast lake before it reflecting the blue canopy above: the mountain from her dream, the mountain that the Spirit had whispered about in her mind as she began this long, exhausting journey.

"I...I don't...what do you mean, launch preparations?"

Lia brought them downward, spiraling into a flat section of land near the mountain's base. In the shadow of the mountain's bulk, a large square of gray was neatly cut out of the otherwise verdant countryside. It was the same gray as Lia's bunker, the same material, she realized. A circular portion of the platform opened, vast doors levering upward from beneath the ground, and shadowed within the deep excavation beneath, the tip of a massive, silvery gray structure could be seen. *The ship. The ship from my dream.*

As Ever looked on in heavy silence, still not understanding completely, night fell in Lia's dreamworld, and the calm gray woman pointed to the evening sky. The dome of the earth was midnight blue, punctuated by the brilliant white and gold of a thousand thousand stars. Ever looked upward in desperate hope, willing herself—willing the Spirit, she realized, to provide some semblance of guidance. *What is happening?* The question seemed to echo in her mind; all useful thought seemed to have vanished. She felt at the mercy of this spectral creation of the ancients.

Despite the fact that she knew, in reality, that he was standing a few feet away from her, Ever wished Jared were there.

"You have a destiny, Ever Oaks," said Lia, her voice clear and dangerous in the starry dark. "You will lead your people to the stars."

Ever Oaks' Diary
10 Thanksgiving Month (9)

I came down from the mountain in a haze. I barely remember it, even though it wasn't an easy climb, up or down. I remember telling them something about what I'd seen, but I got choked up: all of a sudden I just couldn't stop crying. Jared held me—tightly and intimately. No one said anything about it afterward. I still had the ball—the compass—in my hand, though Lia had ended the simulation. She told them what I couldn't, encouraged them to hold the ball themselves and see.

She showed them what she showed me, and more, because they were more patient. Rolan watched it a few times before we finally made him give it up. The others talked about it all the way down to the Valley. Only Sephine and I were silent.

I can't be sure of the date, so I estimated. I lost track at some point. Maybe Jared or Acel knows—I'll ask them if I think of it. I suppose it doesn't matter, really.

I don't fully understand what it is I witnessed on that mountaintop. I understand the plain meaning of most of the words Lia used, the regular words, anyway, but there's a larger message here that I keep missing.

If I'm being honest, the whole idea of this "enterprise" fills me with dread—a sense of foreboding like I've never felt before. It reminds me of Thayne, really: it's all too new and alien and dangerous. I don't know what to do. We left Bountiful to look for a place to move our village, just a new place to live, away from murderers and evil men, and instead we stumbled onto some kind of lost magic that promises the very stars while answering none of our real questions. Why us? Why now? Why me?

It's all too much. It's all just too much.

2 Thanksgiving Month (?)

We gathered today for a memorial service for Mother Greta. The entire Valley was there; I met many of its people for the first time, though they all knew me already. Sephine spoke, tearfully, about Greta's life, and her dedication, and her selflessness. I wanted to listen but I couldn't help but think about the weight on my heart. It's selfish, I know. I should be grateful to Greta, who gave her life for mine, though no one would have known it but for Sephine and I telling them, who sacrificed everything she had just for the dim hope of saving her people. Shouldn't I feel the same way? I wonder now if Greta liked being a leader, or if she wished things were different. I suppose she did, at times, just as I do now. I want nothing but for things to go back to what they were: to wake up in my bed in Bountiful, before Erlan, before this pointless quest. I want to wake up and smell the eggs and bacon Sister Orton is cooking on the griddle, and hear Dallin and Airie laughing in the yard. I want to come out of my room and find Elder Orton buttoning up his vest before heading out to his workshop. I want to wake up and find that my parents never died, and I can still walk down to Brokeneck Beach with my father and hear him tell me stories about the Old People on Golden Neck.

I want. I want to want less.

2 Thanksgiving Month 2

Jared found me in the woods, in the same little clearing Sephine led me to before I went up Tripyramid. I didn't have to tell him what was wrong. He knew, just as he always seemed to know. He just held me, at first, but before either of us knew what was happening we were kissing. His lips were hot on mine and he tasted of the wild mint that Valley people put in everything, and his arms were around me like a vise. I remember wanting him to wrap them tighter, to squeeze until I couldn't breathe anymore; maybe then I'd feel safe.

We stopped, after a while, and lay down among the little star-like flowers and looked up at the sky together. It was a beautiful day. I sent up a wish that we were back home, together like this, that we were to be married...it faded before it reached the treetops. I can't hide from this, I know that much. I've got to face it, somehow, or die trying.

Neither of us had really spoken the whole time; it was only as we walked out that Jared said something.

"Have you prayed about it?" he asked.

I'll admit I was surprised: surprised because Jared, as worthy as he is, is usually not one for prayer and reflection, and because the suggestion honestly hadn't occurred to me. When was the last time I prayed? I asked myself, not just wished for something but really reflected in reverence. It had been so many days ago that I couldn't remember exactly. I felt ashamed, and set out to right it. Half an hour later, kneeling in the field near the gazebo, I twisted my hands in frustration and felt tears coming to my eyes again. It had never been this hard, before. Why now? Why, when I need it most, did it refuse to come?

It was Sephine, in the end, that pointed me in the right direction, though she doesn't know it. I saw her, tall and pretty in the sun across the fields, and I remembered the Scriptures she gave me. Without thinking, I had transferred the little book from my pack to one of my pockets after I got down from the mountain. In hindsight that seems rather providential. I took it out, and opened it to a random page, and this is what I found:

> And I will bring the blind by a way that they knew not; I will lead them in paths that they

> have not known: I will make darkness light before them, and crooked things straight. These things will I do unto them, and not forsake them.

It's from the Book of Isaiah. Greedily, I closed the book and opened it again, and found: "Let not your heart be troubled; ye believe in God, believe also in me. In my Father's house are many mansions: if it were not so, I would have told you. I go to prepare a place for you."

We Blessed may be devout, but we are not a superstitious people. We don't see images of the Savior in our oatmeal, or look for the crucifixion wounds on the hands and feet and sides of our religious leaders. On any other day, had I opened that precious copy of the Scriptures to those two particular passages, I probably wouldn't have thought anything of it. But on that day, at that moment, it was exactly what I needed to hear.

Perhaps there is a place prepared for us. Perhaps it just takes a bit of faith to find it. Perhaps all my people need to get there…is someone to lead them.

THE END of Part 1

The story is continued in Part Two of The Book of Ever, *Extinction*. For news and updates on The Book of Ever and other books by James Cormier, sign up for Jim's mailing list on http://www.jamesdcormier.com.

Made in the USA
Middletown, DE
17 January 2015